"We take C[...]m," he whisp[...]e take [...]ities.

A[...]ndy, *you* ...

[...] have begun."

Something made Ash look up.

She realized a second later that she was following the direction of Daniel de Quesada's bloodshot, ecstatic gaze. Straight up into the blue sky.

Straight into the white-hot blaze of the noon sun.

Tears flooded her eyes. She rubbed her gloved hand across her face. It came away wet.

She saw nothing. She was blind.

"Christ!" she shrieked. Voices howled with her. Close, in the silk-canopied stand; further off, on the tourney field. Screams.

Someone cannoned into her. She grabbed, caught an arm: someone screamed, a whole host of voices screaming, and she couldn't make out what the words were, then:

"The sun! The *sun!*"

Ash raised her head.

In the arch of the sky above her was nothing, nothing at all, except darkness.

Ash whispered, "He put the sun out."

Other Books by
Mary Gentle

A HAWK IN SILVER
SCHOLARS AND SOLDIERS
RATS AND GARGOYLES
THE ARCHITECTURE OF DESIRE
LEFT TO HIS OWN DEVICES
GRUNTS!
GOLDEN WITCHBREED
ANCIENT LIGHT

A SECRET HISTORY

THE BOOK OF ASH, #1

MARY GENTLE

AVON · EOS

For Richard

AVON BOOKS, INC.
1350 Avenue of the Americas
New York, New York 10019

Copyright © 1999 by Mary Gentle
Cover art by Donato
Library of Congress Catalog Card Number: 99-94993
ISBN: 0-380-78869-1
www.avonbooks.com/eos

First Avon Eos Printing: October 1999

AVON EOS TRADEMARK REG. U.S. PAT. OFF. AND IN OTHER COUNTRIES, MARCA REGISTRADA, HECHO EN U.S.A.

Printed in the U.S.A.

WCD   10   9   8   7   6   5   4   3   2   1

Note to the Reader

This 4th edition of the ASH papers contains a facsimile text taken directly from one surviving copy of Pierce Ratcliff's 3rd edition *Ash: The Lost History of Burgundy*, (published, and pulped, 2001). The reader should note that it is, therefore, an exact reproduction of the text.

I have been able to add copies of the original letters and e-mail correspondence between the author and his publisher, and sundry documents of associational interest. The original annotations on those documents are also reproduced here, as found.

It is my hope that, with this new evidence, we will finally be able to understand the extraordinary events surrounding both the original publication of *Ash: The Lost History of Burgundy*, and, indeed, Ash herself.

Dr. Pierce Ratcliff, *ASH: THE LOST HISTORY OF BURGUNDY*, Oxford University Press, 2001. Extremely rare.

The original 2001 edition of Dr. Pierce Ratcliff's *ASH: THE LOST HISTORY OF BURGUNDY* was withdrawn from the publisher's warehouses immediately before publication. All known copies were destroyed. Copies sent out for review were recalled, and pulped.

A percentage of the same material was eventually reissued in October 2005, as *MEDIAEVAL TACTICS, LOGISTICS AND COMMAND, Volume 3: Burgundy*, after the removal of all the editorial notes and the Afterword.

An original copy of the 3rd edition is believed to be available in the British Library, together with facsimiles of the editorial correspondence, but is not available for public consultation.

NOTE: This excerpt from *Antiquarian Media Monthly*, Vol. 2, No. 7, July 2006, is original, glued on to the blank frontispiece page of this copy.

Introduction

I make no apology for presenting a new translation of these documents which are our only contact with the life of that extraordinary woman, Ash (b.1457[?]–d.1477). One has long been needed.

Charles Mallory Maximillian's 1890 edition, *Ash: The Life of a Female Mediaeval Mercenary Captain*, begins with a translation from the mediaeval Latin into serviceable Victorian prose, but he admits that he leaves out some of the more explicit episodes; as does Vaughan Davies in his 1939 collection, *Ash: A Fifteenth Century Biography*. The "Ash" documents badly need a colloquial and complete translation for the new millennium, and one which does not shrink from the brutality of the mediaeval period, as well as its joyfulness. I hope that I have provided one here.

Women have always accompanied armies. Examples of their taking part in actual combat are far too numerous to quote. In AD 1476, it is only two generations since Joan of Arc led the Dauphin's forces in France: one can imagine the grandparents of Ash's soldiers telling war stories about this. To find a mediaeval peasant woman in command, however, without the backing of church or state— and in command of mercenary troops—is almost unique.[1]

The high glory of mediaeval life and the explosive revolution of the Renaissance meet in this Europe of the sec-

---

[1] Not entirely, as we shall see.

ond half of the fifteenth century. Wars are endemic—in the Italian city states, in France, Burgundy, Spain and the Germanies, and in England between warring royal houses. Europe itself is in a state of terror over the eastern threat of the Turkish Empire. It is an age of armies, which will grow, and of mercenary companies, which will pass away with the coming of the Early Modern period.

Much is uncertain about Ash, including the year and place of her birth. Several fifteenth and sixteenth century documents claim to be *Lives* of Ash, and I shall be referring to them later, together with those new discoveries which I have made in the course of my research.

This earliest Latin fragment of the *Winchester Codex*, a monastic document written around AD 1495, deals with her early experiences as a child, and it is here presented in my own translation, as are subsequent texts.

Any historical personage inevitably acquires a baggage-train of tales, anecdotes and romantic stories over and above their actual historical career. These are an entertaining part of the Ash material, but not to be taken seriously as history. I have therefore foot-noted such episodes in the Ash cycle as they occur: the serious reader is free to disregard them.

At the end of our millennium, with sophisticated methods of research, it is far easier for me to strip away the false "legends" around Ash than it would have been for either Charles Maximillian or Vaughan Davies. I have here uncovered the historical woman behind the stories— her real self as, if not more, amazing than her myth.

Pierce Ratcliff, Ph.D. (War Studies), 2001

Dr Pierce Ratcliff Ph. D. (War Studies)
Flat I, Rowan Court, 112 Olvera Street
London W14 OAB, United Kingdom
Fax: ▮▮▮▮▮▮
E-mail: ▮▮▮▮▮▮
Tel: ▮▮▮▮▮▮

Anna Longman
Editor
Oxford University Press
▮▮▮▮▮▮
▮▮▮▮
▮▮▮▮

Copies of some (?) of the original correspondence between Dr Ratcliff and his publisher's editor found inserted between pages of text — possibly in the order in which the original typescript was edited?

29 September 2000

Dear Ms Longman,

I am returning, with pleasure, the contract for our book. I have signed it as requested.

I enclose a rough draft of the translation of Ash's early life: the *Winchester Codex*. As you will see, as further documents are translated, the seed of everything that happens to her is here.

This is a remarkable occasion for me! Every historian, I suppose, believes that one day he or she will make the discovery, the one that makes their names. And I believe that I have made it here, uncovering the details of the career of this remarkable woman, Ash, and thus uncovering a little-known—no, a *forgotten*—deeply significant episode in European history.

My theory is one that I first began to piece together as I studied the existing 'Ash' documents for my doctoral thesis. I was able to confirm it, with the discovery of the 'Fraxinus' document—originally from the collection at Snowshill Manor, in Gloucestershire. A cousin of the late owner, Charles Wade, had been given a sixteenth century German chest before his death and the take-over of Snowshill Manor by the National Trust in 1952. When it was finally opened, the manuscript was inside. I think it must have been sitting in there (there is a steel locking mechanism that takes up the entire inside of the chest's lid!), all but unread *since* the fifteenth century. Charles Wade may not even have known it existed.

Being in mediaeval French and Latin, it had never been translated by Wade, even if he was aware of it—he was one of those 'collectors' who, born in the Victorian age, had far more interest in acquiring than deciphering. The Manor is a wonderful heap of clocks, Japanese armour, mediaeval German swords, porcelain, etc.! But that at least one other eye besides mine has seen it, I am certain: some hand has scribbled a rough Latin pun on the outer sheet—*fraxinus me fecit*: 'Ash made me'. (You may or may not know that the Latin name for the ash tree is *fraxinus*.) I would guess that this annotation is eighteenth century.

As I first read it, it became clear to me that this was, indeed, an entirely new, previously undiscovered document. A memoir written, or more likely dictated, *by the woman Ash herself*, at some point before her death in AD 1477(?). It did not take me long to realise that it fits, as it were, in the gaps between recorded history—and there are many, many such gaps. (And, one supposes, it is my discovery of 'Fraxinus' which encouraged your firm to wish to publish this new edition of the Ash *Life*.)

What *Fraxinus* describes is florid, perhaps, but one must remember that exaggeration, legend, myth, and the chronicler's own prejudices and patriotism, all form a normal part of the average mediaeval manuscript. Under the dross, there is gold. As you will see.

History is a large net, with a wide mesh, and many things slip through it into oblivion. With the new material I have uncovered, I hope to bring to light, once again, those facts which do not accord with our idea of the past, but which, nonetheless, *are* factual.

That this will then involve considerable reassessment of our views of Northern European history is inevitable, and the historians will just have to get used to it!

I look forward to hearing from you,

Pierce Ratcliff

Pierce Ratcliff

PROLOGUE

A.D. c.1465–1467[?]

Psalms 57:4[2]

[2]"My soul is among lions."

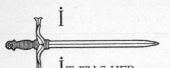

I

IT WAS HER scars that made her beautiful.

No one bothered to give her a name until she was two years old. Up until then, as she toddled between the mercenaries' campfires scrounging food, suckling bitch-hounds' teats, and sitting in the dirt, she had been called Mucky-pup, Grubby-face and Ashy-arse. When her hair fined up from a nondescript light brown to a white blond it was ''Ashy'' that stuck. As soon as she could talk, she called herself Ash.

When Ash was eight-years-old, two of the mercenaries raped her.

She was not a virgin. All the stray children played snuggling games under the smelly sheepskin sleeping rugs, and she had her particular friends. These two mercenaries were not other eight-year-olds, they were grown men. One of them had the grace to be drunk.

Because she cried afterwards, the one who was not drunk heated his dagger in the campfire and drew the knife-tip from below her eye, up her cheekbone in a slant, up to her ear almost.

Because she still cried, he made another petulant slash that opened her cheek parallel under the first cut.

Squalling, she pulled free. Blood ran down the side of her face in sheets. She was not physically big enough to use a sword or an axe, although she had already begun training. She was big enough to pick up his cocked cross-bow (carelessly left ready on the wagon for perimeter defense) and shoot a bolt through the first man at close quarters.

The third scar neatly opened her other cheekbone, but it came honestly, no sadism involved. The second man's dagger was genuinely trying to kill her.

She could not cock the crossbow again on her own. She would not run. She groped among the burst ruins of the first mercenary's body and buried his eating-knife in the upper thigh of the second man, piercing his femoral artery. He bled to death in minutes. Remember that she had already begun to train as a fighter.

Death is nothing strange in mercenary soldier camps. Even so, for an eight year old to kill two of their own was something to give them pause.

Ash's first really clear memory came with the day of her trial. It had rained in the night. The sun brought steam rising from field and distant forest, and slanted gold light across tents, rough bashas, cauldrons, carts, goats, washer-women, whores, captains, stallions and flags. It made the company's colors glow. She gazed up at the big swallow-tailed flag with the cross and beast on it, smelling the cool air on her face.

A bearded man squatted down in front of her to talk to her. She was small, for eight. He wore a breastplate. She saw her face reflected in the curving mirror-shiny metal.

Her face, with her big eyes and ragged long silver hair, and three unhealed scars; two up her cheek under her left eye and one under her right eye. Like the tribal marks of the horse-barbarians of the East.

She smelled grass-fires and horse dung, and the sweat of the armed man. The cool wind raised the hairs on her arms. She saw herself suddenly as if she were outside of it all—the big kneeling man in armor, and in front of him this small child with spilling white curls, in patched hose and bundled into a ragged doublet far too big for her. Barefoot, wide-eyed, scarred; carrying a broken hunting knife reground as a dagger.

It was the first time she saw that she was beautiful.

Blood thundered in her ears with frustration. She could think of no *use* for that beauty.

The bearded man, the Captain of the company, said, "Have you father or mother living?"

"I don't know. One of them might be my father." She pointed at random at men refletching bolts, polishing helmets. "Nobody says they're my mother."

A much thinner man leaned down beside the Captain and said quietly, "One of the dead men was stupid enough to leave a crossbow spanned with a bolt in it. That's an offense. As to the child, the washerwomen say she's no maid, but no one knows her to be a whore either."

"If she is old enough to kill," the Captain scowled through wiry copper-colored hair, "she is old enough to take the penalty. Which is to be whipped at the cart-tail around the camp."

"My name is Ash," she said in a small, clear, carrying voice. "They hurt me and I killed them. If anyone else hurts me, I'll kill them too. I'll kill *you*."

She got the whipping she might have expected, with something added for insolence and discipline's sake. She did not cry. Afterwards, one of the crossbowmen gave her a cut-down jack, a padded cloth jerkin, for armor, and she exercised devotedly in it at weapons practice. For a month or two she pretended the crossbowman was her father, until it became clear that his kindness had been a momentary impulse.

A little later in her ninth year, rumors went through the camp that there had been a Lion born of a Virgin.

II

THE CHILD ASH sat with her back to a bare tree, cheering the mummers. Furs kept some of the ground's ice from her backside.

Her scars were not healing well. They stood out red against the extreme pallor of her skin. Visible breath huffed out of her mouth as she screamed, shoulder to shoulder with all the camp strays and bastards. The Great Wyrm (a man with a tanned horse's skin flung over his back, and a horse's skull fitted by ties to his head) ramped across the stage. The horse skin still had mane and tail attached. They flailed the freezing afternoon air. The Knight of the Wasteland (played by a company sergeant in better armor than Ash had thought he owned) aimed skilful lance blows very wide.

"Oh, *kill* it," a girl called Crow called scornfully.

"Stick it up his arse!" Ash yelled. The children huddling around her tree screamed laughter and disdain.

Richard, a little black-haired boy with a port-wine stain across his face, whispered, "It'll *have* to die. The Lion's born. I heard the Lord Captain say."

Ash's scorn faded with the last sentence. "When? Where? When, Richard? When did you hear him?"

"Midday. I took water into the tent." The small boy's voice sounded proud.

Ash ignored his implied unofficial status as page. She rested her nose on her clenched fists and exhaled warm breath on her frozen fingers. The Wyrm and the sergeant were having it away at each other with more vigor. That was because of the cold. She stood up and rubbed hard at her numb buttocks through her woollen hose.

"Where's you going, Ashy?" the boy asked.

"I'm going to make water," she announced loftily. "You can't come with me."

"Don't *wanna*."

"You're not big enough." With that parting shaft, Ash picked her way out of the crowd of children, goats and hounds.

The sky was low, cold, and the same color as pewter plates. A white mist came up from the river. If it would snow, it would be warmer than this. Ash padded on feet bound with strips of cloth toward the abandoned buildings (probably agricultural) that the company officers had commandeered for winter quarters. A sorry rabble of tents had gone up all around. Armed men were clustered around fire-pits with their fronts to the heat and their arses in the cold. She went on past their backs.

Round to the rear of the farm, she heard them coming out of the building in time to duck behind a barrel, in which the frozen cylindrical block of rainwater protruded up a full handspan.

"And go on foot," the Captain finished speaking. A group of men clattered with him out into the yard. The thin company clerk. Two of the Captain's closest lieutenants. The very few, Ash knew, with pretensions (once) to noble birth.

The Captain wore a close-fitting steel shell that covered all his body. Full harness: from the pauldrons and breastplate enclosing his shoulders and body, the vambraces on his arms, his gauntlets, his tassets and cuisses and greaves that armored his legs, down to the metal sabatons that covered his spurred boots. He carried his armet-type helm under his arm. Winter light dulled the mirrored metal. He stood in the filthy farmyard wearing armor that reflected the sky as white: she had not thought before that this might be why it was called *white harness*. The only color shone from his red beard and the red leather of his scabbard.

Ash knelt back on her knees and toes. Her frozen fingers rested against the cold barrel, too numb to feel the wood staves. The strapped and tied metal plates rattled as the man walked. When his two lieutenants thumped down into the yard, also in full armor, it sounded like muffled pans. Like a cook's wagon overturning.

Ash wanted such armor. It was that desire, more than curiosity, that made her follow them away from the farm buildings. To walk with that invulnerability. With that amount of *wealth* on one's back . . . Ash ran, dazzled.

The sky above yellowed. A few flakes of snow drifted down to lie on top of her untidy hair (less purely white than it), but she took no notice. Her nose and ears shone bright red, and her fingers and toes were blue and purple. This was nothing unusual for her in winter: she thought nothing of it. She did not even pull her doublet tighter over her filthy linen shirt.

The four men—Captain, clerk, two young lieutenants—walked ahead in unusual silence. They passed the camp pickets. Ash sneaked past behind while the Captain exchanged a word with them.

She wondered why the men did not ride. They walked up a steep slope to the surrounding woodland. At the wood's border, confronting the thick bowed branches, the brambles and thorn bushes, the deadwood brushfalls built up over more than a man's lifetime, she understood. You couldn't take a horse into this. Even a war-horse.

Now three of the men stopped and put on their armets. The unarmored clerk fell back a step. Each man kept his visor pinned up, his face visible. The taller of the two lieutenants took his sword out of his scabbard. The bearded Captain shook his head.

The sliding sound of metal on wood echoed in the quiet, as the lieutenant resheathed his blade.

The wood held silence.

All three of the armored men turned to the company clerk. This thin man wore a velvet-covered brigandine and a war-hat,[3] and his uncovered face was pinched in the cold air. Ash sneaked closer as the snow fell.

The clerk stepped confidently forward, into the wood.

Ash had not paid much attention to the hills surrounding the valley. The valley had a clean river, and the lone farmhouse and its buildings. It was good for wintering out of campaign season. What else should she know? The leafless woods on the surrounding high hills had been bare of game. If not hunting, what other reason could take her here, away from the fire-pits?

What reason could take them?

There *was* a path, she decided after some minutes. None of the brambles and thorn bushes on it were more than her own height. Not disused for more than a few seasons.

The armored men pushed unharmed through the briars. The shorter lieutenant swore, "God's blood!" and fell silent, as the other three turned and stared at him. Ash snuck under briar stems as thick as her wrist. Little and quick, she could have out-distanced them, protective armor or not, if she had known where the path went.

With that thought she cast out to the side, wriggled on her belly along the bed of a frozen streamlet, and came out a hundred paces ahead of the leading man.

No snow fell here under the tree canopy. Everything

---

[3]A wide-brimmed steel helmet, identical in shape to the British "Tommy's" helmet of the 1914–1918 World War.

was brown. Dead leaves, dead briars, dead rushes on the
streamlet's edge. Brown bracken ahead. Ash, seeing the
bracken, looked up, and—as she had expected—the tree
cover over it was broken, as it must be to allow its growth.

In the forest glade stood a disused stone chapel,
shrouded in snow.

Ash had no familiarity with the outside or inside of
chapels. Even so, she would have needed to be very familiar indeed with architecture to recognize the style in
which this one had been built. It was ruined now. Two
walls remained standing. Gray moss and brown thorns
covered them, old ice scabbing the vegetation. Two snow-
plastered window frames showed gray, full of winter emptiness. Heaps of snow-rounded rubble cluttered the
ground.

Green color took Ash's eye. Under the thin covering
of snow, all the rubble was grown over with ivy.

Green flowered also at the foot of the chapel walls. Two
fat white-molded holly bushes rooted where the stone slab
of the altar stood against the wall, one on either side of
the cracked slab. Under the snow, their red berries
weighed their branches down.

Ash heard clattering metal behind her. A robin and a
wren took fright and flew out of the holly and away. The
men behind her in the wood began to sing. They were
fifteen feet behind her back, no further away than that.

Ash shot in rabbit-jinks across the rubble. She hit the
snow by the wall and wormed her way in under the lowest
holly branches.

Inside, the bush was hollow and dry. Brown leaves
crackled under her dirty hands. Black branches supported
the canopy of shiny green leaves above her head. Ash lay
flat on her belly and eased forward. Barbed leaves stuck
into her woollen doublet.

She peered from between the leaves. Snow fell now.

The thin clerk lifted a tenor voice and sang. It was a language Ash did not know. The company's two lieutenants stumbled across the broken ground, singing, and it would have sounded better, Ash thought, if they had taken their helmets off instead of just putting up their visors.

The Captain emerged from the wood's edge.

He put his gauntlets up to his chin and fumbled with buckle and strap. Then Ash saw him fiddle with the hook and pin. He opened his helm and took it off, and stood uncovered in the glade. Fat flakes of snow drifted down. They nestled in his hair and beard and ears.

The Captain sang,

"God rest ye merry, Gentlemen, let nothing you dismay;
This darkest hour, the Sun returns; so we salute the Day."

His voice was very loud, very cracked, not very much in tune. The silence of the wood shattered. Ash cried sudden hot tears. He had wrecked his voice bellowing above the noise of men and horses; it was a powerful ruin.

The company clerk came close to the holly bush in which Ash hid. She made herself still. Tears dried on her scarred cheeks. Half of being hidden is to remain utterly, completely still. The other half is to think yourself into the background. *I am a rabbit, a rat, a briar, a tree.* She lowered her mouth into the neck of her doublet so that her white breath would not betray her.

"Give thanks," the clerk said. He put something up onto the old altar. Ash was below and could not see, but it smelled like raw meat. Snow tangled in the man's hair. His eyes were bright. Despite the cold, sweat ran in drops down his forehead, under the brim of his metal hat. The rest of what he said was in the other language.

The taller lieutenant screeched "*Look!*" so loudly that Ash started and jumped. A disturbed twig dumped snow down her face. She blinked it out of her eyelashes. Now I'm discovered, she thought calmly, and put her head out into the glade and found no one even looking in her direction. Their eyes were on the altar.

All three knights went down on their knees in the ivy-covered rubble. Armor scraped and clattered. The Captain's arms fell to his sides, and the helm from his hand: Ash winced as she heard it hit rocky earth and bounce.

The company clerk took off his dish-shaped war-hat and moved to one knee with a singular grace.

Snow whirled faster from the invisible whiteness of the sky into the glade. Snow covered the green ivy, the red berries of the holly. Snow froze on the spindly brown arcs of briar. A great huffing animal breath came down from the altar of the ruined green chapel. Ash watched its whiteness on the air. Animal-breath hit her in the face, warm and wet.

A great paw trod down from the stone altar.

The paw's pelt was yellow. Ash stared at it, two inches from her face. Yellow fur. Coarse yellow fur, paler and softer at the roots. The beast's claws were curved, and longer than her hand, and white with clear tips. Needle tips.

The haunch of a Lion passed Ash's face. Its flank obscured the clearing, the wood, the men. The beast stepped down fluidly from the altar. It threw up its maned head, bolting down whatever the offering had been. She saw its throat move, swallowing.

A coughing roar broke the air a foot away from her.

She pissed the crotch of her woollen hose. Hot urine steamed in the cold, chilled clammily down her thighs, instantly cold in the snowy air. Eyes wide, she could only stare, could not even wonder why none of the kneeling knights sprang up or drew their swords. The Lion's head began to swing around. Ash knelt, paralyzed.

The Lion's wrinkled muzzle swung into the hollow leaves. Its face was huge. Great luminous, long-lashed, yellow eyes blinked. A heavy smell of carrion, heat and sand choked her. The Lion grunted, flinched back slightly from the berry-laden pricking branches. Its black lips writhed back from its teeth. It reached in delicately and nipped the front of Ash's doublet between an upper and a lower incisor.

The Lion's rump went up. Its tail lashed. It pulled her out of the bush. Only a child's weight, no effort—a child snarled up in holly leaves and bramble, pulled forward, in green wool doublet and blue stinking hose, spilled face-down on the snow-shrouded ivy and rocks.

The second roar deafened her.

Ash had become too frightened to move. Now she jammed her arms up over her head, covering her ears. She burst into noisy, uninhibited tears.

A rasping tongue as thick as her leg licked up one side of her scarred face.

Ash stopped wailing. Her sore face stung. She got slowly up onto her knees. The Lion stood twice as tall as she did. She looked up into its golden eyes, whiskered muzzle, curved white teeth. Its great tongue slobbered down and rasped up her other cheek. Her unhealed scars throbbed rawly. She poked at them with fingers blunt and senseless as wood. A robin on the ruined chapel's wall burst into song.

She was young to have such an awareness of herself, but she was perfectly sure of two separate, distinct, and mutually exclusive reactions. The part of her that was camp-child and used to large feral animals, and to hunting in season, froze her body very still: *it hasn't touched me with its claws, I'm too close to run, I mustn't startle it.*

Another part of herself seemed less familiar. It filled with
a burning happiness. She could not remember the words
or language that the clerk had been using. In her utterly
clear voice, she began to sing the Captain's hymn,

> "*God rest ye merry, Gentlemen, let nothing you
>   dismay;*
> *This darkest hour, the Sun returns, so we salute this
>   Day.*
> *We march forth to Your Victory, our foes in
>   disarray!*
> *Oh, his Brightness brings comfort and joy*
> *None can destroy:*
> *Oh, his Brightness brings comfort and joy.*"

The clearing was silent when she ended. She could not
hear the difference between the man's cracked voice and
her own purity. She did not have the age to distinguish
between his bad voice, singing with maturity, and her own
blurring of breath, and pauses, that were a reflection of
rote learning by some campfire.

All the while her young soul sang, her mind whimpered, *no, no.* Remembering a leopard hunt once near Ur-
bino. The cat's claws had sliced open a hound's stomach
in an instant and tangled its stinking intestines in the
grass.

The great head dipped down. For a second she breathed
in fur. She choked, drowned in its mane. The Lion's eyes
looked into hers, with a flat animal awareness of her scent
and presence. The huge muscles clenched and bunched
and the beast sprang over her head. By the time she could
turn, it had crashed through the light underbrush at the
edge of the clearing and vanished.

She sat for a few moments, clearly hearing the dimin-
ishing noise of its departure.

The clatter of metal woke her attention.

Ash sat, legs aspraddle, on snow-smeared rock and ivy. Her head was on a level with the articulated poleyns or knee-armor of the Captain's harness, now that he stood beside her. The silver chape on his scabbard glittered near her eye.

"He didn't speak," she complained.

"The Lion born of a Virgin is a beast," said the clerk, tenor voice loud and flat in the abandoned clearing. "An animal. Lord Captain, I don't understand. The child is known to be no virgin, yet He did not harm her."

The bearded Captain stared down from his great height. Ash felt afraid of his frown. He spoke, but not directly to her.

"Perhaps it was a vision. The child is our poor land, waiting for the breath of the Lion for salvation. This winter barrenness, her spoiled face: all one. I cannot interpret, I have not the skill. It could mean anything."

The company clerk replaced his steel hat. "My lords, what we have seen here was for us alone. And you will let us retire to prayer and seek guidance."

"Yes." The Lord Captain bent and picked up his helmet, brushing the caked snow off the metal. The sun, through an unexpected break in the winter cloud, struck fire from his red hair and beard and hard metal shell. As he turned away, he added, "Somebody bring the brat."

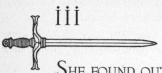

iii

SHE FOUND OUT what she could do with her scar-emphasized child's beauty.

By the age of nine she had a mass of curls that she kept long, halfway to her waist, and washed once a month. Her silver hair had the gray shine of grease. No one in a soldiers' camp could notice the smell. She never showed her ears. She learned to keep dressing in cut-down hose and doublet, often with an adult's jerkin over them. Something in the too-large clothing made her look even more of a little child.

One of the gunners would always give her food or copper coins. He bent her forward over an iron-bound gun carriage, undid the points of her hose, and fucked her up the arse.

"You don't have to be that careful," Ash complained. "I won't have a child. I haven't shown flowers—blood—yet."

"You haven't shown a cock, either," the gunner answered. "Until I find a pretty boy, you'll have to do."

Once he gave her a spare strip of mail. She begged thread from one of the company's clothiers, and a piece of leather from the tanner, and sewed the riveted metal links onto that. She shaped it into a mail standard or collar, tied on to protect the throat. She wore it at every skirmish, every cattle-raid, every bandit ambush where she learned her business—which was, as she had always known, war.

She prayed for war the way other little girls her age, in convents, pray to be the chosen bride of the Green Christ.

Guillaume Arnisout was a gunner in the mercenary company. He never touched her. He showed her how to write her name in Green alphabet: a vertical slash with five horizontal cuts (''the same number as your fingers'') jutting out of it on the right hand side (''*sword* hand side!''). He didn't teach her how to read because he couldn't. He taught her how to figure. Ash thought, *All gunners can calculate to a single powder-grain*, but that was before she understood gunners.

Guillaume showed her the ash tree and taught her how to make hunting bows from that wood (''a *wider* stave than you need for a yew bow'').

Guillaume took her to visit the slaughterhouse, after the August siege at Dinant, before the company went overseas again.

The spring sun shimmered on hawthorn blossom hedging the cattle pastures. A chill wind still blew. The company encampment's noise and smell were carried away, downwind.

Ash rode the cow into the village, sitting sideways on the peaked bone ridge of its back. Guillaume walked beside the cow, on the rutted lane. She looked down at him walking in the dust. He carried a carved stick of a secret black wood, using it at each step for support. Ash knew she had not been born when a poleaxe smashed his knee in a line-fight and he retired to the siege guns.

''Guillaume . . .''

''Urh.''

''I could have brought her on my own. You didn't have to come.''

''Hurh.''

She looked ahead. The double spire of the church was

visible over the trees now. Blue smoke went up. They came to the edge of the cleared ground around the village palisade and the wind changed. The smell of the abattoir was full and choking.

"God's *blood*!" Ash swore. A hard hand clipped her skinny shank. She looked down round-shouldered at Guillaume and let water brim over her lower lids.

"Now that," Guillaume pointed, "is where we're going. Get off that old bag of bones and lead her, for Christ's pity's sake."

Ash kicked her heels out and launched herself into the air. She landed in the dusty road ruts, dipping briefly to steady herself with one hand, and sprang up. She leaped exuberantly around the plodding cow, skipping, and then ran back to the tall man.

"Guillaume." She took his arm, gripping the rusty brown sleeve of his doublet. There was no cloth under the cuff: the gunner had no more shirt to his name at the moment than Ash did. "Guillaume, is it boys you like?"

"Ha!" He stared down at her with his dark eyes. Stringy black hair hung down shoulder-length from his head, except at his crown, where he was balding. He had a habit of shaving himself every so often with his dagger, generally the same day that he remembered to get it sharpened, but his cheeks were brown and leathery and hardly showed one more nick from a blade.

"Do I like boys, missy? Is that you asking me why you can't twist me around your little finger, as you do the rest? Must I like little boys better than little girls for that to be true?"

"Most of them do what I want when I pretend."

He yanked her long silver-white hair. "But I like you the way you are."

Ash pushed her hair back down over her pointed ears. She kicked at the waving heads of grass that grew on the side of the village road. "I'm beautiful. I'm not a woman yet but I'm beautiful. I've got elvish blood in me, look at the hair. Look at my hair, *you* don't care . . ." She sang that to herself for a few minutes, and then looked up with what she knew to be large, widely spaced eyes. "*Guillaume* . . ."

The gunner strode ahead, ignoring her, planting his stick with great firmness in the dust, and then flourishing it to greet the two guards on the village gate. They had iron-shod quarterstaffs, Ash noted, and thick leather jerkins in lieu of armor.

She took the rope that hung around the cow's neck. The cow had been dry for six months. It remained barren now, no matter which town's bull the mercenaries put it to on their way through the countryside. It would make stringy meat, but quite good shoe leather. Ash kicked her bare soles on the earth. Or good leather for sword-belts.

With the smell of the dusty road overcome by the smell of the village's street, she wondered, Is it another place where they shout obscenities at scars, and make the sign of the Horns?

"Ash!"

The cow had drifted to one side of the path, and mouthed grass unenthusiastically. Ash set her bare heels on the path and heaved. The cow's head came up. It drew in a noisy breath and mooed. Ropes of saliva trailed from its jaws. Ash led it toward the village gate and the wattle-and-daub houses, after Guillaume.

Ash had a blade now. She fingered it, staring down the guys on the gate. Someone's twenty-inch dagger originally, so it was more of a short sword for her. At nine she is small, you could take her for seven. It did come with its own scabbard and a loop for hanging it off her belt. She earned it. She steals food, she will not steal weapons. The other mercenaries—she has been thinking of them and herself in those terms recently—regard this as an interesting and peculiar quirk, and take advantage.

It being not long past dawn, few of the village folk were on the street. Ash regretted no one being there to see her.

"They let me enter the village armed," she boasted. "I didn't have to give up my dagger!"

"You're on the books as one of the company." Guillaume had his own falchion at his belt, a meat-cleaver of a blade with a hair-splitter single edge. In the same way that Ash habitually wore over-large doublets and played camp's-little-mascot, she deeply suspected that Guillaume played up to the stereotypical idea that gormless villagers had of mercenaries: filthy dress and spotless weapons. Certainly he did the other thing the yokels expected and cheated them at cards, but badly; even Ash could spot him doing it.

Ash walked with her thin shoulders back and her head up. She stared down a couple of idlers standing under the hanging bush that marked one hut as a tavern.

"If I didn't have this God-rotted barren animal," she yelped at the gunner walking in front of her, "I'd look like a proper contract soldier!"

Guillaume Arnisout laughed briefly. He walked on. He didn't look back.

She worried the complacent cow as far as the abattoir gates before it got its belly full of the smell. The stink of excrement and blood was strong enough to be tangible. Ash's eyes streamed. Something stuck in the back of her throat. She handed the cow's bridle over to a slaughter-man at the gate, coughing.

A voice bawled, "Ash! Over here!"

Ash turned. Something warm and heavy hit her in the face and chest.

Surprise made her gasp, intake a breath. Immediately

she choked on hot liquid. A solid mass of *stuff* slid from her shoulders, down her chest. She ground the heels of her hands into her burning eyes. She coughed, choked again, began to cry. The tears cleared her vision.

Blood soaked the front of her doublet and hose. Hot, steaming blood. Blood stuck her white hair together in crimson tendrils, dripping spatters into the dust. Blood covered her hands. Yellow matter crusted the creases of her clothes. She put her hand up and scooped a mass of matter out of the neck of her doublet: a lump of meat flecked with blood clots the size of her small fist.

The solid mass slid and flopped over her bare feet. It was hot. Warm. Cooling fast. Cold. Pink tubes and red tubes slid to the ground. She moved her foot out from under a kidney-shaped lump that she could not have held in her two hands.

Ash stopped crying.

She did something. It was not new, or she would not have known how to do it now. It might have been something she did just before or after she fired the crossbow point-blank at her rapist and his body exploded in front of her.

She wiped the back of her hand across her chin. Blood tightened on her skin as it dried there. She got rid of the constriction in her throat and the tears pricking behind her eyes.

She stared at Guillaume and the slaughterman, now carrying empty wooden pails.

"That was *stupid*," she raged. "Blood's unclean!"

"Come here." Guillaume pointed to a spot in front of himself.

The gunner was standing at a skinning rack. Timbers as stout as those that made up a siege machine held a chain on a pulley. Hooks hung from the chain, over a gutter dug in the earth. Ash lifted her feet out of pigs' guts and walked toward Guillaume. Her clothes stuck to her. Her nose was ceasing to smell the reek of the slaughterhouse.

"Take out your sword," he said.

She had no gloves. The hilt of her weapon was bound with leather, and slippery in her palm.

"Cut," Guillaume said calmly, pointing at the cow that now hung head-down beside him, still alive, hooves trussed. "Slit her belly."

Ash had not been in a church but she knew enough to scowl at that.

"Do it," he said.

Ash's long dagger was heavy in her hand. The weight of the metal pulled on her wrist.

The cow's long-lashed eyes rolled. She groaned frantically. Her thrashing did no more than roll her from side to side on the hook. A stream of shit ran down her warm, breathing flanks.

"I can't do this," Ash protested. "I can do it. I know how. I just can't *do* it. It's not like she's going to do me any harm!"

"*Do it!*"

Ash flicked the blade clumsily and punched it forward. She leaned all her weight into the point, as she had been taught, and the sharp metal punctured the cow's brown and white pelt. The cow opened her mouth and screamed.

Blood sprayed. Sweat made the dagger grip slide in Ash's hand. The dagger slid out of the shallow wound. She stared up at the animal that was eight times her size. She got a double-handed grip on the blade and cut forward. The edge skimmed the cow's flank.

"You'd be dead by now," Guillaume rasped.

Tears began to leak out of Ash's eyes. She stepped up close to the breathing warm body. She raised the big dagger over her head and brought it down overarm with both hands.

The point of the blade punched through tough skin and the thin muscle wall and into the abdominal cavity. Ash wrenched and pulled the blade down. It felt like hacking cloth. Jerking, snagging. A mess of pink ropes fell down around her in the dawn yard, and smoked in the early chill. Ash hacked doggedly down. The blade cut into bone and stuck. A rib. She yanked. Pulled. The cow's flesh sucked shut on her blade.

"Twist. Use your foot if you have to!" Guillaume's voice directed over her harsh, effortful breathing.

Ash leaned her knee on the cow's wet neck, pressing it back against the wood frame with her tiny weight. She twisted her wrists hard right and the blade turned, breaking the vacuum that held it in the wound, and coming free of the bone. The cow's screams drowned every other sound.

"*Hhaaaaah!*" Both her hands on the dagger-grip, Ash swiped the blade across the stretched skin of the cow's throat. The rib bone must have nicked her blade. She felt the steel's irregularity catch on flesh. A wide gash opened. For a fraction of a second it showed a cross-section of skin, muscle sheath, muscle and artery wall. Then blood welled up and gushed out and hit her in the face. Hot. *Blood heat*, she thought, and giggled.

"Now cry!" Guillaume spun her around and cracked his hand across her face. The blow would have hurt another adult.

Astonished, Ash burst into loud sobs. She stood for perhaps a minute, crying. Then she wept, "I'm not old enough to go into a line-fight!"

"Not this year."

"I'm too little!"

"Crocodile tears, now." Guillaume sighed. "I thank

you," he added gravely; "kill the beast now." And when she looked, he was handing the slaughterman a copper piece. "Come on, missy. Back to camp."

"My sword's dirty," she said. Suddenly she folded her legs and sat down on the earth, in animal blood and shit, and howled. She coughed, fighting to breathe. Great shuddering gasps wracked her chest. Her reddened hair hung down and streaked her wet, scarred cheeks. Snot trailed from her nostrils.

"Ah." Guillaume's hand caught her doublet collar and lifted her up into the air, and dropped her down on her bare feet. Hard. "Better. Enough. There."

He pointed at a trough on the far side of the yard.

Ash ripped her front lacing undone. She stripped off her doublet and hose in one, not bothering to undo the points that tied them together at her waist. She plunged the blood-soaked wool into the cold water, and used it to wash herself down. The early morning sun felt hot on her bare cold skin. Guillaume stood with folded arms and watched her.

All through it she had her discarded sword-belt under her foot and her eyes on the slaughterhouse men.

The last thing she did was wash her blade clean, dry it, and beg some grease to oil the metal so that it should not rust. By then her clothing was only damp, if not dry. Her hair hung down in wet white rats' tails.

"Back to camp," the gunner said.

Ash walked out of the village gate beside Guillaume. It did not even occur to her to ask to be taken in by one of the village families.

Guillaume looked down at her with bright, bloodshot eyes. Dirt lodged in the creases of his skin, clearly apparent in the brightening sun. He said, "If that was easy, think of this. She was a beast, not a man. She had no

voice to threaten. She had no voice to beg mercy. And
she wasn't trying to kill *you*."

"I know," Ash said. "I've killed a man who was."

When she was ten, she nearly died, but not on the field
of battle.

iV

FIRST LIGHT CAME. Ash leaned out over the
stone parapet of the bell tower. Too dark to see the
ground, fifty feet of empty air below. A horse whinnied.
A hundred others answered it, all down the battle-lines.
A lark sang in the arch of the sky. The flat river valley
began to emerge from darkness.

The air heated up fast. Ash wore a stolen shirt and
nothing else. It was a man's linen shirt and still smelled
of him, and it came down past her knees. She had belted
it with her sword-belt. The linen protected the nape of her
neck, and her arms, and most of her legs. She rubbed her
goose-fleshed skin. Soon the day would be burning hot.

Light crept from the east. Shadows fell to the west. Ash
caught a pinprick of light two miles away.

One. Fifty. A thousand? The sun glinted back from helmets and breastplates, from poleaxes and warhammers
and the bodkin points of clothyard arrows.

"They're arrayed and moving! They've got the sun at
their backs!" She hopped from one bare foot to the other.
"*Why* won't the captain let us fight?"

"I don't want to!" The black-haired boy, Richard, now
her particular friend, whimpered beside her.

Ash looked at him in complete bewilderment. "Are you afraid?" She darted to the other side of the tower, leaning over and looking down at the company's wagon-fort. Washerwomen and whores and cooks were fixing the chains that bound the carts together. Most of them carried twelve-foot pikes, razor-edged bills. She leaned out further. She couldn't see Guillaume.

Day brightened quickly. Ash craned to look down the slope toward the river's edge. A few horses galloping, their riders in bright colors. A flag: the company ensign. Then men of the company walking, weapons in hand.

"Ash, why are we so *slow*?" Richard quavered. "They'll be here before we're ready!"

Ash had started to be strong in the last half year or so, in the way that terriers and mountain ponies are strong, but she still did not look older than eight. Malnutrition had a lot to do with it.

She put her arm around him. "There's trouble. We can't get through. Look."

All down by the river showed red in the rising sun. Vast cornfields, so thick with poppies that she couldn't see the grain. Corn and poppies together—the crops so thick and tangled that they slowed down the mercenaries walking with bills and swords and halberds. The armored men on horseback drew ahead, into the scarlet distance, under the banner.

Richard bundled his arms around Ash, pale enough for his birthmark to stand out like a banner on his face. "Will they all die?"

"No. Not everybody. Not if some of the other lot come over to us when the fighting starts. The captain buys them if he can. Oh." Ash's guts contracted. She reached down and put her hand between her legs and took her fingers out bloody.

"Sweet Green Christ!" Ash wiped her hand on her

linen shirt, with a glance around the bell tower to see if anyone had overheard her swear. They were alone.

"Are you wounded?" Richard stepped back.

"*Oh*. No." Far more bewildered than she sounded, Ash said, "I'm a woman. They told me, in the wagons, it could happen."

Richard forgot the armed men moving. His smile was sweet. "It's the first time, isn't it? I'm so happy for you, Ashy! Will you have a baby?"

"Not right now . . ."

She made him laugh, his fear gone. That done, she turned back to the red river fields that stretched away from the tower. Dew burned off in bright mist. Not dawn, now, but full early morning.

"Oh, *look* . . ."

Half a mile away now, the enemy.

The Bride of the Sea's men moving over a slope, small and glittering. Banners of red and blue and gold and yellow gleamed above the packed mass of their helmets. Too far away to see faces, even the inverted V that disclosed mouth and chin when, in the heat, they left off falling-buffs and bevors.[4]

"Ashy, there are so *many*—!" Richard whined.

The Serene Bride of the Sea's host drew up into three. The vaward or advance unit was big enough on its own. Behind it, offset to one side, was the mainward, with the Bride of the Sea's banners and their commander's own standard. Offset again, the rearward was only just in sight as a moving thicket of pikes and lances.

The first rows came on slowly. Billmen in padded linen jacks, their steel war-hats gleaming, bright hook-bladed

---

[4]Armour pieces for the chin and lower face, made of either articulated or solid plate, and often lined with velvet or other cloth; therefore hot to wear.

bills over their shoulders. Ash knew billhooks had some agricultural use, but not what it might be. You could hook an armored knight off his horse with one, and use it to crack his protective metal plates open. Men-at-arms in foot armor, with axes over their shoulders like peasants going out to cut wood . . . And archers. Far too many archers.

"Three battles." Ash pointed Richard bodily, holding him by his narrow shoulders. The little boy trembled. "Look, Dickon. In the front battle. There's billmen, then archers, then men-at-arms, then archers, then billmen, then more archers—all down the line."

A hoarse voice, audible across the whole distance, shouted, "Nock! Loose!"

Ash scratched at her stained shirt. Everything laid itself out, suddenly plain in her head. For the first time, what had been an implicit sense of a pattern found words.

She stuttered into speech, almost too fast and excited to be understood. "Their archers are safe *because* of their men with hand-weapons! They can shoot into us, loose an arrow every six heartbeats, and we can't do anything about it! Because if we *do* try to get up close, their billmen or foot knights will kill us. Then their archers will draw their falchions and get stuck in too, or move out to the flanks and carry on shooting us up. That's why they've put them like that. What can we *do*?"

"If you are outnumbered, you cannot meet them in separate units. Form a wedge. A wedge-shaped formation with the point toward the enemy, then your flank archers can shoot without hitting your men in front. When their foot troops attack, they must face your weapons on each of your flanks. Send in your heavy armored men to break their flank."

Ash found the hard words no more difficult to decipher than discussions she had overheard, lying the grass, back

of the captain's command tent. She puzzled it out, and
said, "How *can* we? We don't have enough men!"

"Ashy," Richard whimpered.

She protested, "What have we got? The Great Duke's
men—about half as many! And the city militia. They just
about know enough not to hold a sword by the sharp end.
Two more companies. And us."

"Ash!" the boy protested loudly. "Ashy!"

*"Then do not array your men too close together. They
are a mass for the enemy to shoot into. The enemy are
out of range. You must move, fast, and close-assault
them."*

She dug with her bare toe in the dust between the
tower's flagstones, not looking at the approaching banners. "There're too many of them!"

"Ashy, stop it. Stop it! Who are you talking to?"

"Then you must surrender and sue for peace."

"Don't tell me! I can't do anything! I can't!"

Richard shrieked, "Tell you what? *Who's* telling?"

Nothing happened for long seconds. Then the mass of
the company moved forward, running, the Great Duke's
troops with them, crashing into the first enemy battle line,
flags dipping, the red of poppies a red mist now; thunder,
iron beating on iron, screams, hoarse voices shouting orders, a pipe shrilling through the dirt rising up a bare few
hundred yards away.

"You said—I heard you!" Ash stared at Richard's
white and wine-colored face. "You *said*—I heard someone saying—Who *was* that?"

The Great Duke's line of men broke up into knots. No
flying wedge now, just knots of men-at-arms gathered
around their standards and banners. In the dust and red
sun, the main battle of the Most Serene Bride of the Sea's
army began to walk forward. Sheaves of arrows thickened
the air.

"But *someone* said—"

The stone parapet smacked her in the face.

Blood smashed across her upper lip. She put one hand to her nose. Pain made her scream. Her fingers spread and shook.

The noise filled her mouth, filled her chest, shook the sky crashing down. Ash touched the sides of her head. A thin, high whine filled her ears. Richard's face streamed tears and his mouth was an open square. She could just hear him bawling.

The corner of the parapet wall fell soundlessly away. Open air gaped in front of her. Dust hung hazy. She got to her hands and knees. A violent whirring whicked past her head, loud enough for her, half-deaf, to hear.

The boy stood with his hands loose at his sides. He stared over Ash's head, out from the broken bell tower. She saw his particolored legs tremble. The front of his cod-flap wetted with urine. With a ripe, wet sound, he shat in his hose. Ash looked up at Richard without condemnation. There are times when losing control of your bowels is the only realistic response to a situation.

"That's *mortars*! Get *down*!" She hoped she was shouting. She got Richard by the wrist and pulled him toward the steps.

The sharp edge of the stone barked her knees. Her sun-blasted vision saw nothing but darkness. She fell down inside the bell tower, cracking her head against the wall of the stairwell. Richard's foot kicked her in the mouth. She bled and yelled and tumbled down to ground-level and ran.

She heard no more gunfire, but when she looked back from the wagon fort, her chest raw inside and burning, the monastery tower was gone, only rubble and dust blackening the sky.

Forty-five minutes later the baggage train were declared prisoners.

Ash ran away, out of their sight, down to the river.

Searching.

Bodies lay so thick on the ground that the air swam with the smell. She clamped her linen sleeve over her mouth and nose. She tried not to step on the faces of the dead men and boys.

Scavengers came by to strip the bodies. She hid in the wet, red corn. Their peasant voices were rapid, inflected music.

She felt the skin across her cheeks and nose crisping in the high summer heat. The sun burned at her calves below the linen shirt, turning her fair skin pink. Her toes burned. The whole world smelled of shit and spoiling meat. She kept spitting without being able to get the taste of vomit out of her mouth. Heat made the air waver.

One of the dying men wept ''Bartolomeo! Bartolomeo!'' and then pleaded with the surgeon's cart, long-handled, dragged on two wheels by a man who grunted and shook his head.

No Richard. No one. The crops were burned black for a mile or more. Ravens dragged bits of two armored horse carcasses apart. If there had been anything else—bombards, bodies, salvageable armor—it had been cleared up or looted.

Ash ran, breathless, back to the company cooking fires. She saw Richard sitting with the washerwomen. He looked up, saw her, and ran away.

Her steps slowed.

Abruptly, Ash turned and tugged the sleeve of a gunner's doublet. Not realising how deaf she was, she shouted, ''Where's *Guillaume*? Guillaume Arnisout?''

''Buried down in the lime pit.''

"*What?*"

The unarmed man shrugged and faced her. She followed his lips as much as the whisper of sound. "Dead and buried in the lime pits."

"Uhh." Air left her lungs.

"No," another man called from beside the fire, "they took him prisoner. The bloody Brides of the Sea have got him."

"No," a third man held his hands apart, "he had a hole in his stomach *this* big. But it wasn't the Most Serene, it was our side, the Great Duke's men, it was someone he owed money to."

Ash left them.

No matter what turf it was set up on, the camp was always the same. She made her way into the middle of the camp, where she did not often go. Now it was full of armed strangers. At last she found a manicured, blond man with a harassed expression, who wore a gold-edged green surcoat over his armor. He was one of the Lord Captain's aides and she knew him by sight, not by name; the gunners referred to him derisively as *tabard-lifter*. She already understood why.

" 'Guillaume Arnisout'?" He put his hand through his thick bobbed hair. "Is he your father?"

"Yes." Ash lied without hesitation. She did the thing she had learned to do and the constriction in her throat went away, so that she could speak. "I *want* him! Tell me where he is!"

The aide pricked down a parchment list. " 'Arnisout.' Here. He was taken prisoner. The captains are talking. I imagine prisoners may be exchanged after a few hours."

Ash thanked him in as quiet a voice as she could manage and returned to the edges of the camp to wait.

Evening fell across the valley. The stench of bodies sweetened the air unbearably. Guillaume did not come

back to camp. Rumor began to say he had died of his
wounds, died of plague caught in the Bride of the Sea's
camp, signed on with the Most Serene as a master gunner
at twice the pay, run off with a noblewoman from the
Duke's city, gone home to his farm in Navarre. (Ash
hoped for a few weeks. After six months, she stopped
hoping.)

By sunset, prisoners moved aimlessly between the
camp's tents, unused to walking around without sword,
axe, bow, halberd. The evening sun lay gold over blood
and poppies. The air tasted of heat. Ash's nose numbed
itself to the worse of the decomposition. Richard stalked
up to her where Ash stood in dung-stained straw, her back
to a cart's wheel, with one of the baggage train's washerwomen dabbing witch hazel on the yellow bruises down
her shins.

"When will we *know*?" Richard shivered, and glared
at her. "What will they *do* with us?"

"Us?" Ash's ears still thinly sang.

The washerwoman grunted. "We're part of the spoil.
Sell us to whorehouses, maybe."

"I'm too young!" Ash protested.

"No."

"Demon!" the boy shrieked. "Demons told *you* we'd
lose! *You* hear demons! *You'll* burn!"

"Richard!"

He ran away. He ran down the earth-track that soldiers'
feet had beaten into existence over the peasants' crops,
away from the baggage wagons.

"Man-bait! He's too pretty," the washerwoman said,
suddenly vicious, throwing her wet rag down. "I wouldn't
be him. Or you. Your face! They'll burn you. If you hear
voices!" She made the sign of the Horns.

Ash leaned her head back, staring up into the endless
blue. The air swam with gold. Every muscle ached, one

wrenched knee hurt, her little toenail had been torn off bloody. None of the normal euphoria of hard exertion over and done with. Her guts churned.

"Not voices. *A* voice." She pushed with her bare foot at the clay pot of witch hazel ointment. "Maybe it was sweet Christ. Or a saint."

"*You*, hear a saint?" the woman snarled incredulously. "Little whore!"

Ash wiped her nose with the back of her hand. "Maybe it was a vision. Guillaume had a vision once. He saw the Blessed Dead fighting with us at Dinant."

The washerwoman turned to walk away. "I hope the Most Serene look at your ugly face and make you fuck their nightsoil men!"

Ash scooped up and hefted the pot of witch hazel in one hand, preparing to throw. "Poxy bitch!"

A hand came out of nowhere and clouted her. It stunned her. She burst into a humiliatingly loud squall, dropping the clay pot.

The man, now visible as wearing the Bride of the Sea's livery, snarled, "You, woman, get up to the center of camp. We're doing shares of spoil. Go! You too, you little scarred freak!"

The washerwoman ran off, laughing too shrilly. The soldier followed.

Another woman, suddenly beside the wagon, asked, "*Do* you hear voices, child?"

This woman had a moon-round, moon-pale face, with no hair showing under her tight headdress. Over her big body a gray robe hung loosely, with a Briar Cross on a chain at her belt.

Ash sniveled. She wiped her dripping nose again. A line of thin, clear snot hung from her nostrils to the shirt's linen sleeve. "I don't know! What's 'hearing voices'?"

The pale moon-face looked avidly down at her.

"There's talk among the men of the Most Serene. I think they're looking for you."

"Me?" A tightness took hold of Ash's ribs. "Looking for *me*?"

A clammily hot white hand reached down, seizing Ash's jaw and turning her face up to the evening light. She strained against the imprint of sharp fingertips, without success. The woman studied her intently.

"If it was a true sending from the Green Christ, they hope you will prophesy for them. If it's a demon, they'll drive it out of you. That could take until morning. Most of them are well gone in drink now."

Ash ignored the grip on her face, her sick fear and her bowels churning. "Are you a nun?"

"I am one of the Sisters of St. Herlaine, yes. We have a convent near here, at Milano."[5] The woman let go. Her voice sounded harsh under the liquid speech. Ash guessed it to be not her first language. Like all mercenaries, Ash

---

[5]Internal evidence therefore suggests this is not one of the Company of the Griffin-in-Gold's contracts with the Burgundian Dukes. Therefore, the battle can be neither Dinant (August 19–25, 1466), or Brustem (October 28, 1467). I theorize that this takes place in Italy, that it is Molinella (1467), a battle in the war between Duke Francisco Sforza of Milan, and the Serenissima or Most Serene Republic of Venice under the condottiere Bartolomeo Colleoni. Colleoni has been falsely credited with the first use of field guns in battle.

The battle is obscure, noted only because of a cynical comment which Niccolò Machiavelli later wrote about the "bloodless wars" of the Italian professional contract soldiers: that only one man died in the battle of Molinella, and that was from falling off his horse. Better sources suggest a more accurate assessment would be around six hundred dead.

The *Winchester Codex* was written around 1495 A.D., some twenty-eight years after this date, and nineteen years after the main body of the 'Ash" texts (which cover the year 1476–1477 A.D.). Some details of the battle depicted here greatly resemble the last conflict in the Wars of the Roses, the Battle of Stoke (1487). Possibly this biography was written by an English soldier who had become a monk at Winchester, and wrote about what he experienced in the English midlands, at Stoke, rather than about Molinella itself.

had the basics of most languages she had heard. Ash understood the big woman as she said, "You need feeding up, girl. How old are you?"

"Nine. Ten. Eleven." Ash dragged her sleeve across her chin. "I don't know. I can remember the big storm. Ten. Maybe nine."

The woman's eyes were light, all light. "You're a *child*. Small, too. No one has ever cared for you, have they? Probably that's why the demon got in. This camp is no place for a child."

Tears stabbed her eyes. "It's my home! I *don't* have a demon!"

The nun put her hands up, each palm to one of Ash's cheeks, surveying her without her scars. Her hands felt both warm and cold on Ash's wet skin.

"I am Sister Ygraine. Tell me the truth. What speaks to you?"

Doubt bit cold in Ash's belly. "Nothing, nobody, Soeur! Nobody was there but me and Richard!"

Chills stiffened her neck, braced her shoulders. Rote words of a prayer to the Green Christ died in her dry mouth. She began to listen. The nun's harsh breathing. Fire crackling. A horse whinnying. Drunken songs and shouting further off.

No sensation of a voice speaking quietly, to her, out of a companionable silence.

A burst of sound roared from the center of the camp. Ash flinched. Soldiers ran past, ignoring them, running toward the growing crowd in the center. Somewhere in a wagon close by, a hurt man called out for his *maman*. Gold light faded toward dusk. The tall sky began to fill with sparks showering up from the campfires, fires let burn too high, far too high; they might burn all the mercenary tents by morning, and think nothing of it but a brief regret for plunder ruined.

The nun said, "They're despoiling your camp."

Not speaking to Soeur Ygraine, not speaking to anyone, she deliberately breathed words aloud: "We're prisoners. What will happen to me now?"

"License, liberty, and drunkenness—"

Ash clamped her hands over her ears. The soundless voice continued:

"—the night when commanders cannot control their men who have come living off the battlefield. The night in which people are killed for sport."

Sister Ygraine shifted her big hand to Ash's shoulder, the grip firm through Ash's filthy-dirty shirt. Ash lowered her hands. A growl in her belly told her she was hungry for the first time in twelve hours.

The nun continued to gaze down at her as if no voice had spoken.

"I—" Ash hesitated.

In her mind now she felt neither silence, nor a voice, but a *potential* for speech. Like a tooth which does not quite ache, but soon will.

She began to hurt for what she had never before given two thoughts to: the solitariness of her soul in her body. Fear flooded her from scalp to tingling fingertips to feet.

She abruptly stuttered, "I *didn't* hear any voice, I didn't, I *didn't*! I lied to Richard because I thought it would make me famous. I just wanted somebody to notice me!"

And then, as the big woman disinterestedly turned her back and began to stride away, into the chaos of firelight and drunken condottieri, Ash shrieked out hard enough to hurt her throat:

"Take me somewhere safe, take me to sanctuary, *don't let them hurt me, please!*"

Dr Pierce Ratcliff Ph.D. (War Studies)
Flat 1, Rowan Court, 112 Olvera Street
London W14 OAB, United Kingdom
Fax: ▮▮▮▮▮▮▮
E-mail: ▮▮▮▮▮▮
Tel: ▮▮▮▮▮

Anna Longman
Editor
Oxford University Press
▮▮▮▮▮▮▮
▮▮▮▮▮
▮▮▮▮▮

9 October 2000

Dear Anna,

It was good to meet with you in person, at last. Yes, I think doing the editing section by section with you is by far the wisest way to go about this, particularly considering the volume of the material and the proposed publication date in 2001, and the fact that I am still fine-tuning the translations.

As soon as my net connection is properly set up I can send work to you direct. I'm glad you're reasonably

44

happy with what you have so far. I can, of course, cut
down on the footnotes.

It's kind of you to admire the 'literary distancing
technique' of referring to fifteenth century Catholicism in
such terms as 'Green Christ' and 'Briar Cross'. In fact,
this is *not* my technique for making sure the readers can't
impose their own preconceptions about mediaeval life on
the text! It's a direct translation of the mediaeval dog-
Latin, as are the earlier Mithraic references. We shouldn't
be too concerned, this is just some of the obviously false
legendary material—supernatural lions and similar—
attributed to Ash's childhood. Heroes always gather
myths to themselves, still more so when they are not
remarkable men but remarkable women.

Perhaps the *Winchester Codex* purports to reflect Ash's
limited knowledge as a child: Ash at eight or ten years
old knows only fields, woods, campaign tents, armour,
washerwomen, dogs, soldiers, swords, saints, Lions. The
company of mercenaries. Hills, rivers, towns—places
have no names. How should she know what year it is?
Dates don't matter yet. All this changes of course, in the
next section: the del Guiz *Life*.

Like the editor of the 1939 edition of the 'Ash' papers,
Vaughan Davies, I am using the *original* German version
of the del Guiz *Life* of Ash, published in 1516. (Because
of the inflammatory nature of the text it was immediately
withdrawn, and republished in an expurgated form in
1518.) Apart from a few minor printing errors, this copy
agrees with the four other surviving copies of the 1516
Life (in the British Library, the Metropolitan Museum of

Art, the Kunsthistorisches Museum in Vienna, and the
Glasgow Museum).

Here, I have a considerable advantage over Vaughan
Davies, who was editing in 1939—I can be explicit. I
have therefore translated this text into modern colloquial
English, especially the dialogue, where I use the educated
and slang versions of our language to represent some of
the social differences of that period. In addition,
mediaeval soldiers were notoriously foul-mouthed. When
Davies accurately translates Ash's bad language as, "By
Christ's bones!," however, the modern reader feels none
of the contemporary shock. Therefore, I have again used
modern-day equivalents. I'm afraid she does say "Fuck"
rather a lot.

Regarding your question about using different
documentary sources, my intention is *not* to follow
Charles Mallory Maximillian's method. While I have a
great admiration for his 1890 edition of the 'Ash'
documents, in which he translates the various Latin
codices, each *Life*, etc., in turn, and lets their various
authors speak for themselves, I feel this demands more
than modern readers are willing to give. I intend to follow
Vaughan Davies' biographical method, and weave the
various authors into a coherent narrative of her life.
Where texts disagree this will, of course, be given the
appropriate scholarly discussion.

I realise that you will find some of my new material surprising, but remember that what it narrates is what these people genuinely *thought* to be happening to them. And, if you bear in mind the major alteration to our view of history that will take place when *Ash: The lost History of Burgundy* is published, perhaps we would be wise not to dismiss anything too casually.

Sincerely,

Pierce

Pierce

Dr Pierce Ratcliff Ph.D. (War Studies)
Flat 1, Rowan Court, 112 Olvera Street
London W14 OAB, United Kingdom

Fax: ▮▮▮▮▮▮▮▮
E-mail: ▮▮▮▮▮▮▮▮
Tel: ▮▮▮▮▮▮▮▮

Anna Longman

Editor

Oxford University Press

▮▮▮▮▮▮▮▮

▮▮▮▮▮▮

▮▮▮▮▮▮

*Previous letter from
A. Longman missing?*

15 October 2000

Dear Anna,

No indeed—although my conclusions will completely supersede theirs, I feel myself very *fortunate* to be following in the academic footsteps of two profound scholars. Vaughan Davies' *Ash: A Biography* was still a set text when I was at school! My love for this subject goes back even further, I must confess—to the Victorians, and Charles Mallory Maximillian's *Ash: The Life of a Female Mediaeval Mercenary Captain*.

Take, for example, Charles Mallory Maximillian on the subject of that unique country, mediaeval Burgundy— because, although the emphasis in the opening part of the main 'Ash' texts is on the Germanic courts, it is with her powerful Burgundian employers that she is finally most associated. Here is CMM in full flood in 1890:—

The story of Ash is, in some ways, the story of what we might call a 'lost' Burgundy. Of all the lands of Western Europe, it is Burgundy—this bright dream of chivalry—which both lasts for a shorter period than any other, and burns more brightly at its peak. Burgundy, under its four great Dukes, and the nominal kingship of France, becomes the last and greatest of the mediaeval kingdoms—aware, even as it flourishes, that it is harking back to another age. Duke Charles's cult of an 'Arthurian court' is, strange as it may seem to us in our modern, smoky, industrial world, an attempt to re-awaken the high ideals of chivalry in this land of knights in armour, princes in fantastic castles, and ladies of surpassing beauty and accomplishment. For Burgundy, itself, thought itself corrupted; thought the fifteenth century so far removed from the Classical Age of Gold that only a revival of these virtues of courage, honour, piety and reverence could make it whole. They did not foresee the printing press, the discovery of the New World, and the Renaissance; all to happen in the last twenty years of their century. And indeed, they took no part in it.

This, then, is the Burgundy which vanishes from memory and history in January, 1477. Ash, a Joan of Arc for Burgundy, perishes in the fray. The great bold Duke dies, slain by his old enemies the Swiss on the winter battlefield at Nancy; lies two or three days before his corpse can be recognised, because foot-soldiers have stripped him of all his finery; and so it is three days, as Commines tells us, before the King of France can give a great sigh of relief, and set about disposing of the Burgundian princes' lands. Burgundy vanishes.

Yet, if one studies the evidence, of course, Burgundy does not vanish at all. Like a stream which goes underground, it runs on through the history of Europe; the northern areas becoming Belgium and Holland; the southern areas merging into that Austro-Hungarian Empire which still—an ageing giant—survives to this day. What one can say is that we *remember* Burgundy as a lost and golden country. Why? What is it that we are remembering?

> Charles Mallory Maximillian (ed.), *Ash: The Life of a Female Mediaeval Mercenary Captain*, J Dent & Sons, 1890; reprinted 1892, 1893, 1895, 1896, 1905.

CMM is, of course, the lesser scholar, full of romantic Victorian flourishes, and I am not depending on him in my translations. Ironically, of course, his narrative history is far more readable than the sociological histories that followed, even if it is more inaccurate! I suppose I am trying to synthesise rigorous historical and sociological accuracy with CMM's lyricism. I hope it can be done!

What he says is all perfectly factual, of course—the collection of counties, countries and duchies that was mediaeval Burgundy *did* 'vanish out of history,' so to speak (although not before Ash fought in some of its most notable battles). It is true in the sense that remarkably little is written about Burgundy after its AD 1477 collapse.

But it was CMM's nostalgic lyricism about a 'Lost Burgundy,' a magic interstice of history, that got me fascinated. Reading through it again, I feel a complete satisfaction, Anna, that I should have found, in my own field, what was 'lost'—and deduced exactly what that discovery implies.

I enclose the next fully translated section, Part One of the del Guiz *Life: Fortuna Imperatrix Mundi*. A point, here—although the main bulk of my new manuscript, 'Fraxinus,' covers events later in 1476, I am able to use parts of it to illuminate these already-existing texts, from where the del Guiz chronicle picks up her adult life in June of that year. You may find there are some surprises even in this 'old stuff' that eluded CMM and Vaughan Davies!

I appreciate that, for your up-coming sales conference, you need to be 'fully briefed,' as you put it, on what my 'new historical theory' arising from 'Fraxinus' is. For various technical reasons, I'm afraid I do not choose to go into the implications in detail just yet.
Sincerely,

Pierce

Pierce

PART ONE

16 June AD 1476(?)–1 July AD 1476

FORTUNA IMPERATRIX MUNDI[6]

[6]"The goddess Fortune is the Empress of this world."

i

"Gentlemen," SAID ASH, "shut your faces!"

The clatter of helmet visors shutting sounded all along the line of horsemen.

Beside her, Robert Anselm paused with his hand to his throat, about to thrust the laminated plate of his steel bevor up into its locking position over his mouth and chin. "Boss, our lord hasn't told us we can attack them . . ."

Ash pointed. "Who gives a fuck? That's a chance down there and we're taking it!"

Ash's sub-captain Anselm was the only rider apart from herself in full armor. The rest of the eighty-one mounted knights wore helmets, bevors, good leg armor—the legs of a man on horseback being very vulnerable—and cheap body armor, the small overlapping metal plates sewn into a jacket called a brigandine.

"*Form up!*"

Ash's voice sounded muffled in her own ears by the silver hair she wore braided up as an arming-cap, padding the inside of her steel sallet.[7] Her voice was not as deep as Anselm's. It came resonant from her small, deep chest cavity; piercing; it sounds an octave above any noise of battle except cannon. Ash's men can always hear Ash.

Ash pushed her own bevor up and locked, protecting

---

[7]Open-faced helmet; in this case with a visor which can be raised or lowered, for visibility or protection.

mouth and chin. For the moment, she left the visor of her sallet up so that she could see better. The horsemen jostled around her in a packed mass on the churned earth of the slope. Her men, in her company's livery: on geldings of mostly medium to good quality.

Down the slope in front of her, a vast makeshift town littered the river valley. Bright under noon sunlight, walled with wagons chained together, and crammed with pennon-flying pavilions and thirty thousand men, women and baggage animals inside it—the Burgundian army. Their camp big enough (confirmed rumor had it) to have *two* of its own markets . . .

You could hardly see the little battered walled town of Neuss inside the enclosing army.

Neuss: a tenth the size of the attacking forces camped around it. The besieged town rested precariously within its gates—rubble, now—and behind its moats and the wide protecting Rhine river. Beyond the Rhine valley, pine-knotted German hills glowed gray-green in the June heat.

Ash tilted her visor down to shade her eyes from the sunlight. A group of about fifty riders moved on the open ground between the Burgundian camp that besieged Neuss and her own Imperial camp that (theoretically) was here to relieve the town. Even at this distance Ash could see the men's Burgundian livery: two red criss-cross slashes, the Cross of St. Andrew.

Robert Anselm brought his bay around in a neat circle. His free hand gripped the company's standard: the azure Lion Passant Guardant on a field Or.[8] "They could be trying to sucker us down, boss."

---

[8] It is worth noting that the Angelotti manuscript's term for the company's main battle standard—*Or, a lion passant guardant azure* (a blue lion, pacing to the viewer's left and looking out, one paw raised)—is unusual. Traditionally in heraldry, the lion passant guardant is referred to not as a lion, but as a leopard.

Deep in the pit of her stomach, expectation and fear churned. The big iron-gray gelding, Godluc, shifted under her, responding. As always in chance ambushes, the suddenness, the sense of moments slipping away and a decision to be made—

"No. Not a trick. They're overconfident. Fifty mounted men—that's someone out with just an escort. He thinks he's safe. They think we're not going to attack them, because we haven't struck a blow since us and Emperor-bleeding-Frederick got here three weeks ago." She hit the high front of the war saddle with the heel of her gauntleted hand, turned to Anselm, grinning. "Robert, tell me what you *don't* see."

"Fifty mounted men, most in full harness, don't see any infantry, no crossbowmen, don't see any hackbutters, don't see any archers—*don't see any archers!*"

Ash couldn't stop grinning; she thought her teeth might be all that was visible under the shadow of her visor, and you could probably see them all the way across the oc-

---

I think it is clear that Ash chooses to refer to hers as a lion for religious reasons.

The standard reproduced in the Angelotti manuscript, a tapering, swallow-tailed banner perhaps six feet long, is charged with the commander's badge, and one version of the company battlecry—"*Frango regna!*": "I shatter kingdoms!"—as well as employers' badges from their various German, Italian, English and Swiss campaigns.

Ash's own personal (rectangular) banner, bearing her badge, is referred to as *Or, a lion azure affronté,* (a blue lion's head, face-on, on a gold field); which seems to be a lion's head cabossed (that is, with no neck or other part of the beast featured). The more correct term would be *Or, a leopard's face azure.* It is clear here that the company livery is gold, and that her men wear, as the badge, the *lion passant guardant azure.*

This combination of blue and gold is especially characteristic of eastern France and Lorraine, and more generally of France, England, Italy, and Scandinavia, in contrast to black and gold, which is more characteristic of the German lands. I can find no reference to "Or, a leopard's face azure" nor "Or, a leopard azure" being associated with any well-known individual other than Ash.

cupied plain to Neuss. ''*Now* you get it. When do we *ever* get to do the pure knightly cavalry-against-cavalry charge in real war?''

''—Without being shot out of the saddle.'' His brows, visible under his visor, furrowed. ''You sure?''

''If we don't sit here with our thumbs up our arses, we can catch them out on the field—they can't get back to their camp in time. Now let's shift!''

Anselm nodded decisive compliance.

She squinted up at the dark blue sky. Her armor, and the padded arming doublet and hose under it, burned as if she stood in front of an armorer's furnace. Godluc's foam soaked his blue caparisons. The world smelled of horse, dung, oil on metal, and the downwind stench of Neuss where they had been eating rats and cats for six weeks now.

''I'm going to boil if I don't get out of this lot soon, so let's *go*!'' She raised her plate-covered arm and jerked it down.

Robert Anselm's thick-necked horse dipped its hind-quarters and then sprang forward. The company standard lifted, gripped high in Anselm's armored gauntlet. Ash spurred Godluc into the thicket of raised lances and through, ahead of her men, Anselm at her shoulder now, half a pace behind her trotting mount. She tapped the long spurs back again. Godluc went from trot to canter. The jolting shook her teeth to her bones and rattled the plates of her Milanese armor, and the wind whipped into her sallet and snatched the breath out of her nostrils.

Percussive concussion shook the world. The hundreds of steel horseshoes striking hard earth threw up showers of clods. The noise went unheard, felt in her chest and bones rather than heard with her ears; and the line of riders—*her* line, *her* men; sweet Christ don't let me get this wrong!— gathered speed down the slope and out onto clear ground.

No rabbit holes, she prayed, and then: Fuck me, that isn't one of their commanders' standards, it's the Duke's banner. Sweet Green Christ! That's Duke Charles of Burgundy himself there!

Summer sun struck brilliances from Burgundian knights in full harness, steel-silver plates from head to toe. The sun winked from the stars that were the tips of their light war lances. Her vision blotted green and orange.

No time for new tactics now. *Anything we haven't practiced, we can't do. This season's training will have to get us through it.* Ash glanced quickly right and left at the riders coming up nose and nose with her. Steel faces, not recognizable now as lance-leaders Euen Huw or Joscelyn van Mander or Thomas Rochester; anonymous hard-riding men, thickets of lances dropping down to attack position.

She brought her own lance down across the bay Godluc's thick arched neck. Her gauntlet-leather over her palm was ridged and wet with sweat where she gripped the wood. The massive jolting of the horse shook her in the high-backed saddle, and the flapping of Godluc's azure caparisons and the rattle of horse armor deafened her already-muffled hearing. She had the smell, almost the taste, of sweat-hot armor in her mouth; metallic as blood. Motion smoothed as she spurred Godluc into full gallop.

She mumbled into the velvet lining of her bevor, "Fifty mounted men. Full harness. Eighty-one with me, medium armor."

"How are the enemy armed?"

"Lances, maces, swords. No missile weapons at all."

"Charge the enemy before the enemy is reinforced."

"What the fuck," Ash shouted happily to the voice in her head, "do you *think* I'm doing? Haro! A Lion! A Lion!" She threw up her free arm and bellowed, "Charge!"

Robert Anselm, half a length to her rear, boomed back in answer, "*A Lion!*" and jammed the staff of the rippling cloth banner up above his head. Half her riders were pelting ahead of Ash now, almost out of formation; too late to think about that, too late to do anything but think *let them learn to stick with the standard!* She dropped the reins over the pommel, brought her free hand up in the automatic gesture over her sallet, slamming the visor fully down, reducing vision to a slot.

The Burgundian flag jerked wildly.

"They've seen us!"

Not clear, least of all to her now, at this speed and this restricted vision, but were they trying to cluster around one man? Move away? Gallop back breakneck toward their camp? Some mixture of all three?

In a split second four Burgundian horses wheeled and came up together and burst into a full gallop toward her.

Foam splattered back on her breastplate. Heat blinded her out of a dark blue sky. It was as real and as solid as bread to her—*those four men galloping toward me on three-quarters of a ton of horse each, with curved metal plates strapped around them, carry poles with sharpened lance-heads as long as my hand, that will hit home with the concentrated momentum of horse and sixteen-stone rider. They will punch through flesh like paper.*

She has a mental flash of the lance tip punching through her scarred cheek, her brain, the back of her skull.

One Burgundian knight hefted his lance, gripping it with his steel gauntlet, couching it on the lance-rest on his breastplate. His head was polished metal, plumed with white ostrich feathers, slit by a bar of blackness—a visor through which not even eyes could be seen. His lance-point dipped straight toward her.

A grim exultation filled her. Godluc responded to her shift of weight and swerved right. She dropped her lance down—down—down again, and took the gray gelding of the leading Burgundian knight squarely under the jaw.

The shaft wrenched out of her hand. His horse reared, skidding forward on broken hind legs. The man went straight over his horse's arse and under Godluc's hooves. Trained as a war-horse, Godluc did not even stumble. Ash slid the lanyard of her mace over her gauntlet to her wrist, swung up the 24-inch shaft, and crashed the small flanged metal head square across the back of the second man's helmet. The metal creased. She felt it give. Something crashed into Godluc's flank: she went careering across grass—hot grass, slippery in the heat, more than one horse missing its footing—and shifted her body-weight again to bring Godluc up beside Robert Anselm. She reached over and hauled on his war-horse's reins, and pulled him up with her. *"There!"*

The confusion of colors, red and blue and yellow liveries and guidons [cavalry lance-pennants], resolved itself into a mass of skirmishing men. First charge over, lances mostly abandoned, except there were the German guys from Anhelt's crew, skimming around the edge of the fray, lances jabbing as if they were boar-sticking—and Josse in the blue brigandine reaching over from his saddle with his hand on the *back*plate of a Burgundian knight, trying to punch his dagger down into the gap between placket and backplate—and a man down, face-down on the dirt—and a spray of red straight up her breastplate, someone hit in a femoral artery, nothing to do with her own wild swing at someone's head—the leather lanyard breaking and her mace flying up in a perfect parabola into the sunlight.

Ash grasped the leather-bound hilt of her sword and whipped it out of its sheath. In a continuation of the same movement she smashed it pommel-first into the face of an armored man. The strike jarred her wrist. She brought her sword around and slammed it down on his right upper arm and elbow. The impact jarred and numbed the whole length of her arm.

He swung his mace up.

The sliding plates of his arm defenses squealed where her blow had crushed metal, and stuck. Jammed.

He could not bring his arm up—or down—

She struck her blade in hard toward his vulnerable underarm mail.

Three wildly plunging horses stampeded through the mass of heaving bodies, pushing them apart. She looked left, right, wildly around: the Lion banner *there*—soul's damnation, if I'm not sticking with the unit banner, how can I expect them to?—and the Duke's standard about twenty yards away, close to the edge of the fight.

She gasped, "Enemy command group—in reach—"

"Then neutralize their unit commander."

"A Lion! A Lion!" Ash stood up high in the stirrups, pointing with her sword. "Get the Duke! Get the Duke!"

Something crashed only glancingly off the back of her sallet, but it knocked her facedown onto Godluc's neck. The war-horse wheeled around and reared up. Busy clinging on, Ash felt his hooves crush something. Screams dinned in her ears, and shouted commands in French and Flemish, and *again* the Lion banner slid off to the side, and she swore, and then saw the Ducal banner jerk and go down, and the knight in front of her threw his sword point-first at her face, and she ducked, and the ground was empty—

Thirty or so horses and men in Burgundian colors galloped, routing, across the packed earth toward their camp. Only minutes, Ash thought, dazed. It's only been minutes, if that!

The little running figures at the Burgundian camp-line resolved themselves into infantry, in the liveries of Philippe de Poitiers and Ferry de Cuisance—archers from Picardy and Hainault.

"Archers—veteran—five hundred—"

"If you do not have sufficient missile troops, withdraw."

"No chance now. Fuck it!" She jerked up her arm, caught Robert Anselm's eye, and threw her whole weight into the gesture of *back*! "Withdraw!"

Two of Euen Huw's lance—a disreputable bunch of

bastards at the best of times—were swinging down from their horses to strip the still-living wounded. Ash saw Euen Huw himself slam a bollock dagger straight down into the visor of an unhorsed knight. Blood sprayed.

"You want to be crossbow meat?" She swung half down from the saddle and pulled the Welshman up. "Bugger off back—*now!*"

The stabbed man was not dead, he thrashed and screamed, and blood jetted up from his visor. Ash hauled herself up into her saddle, rode over him on her way to Robert Anselm's side, and screamed, "Ride back to camp—go!"

The Lion banner withdrew.

A man in a blue livery jacket with a lion on it dragged himself up from under his dead horse. Thomas Rochester, an English knight. Ash sat still in the saddle for one minute, holding Godluc by pressure of her knees, until the man reached her and she pulled him up behind her.

The open ground in front of Neuss was scattered now with riderless horses that abandoned their panic and slowed and stopped.

The man behind her on her horse yelled, "Boss, 'ware archers, let's get out of here!"

Ash picked a careful way across the ground covered by the skirmish. She leaned down, searching among the unhorsed men to see if any of the dead and wounded were hers—or were the Duke—and none were either.

"Boss!" Thomas Rochester protested.

The first Picardian longbowman passed a bush she had privately decided was four hundred yards away.

"*Boss!*"

Thomas must be rattled. He doesn't even want me to stop and capture a stray horse, to replace his. There's money out there on four hooves.

And archers.

"Okay..." Ash turned and rode back, fording the

almost-dry stream of the Erft, and moving on up the slope. She forced herself to ride at walking pace toward the wattle barriers of the Imperial camp's nearest gate. She thumped Godluc's armored neck. "Just as well we fed you up for the practice exercise."

The gelding threw up his head. There was blood at the corners of his mouth, and blood on his hooves.

Men wearing the Blue Lion and carrying bows came crowding out of the Imperial camp—which was a wagon-walled mirror of the Burgundian camp, down on the river plain. Ash rode in through the sentineled gap between their wagons.

"There you go, Thomas." She reined in for the man to slide down, looking back at him. "Lose another horse and you can walk back next time . . ."

Thomas of Rochester grinned. "Sure, boss!"

Figures running, men from her sector of the camp, crowding up to her and Robert Anselm, yelling questions and warnings.

"The damn Burgundians are hardly going to follow us in here. Hang on." The sun blasted down. Ash nudged Godluc a step aside from the crowd, and wrenched her gauntlet buckles open, and then grabbed for her helmet.

She had to lean her head way back to get at the strap and buckle under the chin-piece of her bevor. She yanked the buckle open. The sallet almost fell backwards off her head, but she caught it and put it down over the pommel of the saddle, and then sprang the pin on her bevor and concertina'd the laminations down.

Air. Cool air. Her throat rasped dry and raw. She straightened up in the saddle again.

His Most Gracious Imperial Majesty Frederick III, Holy Roman Emperor, faced her from the war saddle of his favorite gray stallion.

Ash glanced around. A full knightly entourage rode with the Emperor. All bright liveries, and ostrich plumes on their helmets. Not so much as a scratch on the steel. Far too late to join any skirmish. She caught sight of one man at the back—by the look of him, from the Eternal Twilight,[9] in mail hauberk; his eyes bandaged with thin strips of dark muslin—nonetheless wearing a mildly cynical smile.

Sweat stuck her braided-up silver hair to her forehead and cheeks. Her skin felt wet and red as fire. Calm-eyed, she rode toward the Emperor, away from her shouting men. "Majesty."

Frederick's dry little voice whispered, "What are you doing on this side of my camp, captain?"

"Maneuvers, Your Imperial Majesty."

"In front of the Burgundian camp?"

"Needed to practice advancing and retreating with the standard, Your Imperial Majesty."

Frederick blinked. "When you just happened to see the Duke's escort."

"Thought it was a sally against Neuss, Your Imperial Majesty."

"And you attacked."

"Paid to, Your Imperial Majesty. We are your mercenaries, after all."

One of the entourage—the southern mail-clad foreigner—stifled a noise. There was a pointed silence until he muttered, "Sorry, Your Imperial Majesty. Wind."

"Yes . . ."

Ash blinked her indeterminately colored eyes at the little fair-haired man. The Emperor Frederick was not visibly in armor, although his velvet doublet probably concealed mail under it. She said mildly, "Didn't we ride

---

[9]A reference from *Fraxinus*, to an as-yet-unidentified mediaeval myth-cycle or legend. It is also mentioned in the *Del Guiz* text, but absent from the *Angelotti* and *Pseudo-Godfrey* manuscripts.

here from Cologne to protect Neuss, Your Imperial Majesty?"

Frederick abruptly wheeled his gelding and galloped back into the center of the Imperial German camp with his knights.

"Shit," Ash said aloud. "I might have done it this time."

Robert Anselm, helmet at hip, rode up beside her. "Done what, boss?"

Ash glanced sideways at the crop-headed man; twice her age, experienced, and capable. She reached up and pulled her hairpin, and let her heavy braid fall down, unwinding over pauldrons and breastplate as far as the tassets that hung to mid-thigh, and only then noticed that her arms were dripping red to the elbow-couters, and that her silver hair was sopping up the blood.

"Either got myself into deep shit," she said, "or got where I want to be. You know what I want us to get this year."

"Land," Anselm murmured. "Not a mercenary's reward of money. You want him to give us land and estates."

"I want in." Ash sighed. "I'm tired of winning castles and revenues for other people. I'm tired of never having anything at the end of a season except enough money to see us through the winter."

His tanned, creased face smiled. "It isn't every company can do that."

"I know. But I'm good." Ash chuckled, deliberately immodest, getting less of an answering grin from him than she expected. She sobered "Robert, I want somewhere permanent we can go back to, I want to *own* land. That's what all this is about—you get land by fighting, or inheritance, or gift, but you get land and you establish yourself. Like the Sforza in Milan." She smiled cynically.

"Give it enough time and money, and Jack Peasant becomes Sir John Wellborn. *I want in.*"

Robert shrugged. "Is Frederick going to do that? He could be mad as hell about this. I can't tell with him."

"Me either." Heartbeat and breath quieted now, ceasing to thunder in her ears. She stripped one gauntlet off and wiped her face, glancing back at the dismounting knights of the Company of the Lion. "That's a good lot of lads we've got there."

"Haven't I been raising troops for you for five years? Did you expect rubbish?"

It was a remark intended jokingly, Ash noted; but sweat poured down the older man's face, and his eyes flinched away from hers as he spoke. She wondered, *Is he after a bigger share of our money?* and realized, *No, not Robert—so, what?*

"That wasn't war," Ash added thoughtfully, pondering her captain. "That was a *tournament*, not a battle!"

One arm cradled his helmet; the Lion standard was socketed at his saddle. Anselm's blunt fingers prodded under the mail standard at his throat. Its visible rim of leather was black with his sweat. "Maybe a tourney.[10] But they lost knights."

"Six or seven," Ash agreed.

"Did you hear—?" Robert Anselm swallowed. His eyes finally met hers. She was troubled to see his forehead white with sweat or nausea.

"Down there—I took one man in the face with my sword-hilt," he said, and shrugged an explanation: "He had his visor up. Red livery, white harts rampant. I ripped half his face away, just with the cross of my sword. Blinded him. He didn't fall; I saw one of his mates help-

---

[10] A tourney is an organized killing affray. A tournament is an organized killing affray with blunt weapons.

ing him ride off toward their camp. But when I hit him he shrieked. You could hear it, Ash, he knew, right then, he'd been ruined for life. He *knew*.''

Ash searched Robert Anselm's features, familiar to her as her own. A big man, broad across the shoulders, armor bright in the sun, his shaved scalp red with heat and sweat. ''Robert—''

''It isn't the dead ones that bother me. It's the ones who have to live with what I've done to them.'' Anselm broke off, shaking his head. He shifted in his war-horse's saddle. His smile was wan. ''Green Christ! Listen to me. After-battle shakes. Don't take any notice, girl. I've been doing this since before you were born.''

This was not hyperbole but a pure statement of fact. Ash, more sanguine, nodded. ''You should talk to a priest. Talk to Godfrey. And talk to me, later. This evening. Where's Florian?''

He appeared slightly reassured. ''In the surgeon's tent.''

Ash nodded. ''Right. I want to talk to the lance-leaders, we were all over the place down there. Take company roll-call. Find me back at the command tent. Move it!''

Ash rode on through the young men in armor flinging themselves down from their war saddles, shouting at each other, shouting at her, their pages grabbing their war-horses' reins, the babble of after-battle stories. She banged one hard on the backplate, said something obscene to another of her sub-captains, the Savoyard soldier Paul di Conti; grinned at their yells of approval, dismounted, and clattered up the slope, her steel tassets banging on the cuisses that covered her thighs, toward the surgeon's tent.

''Philibert, get me fresh clothes!'' she yelled at her bob-haired page-boy, who darted away toward her pavilion; ''and send Rickard, I need to get unarmed. *Florian!*''

A boy threw down more rushes as Ash ducked in

through the flap of the surgeon's pavilion. The round tent smelled of old blood and vomit, and of spices and herbs from the curtained-off area that was the surgeon's own quarters. Thick sawdust clotted the floor. The sunlight through the white canvas gleamed gold.

It was not crowded. It was all but empty.

"What? Oh, it's you." A tall man, of slight build, with blond badly cut hair flopping over his eyes, looked up and grinned from a dirty face. "Look at this. Shoulder popped right out of its socket. Fascinating."

"How are you, Ned?" Ash ignored the surgeon Florian de Lacey for the moment in favor of the wounded man.

She has his name to hand: Edward Aston, an older knight, initially a refugee of the *rosbifs*'[11] royal wars, a confirmed mercenary now. The armor stripped off him and scattered on the straw was composite, bought new at different times and in different lands: Milanese breast-plate, Gothic German arm defenses. He sat with the wheat-colored light on his balding head and fringe of white hair, doublet off his shoulders, bruises blacker by the minute, his features screwed up in intense pain and greater disgust. The joint of his shoulder looked completely wrong.

"Bloody warhammer, weren't it? Bloody little Burgundian tyke come up behind me when I were finishing his mate. Hurt my horse, too."

Ash ran over Sir Edward Aston's English lance in her mind. He had raised for her service one crossbowman, one fairly well-equipped longbow archer, two competent men-at-arms, a bloody good sergeant and a drunken page. "Your sergeant, Wrattan, will look after your mount. I'll

---

[11]"Rosbif" or "roast-beef": continental nickname at this time for an Englishman, since they were popularly supposed to eat nothing else.

put him in command of the rest of the lance. You rest up.''

''Get my share, though, won't I?''

''Bloody right.'' Ash watched as Florian de Lacey wrapped both hands around the older man's wrist.

''Now say 'Cristus vincit, Cristus regnit, Cristus imperad,' '' Florian directed.

''Cristus vincit, Cristus regnit, Cristus imperad,'' the man growled, his outdoor voice too loud in the confines of the tent. ''Pater et Filius et Spiritus Sanctus.''

''Hold on.'' Florian planted a knee in Edward Aston's ribs, yanked at full strength—

''*Fuck!*''

—and let go. ''There. Back in its socket.''

''Why di'nt you tell me that was going to hurt, you stupid bugger?''

''You mean you didn't know? Shut up and let me finish the charm.'' The blond man frowned, thought for a second, and bent to murmur in the knight's ear: ''*Mala, magubula, mala, magubula!*''

The older knight grunted and raised thick white eyebrows. He gave a sharp nod. Ash watched Florian's long strong fingers firmly bind the shoulder into temporary immobility.

''Don't worry about it, Ned,'' Ash said, ''you're not going to miss much fighting. It took Frederick-our-glorious-leader seventeen days to march the twenty-four miles from Cologne to here; he's not exactly raring for glory.''

''Sooner have my pay for *not* fighting! I'm an old man. You'll see me in my fucking grave yet.''

''Fucking won't,'' Ash said. ''I'll see you back on your horse. About—''

''About a week.'' Florian wiped his hands down the front of his doublet, smearing the red wool, red lacing, and white linen undershirt with dirt. "That's it, except an arm fracture, which I fixed up before you got here." The tall master surgeon scowled. "Why don't you bring me back any interesting injuries? And I don't suppose you bothered to recover any dead bodies for anatomizing?"

"They didn't belong to me," Ash said gravely, managing not to laugh at Florian's expression.

The surgeon shrugged. "How am I ever going to study fatal combat injuries if you don't bring me any?"

Ned Aston muttered something under his breath that might have been "fucking ghoul!"

"We were lucky," Ash stressed. "Florian, who's the arm fracture?"

"Bartolomey St. John. From van Mander's Flemish lance. He'll mend."

"No permanent cripples? No one dead? No plague outbreak? Green Christ loves me!" Ash whooped. "Ned, I'll send your sergeant up here for you."

"I'll manage. I'm not dead yet." The big English knight glowered at Florian de Lacey in disgust as he left the surgeon's tent, something to which the anatomist-surgeon remained apparently oblivious, and had done as long as Ash had known him.

Ash spoke to Florian, watching Ned Aston's retreating back. "I haven't heard you use that charm for a battle injury before."

"No . . . I forgot the charm for bloodless injuries. That one was for *farcioun*."

" 'Farcioun'?"

"It's a disease of horses."[12]

"A disease of—!" Ash swallowed a very unleaderlike snuffle of laughter. "Never mind. Florian, I want to get out of this kit and I want to talk to you. *Now*."

---

[12]Uncertain: possibly glanders.

Outside, the sun hit like a dazzling hammer. Heat stifled her, in her armor. Ash squinted toward her pavilion tent and the Lion Azure standard limp in the airless noon.

Florian de Lacey offered his leather water bottle. "What's happened?"

Unusual for Florian, the coistrel did indeed contain wine thoroughly drowned by water.[13] Ash doused her head, careless of spillage over steel plate. She gasped as the warm water hit. Then, swallowing greedily, she said between gulps, "Emperor. I've committed him. No more sitting around here—hinting to the Burgundians that Neuss is a free city—and Herman of Hesse is our friend— so would they please go home? *War.*"

"Committed? You can't tell with Frederick." Florian's features, pale and fine-boned under the dirt, made a movement of disgust. "They're saying you nearly got the Burgundian Duke. That right?"

"*Damn* near!"

"Frederick might approve of that."

"And he might not. Politics, not war. Aw, shit, who *knows*?" Ash drank the last of the water. As she lowered the bottle, she saw her other page Rickard running toward her from the command tent.

"Boss!" The fourteen-year-old boy skidded to a halt on dry earth. "Message. The Emperor. He wants you at his tent. Now!"

"He say why?"

"That's all the guy told me, boss!"

Ash stuffed her gauntlets into her inverted helmet and tucked the helmet under her arm. "Okay. Rickard, get my command lance together. *Fast.* Master surgeon, let's go. No." She halted, boot heels skidding on glassy summer

---

[13]Water was usually drunk at this period only when tiny amounts of alcohol were included, to prevent water-borne infections.

grass. "Florian. *You* go and change out of those clothes!"

The surgeon looked amused. "And I suppose I'm the only one?"

Ash surveyed her armor. The shining metal was brown now with drying blood. "I can't get out of harness in time. Rickard, get me a bucket!"

A few minutes saw her armor sluiced down, head to foot; the warm water, even the dampness of her soaked arming doublet, welcome in the noonday heat. Ash wrung out her thick, yard-long mane of hair between her hands, flung it dripping over her shoulder, and set off at a fast stride for the center of the camp, her squire running back to the Lion Azure camp with her messages.

"You're either up for a knighting," Robert Anselm growled, as she arrived, "or an almighty bollocking. Look at 'em!"

"They're here to watch something, all right . . ."

An unusually large crowd waited outside the Emperor's four-chambered striped pavilion tent. Ash glanced around as she joined them. Noblemen. Young men in the V-fronted laced doublets of high fashion, with parti-colored hose; bareheaded and with long curls. All wore breastplates at the least. The older men sweated in pleated full-length formal gowns, and rolled hats. This square of grass in the camp center was clear of horses, cattle, women, bare-arsed babies playing, and drunken soldiers. No one dared infringe the area around the yellow and black double eagle standard. It smelled, nonetheless, pleasantly of warhorse-droppings and sun-dried rushes.

Her officers arrived.

The sun dried her from her armor through to her arming-doublet. Enclosed in form-fitting metal, she found the padded clothing underneath drank up all her sweat; left her not so much hot as unable to get air into her lungs.

I would have had time to change. It's always hurry-up-and-wait!

A broad, squarish, bearded man in his thirties strode up, brown robe flapping about his bare feet. "Sorry, captain."

"You're late, Godfrey. You're fired. I'm buying a better class of company clerk."

"Of course. We grow on Trees, my child." The company priest adjusted his cross. He was deep-chested, substantial; the skin around his eyes creased from far too many years spent under open skies. You would never have guessed from his deadpan expression how long Godfrey Maximillian had known her, or how well.

Ash caught his brown-eyed gaze and tapped a bare fingernail on the helmet tucked under her arm. Metal clicked impatiently. "So what do your 'contacts' tell you—what's Frederick thinking?"

The priest chuckled. "Tell me someone in the last thirty-two years who's ever known that!"

"Okay, okay. Dumb question." Ash planted her spurred and booted feet apart, surveying the Imperial nobles. A few of them greeted her. There was no movement from inside the tent.

Godfrey Maximillian added, "I understand there are six or seven fairly influential Imperial knights in there now, griping to him about Ash always thinking she can attack without orders."

"If I hadn't attacked, they'd be griping about contract soldiers who take the money but won't risk their lives in a fight." Ash added, under her breath, nodding to the only other contract commander outside the Emperor's tent, the Italian Jacobo Rossano, "Who'd be a mercenary captain?"

"You would, madonna," her Italian master gunner, Antonio Angelotti, said. His startlingly fair curls and clear-skinned face made Angelotti stand out in any crowd, and not just for his proficiency with cannon.

"That was a rhetorical question!" She glared at him. "You know what a mercenary company is, Angelotti?"

Her master gunner was interrupted by the arrival of an only slightly cleaner and better dressed Florian de Lacey, on the heels of Ash's remark.

"Mercenary company? Hmm." Florian offered, "A troop of loyal but dim psychopaths with the ability to beat up every other thick psychopath in sight?"

Ash raised her brows at him. "Five years, and you still haven't got the hang of being a soldier!"

The surgeon chuckled. "I doubt I ever will."

"I'll *tell* you what a mercenary company is." Ash jabbed her finger at Florian. "A mercenary company is an immense machine that takes in bread, milk, meat and wine, tentage, cordage and cloth at one end, and gives out shit, dirty washing, horse manure, trashed property, drunken vomit and broken kit at the other end. The fact that they sometimes do some *fighting* is entirely incidental!"

She stopped for breath and to lower her voice. Her eyes gazed around the men there as she spoke, picking out liveries, identifying noble lords, potential friends, known enemies.

Still nothing from the Emperor's tent.

"They're a gaping maw that I have to shove provisions into, each day and every day; a company is always two meals from dissolution. And money. Let's not forget money. And when they *do* fight, they produce wounded and sick men who have to be looked after. *And* they don't do anything useful while they're getting well! And when they *are* well, they're an ill-disciplined rabble who beat up the local peasantry. Argghhhh!"

Florian offered his coistrel again. "That's what you get

for paying eight hundred men to follow you.''

"They don't follow me. They allow me to lead them. It's not the same thing at all.''

In quite a different tone, Florian de Lacey said quietly, "They'll be fine, Ash. Our esteemed Emperor won't want to lose a sizeable mercenary contingent of his army.''

"I just hope you're right.''

A voice not many feet behind her said, completely unselfconsciously, "No, my lord, Captain Ash isn't here yet. I've seen her—a butch, mannish creature; bigger than a man, in fact. She had a waif of a girl with her, when I saw her in the northwest quarter of our camp—one of her 'baggage-train'—whom she caressed, quite disgustingly! The girl was shrinking from her touch. That is your 'woman-soldier' commander for you.''

Ash opened her mouth to speak, registered Florian de Lacey's raised eyebrows, and did not turn to correct the unknown knight. She moved a few steps away, toward one of the older Imperial captains in yellow and black livery.

Gottfried of Innsbruck inclined his head to Ash. "Good skirmish.''

"Hoped we might get reinforced from the town.'' Ash shrugged. "But I guess Herman of Hesse is not coming out to attack.''

The Imperial knight Gottfried talked with his eyes on the entrance to the Emperor's pavilion. "Why should he? He's held out eight months without our help, when I wouldn't have given him eight days. Not a little free city, against the *Burgundians*.''

"A little free city that's rebelling against its 'rightful ruler,' Archbishop Ruprecht,'' Ash said, allowing a large degree of skepticism into her tone.

Gottfried chuckled loudly. "Archbishop Ruprecht is Duke Charles's man, Burgundian to the core. That's why the Burgundians want to put him back in control of Neuss.

Here, Captain Ash, you might like this one—Ruprecht was this Duke's *father's* candidate for the archbishopric; you know what Ruprecht sent the late Duke Philip of Burgundy as a gift of gratitude when he got the job? A lion! A real live lion!''

"But not a blue one," a light tenor voice interrupted. "They say he sleeps like a lion, their Duke Charles, with his eyes open."

Turning to look at the young knight who had spoken, formulating an answer, she suddenly thought, *Don't I know you from somewhere?*

It would not be unusual to recognize a German knight from some other camp, some other campaigning season. She took him in superficially in a glance: a very young man, hardly more than her own age; long-legged and rangy, with a width to his shoulders that would fill out in a year or two. He was wearing a Gothic sallet, which even with the visor up hid most of his face; leaving her to price rich doublet and hose pied in green-and-white, high leather riding boots pointed up under the skirts of his doublet, and a knight's spurs.

And a very fancy fluted Gothic breastplate for a man who hadn't been in any skirmishes today.

Two or three hard young men-at-arms with him wore a green livery. *Mecklenburg? Scharnscott?* Ash ran through heraldry in her mind without success.

She said lightly, "*I* hear Duke Charles sleeps upright in a wooden chair, with all his armor on. In case we take him by surprise. Which some of us are more likely to do than others . . ."

Under his sallet's raised visor, the German knight's expression chilled.

"Bitch in men's clothing," he said. "One day, Captain, you really must tell us what use you have for your cod-flap."

Robert Anselm and Angelotti and half a dozen of Ash's sub-captains moved up so that their armored shoulders touched hers. She thought resignedly, *Oh well . . .*

Ash looked deliberately down between her tassets, at the codpiece on the front of her hose. "It gives me somewhere to carry a spare pair of gloves. I imagine you use yours for the same thing."

"Cunt!"

"Really?" Ash inspected his green and white particolored bulge with visible care. "It doesn't look like one—but I dare say you know best."

Any man drawing his sword among the Emperor's guard is looking to be cut down where he stands: she was not surprised to see the young German knight keep his hand off his sword-hilt. What startled her was the sudden flash of his appreciative grin. The smile of a young man who has the strength to take a joke against himself.

He turned his back, speaking to his noble friends as if she had said nothing at all, pointing with one gauntlet at the pine hills miles to the east. "Tomorrow, then! A hunt. There's a he-boar out there stands high as my bay mare's shoulder—"

"You didn't *have* to make another enemy," Godfrey muttered despairingly, at her ear. Heat or strain whitened his face above the dense beard.

"It's compulsory when they're assholes. I get this all the time." Ash grinned at her company priest. "Godfrey, whoever he is, he's just another feudal lord. We're *soldiers.* I've got 'Deus Vult' engraved on my sword—his has 'Sharp End Towards Enemy.' "[14]

---

[14]In the original, this is a completely untranslatable joke based on a pun between two words in German and an obscure, no longer extant, Flemish

Her officers laughed. A flutter of wind picked up the Imperial standard, so that for a second the sun blazed above her through yellow and black cloth. Smells of roasting beef drifted up from the long tent-lined lanes of the camp. Someone was singing something appallingly badly, not drowned out by a flute now playing in the Emperor Frederick's pavilion.

"I've *worked* for this. *We've* worked for this. It's how the rules of power operate. You're either on your way up or your way down. There's never a place to rest."

She watched the faces of her escort, troops in their twenties for the most part; then her officers, Angelotti and Florian and Godfrey and Robert Anselm as familiar as her own scarred face; the rest new this season. The usual mix of lance-leaders: the skeptics, the over-devoted, the crawlers and the competent. Three months in the field, she knows most of their men by name now.

Two guards in black and yellow left the tent.

"*And* I could do with dinner." Ash felt her hair. They had been standing waiting long enough for the last silver curls to dry after her hasty ablutions. The weight of her hair pulled at her when she turned her head, and the flowing thick skeins caught between the plates of her armor: she risked it for the picture she knew she made.

"And—" Ash glanced about for Florian de Lacey and found the surgeon's face was now missing from the command group. "Fuck it. Where's Florian? He's not pissed *again*—?"

All talk was silenced by a trumpeter. A handful of guards and six of the more influential nobles of Frederick's court came out of the tent with the Emperor himself.

---

dialect. I have therefore substituted something to give the flavor of it. *Deus vult* means "God willing."

Ash straightened up in the blazing heat. She saw the southern foreigner again—a military observer?—still blindfolded with translucent strips of cloth, but walking unerringly in Frederick's footsteps, precisely avoiding the guy-ropes of the pavilion.

"Captain Ash," the Emperor Frederick said.

She went down on one knee, carefully, since she was in armor, in front of the older man.

"This sixteenth day of June, Year of Our Lord 1476,"[15] the Emperor said, "it pleases me to raise you to some mark of distinction, for your valiant service in the field against our enemy, the noble Duke of Burgundy. Therefore I have bethought me much what would be fitting for a mercenary soldier in our employ."

"Money," a pragmatic voice said, behind Ash. She dared not look away from Frederick to glare Angelotti into silence.

The skin at the edges of Frederick's pale eyes crinkled. The little fair-haired man, now in blue and gold pleated robes, put his ringed hands together and gazed down at her.

"Not gold," Frederick said, "because I have none to

---

[15]This account is accurate, with one exception. The skirmish at the siege of Neuss took place, not in 1476, but on 16 June 1475. However, records often pick up an apparent error of a year either way. Under the Julian calendar, in different parts of Europe, the New Year is variously dated as beginning at Easter, on Lady Day (25 March) and on Christmas Day (25 December); and post AD 1583, the Gregorian calendar backdates the beginning of those years to 1 January.

I can do no better than refer the reader to Charles Mallory Maximillian's comment in the *Preface and Notes* to the 1st edition (1890):

"The Germanic *Life* of Ash narrates many startling and, one might think, implausible events. It is, however, verifiable that all these particular exploits of the woman Ash are well-attested to, by a great variety of other trustworthy historical sources.

"One should forgive, therefore, this document's mistake in the mere dating of the events contained therein."

spare. And not estates, because it would not be fitting to give them to a woman with no man to defend them for her.''

Ash looked up in plain, utter amazement and forgot propriety. ''Do I *look* like I need defending?''

She tried to swallow the words even as she was saying them. The dry voice overrode her:

''Nor may I knight you, because you are a woman. But I will reward you with estates, albeit at second-hand. You shall marry, Ash. You shall marry my noble lord here— I promised his mother, who is my cousin in the fourth degree, that I would arrange a marriage for him. And now I do. This is your betrothed, the Lord Fernando del Guiz.''

Ash looked where the Emperor indicated. There was no one there but the young knight in pied green-and-white hose and fluted Gothic breastplate. The Emperor smiled encouragingly.

Her breath sucked in, involuntarily. What little she could see of the young man's face was utterly still under his steel visor, and so white that she could see now that he had freckles across his cheekbones.

''*Marry?*'' Ash stared, dazed. She heard herself say, ''*Him?*''

''Does that please you, Captain?''

Sweet Christ! Ash thought. I am in the middle of the camp of His Grace the Holy Roman Emperor, Frederick III. The second most powerful ruler in Christendom. In open court. These are his most powerful subjects. They're all looking at me. I can't refuse. But *marriage*? I never even *thought* about marriage!

She was aware of the strap of her poleyn cutting into the back of her knee as she knelt; and jeweled, armored, powerful men all looking at her. Her bare hands where they rested together on her thigh armor appeared rough, red stains under her nails. The pommel of her sword tapped against her breastplate. Only then did she realize that she was shaking. *Shit, girl! You forget. You really do forget that you're a woman. And they never do. And now it's yes or no.*

She did the thing that put it all—fear, humiliation, dread—outside herself.

Ash raised her bowed head, looking fearlessly up, perfectly aware of the picture that she made. A young woman, bareheaded, her cheekbones slashed with the fine white lines of three old scars, her silver hair tumbling gloriously about her armored shoulders and flowing like a cloak to her thighs.

"I can say nothing, Your Imperial Majesty. Such recognition, and such generosity, and such honor—they are beyond anything I had expected, and anything I could deserve."

"Rise." Frederick took her hand. She knew he must feel her palm sweat. There might have been an amused movement made by those thin lips. He held out his other hand commandingly, took the much fairer hand of the young man, and placed it over Ash's. "Now let no one gainsay this, they shall be man and wife!"

Deafened by tumultuous and sycophantic applause, and with warm, damp male fingers resting on hers, Ash looked back at her company officers.

What the fuck do I do *now*?

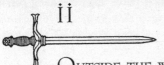

ii

OUTSIDE THE WINDOW of the Imperial palace room in Cologne, rain poured in torrents from gutters and gargoyles to the cobblestones below. It battered loudly, irregular as arquebus[16]-fire, against the expensive glass windows. Biscuit-colored stone finials gleamed with every break in the high cloud.

Inside the room, Ash faced her soon-to-be mother-in-law.

"This is all—very—*well*—" Ash protested through a faceful of azure velvet. She shook herself free of it. "—but I have to get back to my company! I got escorted out of Neuss so fast yesterday, I haven't had a chance to talk to my officers yet!"

"You must have women's clothing for the bridal," Constanza del Guiz said sharply, stumbling over the last word.

"With respect, madam—I have upwards of eight hundred men and women under contract to me, back at Neuss. They're used to being paid! I have to go back and explain how this marriage is going to benefit *them*."

"Yes, yes . . ." Constanza del Guiz had fair hair and lazy good looks, but not her son's rangy build. She was tiny. A soft pink velvet gown fitted tightly around her small bosom, and then flared from her hips to drape voluminously to her satin slippers. She wore a red and silver brocade undergown. Rubies and emeralds ornamented

---

[16]Fifteenth-century man-portable matchlock firearm.

both her padded headdress, and the gold belt that hung down in a V from her hips. A purse and keys hung pendant from the belt-chain.

"My tailor can't work if you keep moving," Constanza pleaded. "Please, stand *still*."

The padded roll of Ash's headdress sat on her braided hair like a small but heavy animal.

"I can do this later. I have to go and sort the company out now!"

"Sweet child, how do you expect me to get a wedding arranged at a week's notice? I could kill Frederick!" Reproachful, Constanza del Guiz looked up at Ash with brimming blue eyes. Ash noted the *Frederick*. "And you don't help, child. First you want to get married in your *armor*..."

Ash looked down at the tailor kneeling with pins and shears at her hem. "This is a robe, isn't it?"

"An underrobe. In your 'livery colors.'" The old woman—fifty, perhaps—put her fingers to her shaking lips, on the verge of tears. "It's taken me all of today to persuade you out of doublet and hose!"

A knock sounded on the door. A square-built, bearded man was admitted by the serving women. Ash turned toward Father Godfrey Maximillian and caught her foot in the sheer linen chemise that tangled her ankles under her full length silk kirtle. She stumbled. "*Fuck!*"

The whole room—tailor, tailor's apprentice, two Cologne serving women, and her prospective new mother—stopped talking and stared at her. Constanza del Guiz's face pinked.

Ash cringed, took a deep breath, and stared out of the window at the rain until someone should start talking again.

"*Fiat lux*, my lady. Captain." Water streamed from Godfrey Maximillian's woollen shoulder-caped hood. He pulled it off phlegmatically, and made the sign of the cross at the Green Man carved in fine stone tracery in the room's shrine. He beamed at the tailors and serving women, including them in his blessing. "Praise the Tree."

"Godfrey," Ash acknowledged. "Did you bring Florian and Roberto with you?"

Anselm had been much in Italy, originally, in tandem with Antonio Angelotti; there were still old company members who did not use the English *Robert*. If she could name one of her officers she was most anxious to talk to now, it was him.

"I can't find Florian anywhere. Robert's acting for the company while you're here."

And where have *you* been? I expected you eight hours ago, Ash thought grimly. Looking respectable. You could at least have cleaned the mud off! I'm trying to convince this woman I'm not a freak, and you turn up looking like a hedge priest!

Godfrey must have read something of this on her face. He said to Constanza del Guiz, "Sorry to be so unkempt, my lady. I've been riding from Neuss. Captain Ash's men need her advice on several things, quite urgently."

"Oh." The old woman's surprise was frank and genuine. "Do they need her? I thought she was a figurehead for them. I would have imagined that a band of soldiers functions more smoothly when women are *not* there."

Ash opened her mouth and the younger serving woman whipped a light linen veil over her face.

Godfrey Maximillian looked up from inadvertently shaking his muddy cloak over the tailor's bales of cloth. "Soldiers don't function with a figurehead in charge, my lady. Certainly they don't raise over a thousand men successfully for three years running and have most of the German principalities bidding for their services."

The Imperial noblewoman looked startled. "You don't mean she actually—"

"I command mercenaries," Ash interrupted, "and that's what I need to get back and do. We've never been paid with a marriage before. I know them. They won't like it. It ain't hard cash."

"Commands mercenaries," Constanza said, as if her mind were elsewhere, and then snapped a blue gaze back to Ash. Her soft mouth unexpectedly hardened. "What's Frederick thinking of? He promised me a good marriage for my son!"

"He promised *me* land," Ash said gloomily. "That's princes for you."

Godfrey chuckled.

Constanza snapped, "There have been women who tried to command in battle. That unsexed bitch Margaret of Anjou lost the throne of England for her poor husband. I could never let you do that to my son. You're rough, unmannered, and probably of peasant stock, but you're not wicked. I can school you to manners. You'll find people will soon forget your past when you're Fernando's wife, and my daughter."

"*Bol*—rubbish!" Ash lifted her arms in response to the tailor's nudge. A blue velvet gown settled over her gold-embroidered underrobe, heavy on her shoulders.

One serving woman began to pull in the laces at the back of the tight bodice. The other draped the gown's gold brocade hanging sleeves to one side and buttoned the undergown's tight-fitting sleeves from fur-trimmed cuff to elbow. The tailor fastened a belt low on Ash's hips.

"I've had fewer problems getting into *armor*," Ash muttered.

"Lady Ash will be a perfect credit to your son Fernando, I'm certain," Godfrey said, straight-faced. "Proverbs, chapter fourteen, verse one: 'every wise woman buildeth her house, but the foolish pulleth it down with her hands.' "[17]

Something in his tone on the last words made Ash look at him sharply.

Constanza del Guiz looked up—and it really is *up*, Ash noted—at the priest. "One moment. Father, you say this girl owns a company of men."

"Under contract, yes."

"And is therefore wealthy?"

Ash snuffled back a laugh, wiping her suntanned wrist across her mouth. Her weather-beaten skin wasn't set off to advantage by silk sleeves and wolf-fur cuffs. She said cheerfully, "Wealthy if I could keep it! I have to pay those bastards. Those men. Oh, shit. I'm no good at this!"

"I've known Ash since she was a child, my lady," Godfrey said smartly, "and she's perfectly capable of adapting herself from camp to court."

Thanks. Ash gave her clerk a look of heavy irony. Godfrey ignored it.

"But this is my only son—" Constanza put her thin fingers to her mouth. "Yes, Father. I'm sorry, I—faced with a wedding in less than a fortnight—and her origins—and no family—"

She dabbed at one eye with the corner of her veil. It was a calculated gesture, but then, as she looked at Ash struggling under the fitting of her headdress, a tension went out of her features. Constanza smiled quite genuinely.

"Neither of us expected this, but I think we can manage. Your men will be a welcome addition to my son's prestige. And you could be lovely, little one. Let me dress

---

[17]Although it is a later translation, some 135 years after the "Ash" texts, I have chosen the King James Authorised Version of the Bible (1611) as more accessible to the modern reader.

you properly and put on a little white lead to hide your blemishes. I would wish you to stand in front of the court as the pride of the del Guiz family, not the shame of it.'' Constanza's plucked brows furrowed. ''Especially if Tante Jeanne comes here from Burgundy, which she might, even with the war between us. Fernando's father's family always think they have a perfect right to come and criticize me. You'll meet them later.''

''I won't.'' Ash shook her head. ''I'm riding back to Neuss. Today.''

''No! Not until I have you dressed and ready for this wedding.''

''Now, *look*—'' Ash planted her feet squarely apart under her voluminous, flowing skirts. She jammed her fists on her hips. The underrobe's close-fitting sleeves suddenly creaked at the shoulder-seams.

Tacking threads snapped.

The azure velvet gown slid up through her hanging belt and bunched at her waist. The sudden weight of the purse pulled her belt skewed. Her heart-shaped horned head-dress, with its padded roll and temple-pieces, slipped to one side and all but fell off.

Ash huffed a breath at the crooked wisp of linen veil that floated down into her eyes.

''Child . . .'' Constanza's voice failed. ''You look like a sack of grain tied with a string!''

''Well, let me wear my doublet and hose, then.''

''*You cannot get married in male dress!*''

Ash broke into an irrepressible grin. ''Tell that to Fernando. I don't mind if he wants to wear the dress . . .''

''Oh!''

Godfrey Maximillian, studying his captain, folded his hands across his robed belly and rather unwisely said aloud what he was thinking. ''I never realized. You look short, in a dress.''

"I'm taller on the goddamn battlefield! Right, that's *it*." Ash wrenched the horned headdress and veils off her head, wincing as the pins pulled out of her hair. She ignored the tailor's protests.

"You *can't* go now!" Constanza del Guiz pleaded.

"Watch me!" Ash strode across the room, the full skirt of her gown flapping about her slippered feet. She picked up Godfrey's wet cloak and slung it around her shoulders. "We're out of here. Godfrey, do we have more than one company horse here?"

"No. Just my palfrey."

"Tough. You can ride pillion behind me. Lady Constanza, I'm sorry—truly." Ash hesitated. She gave the tiny woman a reassuring smile that, she was startled to find, she meant. "Truly. I have to see to my men. I'll be back. I'll *have* to be. Since it's the Emperor Frederick's gift, I can't very well *not* marry your son Fernando!"

There was some debate at Cologne's northwest gate: a lady, with her head uncovered, riding unaccompanied except for a priest? Ash gave them a few coins and the benefit of a soldier's vocabulary, and was put out to have the gate guards then pass her through as a whore accompanied by her pimp.

"Are you going to tell me what's bothering you?" she said over her shoulder to Godfrey, an hour later.

"No. Not unless it becomes necessary."

Rain made the roads into two days' journey, not one. Ash seethed. Deep cart-ruts full of mud tired the horse, until she gave up and bought another at a farm where they stayed, and then she and Godfrey rode on through the downpour, until they smelled the downwind stink of an established camp and knew they must be near Neuss.

"Ask yourself why it is," Ash said, absently grim, "that I know a hundred and thirty-seven different words for diseases of horses? High time we had something more reliable. Get up, there!''

Godfrey reined in his palfrey, waiting. "What did you think of life in the women's rooms in the castle?"

"A day and a half is enough for a lifetime." The roan gelding slowed again as her attention wandered. Ash felt a shift in the air and looked north at breaking cloud. "I've got used to people looking at me as soon as I walk in to a room. Well, no—they *looked* at me in Constanza's solar, but not for the same reasons!" Her eyes slitted with amusement. "I've got used to people expecting me to be in charge, Godfrey. In camp it's *Ash, what do we do now?* And in Cologne, it's *who's this unnatural monster?*"

"You always were a bossy brat," Godfrey remarked. "And, come to think of it, you always were fairly unnatural."

"That's why you rescued me from the nuns, I suppose?"

He ran a hand over his bearded chin and twinkled at her. "I like my women strange."

"That's good, coming from a chaste priest!"

"You want more miracles and grace for the company, you better pray I *stay* chaste."

"I need a miracle, all right. Until I got to Cologne, I thought maybe Emperor Frederick wasn't serious." Ash shifted her heels, bringing the roan from immobility to amble. The rain began to ease

"Ash—are you going through with this?"

"I most certainly am. Constanza was *wearing* more money than I've seen in the last two campaigns."

"And if the company objects?"

"They'll bitch because I didn't let them take prisoners for ransom on the skirmish, that's for sure. I'll bet I'm not flavor of the month. But they'll cheer up when they hear it's a rich marriage. We'll own *land* now. You're the one who objects, Godfrey, and you won't tell me why."

They confronted each other from the saddle: the surprising authority of the young woman, and the reserved concern of the priest. He repeated, "If it become necessary."

"Godfrey, sometimes you're a real godly pain in·the ass." Ash pushed her wet wool hood back. "Now, let's see if we can get all the command lance in one place at the same time, shall we?"

They were in sight of the southeast side of the Imperial wagon-fort now. The small foreign contingent of great-wheeled wagons here, chained together for defense, streamed with the last of the rain. Water ran down the forged iron plates that faced the sides of the war-carts, metal already streaking with orange rust.[18]

Over the sides of the iron war-wagons, inside the immense lager, Ash saw a rainbow of heraldic banners and standards dripping. The canvas cones of the striped tents hung limp from their center poles, ropes stretched and wet. A spatter of rain dashed into Ash's face as they approached the gate. It was a good five minutes before a hail went up from the huddled guards.

Euen Huw, sidling into the gateway past them, with a chicken under his arm, stopped and looked extremely startled. "Boss? Hey, boss—nice dress!"

Ash looked resignedly straight ahead as their horses trudged in down the long wagon- and tent-lined lanes. Antonio Angelotti ran up seconds later, his pale and beautiful hands yellow with sulphur.

---

[18]These improbable vehicles bear some resemblance to the mobile horse-drawn "war-wagons" used by the Hussites in the 1420s, some fifty years earlier than this. The Eastern European fighters appear to have used them as mobile gun-platforms However, the *Del Guiz* "iron-sided" wagons are a mere impossibility—even if constructed, they would have been so heavy that no conceivable team of horses could have moved them.

"Never saw you in a dress before, boss. Looks good.
You missed all the excitement!" His perfect face beamed,
like a down-market angel. "Heralds coming up from the
Burgundian camp. Imperial heralds going down to the
Burgundian camp. Terms put forward."

"Terms?"

"Sure. His Majesty Frederick says to Duke Charles,
pull back twenty miles. Lift the siege. Then in three days,
we'll pull back twenty miles."

"And Duke Charles is still laughing, right?"

Angelotti's yellow curls flew as he shook his head.
"The word is, he'll agree. That it's peace between the
Emperor and Burgundy."

"Oh, *shit*," Ash remarked, in the tone of one who—
two minutes before—had known exactly what eight
hundred-odd men, women and dependent children were
doing for the next three months. And now doesn't, and
will have to work something out. "Sweet Christ. Peace.
There goes our cushy summer siege."

Angelotti fell in to walk beside her gelding. "What's
happening about this marriage of yours, madonna? The
Emperor can't be serious?"

"Yes he fucking can!"

Ten minutes' riding across camp brought them to the
A-frame shelters and horse-lines at the northwest corner.
The voluminous folds of the velvet gown clung wetly to
her legs, rain darkening the cloth to royal blue. She still
wore Godfrey's cloak. It was pulled back by its own
weight of soaked wool, disclosing her kirtle and the wet
linen of her chemise.

The company had separated off a corner of the Imperial
camp with wattle fencing and a makeshift gate, something
which had not pleased the Imperial quartermaster until
Ash truthfully told him it was because her troops would

steal anything not nailed down. A Lion Azure standard now drooped there in the wet.

A redheaded man from Ned Aston's lance, guarding the gate, looked up and executed a perfect double-take.

"Hey—nice dress, boss!"

"*Bollocks!*"

A few minutes saw her in the command tent, Anselm, Angelotti and Godfrey present; Florian de Lacey missing; and the company's other main sub-captains missing.

"They're off muttering in corners. I'd leave them to it until you've got something you can tell them." Robert wrung out his woollen hood. "Tell us how badly we're screwed."

"We're not screwed, this is one *hell* of an opportunity!"

Ash was interrupted by Geraint ab Morgan ducking into the tent. "Yo, boss."

Geraint, new this season, currently overall Sergeant of Archers, was a broad-shouldered man with cropped hair the color of fallen leaves that stood straight up on his skull. The whites of his eyes were perpetually bloodshot. As he came in, Ash noted that the points that joined the back of his hose to the back of his doublet were undone, and his shirt had ridden up out of the gap, disclosing a ragged pair of braies and the cleft of his buttocks.

Aware she had come back unheralded, Ash kept tactfully quiet, except for a glare that had Geraint avoiding her eye and staring up into the conical roof of the tent, where weapons and kit were hung up on the wooden struts out of the wet.

"Day report," Ash said crisply.

Geraint scratched at his buttocks under white and blue wool hose. "The lads have been inside for two days, out of the rain, cleaning kit. Jacobo Rossano tried to poach two of our Flemish lances and they told him to sod off—

he's not impressed. And Henri de Treville is with the provosts, arrested for being drunk and trying to set the cook on fire.''

"You don't mean the cook's wagon, do you?" Ash asked wistfully, "you mean the cook."

"There was some comment about the besieged eating better in Neuss," Florian de Lacey said, as the surgeon entered, muddy to his booted knees. "And words to the effect that rat was a delicacy compared to Wat Rodway's stewed beef . . .''

Angelotti showed white teeth. " 'God sends us meat, and the Devil sends us English cooks.' "

"Enough with the Milanese proverbs, already!" Ash swatted at his head; he dodged. "Good. No one's successfully poaching our lances. Yet. Camp news?"

Robert Anselm volunteered briskly, "Sigismund of the Tyrol's pulling out; he says Frederick isn't going to fight Burgundy at all. Sigismund's been pissed off with Duke Charles since he lost Hericourt in '74. His men have been brawling with Gottfried of Innsbruck's archers. Oratio Farinetti and Henri Jacques have quarreled, the surgeons took up two dead from their men fighting.''

"I don't suppose we've actually fought the enemy?" Ash somewhat theatrically whacked her palm against her forehead. "No, no; silly me—we don't need an enemy. No feudal army does. Christ preserve me from factious nobility!''

A lance of sunlight slanted in through the open tent-flap. Everything Ash could see through the gap was dripping, and jewel-bright. She watched the red brigandines and blue livery jackets of men coming out to coax fires back into life, and tap the beer barrels that stood taller than a man, and fall to playing with greasy cards on the upturned tops of drums. Rising voices echoed.

"*Right*. Robert, Geraint, get the lads out, tell the lance-leaders to split 'em into red and blue scarves, and give them a game of football outside the wagon fort.''

"*Football?* Bloody English game!" Florian glared at her. "You realize I'll have more injuries to deal with than from the skirmish?"

Ash nodded. "Come to think of it . . . Rickard! *Rickard!* Where is that boy?"

Her squire hurtled into the tent. He was fourteen, with glossy black hair and thick winged eyebrows; already conscious of how good-looking he was, and with a growing disinclination to keep it in his codpiece.

"You'll have to run up to the provosts and warn them the noise down here isn't a skirmish, it's a game."

"Yes, my lady!"

Robert Anselm scratched at his shaven head. "They won't wait much longer, Ash. I've had lance-leaders up to the tent every hour on the hour, these past two days."

"I know. *When* they've worked their energy off," Ash continued, "get them all together. I'm going to talk to everybody, not just the lance-leaders. Go!"

"I hope you've got something convincing to tell them!"

"Trust me."

Anselm went out behind Geraint. The tent emptied of all but Ash, her surgeon, priest and page.

"Rickard, on your way out, send Philibert in to dress me." Ash watched her eldest page stomp out.

"Rickard's getting too old," she said absently to de Lacey. "I'll have to pass him on as a squire, and find another ten-year-old page." Her eyes gleamed. "That's a problem you don't have, Florian—*I* have to have body servants under the age of puberty, or all the whore-rumors start up again. 'She's not a real captain, she just shags the company officers and they let her prance around in armor.' Hell-fire!" She laughed. "In any case, young

Rickard's far too good-looking for me to have around. Never fuck your employees!''

Florian de Lacey leaned back in the wooden chair, both palms flat on his thighs. He gave her a sardonic look. ''The bold mercenary captain ogles the innocent young boy—except I don't remember the last time you got laid, and Rickard's been through half the Imperial camp whores and come to me because he caught crab-lice.''

''Yeah?'' Ash shrugged. ''Well . . . I can't fuck anyone in the company because it's favoritism. And anyone who isn't a soldier goes, you're a woman and you're a *what?*''

Florian stood and walked to look out of the tent, cradling a wine cup. Not, after all, a particularly tall man, he had the left-over stoop of a boy who grew tall earlier than his contemporaries and learned not to like standing out in a crowd. ''And now you're getting married.''

''Yippee!'' Ash said. ''It won't change anything, except we'll have revenues from land. Fernando del Guiz can stay in his castle, and I'll stay in the army. He can find himself some bimbo in a stuffed headdress, and I'll be entirely happy to look the other way. Marriage? *No* problem.''

Florian raised a sardonic eyebrow. ''If that's what you think, you haven't been paying attention!''

''I know your marriage was difficult.''

''Oh.'' He shrugged. ''Esther preferred Joseph to me— women often prefer their babies to their husbands. At least it wasn't a man she ignored me for . . .''

Ash gave up her attempt to unlace her bodice herself, and presented her back to Godfrey. As the priest's solid fingers tugged at the cords, she said, ''Before I go out there and talk to the guys—I've been paying attention to one thing, Florian. How come you keep vanishing lately? I turn around and you're not there. What's Fernando del Guiz to you?''

"Ah." Florian wandered in an irritating manner around the kit-cluttered tent. He stopped. He looked coolly at Ash. "He's my brother."

"Your *what?*" Ash goggled.

At her back, Godfrey's fingers were momentarily still on the bodice lacing. "*Brother?*"

"Half-brother, actually. We share a father."

Ash became aware that the top of her gown had loosened. She shook her shoulders in the cloth, feeling it slide away. Godfrey Maximillian's fingers began to untie the fastenings of her underrobe.

"You've got a brother who's noble?"

"We all know Florian's an aristocrat." Godfrey hesitated. "Don't we?" He went around to the trestle table and poured a goblet of wine. "Here. I thought you knew, Ash. Florian, I always thought your family came from one of the Burgundies, not the Empire."

"It does. Dijon, in Burgundy. When my mother in Dijon died, my father remarried a noblewoman from Cologne." The blond man slid a shoulder up in an insouciant gesture. "Fernando's a good few years younger than me, but he is my half-brother."

"Green Christ up a Tree!" Ash said. "By the Bull's Horns!"

"Florian's hardly the only man we've got in the company under a false name. Criminals, debtors and runaways, to a man." Seeing that she would not take the wine, Godfrey gulped it himself. He made a face of disgust. "That sutler's selling us rubbish again. Ash, I assume Florian stays away from his family because no aristocratic family would ever tolerate their son as a barber-surgeon—is that right, Florian?"

Florian grinned. He sat again, sprawling back on Ash's wooden chair, and put his boots on her table. "Your face! It's true. All of the del Guiz family, German and Burgundian, would have a fit if they knew I was a doctor. They'd prefer me dead in a ditch somewhere. And the rest of the medical profession don't like my research methods.''

"One corpse too many gone missing in Padua,[19] I suppose.'' Ash recovered some composure. "Blood! How long have I known you—''

"Five years?'' Florian said.

"And *now* you tell me?''

"I thought you knew.'' Florian stopped meeting her gaze. He scratched at the shin of his torn hose with a hand deeply dirt-ingrained. "I thought you knew everything I had to hide.''

Ash pushed her underrobe and kirtle off her shoulders and stepped out of the vast heap of crumpled silk and brocade, leaving it lying on the rushes. Her linen chemise was fine enough to show her skin as a pink glow under it and to disclose the round swell of her breasts, the darkness of her nipples.

Florian grinned at her, momentarily distracted. "That's what I *call* a pair of tits. Good Lord, woman! Beats me how you ever get those under an arming doublet. One day you really must let me have a closer look . . .''

Ash stripped her chemise off over her head. She stood naked and confident, one fist on her hip, and grinned back at her surgeon. "Yeah, sure—your interest in women's bodies is *purely* professional. That's what all the camp girls tell me!''

Florian leered. "Trust me. I'm a doctor.''

Godfrey did not laugh. He looked out of the tent. "Here's young Philibert. Florian, isn't this ridiculous? You could—mediate with your brother. Isn't this the ideal occasion for a family reunion?''

---

[19]Padua in Italy was at this time a famous center attended by medical students from all over Europe.

All humor gone, Florian said flatly, "No."

"You could be reconciled to your family—bless them which persecute you; bless, and curse not.[20] And then you could *strongly* suggest to your brother that he doesn't marry Ash."

"No. I could not. I recognized who it must be out there by his livery. I haven't met him face to face since he was a child, and I intend to keep it that way."

An edge was apparent in the air, a tension in their voices. Ash glanced from one man to the other, entirely unconscious of being naked. "Don't object to this marriage, guys. It can open up a whole new world for the company. We can be permanent. We'll have land we can go back to in the winter. *And* revenues."

Florian's gaze locked on the priest's face. "Listen to her, Father Godfrey. She's right."

"But she mustn't marry Fernando del Guiz!" The priest's desperate voice went up an octave; he sounded like the young ordinand that Ash remembered meeting in the St. Herlaine convent, eight years ago. "She must not!"

"Why not?"

"Yes, why not?" Ash echoed her surgeon. "Phili, come and sort me out shirt and doublet and hose. The green with the silver points will be suitably impressive. Godfrey, why not?"

"I've been waiting, but you don't—Didn't you recognize his name? Don't you remember his face?" Godfrey was a big man, rather than being fat, and he had all the charisma of a large, powerful body, priest or not. Now there was helplessness in his gestures. He swung around on Florian, jabbing a finger at the willowy man sprawled

---

[20]Romans 12:14.

in the chair. "Ash can't marry your brother because she's met him before!"

"I'm sure our ruthless mercenary leader has met many noble idiots." Florian picked at his dirty nails. "Fernando won't be the first, or the worst."

Godfrey stepped out of the page Philibert's way. Ash hauled a shirt over her head, sat on the wooden chest and pulled on her doublet and hose together—two mismatched shades of green wool; still tied together at the waist with twelve pairs of cords tipped with silver aiglettes. She held her arms out, and the small boy eased her sleeves over them, tying them into the doublet's armholes at the shoulders with more pairs of points.

"Go watch the football, Phili; come and tell me when they're finishing." She ruffled his hair. As he left, and she began lacing up the front of her best puff-sleeved doublet, she said, "Come on, Godfrey, what is it? Yeah, I know I know the face from somewhere. Where do you know him from?"

Godfrey Maximillian turned away, avoiding her eyes. "He . . . won the big tournament, in Cologne, last summer. You remember, child? He unhorsed fifteen; didn't fight in the foot combat. The Emperor presented him with a bay stallion. I—recognized the livery and name."

Ash took his shoulder and turned him to face her again. She said flatly, "Yeah. *And* the rest. What's so special, Godfrey? Where did *I* meet Fernando?"

"Seven years ago." Godfrey took a breath. "In Genoa."

Her belly jolted. She forgot the waiting company. So *that's* what all the adrenalin-powered cheerfulness has been about these past two days. I'm like that when I'm hiding something from myself. I just don't always know that's what I'm doing.

And it's probably why I've been running the company

like a half-arsed excuse for a captain; letting myself be taken off to Cologne—

The memory, chewed dry, comes back to her as it always does, in the same fragments. Sea-water slopping against the stone steps of a dock. Lantern-light on wet cobbles. Male shoulders against the light. Running back to camp afterwards—the camp of her old company, under the Griffin-in-Gold banner—choking, far too ashamed to show rage openly.

"Oh. Yeah. So?" Ash's voice sounded, even to herself, too hurried to be casual. She looked away from Godfrey, out of the tent. "Was *that* del Guiz? That was a long time ago."

"I made it my business afterwards to find out his name."

"Did you?" The back of her throat tightened with malice. "That's the kind of thing you like to do, isn't it, Godfrey? Even then."

In her peripheral vision, Florian de Lacey—now Florian del Guiz, a potential brother-in-law; how strange—stood up. He put his flopping, dirty blond hair out of his eyes, in the so-familiar gesture. "What is it, girl?"

"Didn't I ever tell you? It was before you joined us. I thought I might have got drunk some night and told you." A questioning glance, at which Florian shook his head.

Ash got up from the chest and walked to the tent's entrance. The wet canvas was beginning to dry now, under the afternoon sun. She reached out to test the growing tautness of a guy-rope. A cow moaned, over in the quarter-master Henri Brant's stock pens. The wind brought wet scents of dung. The tents and other shelters—A-frame structures made of canvas pegged down over halberd shafts—were unusually empty. She cocked an ear for the sound of voices shouting at football and heard nothing.

"Well," she said. "Well."

She turned back to face the two men. Godfrey's fingers kneaded obsessively at the cord around the waist of his brown robe. You could still see, in his weather-hardened features, the pallid, plump young man that he had been then. Her rage, hanging fire, snapped.

"And you can take that sheep-face off! I've never seen *you* so happy. You loved me being punished. You could comfort me! You never like me quite so much when I'm not falling apart, do you? Bloody virgin!"

"*Ash!*"

Ebbing, the anger leaves her dry, free of the conviction that the world is full of faces hiding harm, viciousness, persecution.

"Jesus, Godfrey, I'm sorry!"

The priest's face lost a little of its distress.

Florian said, "What did my brother do?"

Ash felt the dry rushes beneath her bare feet as she walked back across the tent. The shadows of clouds move across the canvas; the world bright, then dim, then bright again. She sat on the wooden chest and pulled her boots on, without looking up at the surgeon. "Wine."

"Here." A dirty hand entered her field of vision: Florian holding a goblet.

Ash took it, and watched the red and silver ripples on the surface of the liquid.

"You can't hear it without laughing. No one could. That's the problem." She lifted her head as Florian squatted down on his haunches in front of her; she and the man now level, face to face. "You know, you don't look anything like him. I'd never have taken you on the company books if you had."

"Yes you would." Florian put one hand down to support himself, careless of the mud tracked in on the rushes. He smiled. It showed the dirt in the creases of the skin around his eyes, but made his whole face glow with affection. "How else could you afford a Salerno-qualified doctor, except by finding one with a predilection for cutting up battlefield casualties to see how bodies work? Every mercenary company should have one! And where else are you going to find someone sensible enough to tell you when you're being an idiot? You're an idiot. I don't know my half-brother, but what could he have done—?"

Florian suddenly straightened up and rubbed at his cramped legs. Mud smeared. He picked one or two of the larger clods off his blue hose and watched her out of the corner of his eye. "Did he rape you?"

"No. I wish he had."

Ash reached up and unfastened the tight braids that Constanza's women had done up for her. Her silver hair uncoiled.

This is now. This is now: if I hear birds, they are crows yawping, not gulls. This is now, and this is summer, hot even when it rains. But my hands are cold with humiliation.

"I was twelve; Godfrey had taken me out of St. Herlaine the year before; it was after I'd been apprentice to a Milanese armorer and then found the company of the Griffin-in-Gold again." She heard the sea in her mind. "This was when I still wore women's dress if I wasn't in the camp."

Still sitting, she reached over and picked up her sword, with the swordbelt wound tidily around its scabbard. The round wheel pommel comforted her hand as she rested her palm on it. The leather on the grip was cut and needed redoing.

"There was an inn in Genoa. This boy was there with friends, and he asked me to sit down at their table. I suppose it must have been summer. It was light until late. He had green eyes and fair hair and no particular kind of face, but it was the first time I'd ever looked at a man and got hot and wet. I thought he *liked* me.''

When she has to remember, when something reminds her of it, it is as if she watches what happens from a distance. But it only takes a slight effort to bring back the sweat and the fear, and her whining voice pleading *Let me go! Please!* She pulled away from their hands, and they pinched her breasts, leaving black bruises that she never showed to any physician.

''I thought I was *it*, Florian. I was doing sword-training, and the captain was even allowing me to act as his page. I thought I was *so* hot.''

She couldn't look up.

''He was a few years older, obviously the son of a knight. I did everything to make him like me. There was wine but I never drank it; I just got too high when I thought that he wanted me. I couldn't wait to touch him. When we left, I thought we were going back to his rooms. He took me around the back of the inn, near the dock, and said, 'Lie down.' I didn't care, it could have been there or anywhere.''

Cobblestones: cushioned only by the crumpled cloth of her robe and kirtle and shift. She felt them hard under her buttocks as she lay down and moved her heels apart.

''He stood over me and unlaced his flap. I didn't know what he was doing, I expected him to lie down on top of me. He took it out and he *pissed*—''

She rubbed her hands over her face.

''He said I was a little girl who acted like a man and he pissed on me. His friends came up and watched. Laughing.''

She sprang up. The sword thudded down onto the rushes. Rapidly, she walked to the tent's entrance, looked out, spun around and faced the two men.

''You can't help but laugh. I wanted to die. He held

me down while all his friends did it. On my robe. In my face. The taste—I thought it would be poison, that I'd die from that.''

Godfrey reached out his hand. She stepped back from comfort without realizing that she did so.

''What I don't understand to this day is *why I let it happen.*''

Anguish thinned her voice.

''I knew how to fight. Even if they were stronger, and there were more of them, I knew how to *run.*'' She rubbed her hand hard across her scarred cheek. ''I did scream out to one man walking past, but he just ignored me. He could see what they were doing. He didn't do anything to help. He laughed. I can't be angry about it. *They didn't even hurt me.*''

Sick fear in her stomach kept her from looking at either of them: Godfrey now reminded of a wet, stinking, weeping young woman; and Florian with whom things would not now be the same, not ever, not with him knowing this.

''Christ,'' Ash said painfully, ''if that *was* Fernando del Guiz—he can't remember now or he'd have said something. Looked at me different. Do you think he still has the same friends? Do you think any of *them* will remember?''

Powerful hands closed over her shoulders from behind. Godfrey said nothing, but his grip tightened until she could have cried out. She could feel his mute appeal to Florian. Ash rubbed her flaming cheeks. ''Fuck.''

I've spent five years killing men on the field of battle, and here I am thinking like a green novice, not a soldier—

Godfrey's voice over her shoulder whispered, intensely: ''Florian, find out if he remembers. Talk to him. He's your brother. Buy him off if you have to!''

Florian walked toward Ash. He stopped when he stood directly in front of her. In the light inside the tent, his face looked gray. ''I can't do it. I can't try to persuade him out of it. They'd burn me.''

Ash could only incredulously say, ''*What?*'' still shaking from the rush of memory. The man in front of her reached out. She felt her hand taken. Godfrey's grip from behind tightened again.

Florian's long, surgeon's fingers uncurled her hand. He pulled open the lacing of his doublet and plunged Ash's hand under the gathered neck of his fine linen shirt.

She was touching warm flesh before she said, ''What?''

Under his shirt, Ash's fingers and palm cupped the full, rounded, firm breast of a woman.

Ash stared at his face. The dirty, unshakeable, pragmatic surgeon gripped her hand hard, and was plainly woman—plain as day, a tall woman in man's dress.

Godfrey's puzzled voice rumbled, ''What—?''

''You're a *woman*?'' Ash stared at Florian.

Godfrey gaped at both of them.

''Why couldn't you *tell* me?'' Ash shouted. ''Christ, I needed to know! You might have put the whole company in danger!''

The page Philibert put his head back through the tent flap. Ash snatched her hand away.

The boy looked from one to the other: surgeon, field priest, captain. ''Ash!''

He feels the tension, Ash thought, and then: No, I'm wrong. He's too wrapped up in what he's got to say to notice anything else.

The boy squealed, ''They're not playing football. The men. Everybody. They won't! They're all together, and they say they're not doing anything until you come and speak to them!''

''*Here* we go,'' Ash muttered. She glanced back at Florian, at Godfrey. "Go and tell them I'm on my way. *Now*." And, as the boy Philibert ran out, "It won't wait. They won't wait. Not now. Florian—no—what *is* your name?"

"Floria."

"Floria . . ."

"I don't understand," Godfrey said frankly.

The tall woman re-tied the neck-string of her shirt. "My name is Floria del Guiz. I'm not Fernando's half-brother; he has no brothers. I'm his half-*sister*. This is the only way I can ever practice as a surgeon, and no, my family is not about to welcome me back, not in Burgundy, and certainly not into the Imperial German branch of the del Guizes."

The priest stared. "You're a woman!"

Ash muttered, "That's why I keep you on the company books, Godfrey. Your acumen. Your intelligence. The rapidity with which you penetrate to the heart of the matter." She shot a look at the lantern and its marked hour-candle, burning steadily where it sat on the trestle table. "It's nearly Nones.[21] Godfrey, go and give that unruly mob out there a field-mass. Do it! I need time."

She caught the brown sleeve of his robe as he moved toward the tent-flap. "Don't mention Florian. I mean Floria. You heard it Under the Tree. And get me enough time to arm up."

Godfrey looked at her for a long minute before he nodded.

Ash stared after his departing back as Godfrey stepped out across the rain-wet earth that steamed, now, in the afternoon sun. "Shit on a stick . . ."

"When do I leave?" Floria del Guiz said, behind her.

---

[21]This text often gives the hour of the day by the monastic system: Nones is the sixth office or service of the day, taking place at three p.m.

Ash pressed both index fingers down hard on the bridge of her nose. She shut her eyes. The darkness behind her eyelids speckled with light.

"I'll be lucky if I don't lose half the company, never mind you." She opened her eyes again, dropped her hands to her sides. "You've slept in my tent. I've seen you rat-arsed and throwing up. *I've seen you piss!*"

"No. You're merely under the impression that you have. I've been doing this since I was thirteen." Floria appeared in Ash's peripheral vision, wine cup trailing from her long fingers. "Salerno now trains no Jews, no black Libyans, and no women. I've passed as a man since then. Padua, Constantinople, Iberia. Army doctoring, because nobody *cares* who you are. You and these men. . . . This past five years is the longest I've been able to stay anywhere."

Ash leaned out of the tent and bawled, "*Philibert! Rickard!* Get in here!—I can't make a hasty decision, Florian. Floria."

"Stick with Florian. It's safer. It's safer for *me*."

That rueful tone penetrated Ash's daze. She looked straight at the woman. "I'm female. The world puts up with me. Why shouldn't it put up with you?"

Florian ticked off on her fingers: "You're a mercenary You're a peasant. You're human cattle. You don't have an influential rich family. I *am* a del Guiz. I matter. I'm a threat. If nothing else, I'm the elder: I could inherit at least the estate in Burgundy . . . All this outrage comes down to property in the end."

"They wouldn't burn you." Ash did not sound certain. "Maybe they'd only lock you up and beat you."

"I don't have your facility for being hit without minding it." Florian's fair eyebrows quirked up. "Ash, are you so sure they tolerate you? This idea of a marriage didn't

come out of nowhere. Somebody's put Frederick up to
it.''

"Shit. *Marriage*." Ash moved back across the tent and
lifted her sword up out of the rushes. Apparently absently,
she said, "I heard, in Cologne, that the Emperor knighted
Gustav Schongauer. Remember him and his guys two
years ago at Héricourt?"[22]

"*Schongauer? Knighted?*" Florian, briefly distracted
by outrage, glared at her. "They were bandits! He spent
most of that autumn destroying Tyrolese farms and vil-
lages! How could Frederick ennoble him?"

"Because there's no such thing as legitimate authority
or illegitimate authority. There is only authority." Ash
faced the man who was a woman, still holding her scab-
barded sword between two hands. "If you *can* control a
lot of fighting men—you *will*. And you'll be recognized
and ratified by other controllers. *Like I need to be*. Except
that no king or nobleman is going to knight *me*."

"Knighthood? Boys' games! But if a murdering rapist
can end up as a Graf—!"

Ash waved Florian's shock away. "Yeah, you *are* noble ... How do you think we get new nobles in the first
place? The other Grafs are scared of him. The Emperor
too, for that matter. So they make him one of them. If he
gets too scary, they'll band together and have him killed.
That's the balancing act."

She took the wine cup out of Florian's fingers and
drained it. The buzz was enough to loosen her up, not
enough to make her light-headed.

"It's the law by which chivalry operates." Ash looked
down into the empty cup. "It doesn't matter how generous and virtuous you are. Or how brutal. If you have no

---

[22]Héricourt was a small Burgundian frontier castle put under siege by
the Swiss; their campaign ended with a battle, on 13 November 1474.

powerbase, you'll be treated with disrespect; and if you do have a powerbase, everyone will come to you in preference to anyone else. And power comes from the ability to make armed men fight for you. To reward them with money, yes, but more—with titles and marriages and land. I can't do that. I need to. This marriage—"

Ash abruptly reddened. She scrutinized Floria's face, weighing up secrets known and past confidences not betrayed. Floria, so like the Florian who has shared her tent on many nights, talking into the small hours.

"You don't go, Florian. Unless you want to." She met Floria's gaze, smiled wryly. "You're too good a surgeon, if nothing else. And . . . we've known each other too long. If I trust you to horse-doctor me, I can't stop trusting you now!"

A little shaken, the tall woman said, "I'll stay. How will you manage it?"

"Don't ask me. I'll work something out . . . *Sweet Christ, I can't marry that man!*"

A distant babble of voices became plainly audible outside.

"What are you going to tell them, Ash?"

"I don't know. But they won't wait. Let's move it!"

Ash waited only long enough for Philibert and Rickard to get her undressed and into her arming doublet and hose, and armor, and belt her sword around her waist, gilded sword-pommel catching the canvas-filtered light. The boys did it with never a fumble, rapid fingers tying points, buckling straps, pushing her body and limbs to where would best help them fasten her into her steel shell, all with the ease of practice. Full Milanese harness.

"I *have* to talk to them," Ash added, her tone somewhere between cynicism and self-mockery. "After all— they're the reason why the Holy Roman Emperor calls me 'captain.' And the reason why I can walk through a camp full of armed men without being bushwhacked.''

Florian del Guiz prompted: ''And?''

'' 'And' what?'' Ash left her helmet off, carrying it reversed under her arm, with her gauntlets slung into it.

''Ash, I may be a woman. I've still known you for five years. You have to talk to them because you rely on them—*and?*''

''And . . . I'm the reason they don't go back to being tanners or shepherds or clerks or goodwives. So I'd better see they don't starve.''

Florian del Guiz chuckled. ''That's my girl!''

At the tent-flap, leaving, Ash said, ''Florian, it's the *Emperor's* marriage—I'm finished if I don't go through with it. And damned if I do.''

iii

A BRISK STRIDE took Ash into the center clear ground under the Blue Lion standard. She vaulted up onto the back of an open cart and gazed around at the men variously sitting on barrels and straw bales and wet ground, and standing with their arms folded, faces up-turned grimly to hers.

''Let me recap.'' Her voice was not strained; she spoke distinctly and clearly, could see no one having trouble hearing her. ''Two days ago we fought a skirmish with the Duke's men. This wasn't under orders from our employer. It was my call. It was rash, but we're soldiers, we have to be rash. Sometimes.''

She dropped her voice on the last word, and got chuckles from a group of men-at-arms by the beer barrels: Jan-

Jacob, Gustav and Pieter—Flemish men from Paul di Conti's lance.

"Our employer had two choices then. He could break our contract. In that case we'd go straight across to the other side and sign up with Charles of Burgundy."

Thomas Rochester shouted up, "Maybe we should ask Duke Charles for a contract now, if it's peace here. He's always off fighting somewhere."

"Maybe not *quite* yet." Ash paused. "Maybe we'd better wait a day or two, until he forgets we almost killed him!"

Another laugh, louder; and van Mander's boys joined in—crucial because they were known as hard, and consequently respected.

"We'll sort that out later." Ash went on briskly. "We don't care who's bishop in Neuss, so Frederick knew we'd go if he said the word. That was his first choice, and he didn't take it. Second—he could have paid us money."

"Yeah!" Two female archers (who were known as 'Geraint's women' only when they weren't around to hear about it) raised a cheer.

Ash's heart beat faster. She rested her left hand down on her sword hilt, thumb stroking the ripped leather binding.

"Well, as you all know by now, we didn't get money either."

There were catcalls. The back of the crowd closed in; archers and cross-bowmen, billmen and hackbutters; all shoulder to shoulder now and putting their attention on her.

"For those of you who were with me in the skirmish, by the way, well done. It was fucking amazing. Amazing." Deliberate pause. "I've never seen an encounter won by anybody who did so many things wrong!"

Loud laughter. She spoke over it, picking out individual

men. "Euen Huw, you do *not* get off to loot the bodies. Paul di Conti, you do not start a charge from so far away that your horse is on crutches by the time you finally get to the enemy! I'm surprised you didn't get down and walk. And as for watching your commander for orders!" She let the comments die down. "I should add some remark about keeping your eye on the fucking standard at all times . . ." She cleared her throat.

Robert Anselm deliberately, and helpfully, made himself heard above the racket of several hundred voices. "Yes *you* should!"

There was laughter and she knew the immediate crisis was over. Or holding, at any rate.

"So we'll *all* be putting in lots of skirmish practice." Ash looked out from the back of the cart. "What you guys did *was* fucking amazing. Tell your grandchildren. It wasn't war. You just don't see knight charging knight on the battlefields, because there's all you nasty little fuckers with bows out there! Oh yeah—*and* the hackbutters." A grin at what sounded like cheerful discontent from the gun crews. "I wouldn't recognize a battle without the happy sound of backfiring arquebuses!"

The redheaded man-at-arms from Aston's lance yelled, "Get a fucking axe!" and the foot men took up the chant. The gunners responded variously and profanely. Ash nodded at Antonio Angelotti to quieten them down.

"Whatever it was, it was magnificent. Sadly, it hasn't earned us anything. So the next time we get a chance to stick a lance up Charles of Burgundy's ass, I'll come back and ask if you're going to be *paid* first."

A voice at the back found a moment of silence to call, "*Fuck* Frederick of Hapsburg!"

"In your dreams!"

A roar of laughter.

Ash shifted her weight onto her other hip. The uncer-

tain breeze blew tendrils of hair across her face. She
smelled cooking fires, and horse manure, and the stink of
eight hundred sweaty bodies packed close in a crowd.
They were mostly bareheaded, being in camp and theoretically safe from attack; and their bills and halberds were
piled in stacks a dozen to a tent.

Children ran around the edges, not able to pass through
the packed mass made up of the men and women who
fought. Most of the men and women who didn't, the
whores and cooks and washerwomen, were sitting up on
the sides of wagons at the edge of the camp, listening.
There were—as there always are—some men still intent
on their games of dice, or dead-drunk asleep under wet
canvas, or just off somewhere else, but she had the majority of her company in front of her.

Seeing so many faces that she knew, she thought: The
best thing I have on my side is that they *want* to hear me.
They want me to tell them what to do. Mostly they're on
my side. But they're all my responsibility.

On the other hand, there are always other companies
they can get employment with.

They went quiet, waiting for her. A word here and
there, between mates. There was a lot of shifting of boots
on wet ground, and people watching her, not commenting.

"A lot of you have been with me since I formed the
company three years ago. Some of you were with me
before that, when I raised men for the Griffin-in-Gold, and
the Company of the Boar. Look around you. You're a lot
of mad bastards, and the chances are you're standing next
to some other mad bastards! You *have* to be mad to follow
me—but *if you do*," she increased voice projection: "if
you do, you've always come out of it *alive*—and with a
hell of a *reputation*—and *paid*."

She held up an armored arm, before the level of talk
could rise. "And we will this time. Even if we're being

paid with a marriage! I suppose there's a first time for-everything. Trust Frederick to find it.''

She gazed down at her sub-captains, who stood in a tight little knot, exchanging comments and watching her.

"During the last few days I've been taking chances. It's my job. But it's your future too. We've always discussed in open meeting what contracts we'll take or not take. So now we're going to discuss this marriage.''

The words came as fluently as ever. She never had problems talking to them. Behind the fluency, something tightened and thinned her voice. Ash became aware that her bare hands were clenched, knuckles straining.

What can I tell them? That we have to do this, but I can't do this?

"And after we've discussed it," Ash went on, "then we're going to *vote* on it.''

"Vote?" Geraint ab Morgan yelled. "You mean a real vote?''

Somebody quite audibly said, "Democracy means doing what boss tells you!''

"Yes, a *real* vote. Because if we take this offer, it's *company* lands and *company* revenues. And if we don't take it—about the only excuse the Emperor Frederick is going to accept from me," Ash said, "is 'my company won't let me'!''

She didn't let them think closely about that, but carried on:

"You've been with me, and you've been with merce-nary companies that don't hold together through a season, never mind years. I've always put you in the way of enough loot to keep armor on your backs.''

The clouds, shifting, let sunlight sweep across the wet earth and flash from her Milanese plate armor. It was so pat that she spared a suspicious glance for Godfrey, who stood at the foot of the cart with his hands clasped about his Briar Cross.

The bearded man raised his eyes to the heavens and smiled absently—and followed that with a swift, satisfied glance at the picture she made, standing higher than her men, in bright armor, the Lion Azure a blaze across the sky above her. A very minor miracle.

Ash stood without speaking for a moment to let them notice her armor: its expense and therefore its implications. *I can afford this, therefore I'm good. You really want to be employed by me: honest, guv . . .*

Ash spoke. "If I get married to this man, we can have our own land to go back to in the winter. We can have its crops and lumber and wool to sell. We can," she added thinly, "stop taking suicide contracts just to get the money to reequip ourselves every year."

A man with lank, dark hair and wearing a green brigandine called out, "And what happens next year if we get offered a contract to fight *against* the Emperor?"

"He knows we're mercenaries, for fuck's sake."

A woman archer got her way to the front of the crowd with her elbows. "But that's now, when you're under contract to him. That's not when you're married to one of his feudal subjects." She craned her head back to look up at Ash. "Won't he expect you to be loyal to the Holy Roman Empire, Captain?"

"If I wanted to be *told* who to fight for," a hackbutter shouted, "I'd have joined the feudal levy!"

Geraint ab Morgan growled, "Too late to worry about that; the offer's been made. I vote we join the property game, and don't piss off the Emperor."

Ash looked down from the cart. "I assume we'll just carry on as we are."

A rumble of complaint made itself heard across the field. The archer spun around on her heel. "Can't you motherfuckers give her a chance? Captain Ash, you'll be *married*.''

Ash recognized her now, the fair-haired woman with an odd name: Ludmilla Rostovnaya. She had the crank of a crossbow hanging from her belt. *Crossbowmen from Genoa*, Ash thought, and put both her hands on the side of the cart, dizzy and sick.

Why am I trying to persuade them we should go through with this?

I can't do it.

Not for the world, never mind a poxy little Bavarian estate—

Geraint ab Morgan pushed his way to the front. Ash saw her sergeant of archers look at Florian, and at the priest, as if questioning why they didn't speak.

Geraint yelled, ''Boss, it's fucking obvious someone's landed this one on us because they don't like mercenaries. Remember the Italians, after Héricourt?[23] We can't afford to have Frederick fucked off with us. You're going to have to do this, Captain.''

''But she can't!'' Ludmilla Rostovnaya shouted into his face. There was a rising noise of talk, not everyone being able to hear the quarrel at the front of the crowd. Ludmilla's voice rose clearly over it. ''If she marries a man, her property becomes his. Not the other way around! If she marries him, this company's contract will belong to the del Guiz family! And del Guiz belongs to the Emperor! Frederick just got himself a mercenary company for *nothing*!''

The words went out to the back of the crowd, you could see the intelligence pass.

---

[23]On 24 December 1474, eighteen captured Italian mercenaries who had been fighting for the Burgundians against the Swiss were burned alive at Basel. It was Christmas Eve.

Ash looked down at the eastern woman, always reassured, even in crisis and panic, to see another fighting woman. This one, in her brown padded jack and red hose, with poleyns strapped on her knees, and a sunburned fair-skinned face, now flung up an arm and pointed it at her. "Tell us you've thought about this one, boss!"

Her property becomes *his*—

Frederick is Fernando's feudal lord—we become feudal property. Sweet pity of Christ, this just gets worse!

Why didn't I think of this?

Because you're still thinking like a man.

Ash couldn't speak. Armor demands an upright posture or she would have slumped; as it was, she could only look out at the familiar faces.

Their voices died down. Only children, running and screaming at the edge of the crowd, made any noise. Ash swept her gaze over them, seeing one man with a meat-bone paused halfway to his mouth, another with wine running unnoticed from a wineskin to the earth. The sub-captains were being drawn out of their knot, their men crowding close to ask urgent questions.

"No," she said. "I didn't think about that."

Robert Anselm warned, "That boy won't let you stay in command. You marry Fernando del Guiz, we've lost you."

"Shit!" said a man-at-arms. "She can't marry him!"

"But you fuck off the Emperor and *we're* fucked." Geraint's bloodshot eyes seemed to vanish into his stubbled cheeks as he squinted up at Ash.

She grabbed at a first thought. "There are other employers."

"Yeah, and they're all his second cousins or whatever!" Geraint coughed and spat phlegm. "You know the royal Princes of Christendom. Incest is their middle name. We'll end up only being hired by assholes who call themselves 'noble' because some lord once fucked their grand-mother. We can forget being paid in gold!"

A different man-at-arms said, "We can always split up, hire out to other companies."

His lance-companion, Pieter Tyrrell, yelled, "Yeah, we can go with some stupid fuck who'll get us all killed. Ash knows what she's doing when she fights!"

"Pity she knows fuck-all about anything else!"

Ash turned her head, unobtrusively checking to see where her battle police were, where the gate-guards were, and what the faces of the cooks and the women who washed and mended looked like. A horse neighed. The sky was momentarily full of starlings, moving to another patch of wet, worm-filled earth.

Godfrey Maximillian said quietly, "They don't want to lose you."

"That's because I get them through battles, and I win." Her mouth dried. "Whatever I do here, now, I lose."

"It's a different game. You're wearing petticoats now."

Florian—Floria—growled, "Nine-tenths of them know they couldn't run this company the way you do. The one-tenth that think they can are wrong. Let them talk it out until they remember that."

Ash, stifled, nodded. She raised her voice to battlefield pitch. "Listen up! I'm giving you until Vespers.[24] Come here for Father Godfrey's evening service. Then I'll hear what you decide."

She ducked down from the cart. Florian fell into step beside her. The surgeon even walked like a man, Ash noticed, moving from the shoulders and not the hip. She was dirty enough that you could not see she had no need to shave.

---

[24]Monastic hours: 6 p.m.

The tall woman said nothing. Ash was grateful.

Ash did her rounds, checking the hay and oats for the long lines of horses and the herb-gatherers who collected equally for Wat Rodway and Florian's pharmacy. She checked the water and sand tubs that stood in the open lanes, between tents that might go up like tinder in the brittle summer night. She swore at a seamstress who sat in a wagon with an unshielded candle, until the weeping woman fetched a lamp instead. She checked piled bills and the stock of arrow-heads in the armorer's tents, and the repairs waiting to be done: sword blades to be sharpened, armor to be hammered back into shape.

Florian put a hand on her steel shoulder. "Boss, stop making a frigging nuisance of yourself!"

"Oh. Yeah. All right." Ash let riveted links of mail trail out of her fingers. She nodded to the armorer and left his tents. Outside, she scanned the darkening sky. "I don't think these sorry shites know anymore about politics than I do. Why am I letting them decide this?"

"Because you can't. Or won't. Or daren't."

"Thanks for nothing!"

Ash strode back to the central open area under the standard as lanterns were lit and hung and the end of Godfrey Maximillian's sung mass echoed across the tents. She made her way between the men and women sitting on the chilling earth.

Reaching the standard, under the Blue Lion, she faced about. "Come on, then. This is a company decision? This is all of you?"

"Yeah." Geraint ab Morgan got to his feet, seeming wary of the attention focused on him as spokesman. Ash glanced at Robert Anselm. Her first sergeant was standing in the dark between two lanterns. His face was not visible.

"Lots counted," he called. "It's legit, Ash."

Geraint said in a rush, "It's too big a risk, pissing off

our employer. We vote for you to get married.''

"*What?*"

"We trust you, boss." The big, russet-haired Sergeant of Archers scratched his buttocks unselfconsciously. "We trust you—you can think of some way out of this before it happens! It's up to you, boss. Sort it out before they get the wedding preparations finished. There's no way we're letting them get rid of our captain!"

Fear wiped out thought. She stared around in lantern light at their faces.

"Fucking *hell*. Fuck the *lot* of you!"

Ash stormed off.

If I marry him, he gets the company.

She lay on her back on the hard pallet, one arm under her head, staring up into the roof of the tent. Shadows moved with the shifting evening air. The rope-tied bed frame creaked. Something smelled sweet above the warm body-scent of her own sweat—bunches of camomile, and Lady's Mantle and Self-Heal for wounds, she realized, where they hung tied to the massive struts jutting out from the tent pole. Up among the weapons. It is always easier to lay poleaxes and swords up across the struts rather than lose them in the damp rushes. Camp life means everything goes up out of the mud.

If I marry him, I get a boy who may or may not remember that he's treated me worse than a dockside whore.

The stuffed cloth pallet was hard under her shoulders. She shifted onto fleeces. No better. The air felt damp, but warm. She lay and picked at the metal-tipped points that tied her sleeves into her doublet, until she got them undone and pulled the sleeves off, and lay back again, cooler.

Christ's pity!—I'm in it, and it just keeps on getting deeper—!

Her Milanese harness glinted on its body stand, all

rounded silver curves. She massaged flesh where straps had bit in. There might be rust starting up on the tassets; it wasn't clear in the clay oil lamp's light. Phili would have to scour them with sand again before it bit in, and needed taking to the armorer's to be reground. The armorer would bitch at her if she let them get into that condition.

Ash reached down and rubbed her inner thigh muscles, still aching from the ride back from Cologne.

Striped canvas walls moved in and out with the night air, as if the tent breathed like an animal. She heard occasional voices beyond the walls' illusory security. Enough to let her know there still were guards outside: half a dozen men with crossbows, and a leash of mastiffs apiece, in case someone from the Burgundian camp decided to sneak over and take out a mercenary commander.

She dragged each ankle-high boot off by the heel. They thudded on rushes. She flexed bare feet on the cotton pallet, then loosened the drawstring-neck of her shirt. Sometimes she is just extremely conscious of her body, of muscles knotting with tiredness, of bones, of the weight and solidity of torso, arms and legs in their linen and wool garments. She eased her wooden-handled knife out of its sheath and turned the blade to catch the light, feeling with the edge of a fingernail for nicks. Some knives sit in the hand as if they are born to it.

Cynically, she murmured aloud, "I'm being robbed. Legally. What do I do about *that?*"

The voice that shares her soul sounded dispassionate:

"Not an appropriate tactical problem."

"No shit?" She slid the knife back into its sheath and unbuckled knife, purse and belt all in one heap, shoving up her hips to pull the leather strap out from underneath her. "Tell me about it!"

The clay oil lamp's flame dipped.

She shifted up on one elbow, knowing someone had

entered the main part of the tent beyond the tapestry that curtained off the sleeping area.

In wet summers she put handspan-high raised planking down to floor the tent. The planks shift and creak under footsteps—if the boys were asleep or elsewhere, and the tent's guards gone, she would still be woken up, not taken in her sleep. Rushes are quieter.

"It's me," a voice warned pragmatically, before it approached the tapestry. She lay back down on the pallet. Robert Anselm pushed the hangings aside and stepped in.

She rolled over onto one elbow and looked up. "They send you because you're the most likely to persuade me?"

"They sent me because you're least likely to take my head off." He seated himself with a thump on one of the two massive wooden chests beside her pallet; heavy German chests with locks that take up all the inside of their lids, that she kept chained around the eight-inch tent pole for security.

"Who is this 'they,' exactly?"

"Godfrey, Florian, Antonio. We played cards, and I lost."

"You didn't!" She fell back onto her back. "You didn't. Motherfucker!"

Robert Anselm laughed. His bald head gave him a face all eyes and ears. His stained shirt hung out of the front of his hose and doublet. He had the beginnings of a belly on him now, and he smelled sweetly warm, of sweat, and open air, and wood smoke. There was stubble on his face. One never noticed, looking no further than his cropped scalp and broad shoulders, how his lashes were long and fine as a girl's.

He dropped a hand down and began to massage her shoulder, under the linen and fine wool. His fingers were firm. She arched up into them, shutting her eyes for a second. When his hand slid around to the front of her shirt, she opened her eyes.

"You don't like that, do you?" A rhetorical question. "But you like this." He moved his hand back to her shoulders.

She moved over so that he could dig down into the rock-hard muscles. "I learned the reasons for not sleeping with my sub-commanders from you. Made a mess of that whole summer."

"Why don't you have it written up somewhere: *I don't know everything, I can make mistakes.*"

"I can't make mistakes. There's always someone waiting to take advantage."

"I know that."

His thumbs pressed hard into the knobs of her vertebrae. A sharp click cracked through the tent, ligament sliding over bone. His hands stopped moving. "You okay?"

"What the hell do you think?"

"In the last two hours I've had a hundred and fifty people come and ask to speak with you. Baldina, from the wagons. Harry, Euen, Tobias, Thomas, Pieter. Matilda's people; Anna, Ludmilla . . ."

"Joscelyn van Mander."

"No." He sounded reluctant. "None of the van Manders."

"Uh huh. *Right!*" She sat up.

Robert Anselm's hands moved away.

"Joscelyn thinks because he raised thirteen lances for me this season, he has more say in what we do than I have! I *knew* we were going to have trouble there. I may just pay off his contract and send him over to Jacobo Rossano, make it *his* problem. Okay, okay." She held up both hands, palms out, realizing his reluctance to tell her had been entirely feigned. "Yeah, *okay.* All right! Yes!"

She was conscious of the whole vast engine that was the company, ticking over outside. Rush and hurry around the cook's wagons, the eternal oat-porridge stewing in iron cauldrons. Men on fire-watch. Men taking their horses out to graze on what grass has been left on the banks of the Erft. Men drilling with swords, with bills, with spiked axes. Men fucking the whores that they hold in common. Men with their clothes being sewn by their wives (sometimes the same women, at a later date in those women's lives). Lantern light and campfire light, and the scream of some animal baited for sport. And the sky coursing with stars, over it all.

"I'm good on the battlefield. I don't know politics. I should have *known* I didn't know politics." She met his eyes. "I thought I was beating them at their own game. I don't know how I could have been this stupid."

Anselm clumsily ruffled her silver hair. "Fuck it."

"Yeah. Fuck it all."

Two sentries exchange the day's word outside the tent, giving way to two others. She hears them talking. Without knowing their names, she knows they have unwillingly scoured-clean bodies, full stomachs, swords with nicks carefully sharpened out, shirts on their backs, some kind of body protection (however cheap the armor), the Lion Azure sewn to their tabards. There are men like this all over Frederick III's great military camp tonight, but in this area there would not be, not these particular men— if not for her. However temporary it is, however merce-nary they are, she is what holds them together.

Ash got to her feet. "Look, I'll tell you about . . . the del Guiz family, Robert. Then you tell me what I can do. Because *I don't know*."

Four days after both Charles the Bold of Burgundy's troops and the men of the Emperor Frederick III pulled back from Neuss, effectively ending the siege,[25] Ash stood in the great Green Cathedral at Cologne.

Too many people crowded into the body of the cathedral for the human eye to take in. All shoulder to shoulder, men in pleated gowns of blue velvet and scarlet wool, silver linked chains around their necks, purses and daggers at their belts, and flamboyant rolled chaperon hats with tails hanging down past their shoulders. The court of the Emperor.

A thousand faces dappled with the light slanting from red and blue glass, falling from lancet windows a bowel-twisting height above the tiled floor. Thin stone columns pierced a frightening amount of air, too fragile to support their vaulted roof above. And around the bases of those pillars, men with gold leaf on their dagger pommels, and plenty of flesh on their jowls, stood talking in voices that rose in volume now.

"He's going to be late. He *is* late." Ash swallowed. The pit of her bowels shifted uncomfortably "I don't believe it. He's standing me up!"

"Can't be. You should be so lucky," Anselm hissed, "Ash, you have to do something!"

"Tell me what! If we haven't come up with it in four days, I'm not going to think of it now!"

How many minutes before the power to contract the company passes from wife to husband? All other means exhausted, the only remaining way out of this wedding is for her to walk out of the building. Now.

In front of the Emperor's court.

And they're right, Ash thought. Half the royal families of Christendom are married to the other half; we wouldn't

---

[25]The Gutenburg edition of the Del Guiz *Life* gives the date as 27 June 1476; the siege of Neuss ended, of course, on 27 June 1475. However, all other contemporary sources give the date of the wedding ceremony, four days later, as 1 July 1476.

get another contract from anyone until they'd calmed down. Not until next year, maybe. I don't have enough money put by to feed us if we don't have an employer for that long. Nothing like enough.

Robert Anselm looked past her, behind her head, at Father Godfrey Maximillian. "We could do with a prayer for grace, Father."

The bearded man nodded.

"Not that it matters now, but have you found out who set me up for this?" Ash demanded, quietly enough to be heard only by her supporters.

Godfrey, standing on her right, replied equally quietly. "Sigismund of the Tyrol."

"Goddamn. *Sigismund?* What have we—That man's got a long memory. This is because we fought on the other side at Héricourt?"

Godfrey inclined his head. "Sigismund of the Tyrol is far too rich for Frederick to offend him by refusing a useful suggestion. I'm told Sigismund doesn't like 'mercenaries with more than fifty lances.' Apparently he finds them a threat. To the purity of noble warfare."

" 'Purity' of war? In his fucking dreams."

The bearded priest smiled crookedly. "You mauled his household troops, as I recall."

"I was *paid* to. Christ. It's petty, to give us this much trouble for it!"

Ash looked over her shoulder. The back of the cathedral was also packed with standing men, merchants from Cologne in rich gear, her own lance-leaders who outshone them, and a gaggle of mercenaries who had been made to leave their weapons outside the cathedral, and consequently didn't outshine anyone.

There were none of the bawdy remarks and cheerful grins you would have had with one of her men-at-arms being wedded. Quite apart from endangering their future, she saw how it made them look at her and see a woman, in a city, at peace, where before they had seen a mercenary, in the field, at war, and could therefore avoid considering her sex.

Ash snarled in a whisper, "Christus, I wish I'd been born a man! It would have given me an extra six inches' reach, the ability to pee standing up—and I wouldn't have to put up with any of this crap!"

Robert Anselm's adult, concerned frown vanished in a spluttering burst of laughter.

Ash looked automatically for Florian's cheering skepticism, but the surgeon was not there; the disguised woman had vanished into the mass of the company striking camp at Neuss four days ago and had not been seen since (certainly not during the set-up outside Cologne where, as a number of uninformed mercenaries remarked, there was heavy lifting to be done).

Ash added, "And I *could* take Frederick setting this wedding on St. Simeon's feast-day personally . . . [26] Maybe we could come up with a prior betrothal? Someone to step up to the altar stone and swear we had a prenuptial contract as children."

Anselm, at her left, said, "Who's going to stand up and take the shit for that one? Not me."

"I wouldn't ask it." Ash stopped talking as the Bishop of Cologne came up to the bridal party. "Your Grace."

"Our meek, gentle bride." Tall thin Bishop Stephen reached out to finger the folds of her banner, whose staff Robert Anselm held. He bent to inspect the scarlet lettering embroidered under the Lion. "What is this?"

"Jeremiah, chapter fifty-one, verse twenty," Godfrey quoted.

---

[26]Simeon Salus, died c. 590, is the saint associated with social outcasts, especially harlots His feast-day is celebrated on 1 July.

Robert Anselm growled a translation: " 'Thou art my battle axe and weapons of war; for with thee I will break in pieces the nations, and with thee will I destroy kingdoms.' It's sort of a mission statement, your Grace.''

''How—appropriate. How—pious.''

A new voice whispered dryly, ''Who is being pious?''

The bishop inclined his thin body in its green alb and chasuble. ''Your Imperial Majesty.''

Frederick of Hapsburg limped through the crowds of men, who all got out of his way. He was leaning on a staff now, Ash noted. The little man looked at Ash's company priest as if it were the first time he had noticed the man. ''You, was it? A man of peace in a company of war? Surely not. 'Rebuke the company of spearmen—scatter thou the people that delight in war.' ''[27]

Godfrey Maximillian removed the hood from his robe and stood respectfully bareheaded (if ruffled) before the Emperor. ''But, Your Majesty, Proverbs one hundred and forty-four, one?''

The Emperor rasped a small, dry chuckle. '' 'Blessed be the Lord my strength, which teacheth my hands to war, and my fingers to fight.' So. An educated priest.''

''As an educated priest,'' Ash said, ''perhaps you would tell His Majesty how long we have to wait for a nonexistent bridegroom, before we can all go home?''

''You wait,'' Frederick said quietly. There was a sudden lack of conversation.

Ash would have paced, but the folds of her dress and the stares of the assembly stopped her. Over the altar, the Nine Orders of Angels shone in stone: Seraphim, Cherubim and Thrones, who are closest to God; then Dominions, Powers and Virtues; then Principalities, Archangels and Angels. The Principality of Cologne was sculpted

---

[27]Psalms 68:30.

with arched wings and ambiguous gender, smiling, clutching a representation of Frederick's Imperial crown.

What's Fernando del Guiz playing at?

He won't dare offend the Emperor. Will he? *Will he?*

He is a knight, after all. Maybe he just *won't* marry a peasant-woman soldier. Christ, I hope that's it—

On the altar's left, by some humor of the stonemasons, the Prince of This World was carved offering a rose to the naked figure of Luxury. Toads and serpents clung to the back of his robe's rich stone folds.[28] Ash contemplated the figure of Luxury. There were many women present in stone. In flesh only five, herself and her attendants. The customary maids of the bride's honor stood behind her, Ludmilla (in one of the seamstress's better robes) and the other three: Blanche, Isobel and Eleanor. Women she'd known since they whored together as children in the Griffin-in-Gold. Ash took a certain private satisfaction in how many of the noblemen of Cologne already nervously recognized Blanche and Isobel and Eleanor.

If I have to go through with this damn ceremony, I'm doing it *my* way!

Ash watched the Emperor drift off in conversation with Cologne's Bishop Stephen. Both of them walked as if in a royal hall, not a sacred building.

"Fernando's late. He's not coming!" Joy and relief flooded through her. "Well, hey, *he's* not our enemy . . . Archduke Sigismund did this. Sigismund's making me compete in politics, where I don't know what I'm doing, instead of on the field of battle, where I do."

"Woman, you sweated your guts out to get Frederick to give you land." Godfrey, sounding skeptical enough to

---

[28]No longer extant, but see similar figure at Freiburg-im-Breisgau, sculpted c. AD 1280.

be Florian. "He merely took advantage of that sin of greed."

"Not sin. Stupidity." Ash restrained herself from looking around again. "But it's going to be okay."

"Yes—no. There are people outside."

"*Shit!*" Her sibilant whisper had the front two ranks of men glancing uncertainly at the bride.

Ash wore her silver hair unbound, as maidens do. Because she usually wore it in braids, it took a curl from that, flowing in ripples down over her shoulders, down her back, down, not just to her thighs, but to the backs of her knees. The finest, most transparent linen veil covered her head, and the silver metal headdress that held it in place was wound with a garland of field daisies. The veil was made from flax so fine that the scars on her cheekbones could be seen through it.

She stood stocky and sweaty in the flowing, voluminous blue and gold robes.

Drums sounded, and hurried horns. Her guts jolted. Fernando del Guiz and his supporters hurried up toward the rood-screen—all young noblemen of the Germanies, all wearing more money than she sees in six years of putting her body in the front line of battles for axe and sword and arrow to hit it.

The Emperor Frederick III, Holy Roman Emperor, walked with his entourage to take his regal place at the front. Ash picked out the face of Duke Sigismund of the Tyrol. He did not give her the satisfaction of smiling.

The light slanted down from immense perpendicular lancet windows, dappling green light onto the figure of a woman carved in black marble, riding on the back of the Bull on the altar.[29] Ash looked up with despair at her

---

[29]A direct translation of the original German. No such altarpiece is extant in Cologne.

enigmatic stone smile, and the gold-thread embroidered cloths that hooded her, as the boys in white tunicles came into the choir with their green wax candles burning. She was aware of someone coming to stand beside her.

She glanced to her right. The young knight Fernando del Guiz stood there, staring equally deliberately up at the altar, not looking at her. He looked more than a little ruffled, and he was bareheaded. For the first time she got a clear look at his face.

I thought he was older than me. He can't be. Not by more than a year or two.

Now I remember . . .

It was not his face, older now, clear-skinned and with bold brows, freckles across his straight nose. Nor his thick gold hair, trimmed short now to touch his shoulders. Ash watched the embarrassed hunch of his wide shoulders, and his rangy body—grown from boy almost to man, now— shifting from foot to foot.

That's *it*. That's it . . .

She found her hand aching to reach up and ruffle his hair out of its combed order. She caught his male scent, under the sweet perfume of civet. *I was a child then. Now . . .* Of themselves, her fingertips told her what it would feel like to unlace his velvet pleated doublet that needed no padding at his broad shoulders, unfasten it down to his narrow waist, and untie the points of his hose . . . She let her gaze slide down the triangular line of his male body, to his strong rider's thighs in finest knitted hose.

Sweet Christ who died to save us. I am as much in lust with him as I was at twelve.

"Mistress Ash!"

Somebody, plainly, had asked her a question.

"Yes?" Ash agreed absently.

Light broke in on her. Fernando del Guiz: lifting up her

fine linen veil. His eyes were green, stone-green, dark as the sea.

"You are wed," the Bishop of Cologne pronounced.

Fernando del Guiz spoke. Ash smelled wine warm on his breath. He said, in a perfectly clear voice, into the silence, "I would sooner have married my horse."

Robert Anselm, *sotto voce*, muttered, "The horse wouldn't have you."

Someone gasped, someone laughed; there was one delighted, dirty guffaw from the back of the cathedral. Ash thought she recognized Joscelyn van Mander.

Not knowing whether to laugh or cry or hit something, Ash stared at the face of the young man she had just married. Looking for a hint—only a hint—of the complicit, humorous grin he had given her at Neuss.

Nothing.

She was unaware that her shoulders straightened, and her face took on something of the look she wore around the company's camp. "You don't talk to me like that."

"You're my wife now. I talk to you any way I please. If you don't like it, I'll beat you. You're my wife, and you'll be docile!"

Ash couldn't help a loud blurt of laughter. "I will?"

Fernando del Guiz ran his finger, in its fine leather glove, from her chin down to the linen neck of her chemise. He made a show of sniffing at his glove. "I smell *piss*. Yes I do. I smell piss . . ."

"Del Guiz," the Emperor warned.

Fernando turned his back and walked away, across the flagstone floor to Frederick of Hapsburg and a tearful Constanza del Guiz (the court's ladies now entering the nave, the ceremony over). None of whom did more than glance sideways at the bride left standing alone.

"No." Ash put her hand on Robert Anselm's arm. She

gave a quick look that included Godfrey. "*No*. It's all right."

" 'All right'? You ain't going to let him do that!" Anselm had his shoulders hunched almost up to his protuberant ears, all his body yearning toward crossing the nave and knocking Fernando del Guiz over.

"I know what I'm doing now. I've just seen it." Ash increased the pressure of her fingers on his arm. There were mutters from her company, at the back.

"I would be an unhappy bride," Ash said quietly. "But I could be a really cheerful widow."

Both of the men startled. It was almost comical. Ash continued to look at them. Robert Anselm jerked his head once, briefly, satisfied. It was Godfrey Maximillian who coldly smiled.

"Widows inherit their husbands' businesses," Ash said.

"Yeah . . ." Robert Anselm nodded. "Better not mention it to Florian, though. The man *is* his brother."

"So don't tell h-him." Ash did not meet Godfrey's eyes. "It won't be the first 'riding accident' among the German nobility."

Ash paused under the vast vaults of the cathedral, momentarily unaware of her companions, of what she had said; seeking out Fernando where he stood, his back to her, weight on one hip, towering over his mother. Her body roused at the sight of him, at just the way the tall young man posed.

This will not be easy. Either way, this will not be easy.

"Ladies. Gentlemen." Ash glanced back to check that Ludmilla and Blanche and Isobel and Eleanor were holding up her train so that she could walk, and rested her ringed fingers on Godfrey's arm. "We're not going to skulk in corners. We're going to go and thank people for coming to my wedding.''

Her guts clenched. She knew the picture she made: young bride, veil back, silver-blonde hair a glorious cloud. She did not know her scars stood out silver-red against her pale cheeks. She went first to her lance-leaders, where she would feel at ease: the men spoke a word here, a small joke there, exchanged a hand-clasp.

Some of them looked at her with pity.

She couldn't help it, she continued to stare anxiously through the crowd for Fernando del Guiz. Now she saw him angel-bright in a lancet window's beams, talking to Joscelyn van Mander.

Van Mander kept his back to her.

''*That* didn't take very long.''

Anselm shrugged. ''Van Mander's contract belongs to del Guiz now.''

She heard a whisper from behind her. The heavy material of her train, suddenly unattended, pulled back on her neck. She glared back at Big Isobel and Blanche. The two women mercenaries did not look at her; they had their heads together and whispered, their eyes fixed on a man some distance away, with expressions Ash put somewhere between awe and fear. She recognized him as the southerner who had been present at Neuss.

Little Eleanor whispered explanatorily to Blanche, ''He's from the lands Under the Penitence!''

The reason for the dark muslin cloth knotted ready for use about his neck belatedly dawned on Ash. She said tightly, ''Oh, Green Christ, they're hardly *demons* down in Africa—let's get moving, okay?''

Ash moved on through the nave, greeting the minor nobles of free cities in their best robes, and their wives in towering horned, veiled headdresses. This is not where I belong, she thought, talking politely, aimlessly; speaking to the ambassadors from Savoy and Milan, watching how shocked they were that a *hic mulier*[30] could wear robes, could speak their languages, and did not in fact have a demon's horns and a tail.

What do I do? What do I *do*?

A new voice spoke behind her, with an accent. "Madam."

Ash smiled a farewell to the Milanese ambassador—a boring man, and afraid, too, of a woman who has killed in battle—and turned.

The man who had spoken was the southerner—pale-haired, with a face burned brown by harsh sun. He wore a short white robe, over white trousers with greaves bound around them, and a mail hauberk over all. The fact that he was dressed for war, although without weapons, put her at her ease.

In the light from the lancet windows, the pupils of his light-colored eyes were contracted to pin-points.

"New here from Tunis?" she guessed, speaking her accurate, but uneducated mercenary's version of his language.

"From Carthage," he agreed, giving the city its Gothic[31] appellation. "But I am adjusted, I think, to the light, now."

"I'm—oh *shit*," Ash interrupted herself rapidly.

A solid, man-shaped figure stood behind the Carthaginian. It over-topped him by a head or more: Ash judged it seven or eight feet tall. At first glance she would have

---

[30]Latin: a "mannish" or "man-aping" woman.

[31]Text uncertain here. Charles Mallory Maximillian has "Visigoth," the "noble Goths." Although it is couched in terms of mediaeval legend, I believe the mention of "Visigoths" to have aspects we would do well to consider.

thought it a statue made out of red granite: the statue of a man, with a featureless ovoid for a head.

Statues do not move.

She felt herself coloring; felt Robert Anselm and Godfrey Maximillian crowding in close to her shoulders, staring behind the newcomer. She found her voice again. "I've never seen one of those up close before!"

"Our golem?[32] But yes."

With an amused look in his pale eyes, as if he were used to this, the man beckoned with a snap of his fingers. At the Carthaginian's signal, the figure took a step forward into the shaft of window light.

Stained glass colors slid over the carved red granite body and limbs. Each joint—at neck, shoulders, elbows, knees, ankles—gleamed brass; the metal jointed neatly into the stone. Its stone fingers were articulated as carefully as the lamés of German gauntlets. It smelled faintly of something sour—river mud?—and its tread on the tiny tiles of the cathedral floor echoed heavily, with an impression of enormous weight.

"May I touch it?"

"If you wish to, madam."

Ash reached out and put the pads of her fingers against the red granite chest. The stone felt cold. She slid her hand across, feeling sculpted pectoral muscles. The head tilted downwards, facing her.

In the featureless ovoid, two almond-shaped holes opened, where eyes might have been on a man. Her body

---

[32] I prefer this term, with its suggestion of the organic, to Vaughan Davies's "robot," or Charles Mallory Maximillian's "clay man"

This quasi-supernatural appearance is, of course, one of the mythical accretions which attach themselves to histories such as Ash's; and should not be taken seriously, except in so far as it reflects the mediaeval psychological preoccupation with a lost Roman "Age of Gold."

shocked, anticipating white of eye, pupil, focus.

The eyes behind the stone lids were full of red sand.
She watched the granules swirl.

"Drink," the man from Carthage ordered.

The arms swiveled up noiselessly. The moving statue
held out a chased golden goblet to the man whom it attended. The Carthaginian drank and gave it back.

"Oh yes, madam, we are allowed our golem-servants
with us! Although there was some debate about whether
they would be allowed within your 'church.'" He surrounded the word delicately with nuances of sarcasm.

"It looks like a demon." Ash stared up at the golem.
She imagined the weight of the stone articulated arm if it
should rise and fall, if it should strike. Her eyes gleamed.

"It is nothing. But you are the bride!" The man picked
up her free hand and kissed it. His lips were dry. His eyes
twinkled. In his own language, he said, "Asturio, madam;
Asturio Lebrija, Ambassador from the Citadel to the court
of the Emperor, however briefly. These Germans! How
long can I bear it? You are a woman of your hands, madam. A warrior. Why are you marrying that boy?"

Waspishly, Ash said, "Why are you here as an ambassador?"

"One who had power sent me. Ah, I see." Asturio
Lebrija's sunburned hand scratched his hair which, she
noted, was cropped short in the North African fashion for
one who customarily wears a helmet. "Well, you are as
welcome here as I, I think."

"As a fart in a communal bathtub."

Lebrija whooped.

"Ambassador, I think they're afraid that one day your
people will stop fighting the Turks and turn into a problem." Ash registered Godfrey moving aside to talk to Lebrija's aides. Robert Anselm remained, looming, at her
shoulder, his gaze fixed on the golem. "Or it's because

they envy you Carthage's hydraulic gates and underfloor hot water and everything else from the Golden Age.''

"Sewers, batteries, triremes, abacus-engines . . ." Asturio's eyes danced as he assured her of it. "Oh, we are Rome come again. Behold our mighty legions!"

"Your heavy cavalry aren't *bad* . . ." Ash stroked her hand over her mouth and chin but couldn't smother her smile. "Oops. It's a good job you're the ambassador. That was hardly diplomatic.''

"I have met women of war before. I would sooner meet you in the court than on the battlefield.''

Ash grinned. "So. This northern light too bright for you, Ambassador Asturio?''

"It's hardly the Eternal Twilight, madam, I grant you—"

An older male voice behind Lebrija bluntly interrupted. "Get the fuck over here, Asturio. Help me out with this damned conniving German!"

Ash blinked, realizing almost immediately that the new man spoke in the Visigoth language, that his tone was sweetly pleasant, and that her own mercenaries were the only people present who had understood him. She glared at Isobel, Blanche, Euen Huw and Paul di Conti. They subsided. As she turned back to him, Asturio Lebrija bowed a flamboyant farewell and moved to join what must be the senior ambassador in the Visigoth delegation at the Emperor Frederick's side. The golem followed with heavy soft tread.

"Their heavy cataphracts *aren't* bad," Robert Anselm said in her ear. "Never mind all their fucking ships! And they've had a military build-up going on there these last ten years."

"I know. It's all going to turn into another Visigoths-fighting-Turks war for control of the Mediterranean, with undisciplined serfs and light cavalry knocking hell out of

each other for no result. Mind you,"—a sudden hope—
"there might be some business down there for us."

"Not 'us.'" Anselm's features twisted with disgust.
"Fernando del Guiz."

"Not for long."

On the heels of that, another voice echoed through the
huge spaces of the cathedral, echoing from crypt to barrel
vaults. *"Out!"*

Frederick of Hapsburg—shouting.

Conversation drained swiftly into silence. Ash went forward through the crowd. A foot trod on her trailing train,
bringing her up short. Ludmilla muttered something as she
picked the cloth up off the flagstones and flung the whole
weight of it over her arm. Ash grinned back at big Isobel,
and caught up with Anselm, edging her way between him
and Godfrey to the front of the crowd.

Two men had Asturio Lebrija with his arms twisted up
behind his back, forcing the man in the mail shirt to kneel.
Also down on the stone floor, the older Visigoth Ambassador had a bill-shaft held across his throat, and Sigismund of the Tyrol's knee in his back. The golem stood
as still as the carved saints in their niches.

Frederick's sibilant voice echoed among the soaring
pillars, still shaking with the reimposition of a control Ash
had not heard him lose before. "Daniel de Quesada, I may
hear you say your people have given mine medicine, masonry and mathematics; I will not stand here in this most
ancient cathedral and hear my people maligned as barbarians—"

"Lebrija did not say—"

Frederick of Hapsburg overrode the older Ambassador:
"—my fellow sovereign Louis of France called 'a spider,'
or be told to my face I am 'old and covetous'!"

Ash glanced from Frederick and his bristling nobles to
the Visigoth ambassadors. Far more likely that Asturio

Lebrija had momentarily and catastrophically forgotten which language he was speaking, than that the older man—bearded, with the look of a battle veteran—would deliberately allow him to insult the Holy Roman Emperor.

She murmured to Godfrey, "Someone's picking a fight here. Deliberately. Who?"

The bearded priest frowned. "I think, Frederick. He doesn't want to be asked to lend military aid in Visigothic North Africa.[33] But he won't want to be heard refusing the ambassadors' request, in case it's supposed he's refusing because he hasn't got the troops to send, and is therefore weak. Easier to buy himself time like this, given this excuse, with false anger over an 'insult.' "

Ash wanted to say something on behalf of Asturio Lebrija, whose face reddened as he strained to get out of the grip of two German knights; nothing immediately useful came to mind.

The Emperor snapped peevishly, "I will leave you both your heads! You are returned home. Tell the Citadel to send me civil ambassadors in future!"

Ash flicked a glance sideways, not realizing that her whole stance changed: alert, balanced, and not usual for someone in bridal robes. The golem stood silent and motionless behind the two ambassadors. If *that* should move—Her fingers closed automatically, seeking a sword-hilt.

Fernando del Guiz straightened up from leaning on a cathedral pillar. Caught by the movement, Ash watched him helplessly. *No different from a hundred other young German knights here*, she protested to herself; and then, *But he's golden!*

---

[33]According to conventional histories, the Germanic Visigothic tribes did not settle in North Africa. Rather the reverse—with the Muslim Arab invasion of Visigothic Spain, in AD 711.

Gold light from the windows catches his face as he turns, laughing at something one of the squires clustered around him has said. She sees a snap-shot image of light limning the edge of sun-browned masculine brow, nose, lip; warm in the cold cathedral dimness. And his eyes, which are merry. She sees him young, strong, wearing fluted armor with complete naturalness; thinks of how he knows the outdoor months of campaigning as well as she does, the sunny ease of camp life and the blood-teasing exultation of battle.

Why despise me, when we're the same? You could understand me better than any other woman you could have married—

Fernando del Guiz's voice said, "Let me be the escort for the ambassadors, Your Imperial Majesty. I have some new troops I need to knock into shape. Entrust me with this favor."

It was ten heartbeats at least before Ash replayed "new troops" in her mind.

"*He means my company!*" She exchanged glances with Robert Anselm and Godfrey Maximillian, both men frowning.

"It shall be your bridal gift, del Guiz," Frederick of Hapsburg agreed, something sardonic in his expression. "And a honeymoon for your and your bride." He gathered his nine-yard velvet gown about himself, with the aid of two small boy pages, and without looking over his shoulder, said, "Bishop Stephen."

"Your Imperial Majesty?"

"Exorcise *that*." A twig-thin finger flicked toward the Visigoth golem. "And when you have done it, command stonemasons with hammers, and have it broken into gravel!"

"Yes, Your Imperial Majesty!"

"Barbarian!" The older Visigoth ambassador, Daniel

de Quesada, spluttered incredulously. "*Barbarian!*"

Asturio Lebrija looked up with difficulty from where he was pinned on his knees. "I spoke no lie, Daniel: these damned Franks[34] are children playing in ruins, destroying whatever comes to their hands! Hapsburg, you have no *idea* of the value of—"

Frederick's knights slammed Lebrija facedown on the tiles. The sound of blows echoed through the vaulting heights of the cathedral. Ash took a half-step forward, only to be nearer, and caught her heel in the brocade hem and stumbled, grabbing Godfrey's arm.

"My lord del Guiz," the Emperor Frederick said mildly, "you will escort these men to our nearest port, in chains, and ensure they are deported by ship to Carthage. I wish them to live to carry their disgrace home with them."

"Your Majesty." Fernando bowed, still something coltish about him, for all the breadth of his shoulders.

"You will need to take command of your new troops. Not all, not all. These men—" Frederick of Hapsburg lifted his fingers very slightly, in the direction of Ash's lance-leaders and men-at-arms, crowding in at the rear of the cathedral, "—are now by feudal right yours, my lord. And as your liege lord, they are also ours. You shall take some of them upon this duty, and we shall retain the remainder: we have tasks that they can do, order not yet being secure in Neuss."

Ash opened her mouth.

Robert Anselm, without moving his rigid, eyes-front gaze, rammed his elbow into her ribs.

"He can't do this!" Ash hissed.

"Yes. He can. Now shut *up*, girl."

Ash stood between Godfrey and Anselm, her heavy

---

[34]A term used in this text for Northern Europeans in general.

brocade gown stifling her. Sweat dampened her armpits. The knights, lords, merchants, bishops and priests of the Imperial court began to move off in Frederick's wake, talking between themselves, a great throng of richly dressed men, their voices traveling up into the silence of the fan-vaulting and the saints in their niches.

"They can't just split us up like this!"

Godfrey's hand closed painfully tightly around her elbow. "If you can't do anything, *don't* do anything. Child, listen to me! If you protest now, everyone will see that you lack the power to alter this. Wait. *Wait.* Until you can do something."

The departing Imperial court took as little notice of one woman and a cluster of soldiers as they did of the stone saints above.

"I can't leave it!" Ash spoke so that only the priest and Anselm could hear. "I built this company up from nothing. If I wait now, either they're going to start deserting, or they're going to get used to del Guiz in command!"

"You could let them go. It is their right," Godfrey said mildly. "Perhaps, if they no longer wish to be men of war—"

Both Ash and Robert Anselm shook their heads.

"These are men I know." Ash wiped her hand across her scarred cheek. "These are men hundreds of leagues from whatever poxy farm or town they were born in, and fighting's the only trade they've got. Godfrey, they're my people."

"Now they are del Guiz men-at-arms. Have you considered, child, that this may be better for them?"

This time it was Robert Anselm who snorted.

"I know young knights with their arses on their first war-horse! That young streak of piss and wind couldn't restrain *himself* in battle, never mind his men! He's a heroic disaster looking for a place to happen. Captain, we've got time. If we're leaving Cologne, that's good.'' Anselm stared after Fernando del Guiz, walking down the nave with Joscelyn van Mander, never a glance back for his bride. ''See how you like it out on the road, city boy.''

Ash thought, *Shit*.

They're splitting up my company. My company isn't mine anymore. I'm married to someone who *owns* me— and there's no way I can play court politics to change the Emperor's mind, because I'm not going to be here! I'm going to be dragged off with disgraced Visigoth ambassadors to Christ alone knows where—

Ash glanced out of the cathedral's open doors, under the unfinished west front,[35] out at the sunlight. ''Which *is* the nearest port from here, on Empire territory?''

Godfrey Maximillian said, ''Genoa.''

---

[35]As with the nave, this was in fact left unfinished until the nineteenth century.

*[E-mail printouts included in correspondence found inter-
polated in this copy of the 3rd edition.]*

Message: #5 (Pierce Ratcliff/misc.)
Subject: Ash, historical documents
Date: 2/11/00 at 8.55 p.m.
From: Longman@   *format address and
                               other details
                               non-recoverably deleted*

Pierce--

Sorry to contact you out of office hours, but I *must* talk to you about
the translation of these documents.

I have very fond memories of 'doing' Ash at school. One of the
things I like about her, which comes through strongly in your
translations of these texts, is that she's a jock. Basically. She doesn't
read, she can't write, but boy can she hit things. And she has a
complex character despite that. I love this woman! I still think that a
modern translation of ASH, with your new document discovery, is one
of the best and most commercial ideas that's come my way in a long
time. You know I'm supporting you here, in the editorial discussions,
despite not being fully briefed yet.

However. These sources—

I can cope with the odd mistake in dating, and with mediaeval
legends. This is, after all, how those people *perceived* their
experiences. And what we have here, with your prospective new
theory of European history, is brilliant stuff!—But it's for this very
reason that each deviation from history must be carefully documented.
Provided the legends are clearly noted as such, we have a cracking
good history book for the marketing department to sell.

But—

GOLEMS???!!!

In mediaeval Europe?!

What next—zombies and the undead?!! This is fantasy!
HELP!

--Anna

- -

Message: #1 (Anna Longman/misc.)
Subject: Ash, historical documents
Date: 3/11/00 at 6.30 p.m.
From: Ratcliff@ *format address and other details non-recoverably deleted*

Anna--

This is what comes of getting connected to e-mail, one then forgets to check it! I am *so* sorry not to have answered you yesterday.

About 'golems.' I am following Charles Mallory Maximillian's translation here (with a little FRAXINUS). He refers to them in 1890 as 'clay walkers,' very much the legendary Cabalistic magical servant as featured in the legend of the Rabbi of Prague. (We should remember that when Maximillian did his translation, the Victorian era was gripped in the fin-de-siècle occult revival craze.)

Vaughn Davies, in his later translation, rather unfortunately calls them 'robots,' a reference which in the late 1930s was not as hackneyed as it now appears.

I intend to use the term 'golem,' in this third edition, unless you think it too unscholarly. I am aware that you would like this book to have a wide readership.

As regards what these 'golem' or 'walkers' may, historically, have actually been, I think they are a mediaeval confabulation of something undoubtedly real with something legendary. The historical reality is mediaeval Arabic engineering.

You will no doubt be aware that, as well as their civil engineering, the Arabic civilisations practised a kind of fine engineering, making fountains, clocks, automata, and many other devices. It is quite certain that, by the time of al-Jazari, complex gear trains existed, also segmental and epicycle gears, weight drives, escapements and pumps. The Arabs' celestial and biological models were largely water-powered, and invariably—obviously—stationary. However, the European mediaeval traveller often reported the models to be *mobile* figures of men, horses, singing birds, etc.

My research indicates that the del Guiz LIFE has conflated these travellers' tales with mediaeval Jewish stories of the golem, the man of clay. This was a magical being with, of course, no basis in fact.

If there *had* been a 'walker' or 'servant' of some sort, I imagine it could conceivably have been a *vehicle*, wind-powered like the sophisticated pole-mills of the period—but then, it would require wheels, sophisticated road-surfaces, and a human driver, to function as any kind of message-carrying device, and could perform no indoor tasks at all. And you may say, rightly, that this is stretching historical speculation unaccountably far. No such device has ever been discovered. It is chroniclers' licence.

As a legendary part of the Ash cycle, I like my golems, and I hope you will let me keep them. However, if too much emphasis on the 'legendary' aspect of the texts is going to weaken the historical *evidence* which I am drawing from the del Guiz text, then let's by all means cut the golems out of the finished version!

--Pierce Ratcliff

Message: #6 (Pierce Ratcliff/misc.)
Subject: Ash, historical background
Date: 3/11/00 at 11.55 p.m.
From: Longman@   format address and
                            other details
                            non-recoverably deleted
Pierce--

I wouldn't know a segmental gear if it bit me! But I'm prepared to credit that these 'golems' are a mediaeval legend based on some kind of reality. Any study of women's history, black history, or working class history soon makes you see how much gets dropped from conventional histories, so why should engineering history be any different?

But I guess it's safer to leave them out. Let's not confuse mediaeval legend with mediaeval fact.

One of my assistants has raised a further query about the 'Visigoths' today. She's concerned that, since they were a Germanic tribe who died out after the Roman Empire, how can they still be around in 1476?

Another query, from me—I'm not a Classicist, it's not my period, but don't I remember Carthage being *wiped out* in Roman times? Your manuscript speaks as if it still exists. But it makes no mention of the ARAB cultures of North Africa.

Is all this going to be made clear? Soon? PLEASE?!

--Anna

- -

Message: #3 (Anna Longman/misc.)
Subject: Ash, theory
Date: 4/11/00 at 9.02 a.m.
From: Ratcliff@   *format address and other details non-recoverably deleted*

Anna--

I didn't realise that publishers' editors worked such unnatural hours. I hope you aren't working too hard.:)

You ask me for a statement of my theory—very well. We probably can't proceed in our working relationship without one. Bear with me for a moment, and I'll give you some necessary background:

The arrival of what the LIFE calls the 'Gothic' ambassadors DOES present an apparent problem. I believe that I have solved this problem, however; and, as you imply, it is a key factor in my reassessment of European history.

While the ambassadors' presence at Frederick's court is verified by references in both the CHRONIQUE DE BOURGOGNE and the correspondence between Philip de Commines and Louis XI of France, I at first found it difficult to see where these 'Goths' (or, as I prefer Charles Mallory Maximillian's more precise translation, 'Visigoths': the 'noble Goths') might originate.

The Germanic Gothic barbarian tribes did not so much 'die out,' as your assistant suggests, as become absorbed into the ethnic mix of the lands they moved into after Rome fell. The Ostrogoths in Italy, for example; the Burgundians in the Rhône Valley, and the Visigoths in Iberia (Spain). They continued to rule these territories, in some cases for centuries.

Maximillian thus suggests these 'Visigoth' ambassadors are Spanish. I was not completely happy with that. CMM's rationale is that, from the eighth century on, Spain is divided between a Christian Visigoth knightly aristocracy, and the Arabic dynasties that follow their own invasion in AD 711. Both the numerically inferior Muslim and Visigoth aristocratic classes ruled over a great mass of Iberian and Moorish peasantry. Therefore, Maximillian says, since there were 'Visigoths' of this kind left until well into the late fifteenth century, there might also have been mediaeval rumours that either these Christian Visigoths or the 'heathen Saracen' (Muslims) retained some 'engines and devices' of Roman technology.

It is actually not until fifteen years after Ash's death that the last Arab Muslims are finally driven out of the Iberian peninsula in the 'Reconquista' (1488–1492). The Visigoth ambassadors to the court of the Emperor Frederick *could* therefore be supposed to come from Iberia.

However, I personally then found it very puzzling that the ASH texts directly state that they come from a settlement which must have been on the coast of North Africa. (Even more puzzling since they are plainly not Arab!)

The author of the 1939 2nd edition of the ASH documents, Vaughan Davies, basing HIS theory on not much more than the text referring to Northern Europeans as 'Franks,' treats the Visigoths as the standard Saracen knights of the Arthurian legends—the 'Saracens' are mediaeval Europe's idea of the Arab cultures, mixed with folk-memories of the crusades to the Holy Land. I don't think Davies does anything at all scholarly to address this problem.

Now, we include the other problem—Carthage! The original North African Carthage, settled by the Phoenicians, WAS eradicated, as you point out. The Romans rebuilt a city on that site.

The interesting thing is that, after the last Roman Emperor was deposed in AD 476, it was the Vandals who moved in and took over Roman North Africa—the Vandals being, like the Visigoths, a Gothic Germanic tribe.

They moved in as a small military elite, to rule and enjoy the fruits of this great African kingdom, under their first king, Gaiseric. Although they remained somewhat 'Germanised,' Gaiseric did bring in an Arian priesthood, make Latin the official language, and build more Roman baths. Vandal Carthage became a great naval centre, Gaiseric not only controlling the Mediterranean, but at one point sacking Rome itself!

So you can see that we already have had a kind of 'Gothic Tunisia.' The last (usurping) king, Gelimer, lost Vandal Africa in three months to the Byzantine Empire in AD 530 (and was last heard of enjoying several large Byzantine estates). The Christian Byzantines were duly driven out by the surrounding Berber kingdoms, and Islam (chiefly by the military use of the camel) in the 630s. All trace of Gothic was eradicated from Moorish culture from then on; not even occasional words survive in their language.

Ask yourself, where could Germanic Gothic culture have survived after AD 630?

In Iberia, close to North Africa, *with the Visigoths*.

As you are aware, I believe that the entire field of academic research on northern European history is going to have to be modified once my ASH is published.

Briefly: I intend to prove that there was a Visigothic settlement on the Northern coast of Africa as late as the fifteenth century.

That their 're-settlement' took place much later than Vandal North Africa, after the end of the Early Middle Ages; and that their period of military ascendancy was the 1400s.

I intend to prove that in AD 1476 there was an actual, historical mediaeval settlement, peopled by the survivors of the Roman Visigoth tribes—with no 'golems,' no legends about 'twilights.'

I believe it to have been peopled by an incursion of Visigoth-descended Iberians from the Spanish 'taifa' (mixed/border) states. One might reasonably think this, from the racial type described here. The Fraxinus text calls the settlement 'Carthage,' and indeed it may have been close to the site of the original Phoenician or Roman or Vandal Carthages.

I believe that this Gothic settlement, intermingling with Arab culture (many Arab military terms are used in the del Guiz and Angelotti manuscripts) produced something unique. And I believe that it is perhaps not the fact of this settlement's existence that is so controversial, so much as (shall we say) what this culture did, and their contribution to our culture as we live in it today.

There will be a Preface, or Afterword, perhaps, setting out the implications fully, that will go with the ASH documents; this is as yet unfinished.

I am sorry to be so cagey about those implications at this stage. Anna, I do not wish someone else to publish ahead of me. There are days when I simply cannot believe that no one else has read the ASH 'Fraxinus' manuscript before I saw it—and I have nightmares of opening the GUARDIAN to a review of someone else's new translation. At the moment, I would rather not put my complete theory on electronic media, where it could be downloaded. In fact, until I have the whole translation complete, word-perfect, and the Afterword at first-draft stage, I am reluctant to discuss this editorially.

Bear with me, please. This has to be rigorous and water-tight, or I shall be laughed out of court—or at least, out of the academic community.

For now, here is my first attempt at transmitting translated text to you: Section 2 of the del Guiz LIFE.

--Pierce

- -

Message: #12 (Pierce Ratcliff/misc.)
Subject: Ash, historical background
Date: 4/11/00 at 2.19 p.m.
From: Longman@   *format address and other*
                           details non-recoverably deleted

Pierce--

Vandals, yes, but I can't find *any* hint in my books on European or Arabic history, no matter where I look—*WHAT North African 'Visigoths'?*

Are you SURE you've got this right?

I have to be honest and say that we don't need any controversy about the scholarship associated with this book. *Please* reassure me on this. Today if possible!

- -

Message: #19 (Anna Longman/misc.)
Subject: Ash, historical background
Date: 4/11/00 at 6.37 p.m.
From: Ratcliff   *(format address and other*
                            details non-recoverably deleted)

Anna--

Initially, I had all the same doubts that you have. Even the Vandals had, by the fifteenth century, been gone from an entirely Islamic Tunisia for nine centuries.

At first, you see, I thought the answer must lie in the mediaeval mindset—let me explain. For them, history isn't a progress, a sequence of things happening in a particular order. The fifteenth century artists who illuminated histories of the Crusades put their twelfth century soldiers into fifteenth century clothes. Thomas Mallory, writing his MORTE D'ARTHUR in the 1460s, puts his sixth century knights in the same armour as his own Wars of the Roses period, and they speak as knights in the 1460s spoke. History is *now*. History is a moral exemplar of the present moment.

The 'present moment' of the Ash documents is the 1470s.

Initially, therefore, I thought the 'Visigoths' referred to in the texts must be, in fact, Turks.

We can't easily imagine, now, how *terrorised* the European kingdoms were when the vast Turkish Empire besieged and took Constantinople (AD 1453), the 'most Christian city.' To them, it literally was the end of the world. For two hundred years, until the Ottoman Turks are finally beaten back from the gates of Vienna in the 1600s, Europe lives in absolute dread of an invasion from the east—it is their Cold War period.

What I thought at first, then, was that it was not too surprising if Ash's chroniclers decided that she (simply because she was a famous military commander) *must* have had some hand in holding the Turks back from defenceless Europe. Nor that, fearing the Turkish Empire as they did, they concealed its identity under a false name, hence 'Visigoths.'

Of course, as you know, I had later to revise this.

--Pierce Ratcliff, Ph.D.

- -

Message: #14 (Pierce Ratcliff/misc.)
Subject: Ash
Date: 5/11/00 at 8.43 a.m.
From: Longman   *format address and other details*
                                            non-recoverably deleted

Pierce--

I have no idea how I can explain to my editorial director, never mind sales and marketing, that the Visigoths are actually Turks, and that this whole history is a farrago of lies!

- -

Message: #20 (Anna Longman/misc.)
Subject: Ash
Date: 5/11/00 at 9.18 a.m.
From: Ratcliff   *format address and other*
                                      details non-recoverably deleted

Anna--

No, no, they're NOT Turks! I just thought that they MIGHT be. I was WRONG!

My theory posits a fifteenth century Visigoth enclave on the North African coast. It is my *point* that the evidence for this has been shuffled under the academic carpet.

This happens—it happens with many things in history. And events and people not only get deliberately written out of history, as with Stalinism, they seem almost to slip out of sight when the attitude of the times is against them—I could cite Ash herself as an example of this. Like most women who have taken up arms, she vanishes from history during patriarchal periods, and during more liberal times, still tends to appear only as a 'figurehead' warrior, not involved in actual killing. But then, this happens to Joan of Arc, Jeanne de Montfort, Eleanor of Aquitaine, and hundreds of other women who were not of sufficiently high social class that their names couldn't be ignored.

At various times I've been fascinated both by the PROCESS of how this happens—cf my thesis—and by the DETAILS of what gets written out. If not for Charles Mallory Maximillian's ASH (given to me by a great-grandmother who, I think, had it as a school prize in 1892), then I might not have spent twenty years exploring 'lost' history. And now I've found it. I've found a 'lost' piece of sufficient significance that it will establish my reputation.

I owe it all to 'Fraxinus.' The more I study this, the more I think its provenance with the Wade family (the chest in which it was found supposedly brought back from an Andalusian monastery, on a pilgrimage) is accurate. The mediaeval Spains are complex, distant and fascinating; and if there were to have been some Visigoth survivals—over and above the bloodlines of these Roman-era barbarians in the Iberian ruling classes—this is where we might expect to find it recorded: in little-known mediaeval manuscripts.

Naturally, the ASH manuscripts contain exaggerations and errors—but they contain a coherent and ESSENTIALLY true story. There WAS at least a Visigoth city on the North African coast, and possibly a military hegemony to go with it!

--Pierce

- -

Message: #18 (Pierce Ratcliff/misc.)
Subject: Ash, theory
Date: 5/11/00 at 4.21 p.m.
From: Longman@   *(format address and other
                              details non-recoverably deleted)*

Pierce--

Fine.

MAYBE.

How could something of this magnitude just VANISH out of history???

--Anna

- -

Message: #21 (Anna Longman/misc.)
Subject: Ash
Date: 6/11/00 at 4.07 a.m.
From: Ratcliff   *format address and other details*
                             non-recoverably deleted

Anna--

Apologies for answerphone. I'd left this line switched over to fax. I want to reassure you, but

You see, the thing is, it's EASY to vanish from history. BURGUNDY does it, for God's sake. There it is, in 1476, the wealthiest, most cultured, most militarily organised nation in Europe—and in January 1477 their Duke gets killed, and Charles Mallory Maximillian was right, NOTHING EVER GETS WRITTEN ABOUT BURGUNDY AGAIN.

Well, no, that's not entirely true. But most educated people's concept of European history is that north-west Europe consists of France and Germany, and has done from the fall of the Roman Empire. Burgundy is the name of a wine.

You see, what I'm trying to say is

It actually took Burgundy about a generation to vanish totally. Charles's only child Mary married Maximillian of Austria, and they became the Austro-Hungarian Hapsburgs, which last until World War One, but the POINT I wanted to make is

The point is, if you didn't know Burgundy was a major European power, and that we came THIS close to having five hundred years of

Burgundy instead of France—well, if you didn't know it, you wouldn't learn it. It's as if the whole country is FORGOTTEN the moment that Charles the Bold dies on the battlefield at Nancy.

No one has ever satisfactorily explained this! Some things just don't get into history

I think something similar happens with the 'Visigoth' settlement

Here I am babbling away at the keyboard in the early hours, you're going to think I'm an idiot

Excuse me, please. I'm exhausted. I've got a seat on a plane at Heathrow, I only have an hour to pack, the taxi's due about now, and then I decided to check my phone, and found your last message.

Anna, the most amazing, wonderful thing has happened! My colleague Dr Isobel Napier-Grant telephoned me. She's in charge of the diggings outside Tunis—the GUARDIAN's been running stories on their latest discoveries, you may have seen—and she's found something that may be one of the 'clay walkers' in the del Guiz text!

She thinks it *just might have been* an actual *mobile* piece of technology!!!—maybe mediaeval—post-Roman—or it may be complete nonsense, some weird Victorian invention or forgery that's only been in the ground a hundred years

Tunis, of course, is near the historical ruins of Roman Carthage

Taxi's here. If this damn thing works, I've sent you the next translated section Ash. Phone as soon as back from Tunisia.

anna—if the golem are true—what else is?

PART TWO

July 2, 1476 AD–July 22, 1476 AD

HECUBA REGNINUM[36]

[36]"Hecuba (the Goddess of Hell) reigns (on earth)."

i

AFLOAT ON THE Rhine river, the barge shifting underfoot, Ash lifted her chin and unbuckled her sallet. "What hour is it?"

Philibert took it from her. "Sunset."

On my wedding night.

The little page-boy, with the help of the older Rickard, unbuckled the straps of her brigandine, unlaced the mail standard around her throat, unbuckled her sword-belt, and took her weapons and armor off her body. She sighed, unconsciously, and stretched her arms out. Armour is not heavy when you put it on, weighs nothing ten minutes afterwards, and when you take it off is the weight of lead.

The Rhine River barges presented problems enough: two hundred men of the Lion company detailed off—at Fernando del Guiz's perfectly legal insistence—as escort for the disgraced Visigoth ambassadors, traveling from Cologne to the Swiss Cantons, over the pass and down to Genoa. Therefore two hundred men, their gear and horses, to be organized. And a deputy commander to be left behind with the rest of the company: in this case, her unilateral decision appointed Angelotti, with Geraint ab Morgan.

Outside, there was a solid grunt and the sound of weight slumping to the deck: her stewards, pole-axing the last of the bullocks to be brought on board. She heard footsteps, water sloshed from leather buckets to clean the barge's deck, where basins do not catch all the blood: the rip of skin as the butcher's knife is taken to the carcass.

"What will you eat, boss?" Rickard shifted from one foot to the other, obviously anxious to get out on deck with the rest of the company. Men gambling, drinking; whores enjoying the night on the slow-flowing river.

"Bread, wine." Ash gestured abruptly. "Phili will get it for me. I'll call for you if I need you."

Philibert put a pottery plate into her hands, and she paced up and down the tiny cabin, cramming the crusts of bread into her mouth, chewing, spitting out a crumb and washing it all down with wine; all the time frowning and moving—with a memory of Constanza, in her solar in Cologne—not like a woman, but like a long-legged boy.

"I called an officer meeting! Where the fuck are they?"

"My lord Fernando rescheduled it to the morning."

"Oh, he did, did he?" Ash smiled grimly. Her smile faded. "He said 'not tonight' and made bad jokes about bridal nights—right?"

"No, boss." Phili looked pained. "His friends did. Matthias and Otto. Boss, Matthias gave me sweetmeats. Then he asked me what the whore-captain does. I don't tell him. Can I lie to him next time?"

"Lie yourself blue in the face if you like." Ash grinned conspiratorially to an answering pleased wicked grin from the boy. "That goes for Fernando's squire Otto, too. You keep 'em guessing, kid." *What the whore-captain does . . . ?* Well, what *do* I do?

Be a widow. Confess, do penance. People do.

"Fucking Christ!" Ash threw herself down on the cabin's box-bed.

The wood of the Rhine barge creaked gently. Night air breathed off the unseen water, making the canvas-roofed cabin pleasantly cool. A part of her mind registered the creak of ropes, horses shifting their hooves, a man praising wine, another man devoutly praying to St. Catherine, other barges; all the night noises of two hundred men of the company traveling south upriver, as the long train of barges pulled away from Cologne.

"Fuck!"

"Boss?" Philibert looked up from sanding a rust-spotted breastplate.

"This is bad enough without—!" *Without everybody confused about who they're supposed to be taking orders from, me—or him.* "Never mind."

Slowly, unaware of the boy's fingers undoing her points, she dragged off doublet and hose together, and sprawled back in her shirt. A burst of laughter on deck shattered the comparative quiet. She was not aware that she flinched. One hand unconsciously tugged the hem of her long gathered shirt down over her bare knees.

"Boss, you want the lanterns lit?" Phili rubbed his knuckle into his eye-socket.

"Yeah." Ash watched without seeing as the scruffy-haired page hung the lanterns on their hooks. A buttery yellow light illuminated the opulent quarters, the silk pillows, the furs, the box-sided bed, the canvas canopy with the green and gold colors of del Guiz quartered with the Hapsburg yellow and black.

All of Fernando's traveling chests were thrown carelessly open, crowding the small cabin, his doublets spilling out, every surface covered with his possessions. She inventoried them automatically in her head—a purse, a shoeing horn, a bodkin; a cake of red wax, shoemaker's thread; a bag, a silk-lined hood, a gilded leather halter; sheaves of parchment; an eating-knife with an ivory handle . . .

"I could sing for you, boss."

She reached out with her free hand and patted Philibert on the hip. "Yeah."

The little boy pulled his caped hood off over his head and stood in the lamplight with his shaggy hair sticking up. He squeezed his eyes shut and began to sing unaccompanied:

> *"The thrush she sings from the fire,*
>   *'The Queen, the Queen's my bane—' "*

"Not that one." Ash swung her legs over and sat on the edge of the box-bed. "And that's not the beginning of that song. That comes near the end. It's okay, you're tired. Go sleep."

The boy looked at her with stubborn dark eyes. "Rickard and I want to sleep in here like always."

She has not slept alone since she was thirteen.

"No. Go sleep with the squires."

He ran out. The heavy tapestry curtain let in a burst of sound as it opened, cut it off as it swung to. A far more graphic and biologically descriptive song than Philibert's old country tragedy was being sung out on deck. He probably knows the words to this one too, she thought; but he's been walking around me today like I was Venetian glass. Since this morning, and the cathedral.

Footsteps sounded outside on the deck. She recognized the sound: all her skin shivered. She lay back down on the mattress.

Fernando del Guiz pushed the curtain open, bawling something over his shoulder that made Matthias—a not-very-noble young male friend, Ash thought—howl with laughter. He let the curtain drop behind him, closing his eyes and swaying with the ship.

Ash stayed where she lay.

The curtain stayed undisturbed. No squire, no page; none of his court friends, young boisterous German knights. No very public aristocratic bridal customs? she wondered.

No—no, you won't will you? Drag the sheets out of here and show there's no virgin bloodstains? You won't want to listen to people saying *his wife's a whore*.

"Fernando—"

His large hands unbuttoned the front of his puff-sleeved satin doublet, and he shrugged it back off his shoulders. Fernando smiled a particularly knowing smile. "That's 'husband' to you."

Sweat stuck his yellow hair to his forehead. He struggled with the points at his waist, abandoned them halfway—cloth ripped as he tore his arm out of his shirt. Even rangy in build, with his body not yet filled out to his adult weight, Ash found him just plain *big*: male chest, male torso, the hard muscles of male thighs when the man is a knight and rides every day.

He didn't bother to unlace his cod-flap, he reached in and hitched his stiffening cock out over the top of the fabric, clutching it in his hand, and clambered one-handed onto the tiny box-bed toward her. The yellow lantern light turned his skin into oiled gold. She inhaled. He smelled male, smelled also how linen shirts smell, when they are left to dry in the open air.

With her own hands she pulled up her shirt, under which she was naked.

He reached down and wrapped his hand around his thickening purple cock, lifted her hips with his other hand, guided his thrust with an inexpert shove.

More than ready—ready since the realization that it was his footsteps outside—she received the whole thick length of him thrust into her, shivered, hot as fever. Impaled, she enclosed his solidity.

His face lowered, inches from hers. She saw, in his

eyes, his realization of her wetness. He murmured, "Whore . . ."

His thumb stroked her scarred cheekbones, an old scar at the base of her neck, a curve of black bruises where a blow at Neuss had driven her breastplate in under her arm. His slurred young voice mumbled, "You got a *man's* body."

The points of his hose at his waist, and at his cod-flap, pulled tight. The fine wool ripped down the inner seam, exposing the hard flesh of his thigh. His torso fell across her. His weight made her struggle to breathe. She dug her fingers into the big muscles of his upper arms, hard. His skin under her hand was velvet over hardness, silk over iron. Her head fell back on the silk pillows. She moaned in her throat.

The man thrust, two or three times. Her wet, pulsing cunt held him; a shiver of presensation began to loosen her muscles; she felt herself opening, flesh unfolding.

He jerked twice, like a poacher's rabbit from the killing blow, and his hot seed flooded her, copious, slicking down her thighs. His heavy body sprawled over her.

She smelled—almost tasted—thin German beer on his breath.

His cock slid out of her, limp.

"You're *drunk!*" Ash said.

"No. You wish I was. I wish I was." He looked down at her from a blurred face. "This is my duty and it's done. And that's it, madam wife. You're mine now, sealed by blood—"

Ash said dryly, "I don't think so."

His expression changed: she could not read it. Arrogance? Revulsion? Confusion? A simple, selfish desire not to be here, not to be on this barge, in this bed, with this problematical she-male?

If I was hiring him, I could read him. What's the matter with me?

Fernando del Guiz rolled off her, sprawling facedown and semi-clothed on the mattress. Only his wet semen marked the linen. "You've been with men before. I hoped there was an outside chance it might be a rumor, that you weren't really a whore. Like the French king's maid. But you're not a virgin."

Ash shifted to face him. She merely blinked at him. Both her gaze and her voice were level, flat, very slightly tinged with black humor. "I haven't been a virgin since I was six. I was raped for the first time when I was eight. Then I stayed alive by whoring." Looking for comprehension in his expression, she saw none. "Have you ever had a little maid?"

His fair skin flushed and he colored pink from cheeks to brow to the back of his neck. "I have not!"

"A little girl of nine or ten? You'd be surprised how many men want that. Although, to be fair, some of them didn't care whether it was woman, child, man or sheep, so long as they got to stick their cocks in something warm and wet—"

"God and His angels!" Sheer, appalled shock. "*Shut up!*"

She felt the whisper of air as his fist moved; her own arm came up by reflex, and the blow was all but absorbed by the fleshy part of her forearm. She is muscular there. Only his knuckles brush her scarred cheek. That touch jolts her head back.

"Shut up, shut up, shut up—"

"Whoa!"

Panting, with bright unspilled tears in her eyes, Ash shifted her body back from him. Back from warm, silken skin over hard muscle: from the body that she longs to wrap herself around.

Bitter, all feudal privilege now, he spat, "How could you *do* all that?"

"Easily." Again, it is the commander's voice: acerbic, pragmatic, and with a conscious humor. Ash shook her head to clear it. "I'd rather have had my life as a whore than be the kind of virgin you were hoping for. When you understand why, we might have something to talk about."

"Talk? To a *woman*?"

She might have forgiven him if he had said "to you," even in that tone of voice, but the way that he said "woman" made her mouth curl up at one corner, without humor.

"You forget who I am. I'm Ash. I'm the Lion Azure."

"You *were*."

Ash shook her head. "Well, fuck me. This is some wedding night."

She thought she had him, swore she came within a bowstring's width of Fernando bursting out laughing—of seeing that generous, acknowledging grin she had seen at Neuss—but he threw himself back across the truckle-bed, limbs sprawling, one arm over his eyes, and exclaimed, "*Christus Imperator!* They made me one flesh with *this*."

Ash sat up, cross-legged on the palliasse, easily limber. She was entirely unconscious of being naked while he was still partly clothed, until the sight of him sprawled out in front of her, and his naked thigh and belly and cock in the lantern-light, made a hot wetness grow in her cunt, and she colored, and shifted to sit differently. She put her hands down in front of her, the unsatisfied ache hot in her vagina.

"Fucking peasant *bitch*!" he exclaimed. "Bitch on heat! I was right the first time I met you."

"Oh, bloody *hell* . . ." Her face flamed. She put her hands over her cheeks, and her fingertips felt that even her ears were hot. She said hurriedly, "Never mind that."

Without taking his arm away from his face, he groped and pulled a blanket half over his body. She could feel the skin of her face heating. She locked her hands about her own ankles, to keep from reaching out to touch the hard velvet of his skin.

Fernando's breathing shifted to a snore. His heavy sweating body slumped further down in the bed, deeply and instantly asleep.

After a while she wrapped her hand around the saint's medallion at her throat and held it. Her thumb caressed the image of St. George on one side, the ash-rune on the other.

Her body screamed at her.

She did not sleep.

Yes, I am probably going to have to have him killed.

It's no different from killing on the field of battle. I don't even *like* him. I just want to fuck him.

More hours later than a marked candle could count, she saw summer light around the edges of the tapestry curtain. Dawn began to lighten the Rhine river valley, and the cavalcade of ships moving upstream.

"So what are you going to do?" She said it quietly and rhetorically to herself.

She lay, naked, facedown on the pallet, reaching out for her belt where it lay on her piled doublet and hose. The sheath of her knife came easily to her hand. Her thumb stroked the rounded hilt of the bollock dagger, slipped down to press it an inch or so out of the scabbard. A gray metal blade, with harsh silver lines on the much-sharpened edge.

He's asleep.

He didn't even bring a page in with him, never mind a squire or a guard.

There's no one to shout an alarm, never mind defend him!

Something about this sheer depth of ignorance, his inability to even conceive that a woman might kill a feudal knight—*Green Christ, hasn't he ever thought he might be knifed by a whore?*—and his forgetfulness in merely falling asleep, as if this were any night between a married pair: something in that touched her, despite him.

She rolled over, drawing the dagger. Her thumb tested the edge. It proved keen enough to slice the first layers of dermis, at a touch, without penetrating to the red meat below.

What I ought to think is *Died of arrogance*, and kill him. If only because I might not get another chance.

I wouldn't get away with it; naked and covered in blood, it's going to be kind of obvious who did it—

No. That isn't it.

I know damn well that once it was done, a fait accompli as Godfrey would call it, then my lads would tip the body over the side, shrug, and say, "Must've had a boating accident, my lord," to anybody who asked; up to and including the Emperor. Once it's done, it's done; and they'd back me.

It's doing it. That's the objection I have.

Christ and His pity know why, but I don't want to kill this man.

"I don't even know you," she whispered.

Fernando del Guiz slept on, his face in repose unprotected, vulnerable.

Not confrontation: compromise. Compromise. Christ, but don't I spend half my life finding compromises so that eight hundred people can work together? No reason to leave my brains behind just because I'm in bed.

So:

We are a split company: the others are in Cologne: if I kill Fernando there'll be someone who objects—there's always someone who objects to anything—and if it were van Mander, for example, there's another split: his lances may be following him, not me. Because he likes del Guiz: he likes having a man, and a noble man, and a real live knight for a boss. Van Mander doesn't much like women, even if they are as good on the field of battle as I am.

This can wait. This can wait until we've dumped the ambassadors in Genoa and got back to Cologne.

Genoa. *Shit*.

"Why did you do that?" She spoke in a whisper, lying down beside him, the electric velvet of his skin brushing hers. He shifted, rolling over, presenting her with a freckled back.

"Are you another one like Joscelyn—nothing I do will ever be enough, because I'm a woman? Because the one thing I can't be is a man? Or is it because I can't be a *noble* woman? One of your own kind?"

His soft breathing filled the tented cabin.

He rolled back again, restless, his body pressing up against hers. She lay still, half under the warm, damp, muscular bulk of him. With her free hand, she reached up to brush fine tendrils of hair out of his eyes.

I can't remember what his face looked like then. I can only see in my mind what he looks like now.

The thought startled her; her eyes flicked open.

"I killed my first two men when I was eight," she whispered, not disturbing his sleep. "When did you kill yours? What fields have you fought?"

I can't kill a man while he's sleeping.

Not out of—

The word eluded her. Godfrey or Anselm might have said *pique*, but both men were on other barges in the river convoy, had found things to do that would take them as far from the command barge as possible, this first night after her wedding.

I need to think this through. Talk it through with them.

And I can't split the company. Whatever we do will have to wait until we get back to the Germanies.

Ash's hand, without her volition, stroked the sweat-damp strands of hair back from his brow.

Fernando del Guiz shifted in his sleep. The narrow bed necessarily threw their bodies together on the piled palliasses; skin against skin; warm, electric. Ash, without much thinking about it, leaned down and put her mouth to the back of his neck, her lips to his soft moist skin, breathing in the scent and feel of the finest hair at his nape. Vertebrae made hard lumps between his freckle-spotted shoulders.

With a great sigh he rolled over, put his arms around her waist and drew her to his hot body. She pressed against him, breast and belly and thighs, and his cock hardened and jutted up between them. Still with his eyes shut, one of his narrow strong hands probed her between the thighs, fingers dipping into her wet warm cleft, stroking her. The early light hazing the cabin illuminated his fair lashes, fine on his cheeks; *so young*, she thought, and then, *aah!*

One tilt of his hips put his swollen cock up inside her. He rested, still holding her close in his arms and within minutes began rocking his body, pushing her up to a mild, unexpected, but completely pleasurable orgasm.

His head dipped, face coming to rest against her shoulder. She felt the brush of his lashes against her skin. Eyes still closed, half asleep, he slid his hands over her shoulders, down her arms, around her back. A warm, valuing touch. Erotic, and *kind*.

He is the first man my age to touch me kindly, she realized; and as Ash opened her eyes, taken equally by surprise to find herself smiling at him, he thrust harder and deeper and came, and sank back from his peak into deeper sleep.

"What?" she leaned down, hearing him mumble.

He said it again, slipping down into an exhausted sleep, too unconscious to be reached again.

What she thought she heard was, "They have married me to the lion's whelp."

There were tears of humiliation, bright and wet, standing on his lashes.

Ash, waking again an hour later, found herself in an empty bed.

Fifteen days later—fifteen nights of empty beds—on the feast-day of St. Swithun,[37] they arrived within five miles of Genoa.

ii

ASH THUMBED UP the visor of her sallet, in the dew-wet early morning. The sun was not a finger's breadth above the horizon. Some coolness was still in the air. Around her, men walked and rode, wagons creaked; a wind blew her the noise of a shepherd on a distant hillside, singing as he surely would not if the country were not peaceable.

Robert Anselm rode up, past the wagons and horsemen, from the rear of the column, his open-faced sallet lodged in the crook of his arm. The southern sun had reddened his bald scalp. One of the men walking with a bill over his shoulder whistled like a blackbird and shifted into the opening bars of *Curly Locks, Curly Locks, wilt thou be*

---

[37]Celebrated on 15 July; thus an internal reference for the date of the company's arrival outside the port-city of Genoa.

mine? as Anselm trotted past, only apparently oblivious. Ash felt a smile tug at her mouth, the first for over a fortnight.

"Okay?"

"I found four of these assholes dead drunk in the steward's wagon this morning. They didn't even get out to sleep it off somewhere else in the camp!" Anselm squinted against the morning sun, riding knee to knee with her. "I've got the provosts disciplining them now."

"And the thefts?"

"Complaints, again. Three different lances: Euen Huw, Thomas Rochester, Geraint ab Morgan before we left Cologne—"

"If Geraint had more complaints about this before we left Cologne, why didn't *he* take action?"

Ash looked keenly at her second-in-command.

"How's Geraint Morgan working out?"

The big man shrugged.

"Geraint's not keen on discipline himself."

"Did we know that when we took him on?" Ash frowned at the thickening dawn mist. "Euen Huw vouched for him . . ."

"I know he got slung out of King Henry's household after Tewkesbury. Drunk in charge of a unit of archers— *on* the field. Went back into the family wool business, couldn't settle, ended up a contract soldier."

"We didn't hire him just because he's an old Lancastrian, Roberto! He has to pull his weight, same as everyone else."

"Geraint's no Lancastrian. He fought with the Earl of Salisbury at Ludlow—for the Yorkists, in fifty-nine," Anselm added, apparently none too confident of his captain's intricate knowledge of *rosbif* dynastic struggles.

"Green Christ, he started young!"

"He's not the only one . . ."

"Yeah, yeah." Ash shifted her weight, bringing her horse back toward Roberto's flea-bitten gray. "Geraint's a violent, lascivious, drunken son-of-a-bitch—"

"He's an archer," Anselm said, as if it were self-evident.

"—and worst of all, he's a mate of Euen Huw," Ash continued. Her twinkle died. "He's shit-hot on the field. But he gets a grip, or he goes. Damn. Well, at least I've left him in joint command with Angelotti . . . Come on then, Robert. What about this thief?"

Robert Anselm squinted up at the obscuring sky, then back at her. "I've got him, Captain. It's Luke Saddler."

Ash recalled to her mind his face: a boy not yet fourteen, mostly seen around the camp flushed with ale, wet-nosed and avoided by the other pages; Philibert had had tales to tell to twisted arms, hands touching cods. "I know him. Aston's page. What's he taking?"

"Purses, daggers, someone's *saddle*, for Christ's pity's sake," Anselm remarked. "He tried to sell that. He's in and out of the quartermaster's all the time, Brant says, but it's mostly the lads' personal kits."

"Crop his ears this time, Roberto."

Anselm looked a little grim.

Ash said, "You, me, Aston, the provosts—we can't stop him thieving. So . . ."

She jerked a thumb back at the men riding and walking; hard men in dusty leather and linen, sweating in the early Italian morning, shouting comments to each other about anything they passed, loud voices careless of rebuke.

"We have to act. Or else they'll do it for us. And probably bugger him into the bargain: he's a pretty kid."

Frustrated, she remembers Luke Saddler's sullen, shifty expression when she had had him into the command tent, to see if the full weight of the commander's displeasure might move him; he had smelled of Burgundian wine that day and giggled inanely.

Pricked by an inadequate feeling of having failed the boy, she snapped, "Why tell me, anyway? Luke Saddler's not my problem. Not now. He's my *husband's* problem."

"As if you cared two tits about that!"

Ash looked down rather pointedly at the front of her brigandine. It was not proving very much less hot to wear than plate. Robert Anselm grinned at her.

"As if you're going to let del Guiz worry about this mob," he added. "Girl, you're going demented, running around picking up after him."

Ash stared ahead through the morning sea-mist, thickening now on the road, just making out the figures of Joscelyn van Mander and Paul di Conti riding with Fernando. Unconsciously, she sighed. The morning smelled of sweet thyme, from where the cartwheels crushed it at the edges of the wide merchants' road.

Her husband Fernando del Guiz rode laughing among the young men and servants of his entourage, ahead of the wagons. A trumpeter rode with him, and a rider carrying the banner with the del Guiz arms. The Lion Azure company standard rode a few hundred yards back, between the two wagon lines, whitening with the dust he kicked up.

"Sweet Christ, it's going to be a long bloody trek back to Cologne!"

She shifted by unconscious habit with the movements of her mount, a riding horse she had long ago nicknamed The Sod. She smelled sea nearby; so did he, and moved skittishly. *Genoa and the coast no more than four or five miles away now? We could arrive well before noon.*

Sea-mist dampened down the dust kicked up by lines of plodding horses and the twenty-five lances who rode in groups of six and seven between them.

Ash sat up in the saddle, pointing. "I don't recognize that man. There. Look."

Robert Anselm rode up beside her and looked where she looked, narrowing his eyes to bring the outer line of wagons into focus—wagons driven with shields still strapped to their sides, and handgunners and crossbowmen riding inside them on the stores.

"Yes, I do," she contradicted herself, before he could answer. "It's Agnes. Or one of his men, anyway. No, it's the Lamb himself."

"I'll bring him through." Anselm tapped his long spurs into his bay's flanks and cantered across the lines of moving carts.

Even with the droplets of mist, it was too hot to wear a bevor. Ash rode in sallet and a blue velvet-covered brigandine, the gilt rivet-heads glinting, with her brass-hilted bastard sword strapped to her side. She eased her weight back, slowing, as Robert Anselm brought the newcomer back inside the moving camp.

She watched Fernando del Guiz. He didn't notice.

"Hello, She-male!"

"Hello, Agnes." Ash acknowledged her fellow mercenary commander. "Hot enough for you?"

The straggle-haired man made a gesture that took in the full suit of Milanese plate that he rode in, the armet helm he currently carried on the pommel of his saddle, and the black iron warhammer at his belt. "They've got Guild riots down at Marseilles, along the coast. And you know Genoa—strong walls, bolshie citizens, and a dozen factions always fighting to be Doge. I took out the head of the Farinetti in a skirmish last week. Personally!"

He tilted his hand in his Milanese gauntlet, as far as the plates would allow, and made an imaginary illustrative thrust. His lean face was burned black from fighting in the Italian wars. Straggling black hair fell past his pauldrons. His white livery surcoat bore the device of a lamb, from whose head radiated golden beams embroidered all over in black thread with "*Agnus Dei.*"[38]

"We've been up at Neuss. I led a cavalry charge against Duke Charles of Burgundy." Ash shrugged, as if to say *it was nothing, really.* "But the Duke's still alive. That's war."

Lamb grinned, showing yellow broken teeth through his beard. In broad northern Italian, he remarked, "So now you're here. What is this—no scouts? No spies? Your guys didn't spot me until I was on top of you! Where the hell are your aforeriders?"[39]

"I was told we don't need any." Ash made her tone ironic. "This is a peaceful countryside full of merchants and pilgrims, under the protection of the Emperor. Didn't you know?"

Lamb (she had forgotten his real name) squinted through the mist to the head of the column. "Who's the bimbo?"

"My current employer." Ash didn't look at Anselm as she spoke.

"Oh. Right. He's one of *those* employers." Agnus Dei shrugged, which is a fairly complicated process in armor. His black eyes flashed at her. "Bad luck. I'm shipping out, down to Naples. Bring your men with me."

"Nah. I can't break a contract. Besides, most of my guys are back at Cologne, under Angelotti and Geraint ab Morgan."

A movement of the Lamb's lips, regretful, flirtatious. "Ah well. How was the Brenner Pass? I waited three days for merchants going down to Genoa to get their wagons through."

"We had it clear. Except that it snowed. It's the middle of fucking *July* for Christ's sake—sorry, Lamb. I mean,

---

[38] "The Lamb of God."

[39] Outriders, scouts.

it's the middle of July. I hate crossing the Alps. At least nothing fell on us this time. You remember that slide in seventy-two?''

Ash continued to talk civilly, riding beside him, aware of Anselm glowering on her other side, his bay plodding, horse and rider creamed white with chalk dust. From time to time her gaze flicked ahead, through the opalescent pearl of the mist, to the blurs of sunlight breaking through. Fernando's bright silks and satins glowed where he rode helmetless in the morning. The creak of wheels and the loud voices of men and women calling conversation echoed flatly. Someone played a fife, off-key.

After some professional conversation, Lamb remarked, "Then I shall see you on the field, madonna. God send, on the same side!''

"God willing," Ash chuckled.

The Lamb rode off southeast, in what she supposed must be the direction of his troop.

Robert Anselm remarked, "You didn't tell him your 'current employer' is also your husband."

"That's right, I didn't."

A dark, short man with curly hair rode up beside Anselm, glancing to either side before he spoke. "Boss, we must be nearly in Genoa!"

Ash nodded to Euen Huw. "So I assume."

"Let me take him out hunting." The Welshman's thumb slid down to caress the polished wooden hilt of his bollock dagger. "Lots of people have accidents when they're hunting. Happens all the time."

"We're twenty wagons and two hundred men. Listen to us. We've scared the game off for miles around. He wouldn't buy it. Sorry, Euen."

"Let me saddle up for him tomorrow, then, on the way back. A bit of mail wire around the hoof, under the hock—aw, boss, go on!"

Her gaze could not help but be calculating when she looked through the mist at which of the lance-leaders rode with her and which rode with Fernando del Guiz and his squires. It had been a frightening drift the first couple of days; then the Rhine river journey presented enough problems to keep every man occupied, and now it had stabilized.

You can't blame them. Whatever they ask me, he makes me clear all orders through him now.

But a divided company can't fight. We'll get cut up like sheep.

A man with potato features and a few wisps of white hair protruding under the rim of his sallet nudged his roan gelding up level with Ash. Sir Edward Aston said, "Knock the bloody little bugger off his horse, lass. If he keeps us riding without scouts, we'll be up to our necks in trouble. And he hasn't had the lances drill any night we've made camp."

"*And* if he keeps paying over the odds at every town we stop at for food and wine, we're in trouble." Ash's steward, Henri Brant, a middle-aged stocky man with no front teeth, nudged his palfrey closer to her. "Doesn't he know the value of money? I don't dare show my face among the Guilds on the way back. He's spent most of what I had put by to last us until autumn in these past fifteen days!"

"Ned, you're right; Henri, I *know*." She tapped spurs and shifted her weight left. Her gray gelding sneaked its head out and nipped Aston's roan on the shoulder.

Ash belted The Sod between the ears and spurred off, kicking up gouts of wet dust, the cool air welcome on her face.

She slowed momentarily beside the wagons that held the Visigoth ambassadors. Tall wheel rims jolted in the ruts of the high road, sending the cart one way and then the other.

Daniel de Quesada and Asturio Lebrija lay bound hand and foot with hemp rope, rolling with every jolt.

"Did my husband order this?"

A mounted man riding with his crossbow across his saddle spat. He didn't look at Ash. "Yeah."

"Cut them loose."

"Can't," the man said, even as Ash winced mentally and thought, *What's the first rule, girl? Never give an order you don't know will be obeyed.*

"Cut them loose when Lord Fernando sends word back to you," Ash said, hitting The Sod with a gloved hand again as the gelding tried to sidle up to the crossbowman's mount, a wicked light in its eye. "Which he will—*you* need a gallop to shake the temper out of you, you sod. *Hai!*"

The last remark Ash addressed to her horse. She spurred him from trot to canter to gallop, weaving a thunderous way between the lines of moving carts, ignoring the coughs and curses of those in her dust. The mist began to lift as she galloped. A dozen lance-pennants became clear above the wagons.

Fernando's bright bay pushed ahead of the group, throwing its head up and fretting at the bit, the reins looping dangerously down. Ash noticed that he had given his helmet to his squire, Otto, and that Matthias—neither knight nor squire—carried his lance. The fur of the foxtail pennant shone dully, in wet mist, drooping from its shaft above his head.

Her heart stirred immediately she saw him. *Golden boy*, she thought. The absolute picture of a knight: glowing with strength. He rode easily, and bareheaded. His Gothic plate showed rich, fine workmanship: fluted pauldrons and cuisses, each hinge flanged with decorative pierced metal. Condensation gleamed on the curve of his breastplate, and his tangled gold hair, and the polished brass fleur-de-lis that rimmed the cuffs of his gauntlets.

I was never that careless, she thought, with pinched envy. He's had this since birth. He doesn't even have to *think* about it.

"My lord." She rode up. Her husband's head turned. His cheeks were rough with gold stubble. Ignoring her, he half-turned in his saddle to speak to Matthias, and the long riding sword that swung at his hip banged against the bay's flank. The horse kicked out in aggravation and the whole group of young men swirled into movement, shouting good-naturedly, and re-formed.

The group of squires riding around Fernando seemed reluctant to let her in. A loosening of her rein allowed The Sod's head to snake out and nip the haunch of one.

"Fuck!" The young knight sawed at his reins as his horse reared. Mount and rider staggered away, curvetting in circles.

Ash slid in neatly beside Fernando del Guiz. "A messenger came in. There's been trouble at Marseilles."

"That's leagues away from here." Fernando rode using both hands to hold up a wine skin and tip it with his arms at full extension. The first streams hit him in the mouth; he coughed; straw-colored wine spilled down the front of his fluted breastplate.

"You win, Matthias!" Fernando dropped the half-full wine skin. It thudded to the ground and burst. He threw a handful of coins. Otto and another page rode in close to undo straps, cut points, take pauldrons and breast- and backplate off him. Still wearing arm-defences, Fernando slit the arming doublet's lacing and the points at his waist with his dagger and ripped off the wet doublet. "Otto! It's too hot for harness.[40] Have them put my pavilion up. I'll change."

---

[40] A "harness" is the common term for a suit of armor. Thus the expression, "died in harness," meaning "died while wearing armor."

The spoiled garment went down into the dust as well. Fernando del Guiz was riding in his shirt now, the white silk bunching at his waist where it rode up out of his hose. His hose slid down to his cuisses, the material of the cod-flap stretched tight across his groin. When he dismounted, it would fall; he would strip it off and walk, unconcerned, in his shirt. Ash shifted in her saddle.

She wanted to reach out to his saddle and put her hand between his legs.

The trumpeter wheeled, sounding a long call.

Ash, jolted, said, "We're stopping?"

Fernando's smile took in those of her lance-leaders riding with him as well as his squires and pages and young noble friends. "I'm stopping. The wagons are stopping. You may do what you please, of course, lady wife."

"You want the ambassadors fed and watered while we stop?"

"No." Fernando reined in as the lead wagons stopped.

Ash sat astride The Sod, casting a glance around. The morning mist continued to lift. Broken ground, yellow rocks, scrub dried brown from the long summer's drought. A few copses of bushes—they could hardly be called trees. Higher ground two hundred yards from the wide road. A paradise for scouts, spies, and dismounted men. Maybe even mounted bandits could sneak up.

Godfrey Maximillian plodded up to her on his palfrey. "How close are we to Genoa?"

The priest's beard was white, and the damp dust settled in the creases of his face gave her a premonition of how he would look if he reached sixty.

"Four miles? Ten? Two?" She fisted her hand, punched her thigh. "I'm blind! He forbids me to put scouts out, he forbids me to hire local guides; he's got this damn printed itinerary for pilgrims going to ports for the Holy Land, and *he* thinks that's all we need! He's a

noble *knight*, no one's going to bushwhack *him*! What if
it hadn't been Lamb's men out there? What if it had been
some bandit?''

She stopped as Godfrey smiled, and shook her head.
"Yeah, okay, I grant you, the difference between Lamb
and a bandit is a bit hard to spot! But hey, that's Italian
mercenaries for you."

"A baseless slander. Probably." Godfrey coughed,
drank from his jug, and handed it up to her. "We're making camp two hours after we get started?"

"My lord wants to change his clothes."

"Again. You should have tipped him over the edge of
a barge into the Rhine before we ever got to the Cantons,
never mind crossed the Alps."

"That isn't very Christian of you, Godfrey."

"Matthew ten, thirty-four!"[41]

"I don't think that's *quite* how Our Lord meant that
one . . ." Ash lifted the pottery jug to her lips. The small
beer stung her mouth. It was tepid, vaguely unpleasant,
and (being wet) still extremely welcome for all that.
"Godfrey, I can't push it, not right now. This is no time
to ask my people to start picking sides between me and
him. It'd be chaotic. We've got to at least *function* until
we get back from this idiot's errand."

The priest slowly nodded.

Ash said, "I'm going to ride up to the top of the next
ridge while he's busy. We're wandering around in a mist
in more ways than one. I'll go take a look. Godfrey, go
show your Christian charity to Asturio Lebrija and his
mate. I don't think my lord husband had them fed this
morning."

---

[41]Matthew 10:34. "Think not that I am come to send peace on earth: I
came not to send peace, but a sword."

Godfrey's palfrey plodded back down the column.

Jan-Jacob Clovet and Pieter Tyrrell caught Ash up as The Sod skittered unwillingly up the slope—two fair-haired, almost identical young Flemish men, with unshaven faces, and tallow candle droppings on the sleeves under their brigandines, and crossbows at their saddles. They smelled of stale wine and semen; she guessed they had both been rousted out of a whore's cart before daybreak; probably, if she knew them, from the same woman.

"Boss," Jan-Jacob said, "do something about that son of a bitch."

"It'll happen when the time's right. You move without my word, and I'll nail your balls to a plank."

Normally, they would have grinned. Now Jan-Jacob persisted, "When?"

Pieter added, "They're saying you're not going to kill him. They're saying you're cock-struck. They're saying what can you expect from a woman?"

And if I ask who "they" are, I'll get evasive answers or no answers at all. Ash sighed.

"Look, guys . . . have we ever broken a contract?"

"No!" They spoke simultaneously.

"Well, you can't say that for every mercenary company. We get paid because we don't change sides once we've signed a contract. The law is the only thing we have. I signed a contract with Fernando when I married him. There's one reason why this isn't easy."

She urged The Sod on up toward the lightening skyline.

"I was kind of hoping that God would do it for me," she said wistfully. "Hard-drinking reckless young noblemen fall off their horses and break their necks every day; why couldn't he be one of them?"

"Crossbows work." Pieter patted the leather case of his.

"No!"

"Does he fuck good?"

"Jan-Jacob, get your mind out of your codpiece for once—fucking *hell*!"

The breeze took the mist as they came up to the top of the ridge, rolling it forward, away out to sea. Mediterranean sun blazed back from ocher hills. A blurred blue sky shone, and—no more than two or three miles ahead—the light fractured off creeping waves. The coast. The sea.

A fleet covered the bay, and all the sea beyond.

Not merchant ships.

Warships.

White sails, and black pennants. Ash thought in a split second *that's half a war fleet down there!* and *Visigoth pennants!*

The wind blew the taste of salt against her lips. She stared for a long, appalled, frozen second. The knife-sharp prows of black triremes cut the flat silver surface of the sea. More than ten in number, less than thirty. Among them, huge quinquiremes—fifty or sixty ships. And closer inshore, great shallow-draft troopships vanished from her sight behind the walls of Genoa, the wheels that drove them dripping rainbow sprays of seawater. Dimly, across all the intervening distance, she heard the *thunk-thunk* of their progress.[42]

And she registered black smoke rising from the tiled roofs of the walled port city, and saw moving men among the painted plaster walls and winding streets of Genoa.

Ash whispered, "Troopships unloading, number un-

---

[42]Plainly, this is another intrusion of mediaeval legend into the text. Given the earlier inclusion of the name "Carthage," I suspect that this is in fact a dim memory, preserved in monastery manuscripts, of the sea-power of the historical Carthaginians in the Classical period; when it dominated the Mediterranean before being destroyed by the Roman

known, fleet attacking, no allied vessels; my strength is two hundred men.''

"Withdraw, or surrender."

She still gaped at the coastline below the hills, the sound of the voice in her head almost ignored.

"The Lamb's run right into them!" Aghast, Jan-Jacob pointed at the standard with the white Agnus Dei, a mile ahead. Ash made a quick mental count of his groups of running men.

Pieter already spurred in a circle, his mare hardly under control. "I'll sound the alarm!"

"Wait." Ash held up one hand, palm outward. "Now. Jan-Jacob, get the mounted archers formed up. Tell Anselm I want the knights up and armed, under him as captain! Pieter, tell Henri Brant that all wagons are to be abandoned, everybody on them is to be issued with weapons and told to ride. Ignore anything you hear from anyone with del Guiz livery—I'm going to talk to Fernando!"

She galloped down to the Lion Azure standard in the center of the wagons. Among the milling men she spotted Rickard, yelled at the boy to bring Godfrey and the foreign ambassadors, and pelted on toward the green-and-gold striped pavilion that was being put up in a confusion of struts and ropes and pegs. Fernando sat his horse, sunbright, cheerfully talking to his companions.

"Fernando!"

"What?" He turned in his saddle. An arrogant shape took his mouth, a discontent foreign to what she was beginning to think was only a careless nature. *I bring out*

---

fleet at Milazzo (263 BC), chiefly by the use of the Roman boarding-spike or *corvus*. It would not seem strange to a mediaeval chronicler to include such anachronisms.

the cruelty in him, she thought, and threw herself out of the saddle, quite deliberately on foot and catching his reins, so that she had to lift her head to look up at him.

"What is it?" He hitched at his falling hose, that now rucked down around his buttocks. "Can't you see I'm waiting to dress?"

"I need your help." Ash took a deep breath. "We've been tricked. All of us. The Visigoths. Their fleet. It *isn't* sailing for Cairo, against the Turks. It's *here*."

"Here?" He looked down at her, bewildered.

"I counted at least twenty triremes—and sixty fucking big quinquiremes! *And* troopships!"

His face became open, innocent, bemused. "Visigoths?"

"Their fleet! Their guns! Their army! It's a league up the road *that* way!"

Fernando gaped. "What are *Visigoths* doing *here*?"

"Burning Genoa."

"*Burning*—"

"Genoa! It's an invasion force. I have never seen so many ships in one place—" Ash wiped a crust of dust off her lips. "The Lamb's run into them. There's fighting going on."

"Fighting?"

The man Matthias, in a south German dialect, said, "Yes, Ferdie, *fighting*. You remember. Training, tournaments, wars? That sort of thing?"

Fernando said, "War."

The young German scowled, good-naturedly. "*If* you could be bothered. *I* train more than you do! You're so Boar-damned *lazy*—"

Ash cut across their languid conversation. "My lord husband, you have to see this. Come on!"

She mounted up, spun The Sod, and spurred him un-mercifully, being rewarded by a kick-out (for temper's sake) and then a long, low, hard gallop up the slope, to arrive sweating and anxious, and peer down the long slope to Genoa.

She expected Fernando beside her in heartbeats: it seemed long minutes until he rode up, back-and-breast plates strapped onto his body almost anyhow, and the bleached linen of his shirt sleeves puffing out between the plates on his arms.

"Well? Where—" His voice died.

The foot of the slope was black with running men.

Otto, Matthias, Joscelyn van Mander, Ned Aston and Robert Anselm all arrived beside her in a flurry of manes and wet dust kicked up. They fell silent in the misty morning. Ahead, the smoke from Genoa smirched the sky.

In an identical bewildered tone to Fernando del Guiz, Joscelyn van Mander said, *"Visigoths?"*

Robert Anselm said, "They were either coming for us or the Turk. Turned out to be us."

"Listen." Ash's knuckles whitened on her reins. "A dozen mounted men riding on their own can move faster than this company. Lord husband, Fernando—ride back, tell the Emperor, he has to know about this *now*! Take de Quesada and Lebrija with you as hostages! You can do it in a few days if you ride post."

He stared down from his horse at the approaching banners. Behind him, the lance-leaders and men of the Lion Azure were a mass of steel helmets and dusty flags and the heads of polearms wavering in the heat. Fernando said, "Why not you, *Captain*?"

Poised above the dusty ruts, smelling of horse, wet with sweat, Ash felt a sensation as of putting her hand to a familiar sword grip: a sensation of control not felt since they left Cologne a fortnight ago.

"You're a knight," she said, "not a peasant, not a mercenary. He'll listen to *you*."

Anselm managed a servile, "She's right, my lord." Roberto didn't meet Ash's eye, but she read what he was thinking with the clarity of long knowledge of the man. *Don't let this boy get any ideas about death-or-glory charges against that lot!*

"There are sixty quinqueremes..." Van Mander sounded stunned. "Thirty thousand men."

Fernando gazed down at Ash. Then, as if no one had spoken, as if it were his own decision, he shouted at her, "*I'll* take my Imperial cousin the news! You fight these bastards for me. I *order* it."

Got him! she thought, exultant, and stared down Joscelyn van Mander, who had very plainly heard his order.

They wheeled their horses by unspoken consent, trotting back down the slope. Early humid heat brought a cream sweat to the horses' flanks. The sea-mist from the Mediterranean coast thinned still more. A harsh sunlight stung her eyes.

She beckoned Godfrey Maximillian as he strode up, the two Visigoth men stumbling beside him. "Get them on horses. Chain their wrists. Go!"

Ash slapped her gloved hand against The Sod's satin neck. She couldn't stop grinning. The gelding whickered and mouthed at her, immense teeth clicking on the metal greaves covering her shins. "All right, you sod, so you like people—why the fuck can't you put up with other horses? One of these days you'll be stew. Stand *still*."

A hard object thunked between her shoulders, chinking the metal plates inside the brigandine. Ash swore. The spent arrow fell to the earth.

She brought the gelding around with her knees.

A line of light horses and riders in black livery were skylined at the top of the slope ahead. Mounted archers.

"Stop!" she yelled at Henri Brant, seeing the steward bawling at the drovers and men-at-arms to haul the big-wheeled vehicles around into wagon-fort formation. "You can forget that. That's a fucking army down there! Take what you can carry on packhorses. We'll leave the rest."

She spurred forward to where Anselm drew up a long line of mounted knights at the bottom of the slope, Jan-Jacob and Pieter out to either wing with mounted archers.

She kneed The Sod ferociously, wished that she was riding Godluc—*fucking Fernando, "Don't bring war-horses, we're riding in peace"!*—and her bastard sword was in her right hand, she didn't remember drawing it; and her unprotected hands wore nothing but leather riding gloves: her stomach clenched with the sheer terror of their vulnerability to chopping edged weapons. She spared one glance to see the dozen young German knights riding hell for leather back down the road, lost in plumes of dust; then she galloped across the battle line and out to the flank, and stared toward the sea.

Dark banners with clusters of men under them scrambled across the rocky slopes toward her. The sun winked off their weapons. A couple of thousand spear, at least.

She galloped back to the Lion Azure standard, finding Rickard also there, with her personal banner. Coming up with Robert Anselm, she called, "There's trees, two miles back! Henri, everyone on wagons is to cut their horses' traces, load up what they can, and ride. When you get to the bend about a mile back, leave the road and ride for the hills. We'll cover your backs."

Ash whirled The Sod on the spot, on his hind hooves, and rode out in front of the line. She faced them: about a hundred men in armor on horseback, another hundred out to the wings, with bows. "I always said you bastards would do anything for wine, women and song—and that's your wine, headed for the woods back there! In a minute, we're going to follow it. First, we're going to give this lot of southern bastards enough of a hard time that they won't *dare* come after us. We've done it before, and now we'll do it again!''

Rough voices bawled, "Ash!"

"Archers up on the ridge, there—move it! Remember, we don't go back until the standard goes back. And then we go back steady! And if they're stupid enough to follow us into the forests, they deserve everything they get. Okay, here they come!"

Euen Huw bawled, "Nock! Loose!"

The fine whistle of an arrow split the air, followed by two hundred more. Ash watched a rider in Visigoth livery on the ridge throw up his arms and fall, crossbow-bolt flights feathered in under his heart.

A crowd of spearmen on the ridge ran back.

Anselm yelled, "*Keep the line!*"

Ash, out to one side, saw more Visigoths on horses, small recurved bows in their hands. She muttered, "About sixty men, they can shoot from horseback."

If they rally, charge them with knights. If they run, retreat.

"Uh huh," she murmured thoughtfully to herself, and signaled the Lion Azure standard to pull back. She signaled the column to mount up. A half mile at walking pace, with her eyes on the Visigoth cavalry archers—who didn't follow.

"I don't like that. I don't like that at all . . ."

"Something's odd." Robert Anselm reined in beside her as the men-at-arms rode past, on rising ground. "I expected the bastards to come down on top of us."

"They're outnumbered. We'd cut them to pieces."

"That never stopped Visigoth serf-troops before. They're an undisciplined shower of shite."

"Yeah. I know. But they're not acting like it today." Ash raised her hand and brought the sallet's visor down a touch, shading her eyes with the metal peak. "Thank

Christ he went—I swear I thought my lord husband was going to order us to charge straight into that lot.''

Far ahead, toward Genoa's burning buildings, she saw standards. Not pennants, but Visigoth flags crowned with what might—the distance being deceptive—be gilded eagles.

A movement beneath the eagles caught her eye.

Seen on its own, it could have been a man. Seen with the Visigoth commanders on the distant moorland, it was plainly a head taller. The sun shone on its ocher and brass surfaces. She knows that silhouette.

Ash watched as the clay and brass golem began to stride out to the southeast. It walked no faster than a man, but its ceaseless movement ate up the ground, never faltering over rocks or banks, until she lost it in the haze.

"Shit," she said. "They're sending them out as messengers. That means this isn't the only beach-head."

Anselm tapped her on the shoulder. She followed his pointing arm. Another golem strode off, this one heading northwest, along the coastline. As fast as a trotting man. Slower than a horse—but untiring, needing no food or rest, traveling as well at night as in the day. A hundred and twenty miles in twenty-four hours, and carrying, in stone hands, written orders.

"Nobody's prepared!" Ash shifted in her war-saddle. "They didn't just fool *our* spy networks, Robert. The banks, the priests, the princes . . . God help us. They aren't after the Turks. They never *were* after the Turks . . ."

"They're after us," Robert Anselm grunted, and wheeled to ride with the column. "It's a fucking invasion."

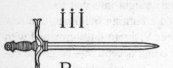

iii

BY THE TIME they caught the hastily loaded baggage train on the low slopes of the foothills, the head of the column was already vanishing up into a cliff-topped valley. Ash rode between a hundred archers and a hundred men-at-arms. Wheel ruts churned the road and the low gorse, the last abandoned wagons marking where the pack animals had left the high road. Ash squinted through air that began to waver as the morning grew hot. Probably a river flowed down through the valley, in winter. Dry, now.

Robert Anselm, Euen Huw, Joscelyn van Mander, her pages and the steward Henri Brant clustered under her banner as two hundred armed men rode by. Tack jingled.

Ash thumped her fist on her saddle. Her breath came short. "If they're burning Genoa, they're prepared to be at war with Savoy, France, the Italian cities, the Emperor . . . sweet Green Christ!"

Van Mander scowled. "It's impossible!"

"It's *happening*. Joscelyn, I want your lances up front as the vaward. Euen, take charge of the archers; Robert, you have the mounted men-at-arms. Henri, can the pack animals keep up?"

The steward, in ill-fitting padded armor now, nodded his head enthusiastically. "We can see what's behind us. They'll keep up!"

"Okay, let's go."

Not until she rode into the steep sided valley, and its shelter, did she realize how the increasing breeze had drummed in her ears, out on the moor. The silence here

194

now echoed with horses' hooves, harness jangling, men muttering. Sun slanted through sparse pines on the valley floor. The promontories either side were thick with pine trees, broken deadfalls. And thick with undergrowth, at the cliff edges, where the trees didn't rob briars of sustenance.

Her neck prickled. With complete clarity, Ash thought, *shit, that's why they didn't attack; they've bounced us back into an ambush!* and opened her mouth to yell.

A storm of eighty arrows blacked the air. A throng of shafts hit home, all in Joscelyn van Mander's lead lance. For a second it was as if nothing had happened. The whirring whine died. Then, a man screamed, metal flashed; another thicket of shafts jutted from horses' flanks, from men's shoulders, from the visor of a sallet; seven horses screeched and reared and the head of the column became a chaos of men running, dismounted, trying to control fear-stricken horses.

Ash lost The Sod's rein. The gray gelding bucked and sprang straight up, all four hooves off the ground, came down on age-hardened pine tree roots—six black-fletched arrows sticking out of his neck and front quarters—and she felt the bone of his hind leg shatter.

She went sideways out of the saddle as he went down. One glimpse let her see men up high on the steep sides of the valley, shooting wicked small recurved bows, and the next mass arrow-flight shrieked down through the sparse trees and took Ned Aston's rearward lance into rioting horses and falling men and sheer, bloody chaos.

She hit the foot of a tree with a metallic crunch, hard enough to compress the plates in her brigandine. A dismounting man hauled her up onto her feet—Pieter?—her personal banner gripped in his other hand.

Her gray horse screamed. She leaped back from his thrashing smashed legs; stepped in, sword in hand—how?

when?—and slashed open the big vein in his throat.

The whole length of the valley seethed with screaming, rioting horses. A bay mare broke past Aston, running toward the moorland.

An arrow took it down.

Every exit blocked.

She steadied herself, body clamped tight up to the sticky resinous trunk of a pine tree, visor slammed up, staring around in desperation. A dozen or more men down, rolling on the dirt; the rest wheeling their mounts, looking for cover—but there is no cover—riding toward the foot of the seventy-degree slope—but no way up it. Bodkin-headed arrows thunked into flesh, bristled from the hastily roped towering loads on the mules.

The way ahead—blocked. A huddle of men, van Mander down; six of his men trying to drag him under the lip of the dry river bed, as if six inches of earth could protect them from a hundred murderous, razor-sharp arrow-heads—

Big Isobel, hauling on the reins of a mule, threw up her arms and sat down. A wooden shaft, as thick around as a man's thumb, stuck through her cheek, and through her mouth, and out of the back of her skull. Vomit and blood spilled over her brown linen bodice. The metal arrow-head dripped.

Ash slammed her visor down. She risked a look up at the cliff edge. Light glinted from a helmet. An arm moved. The tops of bows were a moving thicket. One man stood up to shoot, and she could barely see his head and shoulders. How many up there: fifty? A hundred?

Coldly realistic, she thought: Girl, you're not so special that you can't die yet, shot to pieces in some stupid ambush in some nameless hills. We can't shoot back, we can't get up the sides, we're fish in a barrel, we're dead.

No, we're not.

That simple: not even time to formulate a question for her saint's voice. She grabbed the banner-bearer's arm, her idea fully formed, plain, obvious and dirty.

"You, you and you; with me, *now!*"

She ran fast enough that she outdistanced her banner-bearer and two squires, thumping down behind the baggage mules as the Visigoth arrow-storm shrieked overhead.

"Get the torches out!" she screamed at Henri Brant. Her steward stared, gap-toothed mouth wide open. "The fucking pitch *torches*, now! Get Pieter!"

She grabbed Pieter Tyrrell as Rickard ran back with him, all of them crouching crammed behind the squealing pack mules. Her banner-bearer gripped the pole in gauntleted hands and ducked his head against arrows. The air stank of mule dung, and blood and the fierce resin of the chine's forested slopes.

"Pieter, take these—" she dug in her pack for flint and steel, could only jerk her chin at the bundles of torches with pitch-soaked heads that Henri Brant slashed free from binding cords with his dagger. "Take these and take six men. Ride like hell *up* this valley, ahead of us—look like you're running away. Climb the slope. Fire the trees on the cliff-top. Drag the torches on ropes behind your horses. As soon as there's a fire, cut around northwest. If you don't pick us up on the north road, wait for me at the Brenner. Got all that?"

"Fire? Christ, boss, a forest *fire?*"

"Yes. Go!"

Flint and steel sparked. The soft tinder in the box glowed, red and black.

"It's done!" Pieter Tyrrell swung around, crouching, to yell out half a dozen names.

Ash scuttled across the slope. A Visigoth crossbow bolt blew an explosion of splinters off a pine trunk, a yard

ahead of her and the banner. She flung up an arm, cring-
ing. Splinters rattled across her breastplate and vambraces.
The soles of her riding boots skidded on the needle-
covered slope. She slammed down beside Robert Anselm,
behind a semi-fallen pine. "Have them ready to attack
when I give the word."

"That's a fuck of a slope! We'll be cut to pieces!"

Ash glanced around at sweating, swearing men-at-arms,
mostly in brigandines and long riding boots over leg armor, and carrying polearms that suddenly seemed clumsy
under the low, stark branches of dry pines. Their faces
turned to her. She slitted her eyes and stared up the gorge-
like slopes of the dry river chine. You couldn't ride up
this slope, or run up it: too steep. Weapon in one hand,
the other to help scramble up. And so few trees for cover,
so exposed, exhausted before you hit the men up there in
cover—

"You're going in under cover of bows and arquebuses.
Those fuckers will be too busy to see you coming!" It
was a lie, and she knew it. "Robert, watch me for the
signal!"

Ash sheathed her sword. Its scabbard rattled against her
legs as she flung herself again across empty ground.
Someone shrieked up on the top of the valley. Puffs of
dust went up from the earth, and she caught her foot on
an arrow buried to the fletching and stumbled behind the
second line of braying pack-mules to the archers.

She was grinning so hard it hurt.

"Okay!" Ash slid to a halt beside Euen Huw, de facto
captain of archers. "Oil pots and rags. Try for fire-
arrows."

Henri Brant, unexpectedly still with her, yelled, "We
don't have proper fire-arrows here! We weren't expecting
a siege, so I didn't bring any!"

She slammed her arm around the steward's shoulders.

"Don't matter! Do your best. With luck, we won't need it. Euen, how are we on ammunition?"

"Hackbutters are low. Bolt and arrows enough, though. Boss, we can't stay here, we're getting cut to pieces!"

A man in Blue Lion livery screamed and ran down the slope, arms flailing, toward the bottom of the valley. His boots skidded in the dry river course. A dozen arrows thunked into his legs. He hit dirt, rolled, took a bolt in the face, and lay thrashing and screeching.

"Keeping shooting! Hard and fast as you can. Give those fuckers up there hell!" She grabbed Euen by the arm. "Hold on for five minutes. Be prepared to remount and *go* when I give the signal!"

Ash put her free hand on her bollock dagger, half intending to drop down to the dry river course and the dying man. A figure in padded armor and wearing a woollen hood shot past her. Ash, halfway back to the men-at-arms, her group dodging from tree to tree, suddenly thought *why the hood?* and realized she knew the long, loping run: *Fuck, that's Florian!*

She took one look over her shoulder and saw the surgeon with the man's arm over her shoulder. He—*she*—bodily dragged the man under fallen, dead pine branches. Arrows chipped and thunked into the wood.

Come on, Pieter! Two more minutes and I'm going to *have* to attack, we're being slaughtered down here!

Acrid air rasped her throat.

The skyline above burst into flame.

Ash coughed. She wiped streaming eyes and looked up at the cliff-top. One minute a wisp of black smoke, the air shimmering hard enough to make seeing anyone up on the cliff-top impossible. The next—red fire spouted from branches, from brush, from the deadfalls of old, dry pine branches. A resin-impregnated roar blasted the air.

She had an instant's vision of a man with his recurved

bow raised, a hundred black-fletched arrows whistling between the trees—one magnificent roll of smoke and super-
heated air—

Red flames roared up, obliterating the tree-line at the
top of the cliffs.

Up there on the cliff-top, from further back, came the
terrified screeching of horses.

Her eyes streaming, she prayed, *Thank you, Christ, I
don't have to try to send people up that slope!*

"Okay, let's go!" Her voice was hard, loud and shrill.
It carried over the squeals of mules, the shrieks of mutilated men, the last two shots from an arquebus.

She seized the arm of the standard-bearer, pushing him
and the twelve-foot Blue Lion flag on up the valley path
ahead.

"Mount up! Ride! *GO!*"

The world was a chaos of men on horses, men running
for horses, the thrum of arrows, a piercing long shrill
scream that brought her gut up into her throat, the creak-
ing whine of mules, and men she knows yelling orders:
Robert Anselm with the men-at-arms mounted up and
moving under the Lion standard, Euen Huw cursing the
archers in Welsh and fluent Italian; the pack beasts moving, Father Godfrey Maximillian hauling them, with one
body slumped over the front of a framework packed eight-
foot-high with bundles; Henri Brant with two arrows jutting out from his ribs under his right arm.

A scream broke her concentration. Two men in black
livery broke cover on the skyline. They tumbled down the
slope toward her banner, and her. Ash yelled "Shoot!"
even as a dozen clothyard arrows with bodkin heads
punched through mail shirts and into their bodies, one
man cartwheeling, the other sliding down on his back in
a rumble of clods of earth, one leg in front, one trailing

behind under his body, broken and dead before he stopped
moving—

Ash whipped around, seized the rein of a roan that Philibert thrust at her, and hoisted herself into the saddle. One
slap sent the boys' mounts ahead, on up the valley. She
dug in spurs, aware of her banner-bearer running for his
horse; then the pack train moved, the mounted archers
shot past her in a thunder of hooves, Euen whooping and
the men-at-arms at full gallop, twenty or more of them
riding double with wounded or dead men over the front
of their saddles. The women and Godfrey and Floria del
Guiz ran past, more wounded men over the backs of
mules, abandoned stores spilling halfway down the valley
back to the Genoese moors.

"What the fuck are you doing here?" Ash bawled at
Florian. "I thought you stayed in Cologne!"

The surgeon, one of her arms over the back of a blood-
soaked man on a mule, grinned up at Ash from a filthy
face. "Someone has to keep an eye on you!"

The main body of men-at-arms galloped past, a hundred and fifty men shouting; Ash reined in for a second
for her banner-bearer and half a dozen knights to catch
up. Her eyes poured water. She wiped her face on her
leather gauntlets. The top of the cliff swam. Fire licked
out, catching the tops of the pines lower down the
slope, nearer to her; the pines that grew tall out of the
valley, reaching up for the light.

A man on fire ran off the steep edge of the cliff, cartwheeling down, arms and legs and body blazing. His
corpse slid to a halt three yards away from her, blackened
skin still bubbling.

Behind her, a trail of broken stores, thrashing horses
and dead and wounded men's bodies lay strewn back
down the valley. Heat from the fire brought sweat to her
face. She wiped her mouth and took her glove away black.

"GO!" she yelled, and the roan danced in a circle before she could bring it up and spur in the wake of two hundred men riding up the bed of the dry chine. Smoke stank.

A stag broke cover further up the line, springing straight through the line of galloping archers; and the air above the tree tops shrieked full of kestrels, owls, buzzards.

She coughed. Her eyes cleared.

A hundred yards: a quarter of a mile: the path rising—

A faint wind from the north freshened her face.

In the forest above—and *behind* her, now—the fire roared.

The valley steepened at the end of the chine, and she caught up with Robert Anselm and Euen Huw, under their respective pennants, hurrying the column on and up the earthy cliffs.

"Stick to the dry river bed," she yelled over the thump of hooves, exultant. "Don't stop for anything. If the wind changes, we're fucked!"

Anselm jerked a thumb at the slope in front of him, and a dead man. "We're not the first through here. Looks like your *husband* had the same idea."

Something about the fallen body made her check her horse. Ash leaned to peer down between shifting hooves. A dead man—lying back over the low fork of a pine tree, spine snapped. With his face bashed in, there was no telling what color his hair or skin had been, under the red and black clots. His clothing had been white. Tunic and trousers, under mail. She recognized the livery.

"That's Asturio Lebrija." Ash, oddly moved, shifted her weight, steadying the roan. Foam flew back as the horse lifted and shook his head.

"Maybe young del Guiz didn't make it." Anselm's grim pleasure was evident in his voice. "There could be

Visigoth patrols all over. They won't want news of the invasion getting out.''

Her roan jerked at the crackling of the fire. Ash reined back, letting the last of van Mander's two lances pass her. The men's mounts scrambled, hooves sliding on the thick coat of needles on the sloping forest floor. The air stank of pitch and resin.

I've done it, I've got them out, I can't let it slip now!

We can be caught before we reach the mountains. We can find the passes closed, even in summer. Or that fucking wind can change, and we can fry.

''Get up front, see they don't bog down! Keep them going up into the hills. I want to get above the tree-line, *fast*.''

Robert Anselm was gone almost before she finished speaking.

Ash gazed down now. Between the thin tops of pine trees below her on the slope, oddly undramatic from here: coils of black smoke, drifting up to smudge the sky, and the occasional flicker of red. This fire will burn the hills black. It is unstoppable, and she knows it. There will be peasants who own olive groves, vineyards, sick or weak families, who will curse her name. Huntsmen, charcoal-burners, goat-herds . . .

She ached in every muscle. Her brigandine and boots stank with her dead horse's blood. She strained her vision, trying to see if, on the coast, more of the golems were moving with their unceasing, mechanical tread.

In the far distance, metal eagle standards winked in the sun. The smoke from Genoa hid anything else.

A rider passed her, a mounted archer with blood running out from under the wrist of his padded jack. No one behind him. The last man out.

''Jan-Jacob!'' Ash steered the roan in beside the archer and caught his reins as he sagged forward. She bent low to avoid jagged pine branches, and rode on up at the back of her column, leading the horse and the semi-conscious man.

Behind her, the North African invasion of Europe began.

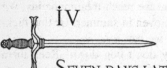

iV

SEVEN DAYS LATER, Ash stood slightly in advance of her lance-leaders, master gunner, surgeon and priest, on the open ground directly in front of a tournament stand at Cologne. The Emperor's household guard surrounded her.

Imperial banners cracked in the wind.

She could smell the scent of the raw wood nailed together into box seating, under Frederick's yellow and black silk canopies. The scent of pine resin made her momentarily shiver. A sound of steel on steel came clashing from the tournament barriers. Play-combat—enough to maim a man, but play-combat all the same.

Her eyes sought the Imperial box, traveled along the rows of faces. All the nobles of the Germanic court and their guests. No ambassadors from Milan or Savoy. No one from any kingdom south of the Alps. A few men from the League of Constance. Some French, some Burgundians . . .

No Fernando del Guiz.

Floria del Guiz's voice, barely loud enough to carry to Ash, murmured, "Seats up the back. On the left. My stepmother. Constanza."

Ash's eyes shifted. Among the hennins and veils of the

ladies, she caught a glimpse of Constanza del Guiz. But not her son. The old woman sat alone. "Right. Let's get this over with. I want a word with her . . ."

Swords clashed a way off, in the wattle enclosure. Coldness lives in her belly, now. Anticipation.

The wind swept over Ash, over the green hills, down toward the white walls of Cologne, containing its tiled blue roofs and the spires of its churches. There were horses on the high road, and in the distance a few peasants in their shifts with hose rolled up were visible, wearing wide straw hats against the heat and cutting a small copse of ten-year-old chestnut trees for fencing.

And what chance of them bringing in this year's wheat harvest?

Ash returned her gaze to Frederick of Hapsburg, Holy Roman Emperor, leaning in his throne to listen to his counselor. He scowled as the advisor concluded.

"Mistress Ash, you ought to have defeated them!" his dry voice raged, loud enough to be heard by all present. "These are just serf-troops from the land of stone and twilight!"

"But—"

"If you can't defeat a scout force of *Visigoths*, for the Green Christ's sake, what are you doing calling yourself a mercenary battle leader?"

"But—!"

"I had thought better of you. But no wise man trusts a woman! Your husband will answer for this!"

"*But*— Oh, fuck it! You mean you think I've made you look bad." Ash rested one steel-plated arm on top of the other and met Frederick's faded blue gaze. She could feel Robert Anselm bristle, without looking at him. Even Joscelyn van Mander's intense florid face scowled—but that might have been pain from his bandaged leg.

"Forgive me if I'm not impressed. I've just come from

calling my muster roll. Fourteen men wounded, who're here in the city hospice, and two so badly mutilated I'll have to give them pensions. Ten men dead. One of them Ned Aston.'' She halted, at a loss, knowing as she spoke that she was making a cock of it: ''I've been in the field since I was a child; this isn't ordinary war. It isn't even bad war. This is—''

''Excuses!'' Frederick spat.

''*No*.'' Ash took a step forward, registering Frederick's household guard shift their stances. ''This *isn't* the way Visigoths fight!'' She gestured at Frederick's captains. ''Ask anyone who's campaigned down south. My guess is they had cavalry squadrons out ready, patrolling for ten or twenty miles inland, all down the coast. They *let* us ride in. They let Lamb in. So they could keep news from getting out until it was too late to do anything about it! They anticipated everything we did. That's way too disciplined for Visigoth slaves and peasant-troops!''

Ash dropped her left hand to grip her scabbard, for comfort. ''I heard news, coming back through the Gotthard monastery. They're supposed to have a new commander. No one knows anything. It's chaos down south! It's taken us seven days to get back here. Have you had post-riders back yet? Has *any* news come north of the Alps?''

The Emperor Frederick held up his goblet for wine and ignored her.

He sat in his gilded chair, among a dazzle of men in fur-trimmed velvet doublets, and women in brocade gowns; those furthest away watching the tournament avidly, those nearest ready to smile or frown as the Emperor might require. There were great papier-mâché models of black Eagles ornamenting the tourney stand above him: the Empire's heraldic Beast.

Under cover of the Imperial servants fussing, just loud

enough for her to hear, Robert Anselm murmured, "How can he be holding a fucking *tournament*, for Christ's sake? There's a fucking *army* on his doorstep!"

"If they haven't crossed the Alps, he thinks he's safe."

Florian del Guiz returned from a brief foray into the crowd. She put her hand on Ash's armored shoulder. "I don't see Fernando here, and nobody will talk to me about him. They all clam up solid."

"Fuck." Ash privately glanced at his sister. With her face washed, you could see the surgeon had her brother's sprinkle of freckles across the nose, although her cheeks had lost the roundness of youth. Ash thought, If *anyone* in this company looks like a woman disguised, it's Angelotti—Antonio's too beautiful to live. Not Florian.

"Can you find anyone to tell you if my husband's come back to Cologne?" Ash looked questioningly back at Godfrey Maximillian.

The priest pursed his lips. "I can't find anyone who spoke to him after his men left the St. Bernard Pass hospice."

"What the *hell* is he doing? Don't tell me: he ran into some more Visigoth aforeriders and decided it was a great idea to defeat the invading army on his own . . ."

Anselm grunted agreement. "Rash."

"He's not dead. I couldn't be that lucky. At least I've got command again."

"De facto,"[43] Godfrey murmured.

Ash shifted from one foot to the other. The Imperial serving of food and drink was obviously designed to keep her standing and waiting. Probably until Frederick devised some suitable penalty for losing a skirmish. "This is just playing games!"

---

[43]Latin: "by the fact (of doing it)," rather than de jure, "by right of the law."

Antonio Angelotti muttered, "Holy Christ, madonna, doesn't this man know what's going on?"

"Your Imperial Majesty!" Ash waited until Frederick glanced down at her. "The Visigoths sent messengers out. I saw clay walkers going west to Marseilles, and southeast toward Florence. I would have sent a raiding party after them, but by then we were in their ambush. Do you really imagine they'll stop with Genoa and Marseilles and Savoy?"

Her bluntness stung him; Frederick blinked. "It's true, Lady del Guiz, there is very little word coming back over the Alps since they closed the Gotthard pass. Even my bankers can tell me nothing. Nor my bishops. You would think they owned no paid watchers. . . . And you: how can you come back and be able to tell me so little?" He pointed a testy finger at her. "*You* should have stayed! You ought to have observed for a longer period of time!"

"If I had, the only way you could reach me now would be through prayer!"

It's about ten heartbeats before she's arrested and thrown out, by her own estimation, but Ash's head is full of Pieter Tyrrell, in a Cologne inn room with thirty gold louis and half his left hand cleaved off: little and ring and middle fingers gone. With Philibert, missing since one snow-bound night on the Gotthard; Ned Aston dead; and Isobel, without even a body for a funeral.

Ash chose her moment and spoke measuredly.

"Your Majesty, I've visited the bishop today, here in the city." She watched the puzzled expression on Frederick's face. "Ask your priests and lawyers, Your Majesty. My husband has deserted me—without consummating our marriage."

Floria made a stifled noise.

The Emperor switched his attention to Floria del Guiz. "Is this true, Master Surgeon?"

Floria said, immediately and without apparent qualm, "As true as I am a man standing here before you, Your Majesty."

"Therefore, I've applied to have the marriage annulled," Ash said rapidly, "I owe you no feudal obligation, Your Imperial Majesty. And the company's contract with you expired when the Burgundian troops withdrew from Neuss."

Bishop Stephen inclined from his seat to speak into the Emperor's ear. Ash watched the Holy Roman Emperor Frederick's lined, dry face harden.

"Well, hey," Ash said, as casual as it is possible to be with eight hundred armed men at one's disposal. "Make me an offer and I'll put it before the men. But I think the Company of the Lion can get work anywhere we want, now. And at a good price."

Anselm, very quietly, groaned, "Shiit . . ."

It is a piece of unwise bravado and she knows it. Political trickery, hard riding and bad food, and the unnecessary fighting; the unnecessary deaths; none of the last month can be paid for by talking back like an unmannerly servant. But some tension leaves her, all the same, with the malice in her tone.

Antonio Angelotti chuckled. Van Mander slapped her backplate. She ignored the two men, her attention on Frederick, relishing how taken aback he looked. She heard Godfrey Maximillian sigh. Jubilant, she smiled at the Emperor. She did not quite dare to say *You forget—we're not yours. We're mercenaries*, but she let her expression say it for her.

"Green Christ!" Godfrey muttered. "It's not enough for you to have Sigismund of the Tyrol as an enemy, you want the Holy Emperor, too!"

Ash moved her hands to cup her elbows: the palms of her gauntlets feeling the cold steel of elbow-counters.

"We weren't getting another German contract, whichever way you look at it. I've told Geraint to get the camp dismount started. We'll go into France, maybe. We're not going to be short of business now."

Casual, ruthless; there is a brutal tone to her voice. Some of it is rough grief for men she knows who are killed or maimed now. Most of it is gut-deep, savage joy that she is still alive.

Ash looked up into Godfrey's bearded face and linked her armored arm with his. "Come on, Godfrey. This is what we do, remember?"

"This is what we do if you're not in a dungeon in Cologne—" Godfrey Maximillian abruptly stopped talking.

A cluster of priests pushed through the crowd. Among the brown cowls, Ash glimpsed one bare head. Something wrong about it . . .

Men jostled, Frederick's Captain of the Guard shouting a challenge; then a space cleared before the stands, and six priests from the St. Bernard hospice knelt before the Emperor.

It was a moment before Ash recognized the bruised, disheveled man with them.

"That's de Quesada." She frowned. "Our Visigoth ambassador. Daniel de Quesada."

Godfrey sounded unusually perturbed. "What's he doing back here?"

"Christ knows. If he's here, where's Fernando? What's Fernando been playing at? Daniel de Quesada . . . There's a man whose head is going home from here in a basket." Automatically, she checked the position of her men: Anselm, van Mander, and Angelotti armed and in armor; Rickard with the banner; Floria and Godfrey unarmed. "He's in shit shape . . . what the hell's happened to him?"

Daniel de Quesada's shaven scalp shone, bloody. Old

brown blood clotted his cheeks. His beard had been ripped out by the roots. He knelt, barefoot, his head up, facing Frederick of Hapsburg and the German princes. His gaze skated across Ash as if he didn't recognize the silver-haired woman in armor.

Some disquiet tugged at her. *Not ordinary war, not even bad war*—What? she thought, frustrated. Why am I worried now? I've got out of this political chicanery. We're mauled, but the Company's been hurt before; we'll get over it. I've won. It's business as usual; what's the *problem*?

Ash stood outside the shade of the tourney stand, in the blazing summer sun. The clash of breaking lances and cheers echoed across from the green grass. A fresh wind brought her a scent of coming rain.

The Visigoth turned his head, surveying the court. Ash saw sweat bead on his forehead. He spoke with a febrile excitement she had seen before, in men who expected to die within the next few minutes.

"Kill me!" de Quesada invited the Hapsburg Emperor. "Why not? I've done what I came to do."

He spoke in fluent German.

"We were a lie, to keep you occupied. My lord the King-Caliph Theodoric sent other ambassadors also, to the courts of Savoy and Genoa, Florence, Venice, Basle and Paris, with similar instructions."

Ash, in her workaday Carthaginian, asked, "What's happened to my husband? Where did you part company with Fernando del Guiz?"

Exactly how much of an unpardonable, irrelevant interruption it was as far as Frederick of Hapsburg was concerned, Ash could see in his face. She held herself in an alert tension, waiting either for his anger, or Daniel de Quesada to reply.

Offhandedly, de Quesada said, "Master del Guiz freed

me when he decided to swear loyalty to our King-Caliph Theodoric.''

"*Fernando?* Swear *loyalty* to—?" Ash stared. "To the *Visigoth Caliph?*"

Behind Ash, Robert Anselm gave a great barking laugh. Ash was unsure whether she wanted to laugh or cry.

De Quesada spoke with a fixed gaze on the face of the Emperor, driving home each word with malice and visible instability. "We—the young man you sent as my escort— met with another division of our army south of the Gotthard Pass. He was twelve men against twelve hundred. Del Guiz was allowed, on condition of his swearing fealty, to live and keep his estate.''

"He wouldn't do that!" Ash protested. She stuttered, "I mean, he wouldn't—he just *wouldn't*. He's a *knight*. This is just misinformation. Rumor. Some enemy's lies.''

Neither the ambassador nor the Emperor heeded her.

"His estate is not yours to give, Visigoth! It's mine!" Frederick of Hapsburg twisted around in the ornamented chair, snarling at his chancellor and legal staff. "Put the young gentleman and his family and estates under an act of attainder. For treason."

One of the fathers from the St. Gotthard hospice cleared his throat. "We found this man Quesada wandering lost in the snow, Your Imperial Highness. He knew no name but yours. We thought it charity to bring him here. Forgive us if we have done wrong.''

Ash muttered to Godfrey, "If they'd met up with Visigoth forces, what was he doing wandering around in the snow?''

Godfrey spread his broad-fingered hands and just shrugged. "My child, only God knows that at the moment!''

"Well, when He tells you, you tell me!''

The little man on the Hapsburg throne wrinkled his lip at Daniel de Quesada, in a quite unconscious disgust. "He is mad, obviously. What can he know of del Guiz? We were hasty—cancel the attainder. What he says is nonsense; convenient lies. Fathers, have him confined in your house in the city. Beat the demon out of him. Let us see how this war goes; he shall be our prisoner, not their ambassador."

"It is no *war*!" Daniel de Quesada shouted. "If you *knew*, you would surrender now, before you take more than a skirmish's casualties! The Italian cities are learning that lesson now—"

One of the Imperial men-at-arms moved to stand behind Quesada where the ambassador knelt, and pricked his throat with a dagger, the thick steel blade old and nicked, but perfectly serviceable.

The Visigoth gabbled, "Do you know what you're facing? Twenty years! Twenty years of ship-building, and making weapons, and training men!"

The Emperor Frederick chuckled. "Well, well, we have no quarrel with you. Your battles with mercenaries are no longer my concern." A dry little smile at Ash, all her earlier malice repaid with interest.

"You call yourself a 'Holy Roman Empire,' " de Quesada said. "You are not even the shadow of the Empty Chair.[44] As for the Italian cities—we find them worth it for their gold, but for nothing else. As for a rabble of farmers on horseback from Basle and Cologne and Paris and Grenada—why should we want *them*? If we wanted to take fools for slaves, the Turkish fleet would be burning now at Cyprus."

---

[44]Context leads me to suspect that this refers, in fact, to the city of Rome—perhaps the Papal throne, the chair of Peter? The textual reference is obscure.

Frederick of Hapsburg waved his nobles down. "You are among strangers, if not enemies. Are you a madman, to behave like this?"

"We don't want your Holy Empire." De Quesada, still on his knees, shrugged. "But we'll take it. We'll take everything that lies between us and the richest of all."

His brown eyes went to the Burgundian guests in the court. Ash guessed them there still celebrating the peace of Neuss. Quesada fixed his gaze on a face she recognized, from other campaigning seasons—Duke Charles of Burgundy's Captain of the Guard, Olivier de la Marche.

Quesada whispered, "Everything that's between us and the kingdoms and duchies of Burgundy, we will take. Then we will have Burgundy."

Of all princedoms of Europe, the richest, Ash remembered someone once saying. She looked from the bloodstained, middle-aged Visigoth man up to the Duke's representative in the tourney stand, whose lugubrious face she also recognized from the tournament circuit. The big soldier in red and blue livery laughed. Olivier de la Marche had a loud, practiced voice from shouting on battlefields; he did not modulate it now. Snickers came from the court hangers-on pressed close around him. Bright surcoats, brilliant armor, the gilded pommels of rich blades, confident clean-shaven faces; all the visible power of knightly chivalry. Ash felt a momentary sympathy for Daniel de Quesada.

"My Duke has recently conquered Lorraine,"[45] Olivier de la Marche said amiably. "Not to mention his defeats of my lord King of France." Tactfully, he avoided looking at Frederick of Hapsburg, or mentioning Neuss. "We have an army that is the envy of Christendom. Try us, sir. Try us. I promise you a warm welcome."

---

[45] In 1475.

"And I promise you a cold greeting." Daniel de Quesada's eyes gleamed. Ash's hand went to her sword hilt, without conscious intention. The man's body movements shouted wrongness, all human caution abandoned. Fanatics fight that way, and assassins. Ash came alive, a snapshot vision took in the men around her, the corner of the tourney stand, the emperor's pennant, the guards, her own command group—

Daniel de Quesada shrieked.

Mouth a wide rictus, he moved nothing else, but the cords of his throat jutted out, his scream lifting above the noise of the cheering crowd, until a silence began to spread out from where they stood. Ash felt Godfrey Maximillian beside her grab at his pectoral cross. The hairs at the back of her neck lifted as if cold air blew over them. Quesada knelt and screamed a pure, uncaring rage.

Silence.

The Visigoth ambassador lowered his head, glaring at them all from bloodshot eyes. The torn skin of his cheeks bled freshly.

"We take Christendom," he whispered, raggedly. "We take your cities. All your cities. And you, Burgundy, *you* ... Now we have begun, I am permitted to show you a sign."

Something made Ash look up.

She realized a second later that she was following the direction of Daniel de Quesada's bloodshot, ecstatic gaze. Straight up into the blue sky.

Straight into the white-hot blaze of the noon sun.

"Shit!" Tears flooded her eyes. She rubbed her gloved hand across her face. It came away wet.

She saw nothing. She was blind.

"Christ!" She shrieked. Voices howled with her. Close, in the silk-canopied stand; further off, on the tourney field. Screams. She rubbed her hands frantically across her eyes. She could see nothing—nothing—

Ash stood for one second, both leather-covered palms across her eyes. Blackness. Nothing. She pressed hard. She felt, through the thin leather, the balls of her eyes shifting as she looked. She took her hands away. Darkness. Nothing.

Wetness: tears or blood? No pain—

Someone cannoned into her. She grabbed, caught an arm: someone screamed, a whole host of voices screaming, and she couldn't make out what the words were, then:

"The sun! The *sun*!"

She was crouching without knowing how, her gauntlets stripped off, her bare hands flat on the dry earth. A body pressed into her side. She gripped at its sweaty warmth.

A thin voice that she almost did not recognize as Robert Anselm's whispered, "The sun's . . . gone."

Ash raised her head.

Prickles of light in her vision resolved into patterns. Faint dots. Not close—far, far away, above the horizons of the world.

She looked down, in faint unnatural light, and made out the shape of her hands. She looked up and saw nothing but a scatter of unfamiliar stars on the horizon.

In the arch of the sky above her was nothing, nothing at all, except darkness.

Ash whispered, "*He put the sun out.*"

*[E-mail printouts included in correspondence found inter-
polated in this copy of the 3rd edition.]*

Message: #19 (Pierce Ratcliff/misc.)
Subject: Ash
Date: 6/11/00 at 10.10 a.m.
From: Longman@   *format address and other details*
                            non-recoverably deleted

Pierce--

THE *SUN* GOES OUT?????
    And you're WHERE?

Message: #22 (Anna Longman/misc.)
Subject: Ash
Date: 6/11/00 at 6.30 p.m.
From: Ratcliff@   *format address and other*
                            details non-recoverably deleted

Anna--

I am stuck in a hotel room in Tunis. One of Isobel Napier-Grant's
young assistants is instructing me on how to download and send e-
mails through the telephone system here—not as easy a task as you
may imagine. The truck doesn't go out to the site until tonight, under
cover of darkness. Archaeological teams can be fanatical about
security. I don't blame Isobel one bit, if she's got what she says she
has.

I'd hoped, when she said she was coming out here, that she might
find confirming evidence—so unlikely anyway, even for a potsherd,

217

with the hundreds of square miles of territory to be searched—but THIS!

'The sun goes out.' Yes, of course. As far as I can discover, there was no actual eclipse visible in Europe in 1475 or 1476; but later chroniclers obviously found it an irresistible piece of dramatic licence. I must say that I do, too.

--Pierce

Message: #20 (Pierce Ratcliff/misc.)
Subject: Ash, historical background
Date: 6/11/00 at 6.44 p.m.
From: Longman@   *format address and other details non-recoverably deleted*

Pierce--

BUT!!! I've been looking this up, Pierce. All the wars I can find, for the whole of 1476–1477, are Duke Charles the Bold of Burgundy's attempts to conquer Lorraine, and link up his 'Middle Kingdom' across Europe. Then there's his defeat by the Swiss at Nancy; and the indecent haste with which his enemies divided up Burgundy between them on his death. There are the usual wars between the Italian city states, but that's it; there's *nothing* about North Africa!

Don't tell me this is Euro-centric historicism! Isn't an invasion of Italy and Switzerland a bit BIG to miss?

I repeat, Pierce, WHAT VISIGOTH INVASION???!!!

--Anna

- -

Message: #23 (Anna Longman/misc.)
Subject: Ash
Date: 6/11/00 at 7.07 p.m.
From: Ratcliff@   *(format address and other details*
                             non-recoverably deleted)

Anna--

I told you that FRAXINUS would cause you to reassess history.

　Very well:

　It is my intention to prove that the North African Visigoth settlement, at one point between approximately AD 1475 and AD 1477, DID mount a military invasion of southern Europe.

　I will be stating that contemporary interest in this raid was lost in the flurry of panic when Charles the Bold was killed in battle in 1477. That was perhaps only to be expected.

　That later historians continue to ignore the episode is due—dare I say—to the preponderance of white, male middle-class academics unwilling to believe that Western Europe might be challenged from Africa? And that a mixed-race culture might prove militarily superior to Caucasian Western Christendom?

--Pierce

- -

Message: #21 (Pierce Ratcliff/misc.)
Subject: Ash, historical background
Date: 6/11/00 at 7.36 p.m.
From: Longman@   *format address and other*
                            details non-recoverably deleted

Pierce--

The problem with this is still that the text gives us an invasion of Europe in 1476 and even the Turks NEVER ACTUALLY SUCCEEDED IN INVADING!!! I know you will say that, according to your present theory, Ash is fighting your North African mediaeval 'Visigoths.' Then WHY IS THERE NO MENTION OF THIS IN MY HISTORY BOOKS?

--Anna

Message: #24 (Anna Longman / ASH)
Subject: Visigoths
Date: 7/11/00 at 5.23 p.m.
From: Ngrant@   *format address and other details*
                            non-recoverably deleted

Anna--

I'm at the site!

Dr Napier-Grant is kindly allowing me to use her satellite notebook PC. There's so much to say that I couldn't wait to try and get a phone call through, the lines here are terrible. Isobel (sorry, that's Dr. N-G, in case you forget) Isobel says I can tell you a bit but she doesn't want it leaking out, because if someone else reads the message then she'll have every archaeologist between here and the North Pole arriving on our doorstep. Those that aren't here already.

I know I'm not supposed to say this, but it's hot and smelly and the only time it's bearable is when we're actually out at the digs—which I'm *not* going to mention the location of, obviously!!! Suffice it to say that we are very near the northern coast of this region of Tunisia. (There are mountains on the southern skyline, they make me think of ice and coldness and somewhere you don't have to stay under shelter between one and five in the afternoon!) Look, you don't want to hear all this, but I can't tell you what I'd like to, and I'm just bursting to

Isobel says that since you're on the verge of ditching the book, I *can* tell you some things. Isobel's a wonderful woman. I've known her since Oxford. She's the last person I can think of who'd get excited unnecessarily. You only have to look at her short hair and sensible shoes. (No, we never did. I wanted to. Isobel isn't keen that way.) And this last twenty-four hours since I got here, she's been skipping about like a schoolgirl! This *could* still turn out to be another Hitler Diaries, but I don't think so.

What have we found? (Not 'we,' of course. Isobel and her wonderful team.)

We've found golems.

Exactly as the text describes them. 'Messenger-golems.' One complete, and some pieces of another. You remember me telling you that Arabic mediaeval engineering was quite up to building singing fountains, and mechanical birds that flap their wings, and all that sort of post-Roman trivia? Very well:

The ASH manuscripts always refer to the 'clay walkers' or 'robots' or 'golem' as *moving* mechanical models of men. This is complete nonsense of course. Imagine building a robot in the fifteenth century! Ornamental devices of some kind, possibly. *Just* possibly. I mean, if you can build metal singing birds—they worked pneumatically or hydraulically, as all the Roman treatises indicate; don't ask me the details, I'm not an engineer!—Then, I suppose, you could build metal models of men, too, like Roger Bacon's Brazen Head, but complete. I don't see why anyone would want to.

That's what I thought, up to twenty-four hours ago. Then there was all the rush of getting a plane out to Tunis, and being driven in some God-awful jeep out to the archaeologists' camp, and then Isobel taking me all the way out here on foot. There are soldiers guarding the camp, all Jeeps and Kalashnikovs, but they don't seem very alert—just a gift from the local government to keep petty pilfering down, I think. Isobel would like to keep it that way. The last thing we want is the military sent into this site. You could destroy the survivals that are five hundred odd years old—

Yes. Isobel's dated them, she's pretty sure they've been in the silt for upwards of four hundred years, and five hundred seems likely; they're not the Victorian curiosities I was afraid I was going to find. These are the messenger-golems of the ASH texts—man-shaped, life-sized carved stone bodies (the complete one is Italian marble), with articulated metal joints at the knees, hips, shoulders, elbows and hands. The stonework on the second one has shattered, but the bronze and brass gears and cogs are complete. *They are golem*!

I confess I don't understand all the professional arguments that are going on between Isobel's team, or rather, I don't understand the technological details. There is a *huge* row breaking out about whether these finds belong to a mediaeval Arab or mediaeval European culture—the Italian marble, you see, although of course Carrara marble was exported across the whole of Christendom at the time, as I've tried to point out. I've given Isobel my copy of the existing ASH translations, indicating that (as I was going to e-mail you to point out) the 'Visigoth' culture of the texts is *not* purely Iberian Gothic, but rather a mixture of Visigothic, Spanish and Arab culture.

I've got this far and I haven't told you the most important discovery so far. You're sitting there in London reading this, and you're thinking, so? So they had mechanical men, as well as mechanical birds, what does this matter?

Isobel has let me examine the surviving golem extremely carefully. This is something that must not get out before she is ready to publish her findings. There are patterns of wear in the metal joints. That isn't all.

There are patterns of wear on the marble surfaces *under* the feet!

The stone is worn away on the carved soles of the feet and under the heels exactly as though this golem has been walking. And I mean walking. Like a man, like you and me, a stone and brass mechanical man, *walking*.

What I have touched—touched, Anna!—is exactly what the ASH texts describe as the Visigoth clay walkers.

They are *real*.

I have to get off this machine, Isobel urgently needs to use it. I'll contact you again as soon as I can. The translations of the documents in section three are in the file I'm sending with this. Don't ditch my book!!! We might have something here that's bigger than anyone ever thought.

What Visigoths? HA!

--Pierce

- -

Message: #28 (Pierce Ratcliff/misc.)
Subject: Ash, media-related projects
Date: 7/11/00 at 6.17 p.m.
From: Longman@

format address and other details non-recoverably deleted

Pierce--

I want you to talk to Dr Napier-Grant, and persuade her that you two should work together, starting NOW. My MD Jonathan Stanley is *very* much in favour of the idea of doing some kind of a tie-in between yourself and Doctor Napier-Grant. She sounds like one of those great British eccentrics who come across brilliantly on the small screen. I can see a possible tv series for her, and there's your original translation of 'Ash'; and then there is what you could do together—a book-of-the-expedition? Do you think you could write a script for a documentary on the expedition? This has *terrific* possibilities!

I'm certain a deal could be arranged. I don't usually say this to my academic authors, but *get yourself an agent*! You need one who handles film and tv rights, as well as non-fiction book translation rights.

It's true we've still got a text that's half mediaeval legend, half historical fact (eclipses!)—and I'm gobsmacked that something like an invasion could be left out of the history books—and how DID these golem MOVE?—but I don't see any of this as a barrier to successful publication. Talk to Dr Napier-Grant about the idea for a joint project and get back to me as soon as you can!

Love, 'Anna

PART THREE

August 1, 1476 AD–August 10, 1476 AD

*"HOW A MAN SCHALL BE ARMYD
AT HIS EASE"*[46]

---

[46]The title of a popular contemporary treatise (c. 1450)
containing instructions for putting on one's knightly armor
for non-cavalry combat: *How a man shall be armed
at his ease when he shall fight on foot.*

i

FORTY PITCH TORCHES flared in the wind under an ink-black daytime sky.

A great lane of people opened in front of Ash as she galloped into the center of the camp outside Cologne. She halted astride Godluc, in full armor, the company banner cracking in the wind above her, the noise loud in the silence. Yellow light blazed across her strained white face. "Geraint! Euen! Thomas!"

Her lance-leader lieutenants ran to stand either side, ready to repeat her words the instant that she spoke, feed them out to the hundreds of her archers and billmen and knights gathering in front of her. Voices began shouting; chaotic in the unnatural dark.

"Listen to *me*. There is," Ash spoke perfectly steadily, "*nothing* for you to be afraid of."

Above, what should have been a June midday blue sky showed only black, empty darkness.

There is no sun.

"*I'm* here. *Godfrey's* here, and he's a priest. You're not damned and you're not in danger—if we were, I'd be the first one out of here!"

No response from any of the hundreds of fearful faces. The torchlight wavers across their shining silver helmets, loses itself in darkness between their crowded, armed bodies.

"Maybe we're going to be like the lands Under the Penance now," Ash continued, "—but—Angelotti's *been*

227

to Carthage, and the Eternal Twilight, and they manage
well enough, and you're not going to let a bunch of
shabby rag-heads outdo the Lion!''

Nothing like a cheer, but they made the first responsive
noise she'd heard out of them: a subdued mutter, full of
fuck! and *shit!* and nobody quite saying the word *desertion*.

"Right," she said briskly. "We're moving. The company's going to strike camp. We've done a night dismount
before; you all know how to do this. I want us loaded and
ready to go at Terce."

A hand went up, just visible in the streaming sooty light
of the makeshift torches. Ash leaned forward in the saddle, peering. She realized it was her steward Henri Brant,
his body still banded with bloodstained cloths, leaning on
the shoulder of her page Rickard. "Henri?"

"Why are we moving? Where are we going?" His
voice sounded so weak, the young black-haired boy beside him shouted his questions up to Ash.

"I'll tell you," Ash said grimly. She sat back in her
saddle, surveying the mass of people, keenly watching for
those slipping away, those already carrying their packs,
those familiar faces she couldn't see present.

"You all know my husband. Fernando del Guiz. Well,
he's gone over to the enemy."

"Is that *true*?" one of the men-at-arms yelled.

Ash, remembering Constanza, rescued from the tourney
field's riot; the tiny woman's absolute distress; her unwillingness to confess to Fernando's peasant wife that the
court nobility knew exactly where her son was—remembering this, she pitched her voice to carry further into the
dark day:

"Yes, it's true."

Over noise, she continued: "For whatever reason, it

seems that Fernando del Guiz has sworn fealty to the Visigoth Caliph.''

She let them take it in, then said measuredly, ''His estates are south of here, in Bavaria, at a place called Guizburg. I'm told Fernando's occupying the castle there. Well—they're not his estates. The Emperor's put him under attainder. But they're still my estates. *Ours*. And that's where we're going. We're going to go south, take what's ours, *and then we'll face this darkness when we're safe behind our own castle walls!*''

The next ten minutes was all shouted arguments, questions, a few ongoing personal quarrels dragged into the discussion, and Ash bellowing at the highest, most carrying pitch of her voice; ram-rodding her authority home.

Robert Anselm leaned from his saddle and murmured in her ear. ''Christ, girl! If we move this camp, we'll have everybody all *over* the place.''

''It'll be chaos,'' she agreed hoarsely. ''But it's this or they panic, run off as refugees, and we're not a company anymore. Fernando's neither here nor there—I'm giving them something we can *do*. Something—*anything*. It really doesn't matter what it is!''

The void above *pulls*, sucks at her. The darkness doesn't fade, doesn't give way to dusk or twilight or dawn; hour upon hour upon hour is going by.

''Doing anything,'' Ash said, ''is better than doing nothing. Even if this *is* the end of the world . . . I'm keeping my people together.''

ii

THE STRIKING OF the Guizburg town clock
reached Ash over the intermittent sound of cannon. Four
bell-chimes. Four hours after what would have been midday.

"It's not an eclipse." Antonio Angelotti, where he sat
at the end of the trestle table, observed without raising his
head: "There's no eclipse due. In any case, madonna, an
eclipse lasts hours at most. Not eight days."

Sheets of ephemerides and his own calculations lay in
front of him. Ash put her elbow on Angelotti's table and
rested her chin on her hand. Inside this room, boards
creaked as Godfrey Maximillian paced up and down. Candlelight shifted. She looked at the shattered frames of the
small windows, wishing for lightening air, for the damp
cold of dawn, the interminable singing of birds, above all
for the sense of freshness, of beginning, that sunrise has
outdoors. Nothing. Nothing but darkness.

Joscelyn van Mander put his head around the door of
the room, between the guards. "Captain, they won't hear
our herald, and they're still shooting at us! The garrison
doesn't even admit your husband's inside the keep."

Antonio Angelotti leaned back in his chair. "They've
heard the proverb, madonna—'a castle which speaks, and
a woman who listens; both will be taken in the end.' "

"They're flying his livery and a Visigoth standard—
he's here," Ash observed. "Send a herald every hour.
Keep shooting back! Joscelyn, let's get inside there *fast*."

As van Mander left, she added, "We're still better off

230

here—as long as we're containing del Guiz, who's a traitor, the Emperor's happy; and we get a chance to stay out of the way and see how hot this Visigoth army really is . . ."

She got up and strode to the window. Cannon fire had exposed the lath and plaster of the wall by the sill, but it would be easy to patch up, she thought, touching the raw dry material. "Angeli, could your eclipse calculations be wrong?"

"No, because nothing that happened accords with the descriptions." Angelotti scratched at the gathered neck of his shirt. Plainly, he had forgotten the ink stone and the sharpened quill: ink liberally dotted his white linen. He looked at his stained fingers in annoyance. "No penumbra, no gradual eating away of the disc of the sun, no uneasiness of the beasts of the field. Just instant, icy lightlessness."

He had bone-framed single-rivet spectacles clamped to his nose for reading. As he squinted through the lenses, in the candlelight, Ash noted the lines at the corners of his eyes, the squinching of flesh between his brows. This is how that face will look in ten years, she thought, when the skin is no longer taut, and the shine is off his gold hair.

He finished, "And Jan tells me the horses weren't bothered beforehand."

Robert Anselm, clumping up stairs and entering the room on the tail of this remark, pulled off his hood and said, "The sun darkened—weakened—once when I was in Italy. We must have had four hours' warning from the horse lines."

Ash spread her hands. "If no eclipse, then what?"

"The heavens are out of order . . ." Godfrey Maximillian did not stop pacing. There was a book in his hands, illuminated in red and blue; Ash might have made the text out with enough time to spell it letter by letter; he paused by one of the candles and flicked from page to page with a rapidity that both impressed her and filled her with contempt for a man who had no better use for his time than to learn to read. He did not even read aloud. He read quickly, and silently.

"So? Edward Earl of March saw *three* suns on the morning of the field of Mortimer's Cross. For the Trinity." Robert Anselm hesitated, as ever, mentioning the current English Yorkist king, then muttered aggressively, "Everyone knows the south exists in an eternal twilight; this is nothing to get worked up about. We've got a war to fight!"

Angelotti took off his spectacles. The white bone frames left a red dint across the bridge of his nose. "I can take down the keep walls here in half a day." On the word *day*, his voice lost impetus.

Ash leaned out of the broken window frame. The town outside was mostly invisible in darkness. She sensed a kind of straining in the air, in the odd warm dusk—cooling, now, perhaps—that wanted to be afternoon. The brown beams and pale plaster of the house's façade were dappled with red, reflections from the huge bonfires burning in the market square below. Lanterns shone at every occupied window. She did not look up at the crown of the sky, where no sun shone, only a deep impenetrable blackness.

She looked up at the keep.

Bonfire-light illuminated only the bottom of the sheer walls, shadows flickering on flints and masonry. Slot-windows were eyelets of darkness. The keep rose into darkness above the town, from steep bare slopes of rock; and the road to the gate ran along one wall, from which the defenders had already shot and dropped more killing objects than she thought they had. A slab-sided building like a block of stone.

That's where he is. In some room behind those walls.

She can envisage the round Norman arches, the wooden floors crammed with bedrolls of men-at-arms, the knights up in the solar on the fourth floor; Fernando perhaps in the great hall, with his dogs and his merchant friends and his handguns . . .

No more than a furlong from where I am now. He could be looking at me.

Why? Why have you done this? What *is* the truth of it?

Ash said, "I don't want the castle damaged so much that we can't defend it when *we're* in there."

All the armed men she could see in the streets near the keep wore livery jackets with the pewter Lion badge fastened to the shoulder; most of those company people who went unarmed—women selling goods, whores, children— had taken up some kind of strips of blue cloth sewn to their garments. Of the town's citizens, she could see nothing, but she could hear them singing mass in the churches. The clock struck the quarter, on the far side of this market square.

She longed for light with a physical desire, like thirst.

"I thought it might end with dawn," she said. "*A* dawn. Any dawn. It still might."

Angelotti stirred his sheets of calculations, scribbled over with the signs of Mercury, Mars, estimations of ballistics. "This is *new*."

Something leonine in the way he stretched his arm reminded Ash of the physical strength he possessed, as well as his male beauty. Points were coming undone at the shoulder of his padded white jack. All the cloth over his chest and arms was pitted with tiny black holes, burned through the linen by sparks from cannon.

Robert Anselm leaned over the master gunner's shoul-

der, studying the scribbled sheets of paper, and they began
to talk in rapid low tones. Anselm thumped the trestle
table with his fist several times.

Ash, watching Robert, was assailed by a paradoxical
feeling of fragility: he and Angelotti were physically large
men, their voices booming now in this room simply because they were used to conversing out of doors. Some
part of her, faced by them, was always fourteen, in her
first decent breastplate (the rest of her harness munition-
quality tat), seeking out Anselm by his campfire after
Tewkesbury and saying, out of the flame-ridden darkness,
raise men for me, I'm fielding a company of my own now.
Asking in the dark because she could not bear a refusal
in cold daylight. And then hours spent sleepless and won-
dering if his curt nod of agreement had been because he
was drunk or joking, until he turned up an hour after sunrise with fifty frowsty, cold, unfed, well-equipped men
carrying bows and bills, whose names she had immediately had Godfrey write onto a muster roll. And silenced
their uncertainty, their jocular complaints and unspoken
hope, with food from the cauldrons she had had Wat Rodway at since midnight. The strands of authority between
commander and commanded are spider-webs.

"Why the fuck doesn't it get light . . . ?" Ash leaned
out further from the broken frame, staring at the castle's
walls above the town. Angelotti's bombard and trebuchet
crews had done no more than knock patches of facing
plaster off the curtain walls, exposing the gray masonry.
She coughed, breathing air that smelled of burning timber,
and pulled herself back into the room.

"The scouts are back," Robert Anselm said laconically. "Cologne's burning. Fires out of control. They say
there's plague. The court's gone. I have thirty different
reports about Frederick of Hapsburg. Euen's lance picked
up a couple of men from Berne. None of the passes south

over the Alps are passable—either Visigoth armies or bad weather.''

Godfrey Maximillian momentarily stopped pacing and looked up from the pages of his book. ''Those men Euen found were part of a procession from Berne to the shrine at St. Walburga's Abbey. Look at their backs. Those lacerations are from iron-tipped whips. They think flagellation will bring back the sun.''

What was similar between Robert Anselm and Godfrey Maximillian, the bald man and the bearded, was perhaps nothing more than breadth of chest, resonance of voice. Whether or not it came from recent sexual activity, after long celibacy, Ash found herself aware now of difference, of maleness, in a way in which she was not used to think; as something pertaining to physicality rather than prejudice.

''I'll see Quesada again,'' she informed Anselm, and turned to Godfrey as the other man strode downstairs. ''If not an eclipse, then some kind of black miracle—?''

Godfrey paused beside the trestle table, as if Angelotti's astrological scribbles might touch somehow on his biblical readings. ''No stars fell, the moon is not as red as blood. The sun isn't darkened because of the smoke of the Pit. The *third* part of the sun should be smitten—that's not what's happening. There have been no Horsemen, no Seals broken. It is not the last days after which the sun shall be darkened.''[47]

''No, not the troubles before the Last Judgment,'' Ash persisted, ''but a punishment, a judgment, or an evil miracle?''

''Judgment for what? The princes of Christendom are wicked, but no more wicked than the generation before

---

[47]See Revelation 6:12; Revelation: 9:12; Revelation: 8:12; and Matthew 24:29, respectively.

them. The common people are venal, weak, easily led, and often repentant; this is no alteration from how things have always been. There is distress of nations,[48] but we have never lived in the Age of Gold!'' His thick fingertips strayed over curlicued capitals, over painted saints in little illuminated shrines. ''I don't know.''

''Then bloody well pray for an answer!''

''Yes.'' He folded the book shut over one finger. His eyes were amber, full of light in the room lit by lanterns and fires. ''What use can I be to you without God's help? All I do is puzzle it out from the Gospels, and I think I am more often wrong than right.''

''You were ordained, that's good enough for me. You know it is.'' Ash spoke crudely, knowing exactly why he had left after instruction. ''Pray for grace for us.''

''Yes.''

A shouted challenge, and footsteps sounded on the stairs below.

Ash walked around and seated herself on the stool behind the trestle table. That put her with the Lion Azure standard, leaning on its staff against the wall, at her back. Sallet and gauntlets rested on the table, with her sword-belt, scabbard, and sword. Her priest praying in the corner at his Green Shrine. Her master gunner calculating expenditure of powder. More than enough for effect, she calculated, and did not look up for a good thirty heartbeats after she heard Floria del Guiz and Daniel de Quesada enter the room.

De Quesada spoke first, quite rationally. ''I shall construe this siege as an attack on the armies of the King-Caliph.''

Ash let him listen to the echo of his voice in silence. The lath and plaster walls muffled shouting and the infre-

---

[48]Luke 21:25.

quent small cannon fire. Finally she looked at him.

She suggested mildly, "Tell the Caliph's representatives that Fernando del Guiz is my husband, that he is now under an act of attainder, that I am acting on my own behalf in recovering what is now my property since he was stripped of it by the Emperor Frederick."

Daniel de Quesada's face was crusted with healing scabs, where the hairs of his beard had been ripped out. His eyes were dull. His words came with an effort. "So you besiege your husband's castle, with him in it, and he is now a sworn feudal subject of King-Caliph Theodoric— but that is not an act of aggression against us?"

"Why should it be? These are my lands." Ash leaned forward over linked hands. "I'm a mercenary. The world's gone crazy. I want my company *inside* stone walls. Then I'll think about who's going to hire me."

De Quesada still had a febrile nervousness, despite Floria's opiates and restraining hand on his arm. The doublet and hose and rolled chaperon hat he had been given sat awkwardly on him; you could see he was not used to moving in such clothes.

"We can't lose," he said.

"I usually find myself on the winning side." That was ambiguous enough that Ash let it rest. "I'll give you an escort, Ambassador. I'm sending you back to your people."

"I thought I was a prisoner!"

"I'm not Frederick. I'm not a subject of Frederick." Ash gave a nod, dismissing him. "Wait over there a minute. Florian, I want to speak with you."

Daniel de Quesada looked around the room, then walked across the uneven floorboards as if across the uncertain deck of a ship, hesitating at the door, finally moving to stand in a corner furthest from the windows.

Ash stood up and poured wine into a wooden goblet

and offered it to Floria. She spoke briefly in English—it
being the language of a small, barbaric, unknown island,
there was a sporting chance the Visigoth diplomat might
not understand it. "How mad is he? What can I ask him
about this darkness?"

"Barking. *I* don't know!" The surgeon hitched one hip
up onto the trestle table and sat, long leg swinging. "They
may be used to their ambassadors coming back God-
struck, if they send them out with messages about signs
and portents. He's probably functional. I can't promise
he'll stay that way if you start asking him questions."

"Tough. We need to know." She signaled the Visigoth.
He came forward again. "Master Ambassador, one other
thing. I want to know when it's going to get light again."

"Light?"

"When the sun's going to rise. When it's going to stop
being dark!"

"The sun . . ." Daniel de Quesada shivered, not turning
his head toward the window. "Is there fog outside?"

"How would I know? It's black as your hat out there!"
Ash sighed. *Evidently I can forget a sensible answer from
this one.* "No, master Ambassador. It's dark. Not foggy."

He huddled his arms around himself. Something about
the shape of his mouth made Ash shiver: adult men in
their right minds do not look like this.

"We were separated. Almost at the top—there was fog.
I climbed." Quesada's staccato Carthaginian Gothic was
barely comprehensible. "Up, up, up. A winding road, in
snow. Ice. Climbing forever, until I could only crawl.
Then a great wind came; the sky was *purple* above me.
Purple, and all the white peaks, so high above—Mountains. I cling. There is only air. The rock makes my hands
bleed—"

Ash, with her own memory of a sky so dark blue it

burns, and thin air that hurts the chest, said to Floria, "He's talking about the Gotthard Pass now. Where the monks found him."

Floria put a firm hand on the man's arm. "Let's get you back to the infirmary, Ambassador."

Half-alert, Daniel de Quesada met Ash's gaze.

"The fog—went." He moved his hands apart, like a man opening a curtain.

Ash said, "It was clear a month ago, when we crossed the pass with Fernando. Snow on the rocks either side, but the road was clear. I know where they must have found you, Ambassador. I've stood there. You can stand and look straight down into Italy. Straight down, seven thousand feet."

The wagons creak, horses straining against the ascent; the breath of the men-at-arms streams on the air; and she stands, the cold striking up through the soles of her boots, and peers down a mottled green-and-white-cliff face, funneling down toward the foothills. But it seems puny to call it a cliff, this southern side of the saddle-pass across the Alps; the mountains rise up in a half-circle that is miles across.

And it is almost a mile and a half straight down.

Sheer rock, moss and ice, and a vastness of empty air so big and deep that it hurts the mind to look at it.

She finished quietly, "If you fell, you'd never touch the earth until you hit bottom."

"Straight down!" Daniel de Quesada echoed. His eyes flashed. "I found I was looking—The road below me, winding down bend upon bend upon bend. There is a lake at the bottom. It is no larger than the nail upon my finger."

Ash remembers the interminable straining fear of the descent, and how the lake, when they got down to it, was quite large, and nestled in foothills: they were not off the mountain even then.

"The fog cleared and *I was looking down.*"

All the room was silent. After a minute, it became apparent to Ash that there was to be no more from him. De Quesada stared with unseeing eyes at the shifting shadows.

As Floria was handing the Visigoth over to one of her aides, Angelotti said, "I've known men blindfold themselves going over the alpine passes, afraid of going mad.[49] I didn't think I should meet one, madonna."

"I think you just have." Ash looked after de Quesada grimly. "Well, picking him up in the riots in the hope he'd be some use wasn't one of my better ideas. I'd hoped he'd negotiate with del Guiz when we got here."

"He's away with the fairies," Floria remarked. "If you want my medical opinion. Not the best qualification for a herald."

Ash snorted. "I don't care if he's nuts. I want *answers.* I don't like this darkness!"

"Who does?" Floria inquired rhetorically. She snorted. "You want to know how many of your men have developed acute attacks of coward's belly?"

"No. Why do you think I want to keep them busy with a siege? They're used to tunneling petards and banging away with cannon; it reassures them . . . That's why the men-at-arms are going through this town street by street commandeering supplies—if they're going to loot the place, it might as well be *organized* looting."

This appeal to her cynicism made Floria chuckle, as Ash had known it would. There was so little difference between Floria and "Florian," even down to the gallantry

---

[49] Recorded in several fifteenth century travelers' accounts of their alpine journeys.

with which the tall woman offered now to pour wine for
Ash herself.

"It's no different from night attacks," Ash added, refusing wine; "which are, God knows, a bitch, but possible. I
want this castle opened up by treachery, not damaged by us
having to storm it. Speaking of which—" the restlessness
that came with her failure to interrogate de Quesada im-
pelled her into action "—you come with me and look at
this. Angelotti!"

They left the room, the gunner with them; Ash glancing
back to see Godfrey Maximillian, broad shoulders bowed,
still at prayer. Outside—walking into a wall of darkness,
pitch-black down in the streets—they silently stood for
some minutes, waiting for night-vision, before stumbling
toward the bonfire-lights.

The town blacksmith's had been taken over by the company armorers, a perpetually black-handed group of men
with straggling hair, hatless, in pourpoints[50] and leather
aprons and no shirts, sweating from the forge, half-deaf
from the ceaseless ringing of hammers. They made way
good-naturedly for Ash, her surgeon and her escort of half
a dozen men and dogs. No commander was ever more
than means to an end for them, this she knew. The latest
project was difficult, welcome because of that, welcome
because unusual.

"A twelve-foot pair of *bolt-cutters?*" Floria surmised,
studying vast steel handles.

"It's getting the blades right?" The company's head
armorer, Dickon Stour, habitually ended on a note of
query, even when not speaking his native English. "To
withstand the pressure, and to cut iron?"

"And those are scaling ladders," Ash said. She pointed
at stout wooden poles with steel hooks on the end, and a

---

[50]Pourpoint: a waistcoat-like garment, to which hose can be tied.

mess of spars attached. Hook it over a wall, tug ropes, and a ladder will unfold from the mess. "I'm going to send people in secretly with black wool over their armor, to cut the big bars on the postern gate from the inside. I would say, at night, but in this darkness—" A shrug and grin. "Stealth knights . . ."

"You're mad. *They're* mad. I want to talk to you!" Floria scowled at the noise from the anvils and pointed, silently, at the street. Ash shook hands, thumped shoulders, left with her escort. Angelotti stayed, discussing metallurgy.

Ash caught up with the surgeon a few yards away, staring up from the cobbled street that ran up the hill, to the shadowy machiolations and timber-works of the castle crowning the heights.

Floria walked fast, a few paces ahead of the men-at-arms and hounds. "Are you really going to try that?"

"We did it before. Two years back, in—where was it?" Ash thought. "Somewhere in southern France?"

"That *is* my brother in there." The woman's voice came masculine out of the dusk, a breathy drop into lower registers that never relaxed, whether the command escort could hear her or not. "Granted I haven't seen him since he was ten. Granted he was a brat. And now he's a shit. But blood's blood. He *is* family."

"Family. Yeah. Tell me how much *I* care about family."

Floria began, "What—?"

"What? Will I give orders for him to be taken prisoner, not killed? Will I let him run, go off and raise men somewhere else to come back and fight me? Will I have him killed? What?"

"All of those."

"It seems unreal." Unreal, when I have had his body inside me, to believe that he could die with an arrow through the throat, a bill-hook slashing his gut, that some-one with a bollock dagger and my express order could make him *not be*.

"Damn it, you can't go on ignoring this, girl! You fucked him. You married him. He's your flesh in the sight of God."

"That's a dumb thing to say. You don't believe in God." Ash could, in the torchlit streets, make out the sudden strain etching itself into the woman's face. "Florian, I'm not likely to go around denouncing you to the local bishop, am I! Soldiers either believe completely, or not at all, and I've got both sorts in the company."

The tall woman continued walking down the cobble-stones beside her, all her balance in her shoulders: gangling and masculine. She made an irritated motion that might have been a shrug or a flinch as Angelotti's siege cannon crashed out smoke and flame, two streets away. "You're *married*!"

"Time enough to decide what to do about Fernando when I've got him and his garrison out of that castle." Ash shook her head as if she could clear it, somehow; clear the oppressive, unnatural darkness out of her skull.

She called the commander of the escort to her as she reached the commandeered town house again, ordering a brazier and food for his men in the street, and then clumped back up the stairs, Floria at her shoulder, only to walk into what seemed an entire company of people crammed between narrow white walls, helmet-plumes rubbing the candle-stained ceiling, voices raised.

"*Quiet!*"

That got silence.

She gazed around.

Joscelyn van Mander, his red-cheeked intense face framed by the brilliance of his steel sallet; two of his men; then Robert Anselm; Godfrey rising from his knees and disrupted prayer; Daniel de Quesada in his badly fitting European clothes—and a new man in white tunic and trousers and riveted mail hauberk, no weapons.

A Visigoth, with leather rank badges laced to his mail shoulders. *Qa'id*, she dredged up out of her memory of campaigns in Iberia: an officer set over a thousand. Roughly the equivalent of her own command.

"Well?" she said, reclaiming her place behind the table, and sitting. Rickard appeared and poured heavily watered wine for her. She dropped without thought into the dialect she had learned around Tunisian soldiers; something as automatic to her as calling a hackbutter an arquebusier in the French King's lands, or a poleaxe *der Axst* here and *l'Azza* to Angelotti. "What's your business, *qa'id?*"

"Captain." The Visigoth soldier touched his fingers to his forehead. "I met my countryman de Quesada and your escort, on the road. He decided to return here with me, to speak to you. I bring news to you."

The Visigoth soldier was small, fair-skinned, hardly taller than Rickard, with the palest blue eyes, and something about him that was undeniably familiar. Ash said, "Is your family name Lebrija?"

He seemed startled. "Yes."

"Continue. What news?"

"There will be other messengers, of your own people—"

Ash's gaze flicked to Anselm, who nodded, confirming: "Yes. I met them. I was on my way here when Joscelyn came in."

"*You* may have the honor of telling me," Ash told the Visigoth *qa'id* mildly, hating to hear news unprepared, hating not to have the few minutes' warning she would have had if Robert had been the one to tell her. Since Joscelyn van Mander seemed intensely worried, she switched back to German. "What's happened?"

"Frederick of Hapsburg has sued for terms."

There was a little silence, essentially undisturbed by Floria muttering "Fuck," and Joscelyn van Mander's demand: "Captain, what does he mean?"

"I think he means that the territories of the Holy Roman Emperor have surrendered." Ash linked her hands in front of her. "Master Anselm, is that what our messengers say?"

"Frederick's surrendered. Everything from the Rhine to the sea is open to the Visigoth armies." In an equally level tone, Robert Anselm added, "And Venice has been burned to the water line. Churches, houses, warehouses, ships, canal-bridges, St. Mark's Basilica, the Doge's palace, everything. A million, million ducats up in smoke."

The silence became intense: mercenaries stunned at the waste of wealth, the two Visigoth men imbued with a silent confidence, being associated with a power to make such destruction.

Frederick of Hapsburg will have heard about Venice, Ash thought, shocked, hearing in her mind the dry, covetous voice of the Holy Roman Emperor; *he's decided not to risk the Germanies!* and then, bringing her gaze snap into focus on the Visigoth soldier, brother or cousin of dead Asturio Lebrija, she realized *The Empire has surrendered and we're caught on the wrong side.* Every mercenary's nightmare.

"I assume," she said, "that a relieving force from the Visigoth army is now on its way here to Fernando?"

Her vision of where they are flips a hundred and eighty degrees. It's no longer a matter of feeling herself safe behind town walls, soon to be safe behind the castle walls. Now the company's caught in between the approaching Visigoth men-at-arms in the countryside beyond the town, and Fernando del Guiz's knights and gunners up in the castle itself.

Daniel de Quesada spoke rustily. "Of course. Our allies must be helped."

"Of course," the brother or cousin of Lebrija echoed.

Quesada could not yet have told the *qa'id* of Lebrija's death, might not know anything, Ash thought, and resolved to keep silent where speech could very likely get her into trouble.

"I'll be interested to talk to your captain when he arrives," Ash stated. She watched her own officers out of her peripheral vision, seeing them draw strength from her confidence.

"Our commander arrives here by tomorrow," the Visigoth soldier estimated. "We are most anxious to talk to you. The famous Ash. That's why our commander is coming here now."

Sun gone out or not, Ash thought, I am not going to get the time I want to consider my decisions. Whether I like it or not, it's happening *now*.

And then:

Sun gone out or not, Last Days or not, it is nothing to do with me: if I stand by my company, we're strong enough to survive this. The metaphysics of it aren't my problem.

"Right," she said. "I'd better meet your commander and open negotiations."

Rickard presented Bertrand, a possible half-brother of Philibert, at thirteen busy growing into a body far too large for him, managing simultaneously to be fat and gangling. They put Ash into her armor and brought Godluc in his best barding; the boys smear-eyed with lack of sleep, at an hour which might have been dawn, if this third day in Guizburg had had one.

"As far as I can tell, their commander's personal name

is actually the name of her rank," Godfrey Maximillian said. "Faris.[51] It means Captain-General, General of all their forces, something like that."

"Her rank? A woman commander?" Ash remembered, then, Asturio Lebrija saying *I have met women of war*, and his sense of humor, which his cousin Sancho (Godfrey reporting the name and fact) did not possess at all. "And she's here now? The boss of the whole damn invasion force?"

"Just down the road from Innsbruck."

"Shit . . ."

Godfrey went to the door, calling a man in from the main room of the commandeered house. "Carracci, the boss wants to hear it herself."

A man-at-arms with startling white-blond hair and high color on his cheeks, who had stripped off all but a minimum of his shabby foot soldier's kit to travel fast, came in and made a courtesy. "I got right up to their command tent! It's a woman, boss. A woman leading their army; and you know how they've made her good? She's got one of those brazen head machines of theirs, it does her thinking for her in battles—they say she hears its voice! She hears it talk!"

"If it's a Brazen Head,[52] of course she hears it talk!"

"No, boss. She doesn't have it with her. She hears it in her head, like God speaking to a priest."

---

[51]This appears to be the del Guiz *Life*'s mistranslation of a Saracen term. Faris is Arabic for "horseman," meaning the ordinary professional cavalry knight, rather than an army commander. However, I have chosen to use *faris* since the better alternative given in the Angelotti manuscript, the Muslim *al-sayyid*, "chieftain" or "master," already exists in European history—as the title of Rodrigo de Vivar: "El Cid."

[52]Fr Roger Bacon (c. 1214–1292) was an early scientist, and the actual European inventor of gunpowder. He was popularly supposed to have been a sorcerer, and was credited with inventing a mechanical speaking head, made of brass; later destroyed.

Ash stared at the billman.

"She hears it like a saint's voice; it tells her how to fight. *That's* why a woman beat us." Carracci suddenly stopped talking, lifted a shoulder, and at last gave a hopeful grin. "Oops. Sorry, boss?"

She hears it like a saint's voice.

A pulse of coldness went through the pit of Ash's stomach. She was aware that she blinked, stared, said nothing; chill with an as-yet unidentified shock. She wet her lips.

"Bloody right you're sorry . . ."

It was an automatic response. This billman, Carracci, had clearly not heard *Ash hears saint's voices!* as a company rumor: most—especially those who had been with her for years—would have done.

Does she hear a saint, this Faris? Does she? Or does she only think it's a useful rumor? Burned as a witch is no way to end . . .

"Thanks, Carracci," she added absently. "Join the escort. Tell them we're riding in five minutes."

As Carracci left, she turned back to Godfrey. *It's difficult to feel vulnerable laced and tied into steel.* She put the billman's words out of her mind. Her confidence came back with her stride across the small room, the trestle bare of waiting armor now, to the window, where she stood and looked out at Guizburg's fires.

"I think you're right, Godfrey. They're going to offer us a contract."

"I've talked to travelers from a number of monasteries this side of the mountains. As I said, I can't get a real idea of their numbers, but there is at least one other Visigoth army fighting in Iberia."

Ash kept her back to him. "Voices. They say she hears voices. *That's* odd."

"As a rumor, it has its uses."

"Don't I know it!"

"Saints are one thing," Godfrey said. "Claiming a miracle voice from an engine, that's another. She might be thought a demon. She might *be* a demon."

"Yes."

"Ash—"

"There isn't the time to worry about this, okay?" She turned and glared at Godfrey. "*Okay?*"

He watched her, brown eyes calm. He did not nod.

Ash said, "We have to make our minds up fast, if the Visigoths *do* make us an offer. Fernando and his men are just waiting to find us caught between hammer and anvil. Then it'll be up with his castle drawbridge, and sally out and take us right in the back. Yippee," she said dourly, and then grinned over her armored shoulder at the priest. "*Won't* he be sick if we're contracted to the same side? We're mercenaries, but he's an attainted traitor—I still reckon this castle's mine."

"Don't count your castles before they're stormed."

"Should that be a proverb, do you think?" She sobered. "We *are* between hammer and anvil. Let's hope they need us on their side more than they need to get rid of us. Otherwise I should have decided to move us out, not stay put. And it's going to be very short and very bloody up here."

The priest's broad hand came down on her left pauldron. "It's bloody where the Visigoths are fighting the Guilds, up near Lake Lucerne. Their commander will probably buy any fighting force they can get, especially one that's got local knowledge."

"And then put us in the front line to die, rather than their own men. *I* know how it goes." She moved cautiously, turning; armor can be considered a weapon in itself, if you are only wearing a brown pleated woollen robe and sandals. Godfrey's hand slid away from the sharp metal plates. She met his brown-eyed gaze.

"It's remarkable what you can get used to. A week, ten days . . . The question no one wants to ask, of course, is—after the sun, what? What *else* can happen?" Ash knelt stiffly. "Bless me before I ride out. I'd like to be in good grace right now."

His deep, familiar voice sang a blessing.

"Ride with me," she directed, a heartbeat after he finished and made for the stairs. Godfrey followed her downstairs and out into the town.

Ash mounted and rode through the streets, with her officers and escort, men-at-arms and dogs. She reined Godluc in when a procession passed, jamming the narrow street, men and women wailing, their woollen doublets and kirtles deliberately slashed, faces streaked with ashes. Merchants and craftsmen. Bare, bloody-footed boys in white carried a Virgin between green wax candles. Town priests whipped them with steel-toothed whips. Ash took off her helmet and waited while the lamenting, praying crowd stumbled past.

When the noise level dropped to the point where she could be heard, she replaced her sallet and called, "On!"

She rode with fifty men, past bone-fires that burned the clock around now, out through the gates of Guizburg. They passed some of her own men coming in from expeditions to untouched forest, dragging loads of pine for torches. What she thought were silver pine-needles were, she saw as she rode close, pine-needles covered in frost. Frost. In July.

The wheel of the mill was silent above where they splashed across the ford; and in the darkness she could just see cows straying, not knowing when to come in to be milked. An odd half-song came from copses, birds uncertain whether to sleep or to claim territory. Oppressiveness prickled her spine under the pinked silk lining of her arming doublet and made her sweat; all this before she saw a thousand torches down the shallow valley, and the silver eagle Visigoth standards, and heard drums.

Joscelyn van Mander demanded reassurance, his eyes on the spearmen and bowmen down the slope. "I never fought Visigoths, what's it like?"

Ash leaned her upright lance back against her armored shoulder. Its foxtail pennant hung in the still air. Godluc frisked, his tail bound up with a chaplet of oak-leaves and folly-bells. "Angelotti?"

Antonio Angelotti rode beside her, armored, a Saint Barbara medal knotted around the cuff of her gauntlet. "When I was with the lord-*amir* Childeric, we put down a local rebellion. I had captaincy of the English hackbutters.[53] The Visigoths are raiders. *Karr wa farr*: repeated attack and retreat. Hit and run, cut your supply lines, deny you the fords, indifferent sieges for a year or three, then take the city by storm. I have not known them seek out the enemy army for a pitched battle. They've changed tactics."

"Evidently." There was a strong smell of unwatered beer from van Mander.

Ash checked back, twisting in the high, upright war-saddle. Apart from the usual command officers, she had brought Euen Huw and his lance; Jan-Jacob Clovet and thirty bowmen; ten men picked from van Mander's band, and her steward Henri Brant—torso swathed in bandages—to oversee on behalf of the noncombatants. A majority of her riders carried torches.

Angelotti said, "You should have let my bombards open up the Guizburg keep. It would be much harder to get us out of that, madonna."

"Try not to think of it as *a* pile of rubble, but as *our* pile of rubble. I'd like it kept in one piece!"

---

[53] "Hackbut": English for "arquebus," a man-portable gun.

Confident of the number and disposition of this part of the Visigoth forces at least, the company's scouts being reliable, Ash rode on down the slope between neatly sectioned fields and wattle-fenced animal pens. The company standard and her personal banner rode in the mass of men, dark against the unnatural dark sky, among the jolting, flaring torches.

They topped a slight rise. Ash kept Godluc moving forward when he would have responded to the shift in her weight as she saw what lay a little distance off. It is one thing to be reliably informed that there is a division of an army, eight or nine thousand men plus baggage train, encamped just off the Innsbruck road. It is another to see a hundred thousand torches, bright bonfires, hear the whickering and stamping from the horse-lines and the shouting of guards; glimpse, in the lightless day, the vast wheel of tents, spidered with guy-ropes, thronging with armed men, and circled with wagons, that is that army in the flesh.

Ash drew rein at the appointed rendezvous, a crossroads milestone, and thumbed her sallet's visor up. All her party rode in full armor, by her orders; horses fully barded and caparisoned; colored silk scarves twisted around helmets, plume-holders on sallets and armets frothing with white ostrich feathers. The mounted crossbowmen had their weapons out of their cases, and bolts close to hand.

"There," she said, straining to see through the darkness.

A rider with a white lance pennant rode up from the Visigoth encampment. After a while she managed to distinguish European armor, the rounded curves of Milanese plate, and a straggle of black hair curling out from under the neck of his armet. "It's Agnes!"

Robert Anselm growled, "Jammy sod. Trust Lamb to get hired."

"In the middle of a fucking battle! He must have signed a contract while they were still having that skirmish." In so far as her armor allowed it, Ash shook her head ruefully. "Don't you just love Italian mercenaries?"

They met in the stink of smoking pine torches. Lamb carefully unpinned the visor of his armet, showing his tanned face. "Planning a quick getaway, are we?"

"Unless the whole Visigoth army down there comes after us, we'd make it back through the town gates." Ash slotted her lance into its saddle holster to give her hands freedom. She spoke mainly for the benefit of her officers. "And unless your employer *really* wants to be sitting in front of one tiny Bavarian castle for the next twelve weeks, I don't think she'll be too interested in trying to prise us out of Guizburg."

"Perhaps." Ambiguous.

"Tell your general that we're understandably not keen about riding into her camp, but if she wants to ride up here, we'll negotiate."

"That's the word I wanted to hear." Lamb wheeled his lean, bony roan gelding, held up his lance, and dipped the white pennant to the dirt. Another group of riders moved out from the wagon fort, perhaps forty strong. Too far away in the darkness to see detail, they could be any group of armed men.

"So how much extra did you get paid for riding up here on your own?"

"Enough. But I'm told you treat hostages well." A flirtatious curve of the lips; Agnus Dei's religious convictions not (by common rumor) extending as far as celibacy. Ash smiled back, thinking of Daniel de Quesada and Sancho Lebrija, now being compulsorily entertained in Guizburg until she should return unhurt.

"Nothing in the city states is holding out now except Milano," Lamb added, ignoring Antonio Angelotti's sudden obscenity, "and of the Swiss Cantons, only Berne."

"They fucked the *Swiss*?" Ash was stunned into momentary silence. "Their lines of supply go back clear across the Mediterranean; they can keep armies like this in the field and still push on north? And hold down territory behind them?"

It was very inelegant fishing for information, or rather, a re-stating of information that her sources informed her was true. Ash's attention fixed on the approaching riders.

Lamb proved close-mouthed. "Twenty years of preparation helps, I think, madonna Ash."

"Twenty years. I find it hard to imagine. That's as long as I've been alive." The mention of her youth was entirely malicious, Lamb being in his early thirties. So young, so famous; better not to be overconfident as well, she concluded, and waited for the riders to come up the slope. A wind swept over the dark grass, rustling the pine forests in the distance. There was a sense in her, almost physical, like the sensation of successfully riding a mettlesome horse of which one is barely in control.

"Sweet Christ," she murmured joyfully, almost to herself, "it's Armageddon. Everything's changing. Christendom being turned upside-down. Who'd be a peasant now?"

"Or a merchant. Or a lord." Lamb drew in his reins. "This is the only trade to be in, *cara*."

"You think so? Fighting's all I can do." A rare moment: she and the straggle-haired man apprehended each other very clearly. Ash said, "Stay in the fighting line until you're thirty and you die, so I command. Stay in command until you're old, forty or so, and you die. Hence—" A wave of her armored hand back at Guizburg. "The game of princes."

"Mmm?" Lamb turned both body and head, in his plate harness, so that he could look directly at her. "Oh yes, *cara*. I heard rumors that half your trouble was, you wanted an estate and title. As for myself—'' He sighed, with some degree of content. ''I have my money for the last two campaigns invested in the English wool trade.''

''Invested?'' Ash stared at him.

''And I own a dye-works in Bruges now. Very comfortable.''

Ash became aware that her mouth was open. She shut it.

''So who needs land?'' Agnus Dei concluded.

''Uh . . . Yeah.'' Ash switched her attention back to the Visigoths. ''You've been with them, what, two weeks or more? Lamb, what's the deal here?''

The Italian mercenary touched the lamb on his surcoat. ''Ask yourself if you have a choice, madonna, and if not, what does my answer matter?''

''She's *good*.'' Ash watched the torchlit procession coming closer. Close enough to see the outriders, four robed and veiled men on mules, with what looked like open-frame octagonal barrels resting on their saddles in front of them. Something wrong about the size of the men's heads and bodies. She identified them as dwarfs a moment after she realized the red and gilded leather sides of the barrels were being struck with sticks, were, in fact, war-drums. The growing vibration made Godluc's ears go back.

Ash said, in a rush, ''She kicked our asses at Genoa. You believe all this stuff about a brazen head machine telling her what to do? Have you seen it?''

''No. Her men say the brazen head, that they call her 'Stone Golem,' isn't here with her. It's in Carthage.''

''But the time you'd spend waiting for an answer— messages, riders on post-horses, pigeons—then she can't be using in the field. Not in real-time *combat*.''

''But her men say she does. They say she hears it *at*

the same time as it speaks in the Citadel, in Carthage."
He paused. "I don't know, madonna. They say she's a
woman, so she can only be this good if it's voices."

Lamb's sly comment stung. Ash momentarily ignored
him, caught up in an idea of what it might mean if one
could be in constant real-time communication with one's
home city and commanders, thousands of miles away.

"A Stone Golem . . ." she said slowly. "Lamb, hearing
Our Lord's saints is one thing; hearing a *machine*—"

"It's probably just the rumor-mill," Lamb snapped.
"Half of what they *say* they have in North Africa, they *don't*
have—just manuscripts and some great-grandfather's memories. This woman is new, and a commander of armies.
There will of course be ridiculous stories. There always
are."

Something about his rapid speech made her glance at
Agnus: the Lamb was undoubtedly on edge. She caught
the gaze of Robert Anselm, Geraint ab Morgan, Angelotti—all her officers in readiness for this, which might
be a negotiation, and might be an ambush, and must in
any case be endured long enough to find out. She looked
down for Godfrey Maximillian's palfrey. The priest was
staring at the approaching torches.

"Pray for us," she ordered.

The bearded man gripped his cross, his lips moving.

More torches bloomed, lower, carried by men on foot.
Ash heard a superstitious oath from Robert Anselm. The
torch-carriers were clay and brass figures of men, golem
bearing streaming pitch-torches whose light flowed over
their featureless red and ocher skins.

"Nice," she admitted. "If I were her, and had something that disconcerting, I'd use it too."

The Visigoth horses came on, between two lines of golem. Little high-stepping horses, with desert blood in
them, and gilded leather tack that lay across their necks

and their rumps, each bit and ring and stirrup flashing in
the torchlight. They brought a smell of spicy horse dung,
perceptibly different to the thick-necked European war-
horses. Godluc stirred. Ash gripped his rein. Some of
those are mares, she thought; and I've never been convinced Godluc realizes he's been cut. The darting shadows bothered Godfrey's palfrey; she indicated a bowman
should get down and hold the bridle, so that Godfrey
could continue uninterrupted prayer.

Behind the Visigoth riders came the standard bearer,
with a black flag and an eagle on a pole. His horse was
armored, and Ash smiled to herself at that, having carried
the standard in a number of battles and come to understand what her voices meant by the term *fire magnet*. An
armored poet rode beside him, singing something too colloquial for her to understand, but she remembered the cus-
tom from Tunis: *cantadors*, for morale.

"What a racket. I wonder if they're trying to impress
us?" Ash sat in the tall saddle, her legs almost straight in
the stirrups, center of gravity at hips or just below: a different feeling to walking in armor. She shifted impercep-
tibly, keeping Godluc still. The Visigoth horses jangled
as they came to a halt. Lances and shields, swords and
light crossbows . . . She studied men wearing mail hau-
berks over padded armor, with white surcoats and open-
face helmets. They leaned from their saddles toward each
other, talking openly, some of them pointing at the European mercenary knights.

"No," Ash said cheerfully, picking one and letting her
voice carry, "we don't, as it happens. Besides, you don't
get goats in these mountains. Male *or* female."

A spurt of laughter, cursing and alarm followed her
speech. Geraint ab Morgan slapped his armored thigh. A
better-armed Visigoth rider under the black pennant-and-

eagle standard spoke to men either side, then urged a chestnut gelding forward.

Not to be outdone, Ash signaled. Euen Huw blew three clear notes on the trumpet he unwillingly carried. Ash rode forward in a clatter of horse barding, six officers with her—Anselm, Geraint, and Joscelyn van Mander in gleaming Milanese full plate; Angelotti in a Milanese breastplate and fluted, intricate Gothic leg harness; Godfrey (still praying, eyes shut) in his best monastic robe; and Floria del Guiz in someone's borrowed brigandine and archer's sallet, looking nothing like a woman, and, sadly, nothing much like a soldier either, Ash had to admit.

"I'm Ash," she said into the silence after the trumpet. "Agnes Dei tells me you're interested in a contract with us."

Ash could not make out the Visigoth leader's face under her helmet in the moving shadows.

The woman wore steel helmet and greaves, banded sabatons visible in her stirrups. Torchlight flowed richly over her crimson velvet-covered body armor: a coat-of-plates with a hundred big flower-shaped rivet heads gleaming gold. Mail was visible under it, at her thigh. A standing plate collar must be a gorget of some sort, Ash surmised; and she noted a tri-lobed gilded sword hilt, sword and dagger scabbards with gold chapes, sword-belt with heavy gold decoration, and the blue-black and white checker of a cloak lined with vair.[54] Ash had the price of each totted up in seconds and was impressed despite herself. She could not help the spasm of pure pleasure she felt at seeing another woman commanding armed troops—especially one foreign enough not to be a competitor.

"You would fight Burgundians." The woman's voice,

---

[54] Back and belly fur of a European squirrel.

penetrating, spoke German with a Carthaginian accent. It argued that she wanted to be understood by those of Ash's entourage who did not speak Carthaginian.

"Fight Burgundians? Not for choice. They're hard bastards." Ash shrugged. "I don't risk my company for no good reason."

"You are 'Ash.' The *jund*."[55] The armored chestnut gelding moved forward, coming into the light of Ash's torches. The woman wore a helmet with a nasal bar and a mail aventail hanging from its edges. A black scarf swathed her shoulders and lower face. There is little detail visible in helmet-framed eyes, which was all Ash could see, but enough to make her suddenly realize *She's young! My God. She's no older than me!*

It explained something of Lamb's edginess: a malicious desire to see these two female freaks, as he undoubtedly considered them, meet each other. Ash, out of pure perversity, immediately warmed to the Visigoth commander.

"Faris," Ash said. "General. Make me an offer. I've tended to fight on the side of the Burgundians when chance offered, but we can handle them if necessary."

"You have my ally here."

"He's my husband. I think that gives me prior claim."

"Your siege must be lifted. As part of the contract."

"Whoa. Too fast. I always consult with my men." Ash put up a hand. Something bothered her about the Visigoth general's voice. She would have edged Godluc closer, but the torchlight flickered on the points of arrows, easily nocked, in some cases lying across Visigoth riders' laps; and some of her own men very definitely had lances in their hands rather than socketed at the saddle. Weapons have their own life, their own tension; she could have said, with complete accuracy, how many Visigoth riders

---

[55]Arabic: a mercenary, a soldier who fights for money or land-grants.

were looking at her and judging distance. She could feel the invisible connection.

Purely from a desire to gain a minute or two to think, Ash found herself asking the question most on her mind. "Faris—when will we see the sun again?"

"When we choose." The woman's young voice sounded calm.

It also sounded, to Ash, like a lie; having told enough lies in public in her own time. *So you don't know either? The Caliph back in Carthage doesn't tell his general everything?* The yellow light of the torches grew to a glare, the clay walkers making a half-circle to either side of their general. Fine-linked mail armor glinted.

"What are you offering?"

"Sixty thousand ducats. Contracted for the duration of this war."

Sixty *thou*—

As plain as if it were her inner voice, she could hear Robert Anselm think *If the bitch has money to burn, don't argue with her!*

Ash gave herself a second or two to consider by reaching up and unbuckling her sallet and taking the helmet off; this also being a sign to her men to stand down—or at any rate not to do anything rash unless aggressive intent became very clear on the Visigoth side.

Lamb stripped a gauntlet off and bit at his fingers.

Ash pushed her bound silver hair (sweaty from its confinement as her helmet lining) out of her face and glanced at the Visigoth general. After a long hesitation the young woman reached up and took off her mail-hung helmet and pulled off her veil.

One of the Visigoth riders swore, violently. His mount lifted both front feet off the earth and cannoned into the man beside him. A strident roar of voices made Ash grab at Godluc's reins, left-handed. Godfrey Maximillian opened his eyes and she saw him look directly ahead.

"Jesus Christ!" Godfrey exclaimed.

The young Visigoth Faris sat her horse in torchlight. She moved her scarlet-armoured body, encouraging the chestnut mare forward a pace, and stared. Shifting shadows and light gleamed from the waterfall of her silver hair.

Her brows were dark, sweeping, definite; her eyes a dark brilliance; but it was the mouth that gave it to Ash. Ash thought, *I have seen that mouth in a mirror every time there has been a mirror to hand*, and she took in the same length of arm and leg, solid small hips, strong shoulders, even—which she had not seen—the same way of sitting a saddle.

She brought her gaze back to the Visigoth woman's face.

No scars.

If there had been scars, she would have fallen off her horse and gone facedown on the earth, praying to the Christ, praying against madness and demons and whatever inhabitant of the Pit this might be. But the woman's cheeks were flawless and unmarked.

The Visigoth woman general wore no expression at all now, her features frozen, stone.

In the same second that armed men in both the European and Visigoth groups crowded their horses closer, Ash realized, *So that's what I look like without scars.*

No scars.

In everything other than that—we are twins.

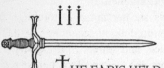

iii

THE FARIS HELD up one arm and said something too sharp and quick for Ash to understand.

"I'll send my *qa'id* to you with a contract!" the Visigoth general added. An urging movement of her body
sent the chestnut Barb around on the spot, haunches
bunched, then galloping away. And the rest of them with
her, instantly. Drums, eagle, dwarfs, poets and armed
thugs, all clattering down the dark slope toward the Visigoth camp.

"Back to town." Ash heard her own voice sharp and
hoarse, in the silence. Thinking, *how many of them saw—
perhaps a few men, close to me—thirty heartbeats—to see
a face in darkness—but word will soon get around, turn
to rumor—*"Back to the town!"

For the next five days she was never at any moment
speaking to less than two people at a time, and sometimes
it was three.

Godfrey brought her the Visigoths' contract for the
company, its meticulous Latin checked for her to sign.
She signed—midway through remonstrating with Gustav
and his foot knights for attempting a last raid on Guizburg
castle, and that itself midway between counting remounts
and sacks of oatmeal with Henri Brant, listening to complaints from hand-gunners about lack of powder, and
hearing from Florian—*Floria!*—how wounds did or did
not mend. By the first midnight, she had visited each lance
of men at their own billets, agreeing the contract.

"We move at night," Ash announced. In part because at night *some* light existed—the moon waning into its last quarter still gave more light than the day did. In part because her men did not like riding under an unnatural daytime black sky, were safer, in her opinion, sleeping by day, no matter how difficult that might be. Shifting a camp of eighty lances and a baggage train each day is bad enough by daylight.

She was never, not for one heartbeat, alone.

She wrapped herself in impenetrable authority. There could be no questions asked. There were none. To herself, she seemed asleep, or sleepwalking at best.

She woke, paradoxically, five days later, out of sheer weariness.

Ash jolted out of a doze and found herself leaning her forehead against the neck of her mare. Conscious that her hand, gripping a horse brush, moved in small circles, decreasing now. Conscious that she had just spoken—but said what?

She raised her head and looked at Rickard. The boy looked frazzled.

Lady butted her with a plush nose, whuffing. Ash straightened. She ran her free hand across the warm, sleek flank, pressed out by the foal within. The mare whickered gently and pushed up against Ash with her golden shoulder. The rushes underfoot smelled pleasantly of horse dung.

Ash glanced down. She wore her high riding boots, the tops pointed in to her doublet skirt to keep them up. They were covered with mud and horse dung to the knee.

"The glorious life of a mercenary. If I'd wanted to spend my life knee-deep in shit, I could have been a peasant on a farm. At least you don't have to *move* a farm fifteen miles every cock-crow. Why am I ass-deep in crap?''

''Don't know, boss.'' It was the kind of rhetorical remark that some would have taken as an invitation to wit; Rickard only looked inarticulate. But pleased, too. This was obviously not what she had been talking about before.

Encouraged, Rickard said, ''She'll drop in around fifteen days.''

Her body was bruised, warm, weary. Pierced iron lanterns shone yellow light onto the moving walls of the canvas stall and the hay jutting from Lady's manger. Pleasant and restful in these early hours.

But if I leave, I won't see dawn breaking. Only darkness.

Ash heard the voices of men-at-arms outside talking, and the whine of dogs; she had not come through camp without an escort, then. *My absence of mind doesn't go that far.* She felt it as a real absence, as if someone had gone traveling and had only now returned.

''Fifteen days,'' she repeated. The handsome boy watched her. His shirt bunched up out of the gap between points at shoulder and lower back, and his face was thinning down, losing child-fat, changing to man. Ash gave him a reassuring smile. ''Good. Listen, Rickard, when you've taught Bertrand to be cup-bearer and page, I'll ask Roberto to take you on as squire. It's past time you trained.''

He said nothing, but his face illuminated, like a page from a manuscript.

After physical exertion, the body relaxes. Ash became aware of her loosened muscles; of the warmth from her demi-gown, made like a doublet with a fuller skirt and with the puffed sleeves sewn in, that was buttoned over her brigandine; of her sleepiness, that did nothing to take the edge off desire. She had an intense, sudden tactile memory: the line of Fernando del Guiz's flank from shoulder to hip, skin hot under her fingertips, and the thrust of his erect member.

"Shit!"

Rickard startled. He ventured, "Master Angelotti wants to talk to you."

Ash's hand went to Lady's neck automatically as the mare nuzzled at her. Touch calmed her. "Where is he?"

"Outside."

"Right. Yes, I'll see him now. Tell everyone else I'm unavailable for the next hour."

Five days unconscious of traveling between sloping walls of bald rock patched in the moonlight with white snow. Unconscious of the road. Cold scrub and heather and alpine weeds, and the clink of stones trickling off cliffs to either side. Moonlight on lakes, far below winding roads and scree. Now, if there was sunlight, she would be looking down into the distance, seeing unfenced green meadows and small castles on hilltops.

Moonlight showed her nothing of the surrounding country as she left the horse lines. From the camp, she could see no distance at all.

"Boss." Antonio Angelotti turned from speaking to her guards. He wore a voluminous red woollen cloak, which he should not need in July, over his brigandine and leg-armour. What crackled under his boots as he walked to her was not the dry rushes, but hoar frost.

The inner and outer circles of the company's wagons bristled with guns, behind pavises big as church doors. Bonfires burned within the central camp, where men slept in their bed-rolls, and burned also beyond the perimeter, by her order, to give sight of the country beyond, and to prevent their being silhouetted against flame for any passing bowman or hand-gunner. She could tell where the huge Visigoth camp was, a mile away, by flaring bonfires,

and by men distantly singing, in drink or in battle ardor—
it was not clear which.

"Let's go." She walked with Antonio Angelotti as far
as the massed cannon and the hand-gunners encamped
around their fires without speaking of more than organi-
zational matters. When the startlingly beautiful man stood
aside for her to go into his small tent, she knew her silence
was about to end.

"Rickard, see if you can find Father Godfrey, and F-
Florian. Send them to me here." She ducked through the
small pavilion's flap and entered. Her eyes adjusted to the
shadows. She seated herself on a wooden chest, bound
with straps and iron, that contained enough powder to
blow her and the hand-gunners outside to the Pit. "What
have you got to say privately?"

Angelotti eased himself into leaning against the edge
of his trestle table, without clipping the top edge of the
cuisses that armored his thighs. A sheaf of paper, covered
with calculations, fell to the rush-strewn earth. He was
incapable, Ash thought, of looking less than graceful in
any situation; but he was not incapable of seeming embarrassed.

"So I'm a bastard from North Africa, instead of a bastard from Flanders or England or Burgundy," she said
gently. "Does it really matter to you?"

He shrugged lithely. "That depends on which noble
family our Faris comes from, and whether they find you
embarrassing. No. In any case, you're a bastard for a family to be proud of. What's the matter?"

"Pr—!" Ash wheezed. Her chest burned. She slid
down the side of the chest and sat, spraddle-legged, in the
rushes, laughing so hard that she couldn't breathe. The
plates of her brigandine creaked with the movement of
her ribs. "Oh, Angel! Nothing. 'Proud.' Such a compli-
ment! You—no, nothing."

She wiped the back of her glove under her eyes. A push with powerful legs hitched her back up onto the wooden chest. "Master gunner, you know a lot about the Visigoths."

"North Africa is where I learned my mathematics." Angelotti was, it became apparent, studying her face. He did not look as though he knew he was doing it.

"How long were you over there?"

Oval lids lowered over his eyes. Angelotti had the face of a Byzantine icon, in this light of candles and shadows, with youth on it like the white film on the surface of a plum.

"I was twelve when I was taken." The long-lashed lids lifted. Angelotti looked her in the face. "The Turks took me off a galley near Naples. *Their* warship was taken by Visigoths. I spent three years in Carthage."

Ash did not have the nerve to ask him more about that time than **he** seemed disposed to volunteer now. It was more than he had said to her in four years. She wondered if he had wished, then, that he had not been quite so beautiful.

"I learned it in bed," Angelotti said smoothly, with a humorous twist to his mouth that made it clear her thinking was transparent to him. "With one of their *amirs*,[56] their scientist-magi. Lord-*Amir* Childeric. Who taught me trajectories for cannon, and navigation, and astrology."

Ash, used to seeing Angelotti always clean (if somewhat singed), and neat, itself a miracle in the mud and dust of the camp, and, above all, private—Ash thought, How badly does he think he needs to break through to me, to tell me this?

---

[56]*Amir* or *emir*: "lord." Arabic. I can find no linguistic proof for the connection either with the Persian *magi* (holy man or magician) in the Angelotti text, or with "scientist"—surely a much later addition to the text, by another hand.

She spoke hurriedly. "Roberto could be right, this could be their twilight . . . *spreading*. Godfrey would call it an Infernal contagion."

"He would not. He respects their *amirs*, as I do."

"What is it you want to say to me?"

Angelotti undid his cord cloak ties. The red wool cloth slid down his back, to the table, and bunched there. "My gunners are mutinous. They don't like it that you called off the siege of Guizburg. They're saying it's because del Guiz is your husband. That you no longer have the smile of Fortune."

"O Fortuna!" Ash grinned. "Fickle as a woman, isn't that what they're saying? All right, I'll talk to them. Pay them more. I know why they're mad. They had galleries dug in almost to the castle gate. I know they were really looking forward to blowing it sky-high . . . !"

"And so they feel cheated." Angelotti appeared extremely relieved. "If you'll talk to them . . . good."

"Is that all?"

"Are your voices the same as hers?"

The slightest tap will shatter pottery, given in the right place. Ash felt cracks crazing out from his question. She sprang to her feet in the cramped pavilion.

"You mean, is my saint *nothing*? Is the Lion nothing? Is it a demon speaking to me? Am I hearing a machine's voice, the way they say she does? *I don't know*." Breathing hard, Ash realized the fingers of her left hand had cramped around the scabbard of her sword. Knuckles whitened. "Can she do what they say she does? Can she hear some, some *device*, halfway across the middle sea? You've been there, you tell me!"

"It could be just a rumor. A complete lie."

"I don't know!" Ash unclamped her fingers slowly. Mutinous or not, she could hear the gunners celebrating one of their obscure saint's day feasts outside;[57] someone was singing something very loud and coarse about a bull being taken to a cow. She realized that the song was calling the bull *Fernando*. One of her dark brows went up. Maybe not so far from mutiny after all.

"The Faris's men have been building brick observation posts all down the roads, on the march." Angelotti spoke loudly over the embarrassing chorus.

"They're nailing this country down." Ash had a moment's sheer panic thinking *But where* are *we*? Fear vanished as the memories of the last few days welled up obediently in her mind. "I guess that's why they want to crown this Visigoth 'Viceroy' of theirs in Aachen."[58]

"The weather's bad. You said they'd have to settle for somewhere closer, and you were right, madonna."

In the moment's silence, Ash heard dogs bark, and friendly greetings from the guards; and Godfrey Maximillian walked in, stripping off sheepskin mittens, with Floria behind him. The surgeon pointed, and the boy Bernard, with a brazier, cleared a space in the tent to put it down, and heaped on more hot coals. At a nod from Angelotti, he clumsily served small beer, and butter and two-day old bread, before leaving.

"I hate bad preaching." Godfrey sat on another wooden chest. "I've just been giving them Exodus chapter ten, verse twenty-two, where Moses calls down a thick darkness from heaven over Egypt. Someone who knows is bound to ask why that only lasted three days, and this has gone on for three weeks."

---

[57]By internal mss. evidence, I calculate this takes place on 9 August, the feast day of King Osward of Northumbria. Born c. 605, died 642 at Maserfeth, St. Osward prayed for the souls of those who fell in battle with him. His cult as a soldier saint was later popular as far as south Germany and Italy.

[58]The coronation-place of Charlemagne.

The priest drank and wiped his beard. Ash carefully checked the distance between the various chests and flasks of powder, and the brazier's burning coals. *Probably okay*, she thought, having no great faith in Angelotti's good sense about gunpowder.

Floria warmed her hands at the brazier. "Robert's on his way here."

This is a meeting convened without my consent, Ash realized. And my bet is that they've been waiting five days to do it. She took a thoughtful bite out of the bread and chewed.

Anselm's voice barked outside. He ducked hurriedly in through the tent flap. "Can't stay, got to go and sort out the gate-guards for tonight—for today." He hauled his velvet bonnet off, seeing Ash. Candlelight shone on his shaven skull and on the pewter Lion livery badge fixed to his hat. "You're back, then."

The odd thing, perhaps, was that no one questioned his choice of words. They turned their faces to her, Angelotti's altar-painting features, Godfrey's crumb-strewn beard, Floria with her expression utterly closed.

"Where's Agnes?" Ash demanded suddenly. "Where's Lamb?"

"Half a mile to the northeast of us, camped, with fifty lances." Robert Anselm hitched his scabbard out of the way and stood beside Floria at the iron brazier. He would move entirely differently, Ash suddenly thought, if he realized Florian wasn't a man.

"Lamb *knew*," Ash snarled. "Motherfucker! He *must* have known, as soon as he saw her—their general. And he let me walk into that without a word of warning!"

"He let their general walk into it, too," Godfrey pointed out.

"And she hasn't hanged him yet?"

"I'm told he claims he never realized how close the

resemblance was. Apparently the Faris believes him.''

''Bloody hell.'' Ash seated herself on the edge of the trestle table, beside Angelotti. ''I'll send Rickard over with a challenge to a personal duel.''

''Not many people know what he did, if indeed he did, and it wasn't just a sin of omission.'' Godfrey licked butter from his white fingertips, his dark eyes keenly on her. ''You have no public need.''

''I might just fight him anyway,'' Ash grumbled. She folded her arms across her brigandine, looking down at the gilded rivet-heads and blue velvet. ''Look. She's *not* my fetch. I'm *not* her devil. I'm just some *amir* family's by-blow, that's all. Christ knows the Griffin-in-Gold went across the Mediterranean often enough twenty years ago. I'll be a bastard second cousin or something.''

She raised her head, catching Anselm and Angelotti exchanging a look that she couldn't read. Floria poked the red coals. Godfrey drank from a leather mug.

''There is something I thought we would say?'' Godfrey wiped his mouth and looked diffidently around the tent, at its shadowed folds and faces profiled in candlelight. ''About our complete confidence in our captain?''

Robert Anselm muttered, ''Fucking hell, clerk, get on with it, then!''

There was an anticipatory silence.

Into it, the last two lines of the hand-gunners' ballad echoed, having the failed bull Fernando being serviced by the cow.

Ash caught Anselm's eye and, poised between absolute rage and laughter, was precipitated into helpless giggles by what must be an exactly similar expression on Robert's face.

''I didn't hear that,'' she decided, cheerfully.

Angelotti looked up from scribbling with a quill, leaning across his trestle table. "That's all right, madonna, I've written it down in case you forget!"

Godfrey Maximillian sprayed bread-crumbs across the tent, whatever he would have said lost or superseded.

"I'm getting a new company," Ash announced, with a deadpan humor, and was disconcerted when Floria, who had remained silent, said flatly, "Yes—if you don't trust us."

Ash saw the absence of five days written into Floria's expression. She nodded slowly. "I do. I trust all of you."

"I wish I thought that you did."

Ash jabbed a finger at Floria. "*You're* coming with me. Godfrey, so are you. And Angelotti."

"Where?" Florian demanded

Ash rattled her fingertips against her scabbard, keeping arrhythmic time to her calculations. "The Visigoth general can't crown her Viceroy in Aachen; it's too far to travel. We're turning west. That means she's going for the nearest city here, which is Basle—"

Godfrey said excitedly, "That would be a useful first move! It fixes the League and the south Germanies under their government. Aachen can come later. Sorry. Go on, child."

"I'm going into Basle. You'll see why in a minute. Robert, I'm giving you temporary command of the company. I want you to make a fortified camp about three miles outside the city, on the western side. You can put my war-pavilion up, tables, carpets, silver plate, the whole works. In case you get visitors."

Anselm's high forehead wrinkled as he frowned. "We're used to being sent off while you negotiate a contract. This one is already signed."

"I know. I know. I'm not changing that."

"It isn't the way we've done it before."

"It's the way we're doing it now."

Ash unfolded her arms and stood up. She glanced around at their faces in the candlelit tent, fixing her gaze briefly on Floria. *There is a lot of history here. Some of it not known to everyone.* She put the problem aside for later.

"I want to talk to the general." Ash hesitated. Then she went on, speaking to each of them in turn.

"Godfrey, I want you to talk to your monastic contacts. And F-Florian, you talk to the Visigoth physicians. Angelotti, you know mathematicians and gunners in their camp; go get drunk with them. I want to know *everything* about this woman!—I want to know what she has to break her fast, what she wants her army to do in Christendom, who her family are, and whether she *does* hear voices. I want to know if *she* knows what's happened to the sun."

Outside, the setting crescent moon argues the arrival of another lightless day.

"Roberto. While I'm *inside* the walls of Basle," Ash said, "I can do with all the implicit threat that I can get, sitting there *outside*."

Going into the city of Basle, Ash could think of nothing else except *She has my face.* I don't have father or mother, there's no one in the world who looks like me, but *she has my face. I have to talk to her.*

Sweet Christ, I wish it would get light!

In the daytime darkness, between its mountains, Basle echoed with the hooves of war-horses and the shouts of soldiers. Citizens leaped out of her way, scurried indoors; or never left their houses, shouted from upper story windows as she rode by. *Whore, bitch,* and *traitor* were most common.

"Nobody loves a mercenary," Ash mock-sighed. Rickard laughed. The company's men-at-arms swaggered.

Crosses marked most doors. The churches were packed.

Ash rode through processional flagellations, finding the civic buildings all shut up except for one guild house. That had black pennants outside.

Ash negotiated climbing the narrow crooked stairs in armor, her escort behind her. Bare oak support beams protruded from the white plastered walls. The lack of space made any weapon a liability. A rising noise came from the upstairs chambers: men's voices speaking Schweizerdeutsch, Flemish, Italian, and the Latin of North Africa. The Faris's council of occupation: somewhere she might be found.

"Here." Ash took off her sallet and handed it to Rickard. Condensation misted the bright metal.

It was, when she entered, no different from any other room in any other city. Stone-framed windows with diamond leaded panes, looking out on rain on the cobbled streets below. Four-story houses across the narrow alley, plaster-and-beam frontages gleaming in the wet—in rain turning to sleet, she suddenly realized. White dots dropped into the circles of lantern light, light from other windows and the pitch torches illuminating the men-at-arms below.

Sloping roofs blocked the black sky above the street. The room sweltered and stank with a hundred tallow candles and rush-lights. When she looked at the marked wax candle, she saw it was just past midday.

"Ash." She produced a leather livery badge. "Condottiere to the Faris."

The Visigoth guards let her pass in. She seated herself at table, her men behind her, reasonably secure in her knowledge that Robert Anselm could handle both Joscelyn van Mander and Paul di Conti; that he would take notice of what the leaders of smaller lances said; that, if it came to it, the company would follow him into an attack. A quick glance around showed her Europeans and Visigoths, but not their Faris.

An *amir* (by his robes) said, "We must arrange this coronation. I appeal to you all for procedure."

Another Visigoth civilian began to read, carefully, from a European illuminated manuscript. " 'As soon as the Archbishop hath put the crown on the king's head, then shall the king offer his sword to God on the altar . . . the worthiest earl that is there present shall . . . bear it naked before the king . . .' "[59]

This is not what I do, Ash thought. How the hell do I get to speak to their general?

She scratched at her neck, under her mail standard. Then she stopped, not wanting to draw attention to rat-nibbled leather and the red dots of flea-bites.

"But why crown our Viceroy by heathen ceremonies?" one of the Visigoth *qa'ids* demanded. "Even their own kings and emperors don't command these people's loyalty, so what good will it do!"

Further down the table, on the far side, a man with yellow hair cut short in the Visigoth military fashion lifted his head. She found herself staring at the face of Fernando del Guiz.

"Ah—nothing personal, del Guiz," the same Visigoth military officer added genially. "After all, you may be a traitor, but, hell, you're *our* traitor!"

A ripple of dry humor went around the wooden table, quelled by the *amir*, who nonetheless glanced at the young German knight quizzically.

Fernando del Guiz smiled. His expression was open,

---

[59]This is similar to the Hastings manuscript Ordinances of Chivalry of the fifteenth century, "The maner and the forme of the Coronacion of kyngis and Quenes in Engelonde."

generous, complicit with the high-ranking Visigoth officer, as if Fernando was seeing the joke against himself.

It was the same disarming smile he had shared with her
outside the Emperor's tent at Neuss.

Ash saw his forehead gleaming in the candlelight: shiny
with sweat.

Not a sign of strength of character. Not at all.

"*Fuck!*" Ash shouted.

" 'And the king shall be'—" A white-haired man, in
a murrey-colored woollen pleated gown, with a silver
linked chain around his neck, looked up from tracing a
handwritten document with his beringed finger. "Your
pardon, Frau?"

"*Fuck!*" Ash sprang up and leaned forward, her gauntleted hands resting on the table. Fernando del Guiz:
stone-green eyes. Fernando del Guiz, in a mail hauberk,
and a white tunic under it; the badge of a *qa'id* laced to
his shoulder, and his mouth now white around the lips.
He met her eyes and she felt it, felt the eye-contact as a
literal jolt under her ribs.

"*You* are *a fucking traitor!*"

The hilt of her sword is solid in her grip, the razor-
sharp blade drawn two inches from the scabbard before
she even thinks about it, every trained muscle beginning
to move. She feels in her body the anticipated jolt of the
sword-point stabbing through his bare, unprotected face.
Smashing cheekbone, eye, brain. Brute force solves so
many things in life not worth wasting time thinking about;
this is what she does for a living, after all.

In the split second before she drew, Agnus Dei—now
visible, sitting in his Milanese armor and white surcoat
beyond the *amir*—gave a shrug that said plainly, *women!*
and said loudly, "Keep your private business for another
time, madonna!"

Ash flicked a glance back to ascertain where her six

men-at-arms were positioned behind her. Impassive faces. Ready for back-up. Except for Rickard. The boy bit on his bare hand, appalled at the silence.

It reached her.

Fernando del Guiz watched, no expression on his face. Safe behind the walls of public protection.

"I will," Ash said, sitting down. Around the low-beamed room, suddenly tense men wearing swords relaxed. She added, "I'll keep my business with Lamb for another time, too."

"Perhaps mercenaries do not need to attend on this meeting, condottieri," the lord-*amir* offered dryly.

"Guess not." Ash braced her hands against the edge of the oak table. "I really need to speak with your Faris."

"She is in the town's great hall."

It was clearly the placation of a quarrelsome mercenary. Ash appreciated it. She pushed herself to her feet and concealed a smile at Agnus Dei having also to gather his men, make his farewells and leave the meeting and the house.

She glanced back as Lamb and his men stepped carefully out onto the cobbles after her. She tugged her cloak around her against the sleet. "All mercenaries out on the street together . . ."

That would either make him fight or laugh.

The creases deepened in his brown face, under his barbute with its sodden plumes. "What's she paying you, madonna?"

"More than you. Whatever it is, I bet it's more than you."

"You have the more lances," he said mildly, pulling on his heavy gauntlets.

Confused by the evaporation of her anger, Ash put on her helm and reached out as Rickard brought Godluc, and mounted quickly and easily. Not that a war-horse's shod hooves were anymore certain on the cobbles than her own slick-soled boots.

Lamb called, ''Did your Antonio Angelotti tell you? They've burned Milano, too. Down to the dirt.''

A smell of wet horse permeated the chill air.

''You were from Milan, weren't you, Lamb?''

''No mercenary is from anywhere, madonna, you know that.''

''Some of us try.'' That brought Guizburg to mind, fifty miles away—shattered town walls and unbreached keep— and another jolt left her breathless: *he is upstairs in that little room and I wish he was dead!*

''Which one of you was it,'' she demanded, ''who let 'twins' meet, without warning either of us?''

Lamb chuckled harshly. ''If the Faris believed it was my fault, madonna, would I be here?''

''But Fernando's still here, too.''

The Italian mercenary gave her a look that said *you are a child* and had nothing to do with her age.

Ash said recklessly, ''What about if I paid you to kill my husband?''

''I'm a soldier, not an assassin!''

''Lamb, I always knew you had principles, if I could only find them!'' She made a joke of it, laughing it away, uncomfortably aware from the look on the Italian's face that he knew it was not a joke.

''Besides, he's the coming man with the Faris-General.'' Agnus Dei touched his white surcoat, his expression changing. ''God judges him, madonna. Do you think you're the only enemy he has, having done this? God's judgment comes on him.''

''I'd like to get in first.'' Ash, grim, watched Agnus Dei and his men mount up. Hooves and voices echoed between high, narrow houses. A bitch of a street to fight along, she thought, and dropped her chin into her mail standard to mutter aloud—purely as a supposition—and for the first time since Genoa: "Six mounted knights against seven—all carrying war-hammers, swords, axes—on very bad ground—"

And stopped. And reached up to jerk the visor of her sallet down, hiding her face. She whirled Godluc, iron shoes striking sparks in the sleet, and slid off at a gallop, men-at-arms following her all anyhow, Lamb's appalled shout lost in the clatter.

No! I said nothing! I don't want to hear—!

Nothing rational: a wall of fear rose up in her mind. She would not consider the reasons why.

It's only the saint I have heard since I was a child: why—

I don't want to hear my voice.

Eventually she let Godluc slow on the dangerous cobbles. Torches flared as Ash led her entourage through narrow, pitch-dark streets. A clock distantly struck two of the afternoon.

"I know where we'll pick up the surgeon on the way," she told Thomas Rochester, having given up *Floria-Florian* as a name that made her speech stumble. Rochester nodded and directed the manner of their riding: himself and another armored horseman before her, two more at the rear, and the two mounted crossbowmen in their felt hats to ride beside her. The road underfoot changed from cobbles to frozen mud ruts.

Ash rode between houses with tiny paned windows illuminated by cheap rush-lights. A black dot jerked and darted across her vision. Godluc tossed his head at its angular flight. Bats, she realized: bats flying out from under the house-caves, in this dark daytime, snatching at insects, or trying to.

Something crunched under the war-horse's shod hooves.

Stretching across the cold dirt in front of them, insects lay like a crisp frost.

Pismires of the air, all dead from cold: honey-bees, wasps, blow-flies. A hundred thousand of them. Godluc's feathered hooves came down on the bright, broken wings of butterflies.

"Here," she directed, at a three-story house with a stack of overhanging windows. Rochester snuffled. She could see little of the dark-haired Englishman's face under his visor, but when she studied the house outside which they had halted, she guessed the reason for his humor. A hundred rush-lights shone in the windows, someone was singing, someone was playing a lute surprisingly well, and three or four men were being sick in the gutter in the center of the alley. Whorehouses always do good business in a crisis.

"You guys wait for me." Ash swung down from the saddle. Light glinted from her steel armor. "And I mean *here*. I don't want to find any of you missing when I come back!"

"No, boss." Rochester grinned.

Thick-necked men in jerkins and hose, backlit, let her pass, seeing armor and livery jacket. Nothing unusual about a boy-voiced knight or man-at-arms in a Basle whorehouse. Two questions got her knowledge of the room occupied by a yellow-haired Burgundian-accented surgeon, two silver coins of indeterminate issue gained silence. She strode up the stairs, knocked once, and went in.

A woman was lying back on a pallet in the corner of the small room, her bodice pulled down and her long veined breasts drooping out. All her chemises and her woolen kirtle were ruffled up about her naked thighs. She might have been anything between sixteen and thirty, Ash couldn't tell. She had dyed yellow hair, and a small plump chin.

The room smelled of sex.

There was a lute beside the whore, and a candle and some bread on a wooden plate on the floor. Floria del Guiz sat cross-wise on the pallet with her back against the plaster of the wall. She drank from a leather bottle. All her points had been unlaced; one brown nipple was visible where her breast lay out of her open shirt.

As Ash watched, the whore stroked Floria's neck.

"Is this a sin?" the girl demanded fiercely. "Is it, sir? But fornication is a sin in itself, and I have fornicated with many men. They are bulls in a field, with their great cocks. She is gentle and wild with me."

"Margaret. Sssh." Floria leaned forward and kissed the young woman on the mouth. "I am to leave, I see. Shall I come back and visit you?"

"When you have the money." A glint, under the bravado, of something else. "Mother Astrid won't let you in if you don't. And come in your man-shape. I don't want to make a bonfire for the church."

Floria met Ash's black look. The surgeon's eyes danced. "This is Margaret Schmidt. She's excellent with her fingers—on the lute."

Ash turned her back on the young whore rearranging her clothes, and on Floria, tying her points with a surgeon's neatness. She walked across the floor. Boards creaked. A deep male voice shouted something from upstairs; there was a series of rising cries, faked, in another upstairs room.

"*I* never whored with women!" Ash turned, stiffly, in metal plates. "I went with men. I never went with animals, or women! How can you *do* that?"

Margaret murmured, shocked, "He's a woman!" to which Floria, now tying on her cloak and hood, said,

"She is, greatheart. If you fancy life on the road, there are worse camps to join."

Ash wanted to shout, but kept her mouth shut, halted by the decisions passing across the young woman's face.

Margaret rubbed her chin. "It's no life, among soldiers. And listen to him, to her, I couldn't be with you, could I?"

"I don't know, sweetness. I've never kept a woman before."

"Come back here before you go. I'll give you my answer then." With remarkable self-possession, Margaret Schmidt tidied the lute and the plate onto an oaken stool in the chiaroscuro of the rush-light. "What are you waiting for? Mother will be sending another one to me. Or she'll charge you double."

Ash didn't wait to see what she thought might be a kiss of parting—except that whores do not kiss, she thought; *I* never—

She turned and stomped down the narrow stairs, between doors sometimes open to men with bottles and dice, sometimes to men fornicating with women—until she stopped and spun around in the hallway, nearly impaling the surgeon on the sharp edge of her steel elbow-couter. "What the *hell* do you think you're doing? You were supposed to be sounding out other physicians, picking up trade gossip!"

"What makes you think I haven't been?"

The tall woman checked belt, purse and dagger with an automatic touch of one hand, the other still clasped around the neck of the leather bottle.

"I got the physician to the Caliph's cousin truly rat-arsed, right here. He tells me in confidence that Caliph Theodoric has a canker, months to live at best."

Ash only stared, the words going past her.

"Your face!" Floria laughed. She drank from the bottle.

"*Shit, Florian, you're fucking women!*"

"Florian's perfectly safe fucking women." She swept her man-cut hair back into her hood, where it framed her long-boned face. "Now wouldn't it be inconvenient if I wanted to fuck men?"

"I thought you were just paying for a room, and her time! I thought it was a trick, to keep up your disguise!"

Floria's expression softened. She patted Ash gently on her scarred cheek and then dropped the empty bottle and whipped her mittens on against the chill seeping in from the street. "Sweet Christ. If I can put it the way our excellent Roberto would—don't be such a humorless hard-ass."

Ash made a half-noise, not speech, all breath. "But you're a woman! Going with another woman!"

"It doesn't bother you with Angelotti."

"But he's—"

"He's a man, with another man?" Floria said. Her mouth shook. "Ash, for Christ's sake!"

An older woman with a tight face under her coif came out from the kitchens. "Are you bravos looking for a woman or wasting my time? Sir knight, I beg your pardon. All our girls are very clean. Aren't they, doctor?"

"Excellently." Floria pushed Ash toward the door. "I'll bring my lord back when our business is done with."

Cold darkness blinded Ash outside the doors; then Thomas Rochester and her men and their pitch-torches dazzled her, so that she hardly saw a boy bring Floria her bay gelding. She mounted and settled herself down in Godluc's saddle.

She opened her mouth to shout. And then realized that

she had no idea what to say. Floria, watching her, looked
supremely unapologetic.

''Godfrey will be at the hall by now.'' Ash shifted,
rousing Godluc to a slow walk. ''The Faris will be there.
Ride on.''

Floria's gelding shivered and flicked its head up. The
white, soundless swoop of a disorientated barn owl curved
past in flight, not a yard from the surgeon's hat.

''Look.'' Floria pointed up.

Ash tilted her head to gaze up at the high gable roofs.

She was not used to noticing the fullness of the summer
skies. Now, every gable line and window ledge clustered
thick with roosting birds—with pigeons, rooks, crows and
thrushes, fluffing out feathers against the chill. Blackbirds,
sparrows, ravens; all, in an uncanny peace, sharing their
perches undisturbed with merlin hawks, and peregrines,
and kestrels. A low, discontented mumbling went up from
the flocks. White guano streaked the beams and plaster.

Above them, the overcast clouds of the day's sky stayed
invisible, and black.

Despite the Visigoth ordinance restricting any noble's escort to six or less, Basle's civic hall was packed with men.
It stank of tallow candles and the remnants of a huge
banquet, and of two or three hundred sweating men
crowded into the space between the tables, waiting to petition the Visigoth Viceroy at the high dais.

The Visigoth general was not visibly present.

''Fucking hell,'' Ash swore. ''Where *is* the woman?''

A fug smudged the heights of the barrel vaulted roof,
with the Empire's and Cantons' banners hanging down
over tapestried stone walls. Ash let her gaze sweep across
rushes and candles and men in European dress, doublet
and hose, and brimless felt hats with tall crowns. Far more

men were wearing southern robes and mail: soldiers and *'arifs* and *qa'ids*. But no Faris.

Ash tilted the visor of her sallet low, leaving only mouth and nose to be seen, her silver hair hidden under her steel helmet. Fully armored, she is not immediately recognizable as a woman, never mind as a woman who bears a resemblance to the Visigoth general.

Around the walls, as servers, stood clay-colored Visigoth golem, eyeless and metal-jointed, their baked skins cracking in the great fireplaces' heat. Lifting herself on armored toes, Ash could see one golem standing behind the white-robed Visigoth Viceroy—who was, she noted with a little surprise, Daniel de Quesada—and holding a brazen head, which de Quesada consulted for a currency exchange as she watched.

Floria took wine from one of the pantlers rushing past, not apparently minding that it came from well below the salt. "How on earth can you tell this lot apart? Bear and swan and bull and marten and unicorn . . . It's a bestiary!"

A fast scrutiny of heraldry on liveries showed Ash that men were present from Berne, Zürich, Neufchatel and Solothurn, and from Fribourg and Aargau . . . most of the Swiss Confederation lords, or whatever one called the lords among the League of Constance, all with an equally shut-faced look to them. Conversations were going on in Schweizerdeutsch and Italian and German, but the main talk—the shouted talk up at the head table—in Carthaginian. Or in North African Latin when the Visigoth *amirs* and *qa'ids* recalled their manners, which nothing forced them to do.

So where do I look for her now?

Thomas Rochester rejoined Ash, moving through the civilian crowd. The lawyers and officials of Basle moved back automatically, as one does from a man in steel plate, but otherwise ignored the mercenary man-at-arms. He lowered his voice to speak to Ash.

"She's been out at the camp, looking for you."

"*What?*"

"Captain Anselm sent a rider. The Faris is on her way back here now."

Ash kept her hand from her sword grip with an effort of mind, such gestures being prone to misinterpretation in a crowded hall. "Did Anselm's message say what her business was?"

"To talk to one of her mercenary *junds*." Thomas grinned. "We're important enough for her to come to us."

"And I'm Saint Agatha's tits!" Suddenly queasy, Ash watched the throng around Daniel de Quesada, which did not grow any the less for being watched. Quesada's face was hardly marred by scars now. His eyes moved very quickly around the hall, and when one of the cocky-tailed white dogs nosing in the rushes yipped, his body startled uncontrollably.

"I wonder who's pulling *his* strings?" Ash thought aloud. "And did she come out just to take a look at me, back at Guizburg? Maybe. Now she's gone out to the camp. That's a lot of trouble to go to, just to look at a bastard one of your family fathered on a mercenary camp-follower twenty years ago."

Antonio Angelotti appeared at her elbow, tall and sweating and swaying. "Boss. 'M going back to camp. It's true. Their armies defeated the Swiss ten days ago."

Knowing it must have happened, and hearing it, were two different things. Ash said, "Sweet Christ. Have you found anyone who was there, who saw it?"

"Not yet. They were outmaneuvered. The *Swiss.*"

"Oh, that's why everyone's creeping up the arses of the King-Caliph. That's why everybody's throwing banquets. Son of a bitch. I wonder if Quesada meant it when he said they intended to war on Burgundy?'' She shook Angelotti's shoulder roughly. ''Okay, go back to camp; you're pissed.''

The master gunner, leaving, drew her eye to the great doors. Godfrey Maximillian strode in, glanced around, and made for the blue Lion liveries. The priest bowed to Ash and glanced at Floria del Guiz before he opened his mouth to speak.

''*That's* the look I hate,'' the disguised woman said, not particularly quietly. ''Every time before you speak to me now. I don't bite, Godfrey. How long have you known me! For Christ's sake!''

Her cheeks flushed, her eyes brilliant. Her bowl-shaped haircut was spiked with damp drizzle. A server and a pantler glanced as they hurried past, their white aprons stained. Seeing what, when they see her? Ash wondered. A man, definitely. With no sword, therefore a civilian. A professional man, because of the well-cut woollen demigown lined with fur, and the fine hose and boots and velvet hat. A livery badge pinned to the upturned velvet hat-brim: therefore a man who belongs to a lord. And— given the prominent Lion—belonged to Ash.

''Quieten down. I've got enough problems here.''

''And I don't? I'm a woman, for fuck's sake!''

Too loud. Ash beckoned Thomas Rochester and Michael, one of the crossbowmen, forward from the rear wall of the hall.

''Take him outside, he's drunk.''

''Yes, boss.''

''Why does everything have to *change*?'' Floria demanded, wrenching her arms away. Thomas Rochester efficiently punched the surgeon in the small of the back, his armored fist hardly moving any distance, and while her face was screwed up in pain, lifted her between himself and Michael and half-carried her out.

"Shit." Ash frowned. "I didn't mean them to man-handle h—— . . ."

"You wouldn't object if you still thought she was a man." Godfrey's hand gripped his cross on his substantial chest. The hood of his robe was far enough forward to give her only a glimpse of beard and lips, nothing of his expression.

"We'll wait till the Faris gets here," Ash said decisively. "What have you heard?"

"That's the head of the goldsmiths' guild." Godfrey indicated with a slight inclination of his hood. "Over there, talking to the Medici."

Ash's gaze searched along the table, identifying a man in a black wool coif, with strands of silver hair wisping out under his ear. He sat within easy whisper of a man in an Italianate gown and a dagged green hood. The Medici sat gray-faced and drawn.

"They trashed Florence, too, to make a point." Ash shook her head. "Like Venice. To say, we don't *need* this. Don't need the money or the armor or the guns. We can just keep pouring it in from Africa . . . I think they can."

"Does it matter?" A man in a scholar's gown first bowed to Ash and then straightened, startled, frowning at the unexpected woman's voice.

Godfrey interposed himself. "Sir, you are?"

"I am—I was—astrologer to the court of the Emperor Frederick."

Ash could not help a snort of cynicism, her eyes traveling to the hall door and the darkness beyond. "Bit redundant, aren't you?"

"God has taken the sun away," the astrologer said. "Dame Venus, the daystar, may still be seen at certain hours, thus we know when morning *would* break, but for

our wickedness. The heaven remain dark, and empty.''
The man wilted a little. ''This is the second coming of
the Christ, and his judgment. I have not lived as I should.
Will you hear my confession, Father?''

Godfrey bowed, at Ash's acknowledgment; and she
watched the two men find a relatively quiet corner of the
hall. The astrologer knelt. After a time, the priest rested
his hand on the man's forehead in token of forgiveness.
He came back to Ash.

''It seems the Turks have paid spies here,'' Godfrey
added. ''Which my astrologer knows. He says the Turks
are much relieved.''

''Relieved?''

''The Visigoths having taken the Italian cities, and the
Cantons, and south Germany; they must either turn east
and strike at the Turk Empire, or west at Europe.''

''If they turn west, then the Turks might face a Visigoth
rather than a Christian Europe, but otherwise no change;
well,'' Ash said, ''since Sultan Mehmet[60] must have
thought all this was intended for him, he will be relieved!''

There were present, Ash saw, a few nervous men of
Savoy and France, as yet untouched, desperate to know
which way the Visigoth invasion was aimed next.

''I hate cities,'' she said absently. ''They're a fire haz-
ard. You can't buy oil or tapers here for gold. I give it
two days before this city burns itself from wall to wall.''

She expected some comment on her grumpiness, given
with ease based on their long knowledge of each other.
What Godfrey said, in a thoughtful tone, was, ''We talk
as if the sun will never shine again.''

Ash stood silent.

''It's still getting colder. I rode through fields on my

---

[60]Mehmet II, ruled the Turkish Empire AD 1451–1481.

way in. The wheat is being blighted, and the vines. Such a famine is coming . . .'' Godfrey's voice rumbled in his resonant chest. "Perhaps I was wrong. Famine is coming, and pestilence with it, and death and war are already here. These *are* the final days. We should be looking to the state of our souls, not picking among the ruins.''

"I want the general of the Visigoths." Ash said speculatively, ignoring him. "And the general of the Visigoths is looking for me.''

"Yes." Godfrey hesitated, watching her survey the town hall. "Child, you are not about to send us away from here.''

"I am, too." The flicker of a grin. "You and Florian. Take her. Ride with Michael and Josse, out to Roberto at the camp, and stay there unless you hear from me. Can't you feel your hackles rising here? Go.''

One thing about the habit of giving orders is that others fall into the habit of obeying them. She could see, under his hood, Godfrey Maximillian smooth his face to a pious unconcern. He made his way deceptively fast through the crowd, to the doors.

That leaves me and an escort of four men, Ash concluded. Yippee. Now we'll see who's a mistrusting bitch.

One could stay standing around at the back of the hall, not being offered salver and cloth to wash one's hands, never mind any meat or the strange foreign dishes spilling on the yellowing linen tablecloths. One could keep waiting. Ash thought, until the sycophancy attendant on Daniel de Quesada's installation lost its first fervor. That might be days. Weeks.

She watched the men from France and Savoy gathering in tiny groups, nittering anxiously.

"I wish I had the French king's intelligence service. Or the Flemish bankers.' " She turned to Thomas Rochester. "Guido and Simon, to the buttery, see what you can hear; Francis and you, Thomas, as and when the shit hits the fan here, we ride like hell for Anselm, got that?''

Rochester looked doubtful. ''Boss, this is dodgy.''

''I know. We ought to leave now. But . . . There might be some privilege in being a bastard from the Faris's family. We might get more money.'' Ash shook her head. The white scars on her face stood out dark, by virtue of her pale skin. ''I just want to *know*.''

She worked the hall for a time. She cornered a merchant and argued a price for goods to make up losses of mules and baggage outside Genoa. The cost of replacement wagons shook her, until the man quoted her his price for broken and schooled horses. *Stealing may be better than buying*, she reflected, not for the first time.

A flurry of servants went past her, replacing burned-down candles and exhausted lanterns, and she stepped back against the wall out of their way, catching her scabbard across someone's knees.

''Pardon—'' She turned, stopped, staring up at Fernando del Guiz. ''Son of a *bitch!*''

''How *is* mother?'' he inquired, mildly.

She snorted, thought: He *meant* to make me laugh.

That realization shocked her into silence. She stood out of the crowd, staring up at his face: Fernando del Guiz in Visigoth military mail and surcoat, the cropped hair making him look oddly younger.

''Christus fucking Imperator! What do *you* want?'' Ash saw Thomas Rochester, still finalizing delivery with the merchant, look over at her inquiringly; she shook her head. ''Fernando—no: what? *What? What* can you possibly have to say to me?''

''You're very angry,'' he remarked. His voice came from above her, where he stared out across the heads of the crowd; and then he suddenly dropped his gaze, impaling her. "I don't have anything to say to you, peasant."

"That's fucking good. Being noble didn't stop you going over to the Visigoths, did it? You *are* a traitor. I thought it was a *lie*." Anger, fueling her, ran out, drained away with the flinch of his eyes. She was silent for a second.

He began to turn away.

"*Why?*" Ash demanded.

" 'Why'?"

"You—I still don't understand. You're a lord. Even if they were going to take you prisoner, they'd have ransomed you back. Or kept you safe in a castle somewhere. Hell, you had armed and armored men with you, you could have broken out, run—"

"From an army?" Humor in his expression now.

Ash put a steel-covered arm in front of his body, so that Fernando del Guiz would have to push past her to get out into the body of the hall. "You didn't run into an army. That's just rumor. Godfrey brought me the truth of it. You ran into a squad of eight men—*eight* men. You didn't even try to fight. You just surrendered."

"My skin's worth more to me than your good opinion." Fernando sounded sardonic. "I didn't know you cared, madam wife."

"I don't! I—Well, it got you a place at this court. With the winners." She nodded at the hall. "Devious. And you were taking a real chance. But then, the Emperor's nobles are all politicians—I should have remembered that."

"It *wasn't*—!" Fernando glared down into her face. The candlelight showed his upper lip beaded with damp.

"Wasn't what?" Ash asked, more quietly.

"Wasn't *political* treason!" Some odd expression crossed his face, in the deceptive light of the candles. He held her gaze. "They killed Matthias! They stuck a

spear into his stomach and he fell off his horse, screaming! They shot Otto with a crossbow bolt, and three of
the horses—''

Ash forced her voice down to a hoarse, outraged whisper:

''Jesus Christ, Fernando, you're not like fucking Matthias. They'd have given you quarter. And what about all
your fancy kit—you were fully armored, for Christ's sake,
up against Visigoth peasants in tunics! You can't tell me
you couldn't have fought your way out! You didn't even
try to bang out of there!''

''I couldn't do it!''

She stared at him: at the sudden, stark honesty on his
face.

''I couldn't do it,'' Fernando repeated, more quietly,
and with a smile that made his face seem older, distressed.
''I filled my hose, and I fell off my horse, and I lay in
front of the peasant sergeant and I begged him not to kill
me. I gave him the ambassador in exchange for my life.''

''You—''

''I gave in,'' Fernando said, ''because I was afraid.''

Ash continued to stare. ''Jesus Christ.''

''And I don't regret it.'' Fernando wiped his face with
his bare hand, bringing it away wet. ''What's it to you?''

''I—'' Ash hesitated. She let her arm drop, not block-
ing his way now. ''I don't know. Nothing. I suppose. I'm
a mercenary; I'm not one of your retainers or your king;
I'm not the one you've betrayed.''

''You don't get it, do you?'' Fernando del Guiz did not
move away from where they stood. ''There were men
with crossbows. Steel arrowheads as thick as my thumb—
I saw a bolt go through Otto's face, straight through his
eye, bang! His *head* exploded. Matthias was holding his
entrails in his hands. Men with spears, like spears I've

hunted with, gutting open animals, and they were going to gut me. I was surrounded by *madmen.*''

"Soldiers," Ash corrected automatically. She shook her head, puzzled. "Everybody craps themselves when there's going to be a fight. I do. Thomas Rochester over there has; so have most of my men. That's the bit they don't put in the chronicles. But fucking hell, you don't have to surrender when there's still a fighting chance!''

"*You* don't.''

His intense expression aged him: a young man grown suddenly old. I've been to your bed, Ash thought suddenly, and it seems I don't know you at all.

He said, "*You* have physical courage. I never knew, until that moment—I've done tournaments, mêlées . . . war's *different.*''

Ash looked at him with complete incomprehension. "Of course it is.''

They stared at each other.

"Are you telling me you did this because you're a *coward*?''

For answer, Fernando del Guiz turned and walked away. The shifting light of candles hid his expression.

Ash opened her mouth to call him back, and said nothing, could think of nothing, for long minutes, that she wanted to say.

Over the hubbub of talk and rattle of papers being signed, she heard Basle's town clock strike four of the afternoon.

"That's long enough." She signaled Rochester, resolutely put del Guiz out of her thoughts. "Wherever the Faris-General is, she's not coming here. Get the lads.''

Thomas Rochester retrieved the men-at-arms from (respectively) the stables, the kitchens, and a maid's dormitory bed. Ash sent Guido out for the horses. She stepped out of the town hall between Rochester and the other crossbowman, Francis, two yards tall, a burly man who looked as if he might not need a crank to cock a bow: he could probably do it with his teeth. The sky above the courtyard was empty. Black. All the shouting of grooms and horses' hooves on stones couldn't cover the silence that seeped down from above.

Francis crossed himself. "I wish the Christ would come. The tribulation first, that scares me. Not the Last Judgment."

Ash caught sight of orange dots all down her vambraces, where sleet falling on her arms had turned to rust spots during her time within the warm civic hall. She muttered an obscenity and scrubbed at the steel with a linen-covered finger, waiting for the horses.

"Captain," a man's accented, Visigothic Latin said. She looked up. She saw in rapid succession that he was an *'arif* commander of forty, that he had twenty men, that all of them had their swords out of their sheaths. She stepped back and drew, screaming at Thomas Rochester. Six or seven mail hauberk-covered bodies hit her from behind and slammed her down on her face.

Her sallet and visor hit the cobbles, slamming her forehead against the helmet's padding. Dazed, she closed her left hand and swung her gauntlet back. Her thick metal fist thunked into something. A voice screamed above her, on top of her. She bent her left arm. Armor is a weapon. The great butterfly-plates of the couter that protect the inner elbow joint flow, at the back, to a sharpened spike. She slammed her bent elbow back and up and felt the spike punch through mail to flesh. A shout.

She thrashed, struggled to bend her legs, searingly afraid of a hamstring cut across the back of her unprotected knee. Two mail-clad bodies lay full-weight across her right arm, across her hand that gripped her sword-hilt. Men shouted. Two or three more bodies hit her in rapid succession, slamming down against her backplate, holding her motionless, pinned, unhurt, a crab in a padded steel shell.

Their hard-breathing weight pinned her absolutely. *So I am not to be killed.*

Weight across her armored shoulders kept her from raising her head. She saw nothing but a few inches of stone, straw and dead cold bees. About a yard away, there was a soft impact and a scream.

I should have made *them let me bring a larger escort! Or sent Rochester away—*

She tightened the grip of her gauntleted right hand on her sword. With her left hand unnoticed for a moment, she folded her fingers under, so that the sharp edge of the plate on the back of her hand jutted forward, and shoved the edge out to where she guessed a man's face to be.

No impact. Nothing.

A heel in a mail sabaton came down on her right hand, trapping her fingers and flesh around the sword's grip, between the steel plates of her gauntlet, between the man's full weight and the hard cobblestones.

She shrieked. Her hand released. Someone kicked the blade away.

A dagger-point stabbed down and into her open visor and stopped a quivering inch away from her eye.

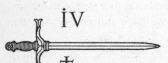

IV

THE WANING MOON cast a faint light, setting over Basle's castle. Far off, away and high over the city walls, the same silver light glimmered on the snow of the Alps.

The tall hedges of the *hortus conclusus* shone with frost. *Frost in summer!* Ash thought, still appalled, and stumbled in the near-darkness. The sound of a fountain plinked out of the dimness, and she heard the shift and clatter of many men in armor.

They have left me my armor, therefore they intend to treat me with some respect; they have only taken my sword; therefore they do not *necessarily* intend to kill me—

"What the fuck *is* all this?" Ash demanded. Her guards didn't answer.

The enclosed garden was tiny, a small plot of grass surrounded by an octagon of hedges. Flowers climbed frames. A cropped grassy bank ran down to a fountain, the jet falling into a white marble basin. The scent of herbs filled the air. Ash identified rosemary and Wound's-Ease individually; underneath their smell was a stench of decaying roses. *Died from the cold, rotting on the stalk*, she surmised, and continued to walk forward into the garden, between her *'arif*'s guards.

A figure in a mail hauberk sat at a low table covered with papers, on top of the grassy bank. Behind her, three stone figures held torches upright in their hands. A trail of hot spitting pitch ran down a torch-shaft as Ash watched, over one figure's clenched brass-geared hand, but the golem did not flinch.

Torch-flame cast flickering yellow light over the young Visigoth woman's unbound silver hair.

Ash could not help herself—her soles slipped on the cropped frozen grass and she stumbled. Recovering, she halted and looked at the Faris. That is my face, that is how I look—

Do I *really* look like that to other people?

I thought I was taller.

"You're my employer, for Christ's sake," Ash protested, aloud, disgusted. "This is completely unnecessary. I would have come to you. All you had to do was say! Why do this?"

The woman looked up. "Because I can."

Ash nodded thoughtfully. She walked closer, feet dipping into the springy cold turf, until the *'arif*'s hand on her vambrace arrested her progress some two yards away from the Faris's table. Her left hand automatically dropped to steady her sword-scabbard and closed on emptiness. Ash planted her boots squarely, getting her balance; ready in any instant to move, and move as fast as armor permits. "Look, General, you're in charge of a whole invasion force here; I really don't think I need your power and influence to be *proved* to me!"

The woman's mouth quirked up at the corner. She gave Ash what was unmistakably a grin. "I think you do need the point driven home, if you're anything like me—"

She stopped, abruptly, and sat up on the three-legged stool, letting her papers fall back onto the small trestle table. She weighted them down with a Brazen Head, against the night breeze. Her dark eyes sought out Ash's face.

"I'm a lot like you," Ash said, quietly and unnecessarily. "Okay, so you're making a point. Fine. It's made. Where's Thomas Rochester and the rest of my men? Are any of them wounded or killed?"

"You wouldn't expect me to tell you that. Not until you've become sufficiently worried about it that you're willing to talk openly to me."

The quirk of an eyebrow, the same as her own—but mirror-image, Ash realized with a shock. Her own self, but reversed. She considered the idea that the general might be a demon or devil.

"They're well, but prisoners," the Faris added. "I have very good reports of your company."

Between relief at hearing her people were—or might be—still alive, and the shock of hearing that voice just not *quite* her own, Ash had to brace herself against dizziness that threatened to blank out her vision. For a moment, yellow torchlight wavered.

"I thought you might be amused to see this." The Faris held out a paper festooned with red wax seals. "It's from the *parlement* of Paris, asking me go to home because I'm a scandal."

Ash snorted despite herself. "Because *what*?"

"You'll appreciate it. Read it."

Ash stepped forward and extended her hand. The *'arif*'s men tensed. She still wore her gauntlets, and her gloved fingers only touched the paper; still, coming within scenting distance of her double—a smell of spice and sweat, like all the Visigoth military men around her—made her hand shake. Her gaze faltered. She looked down hurriedly at the paper.

" 'Since that you are unbaptised and in a state of sin, and since that you have received none of the sacraments, and bear no saint's name for your own; therefore we sternly petition you to return whence you came,' " Ash read aloud, " 'since we would not have our queens and dowagers have unclean intercourse with a mere concubine, nor our clean maidens, true wives and steadfast widows be corrupted by the presence of one who can be no more than a wayward wench or wanton wife; therefore enter not into our lands with your armies—' Oh my lord! 'Wayward wench'!"

The other woman gave vent to a surprisingly deep-chested laugh. *Do I sound like that?* Ash wondered.

"It's the Spider,"[61] Ash murmured, reading through it again, delighted. "Genuine?"

"Certainly."

Ash looked up.

"So whose bastard am I?" she asked.

The Visigoth general snapped her fingers and said something rapid in Carthaginian. One of her men put another stool down beside the trestle table, and all the armed men, whose boots had been stamping divots from the enclosed garden's lawn, filed out through the gate in the hedge.

And if we're actually alone now, I'm the Queen of Carthage.

Armor is a weapon: she considered using it, and as rapidly abandoned the idea. Ash let her gaze stray around in the dark, trying to pick out the points of light that would be reflected by steel arrow-heads or crossbow-bolts. The cool night air shifted across her face.

"This place reminds me of the gardens in the Citadel, where I grew up," the Faris said. "Our gardens are brighter than this, of course. We bring the light in with mirrors."

Ash licked her lips, attempting to moisten a dry mouth. As required by the castle's ladies, little of the outside world could enter this garden. The hedges baffled sound. Now it was true night, and the darkness genuine, and the armed presence for the moment withdrawn, she found herself (despite the golem) insensibly more at ease; felt herself becoming the person who commands a company, not a frightened young woman.

"*Were* you baptised?"

"Oh yes. By what you call the Arian heresy." The

---

[61]Louis XI of France, known to his contemporaries as "the Spider King" because of his love of intrigue.

general held out an inviting hand. "Sit down, Ash."

One does not commonly say one's own name, Ash reflected; and to hear it said in what was almost her own voice, but with a Visigothic accent, sent the hairs on the nape of her neck prickling up.

She reached up to unfasten the strap and buckle of her sallet, easing the helmet off. The night air felt chill against her sweating head and braided hair. She placed the visored sallet carefully on the table, and lifted her tassets and fauld with the ease of long practice to seat herself on the stool. Breast-and backplate kept her posture absolutely upright.

"This *isn't* the way to get your employee's co-operation," she added absently, settling herself. "It really isn't, General!"

The Visigoth woman smiled. Her skin was pale. She had a mask of darker skin around her eyes, tanned honey-brown from long exposure to the sun, where neither steel helm nor mail aventail shielded her face. The mail mittens dangling from her wrists disclosed her hands: pale, with neatly trimmed nails. While it is true that mail sucks onto a human body, clinging to the padded clothing underneath, leaving her looking podgy, Ash judged the woman to have a very similar build to her own; and she was consumed, for a moment, with the sheer reality of the living, breathing, warm flesh sitting opposite her, no more than arm's reach away, looking *so alike*—

"I want to see Thomas Rochester," she said.

The Visigoth general raised her voice very slightly. The wicket-gate opened. A man held up a lantern long enough for Ash to see Thomas Rochester, hands bound behind him, his face bloodied, but well enough apparently to stand without help—the gate closed.

"Happy?"

"I wouldn't describe myself as *happy*, exactly . . . Oh fuck it!" Ash exclaimed. "I didn't expect to like you!"

"No." The woman, who could not be much above her own age, pressed her lips flatly together. An irresistible smile tweaked the corners up. Her dark eyes glowed. "No! Nor did I! Nor did the other *jund*, your friend. Nor your husband."

Ash confined herself to growling, "Lamb's no friend of mine," and left the subject of Fernando del Guiz well alone. A familiar exhilaration began to fizz in her blood: the sheer balance required when renegotiating a trustworthy arrangement with people always more powerful than oneself (or they wouldn't be hiring mercenaries); the necessity of knowing what must be said, and what left unsaid.

"How did you come to have scars?" the Visigoth general asked. "A battle injury?"

Not negotiation, but pure personal curiosity, Ash judged. And as such, probably a weakness to be exploited.

"There was a saint's visitation when I was a child. The Lion came." Ash touched her cheek, something she did not often do, feeling the dinted flesh under her gloved fingertips. "He marked me out with His claws, thus showing I should be a Lioness myself, on the field of battle."

"So young? Yes. I was trained early too."

Ash repeated, using the term quite deliberately, her earlier question. "Whose bastard am I?"

"Nobody's."

"N—?"

The Visigoth general looked as though she were appreciating how taken aback Ash felt. We should read each other very well, Ash thought. But do we? How would I know? I could be wrong.

She let her tongue run on:

"What do you mean, nobody? You can't mean I'm *legitimate*. Whose family is it? What family do you come from?"

"No one's."

The dark eyes danced, without any malice that Ash could detect; and then the other woman heaved a great sigh, and rested her mailed arms on the table, and leaned forward. The light from the golems' torches slid over her silver-blonde hair and her unmarked face.

"You're no more legitimate than me," the Faris said. "I'm slave-bred."

Ash stared, conscious of a shock too great to recognize; so great that it faded into a mental shrug, and a *so what*? and a consciousness only that something, somewhere, had come adrift in her mind.

The Faris continued, "Whoever my parents were, they were slaves in Carthage. The Turks have their Janissaries, Christian children they steal and raise up as fanatical warriors for their own country. My—father—did something very like that. I'm slave-bred," she repeated softly, "a bondswoman: and I suppose you are, too. I'm sorry if you were hoping for something better than that."

The sadness in her tone felt genuine.

Ash abandoned any thought of negotiation or subterfuge. "I don't understand."

"No, why should you? I don't suppose the *Amir* Leofric would be pleased that I'm telling you. His family have been breeding for a Faris for generations. I am their success. You must be—"

"One of the rejects," Ash cut in. "Isn't that it?"

Her heart hammered. She held her breath, waiting to be contradicted. The Visigoth woman silently leaned over and with her own hands poured wine from a bottle into two ash-wood cups. She held out one. Ash took it. The black mirror of the liquid shook with the shaking of her hands. No contradiction came.

"Breeding project?" Ash repeated. And, sharply: "You said you had a father!"

"The *Amir* Leofric. No. I've become used to . . . he isn't my true father, of course. He wouldn't lower himself to impregnate slaves."

"I don't care if he fucks donkeys," Ash said brutally. "That's why you wanted to see me, isn't it? That's why you came all the way to Guizburg, when you're running a damn war? Because I'm your—sister?"

"Sister, half-sister, cousin. Something. Look at us!" The Visigoth general shrugged again. When she lifted her wooden cup, her hand was shaking too. "I don't believe that my father—that Lord-*Amir* Leofric—would know why I *had* to see you."

"Leofric." Ash stared blankly at her twin. Part of her mind rummaged through memories of heraldry. "He's one of the *amirs* at the King-Caliph's court? A powerful man?"

The Faris smiled. "House Leofric has been, time out of mind, close companions to the King-Caliphs. We gave them the golem-messengers. And now, a *faris*."

"What happens to the . . . you said there were others. A project. What happens to the other people like us? How *many*—"

"Hundreds, over the years, I suppose. I never asked."

"You never asked." Incredulous, Ash drained her cup, not noticing whether the wine was good or bad. "This isn't new to you, is it."

"No. I suppose it does seem strange, if you didn't grow up with it."

"What happens to them? The ones that aren't you—what happens to them?"

"If they can't talk to the machine,[62] they're usually

---

[62]The original text uses the Latin *fabricatio*, for a structure made by human hands, not necessarily a machine in the sense that we would think of one.

killed. Even if they can talk to the machine, they usually go mad. You have no idea how lucky I feel that I didn't go insane in my childhood.''

The first thought in Ash's mind was a sardonic. *Are you quite sure about that?* and then more of what the woman had said sunk in. Utterly appalled, Ash repeated, ''Killed?''

Before the Visigoth woman could reply, the impact of one single phrase hit home.

She blurted out, without any intention of doing so, ''What do you mean, *talk to the machine*? What 'machine'? What do you *mean*?''

The Faris folded her fingers around her wooden cup.

''Don't tell me you haven't heard of the Stone Golem?'' she inquired, in a sardonic tone that Ash not only recognized but suspected of being a deliberate parody. ''When I've gone to so much trouble to spread the rumor? I *want* my enemies too terrified to fight me. I *want* everybody to know that we have a great war-machine[63] at home—and that I speak with it whenever I please. Even in the middle of battle. *Especially* in the middle of battle.''

That's it, Ash realized. This is why I'm here.

Not because I look like her.

Not because we're probably kin.

Because she hears voices *and she wants to know if I do, too.*

And what the hell will she do if she knows the truth?

Even knowing it to be a long leap to a conclusion,

---

[63]The Angelotti Latin text has, in its brief and previously obscure mention of this episode, *machina rei militaris*, a ''machine-tactician,'' and *fabricari res militaris*, ''[something] made to [create] tactics.'' ''Fraxinus me fecit'' renders it as *computare ars imperatoria*, or, in a bizarre mixture of Latin and Greek, *computare strategoi*, 'a computor of the ''art of empire'' ' or ''strategy.'' This can be rendered into modern English as ''tactical computer.''

knowing it might be unjustified, panic and uncertainty set her heart thumping, to the point where she was glad to be wearing a mail standard: a pulse would have been clearly visible at her throat.

By reflex, she did the thing she had been doing since she was eight: cutting the linkage between herself and her fears. Her voice came out casually dismissive. "Oh, I heard the rumors. But that's just rumors. You've got some kind of a Brazen Head in Carthage—is it a head?" she broke off to ask.

"You have seen our clay-walkers? It is their great father and progenitor: the Stone Golem. But," the woman added, "our defeating the armies of the Italians and the Swiss is not mere 'rumor.' "

"The Italians! I know why you razed Milan, that was just to cut off the armor trade. I know all about that: I was apprentice to a Milanese armorer once." This fact having failed to distract either the woman or herself, Ash went rapidly on: "I grant you the Swiss. But why shouldn't you be good? After all, *I'm* good!"

She stopped, and could have bitten her tongue hard enough to draw blood.

"Yes. You are good." The Faris said evenly, "I understand that you, also, hear 'voices.' "

"Now that isn't a rumor. That's a downright lie." Ash managed to guffaw coarsely. "Who do you think I am, the Pucelle?[64] You'll be telling me next that I'm a virgin!"

"No voices? Merely a useful lie?" the Visigoth general suggested mildly.

"Well, I'm hardly likely to deny it, am I? The more Godly I sound, the better off I'm going to be." Ash managed, more convincingly, to sound both smug and

---

[64]Joan of Arc (AD 1412–1431).

ashamed of having been caught out telling fibs in public.

The woman touched her temple. "Nonetheless, I *am* in contact with our tactical computer. I hear it. Here."

Ash stared. She must look, she realized dimly, as if she didn't believe a word the woman was saying and thought she must be mad. In fact she was hardly aware of the woman at all.

The chill air moving into the sheltered garden swept over her sweating face. Somewhere outside a horse snorted, wuffing breath into the night sky. The sound of Visigoth soldiers talking was just audible. Ash clung to what she could see and hear as if to her own sanity. The thought formed itself in her mind with absolute inevitability. *If I was bred like her, and she hears voices from a tactical machine, then that's where my voice comes from.*

No!

Ash wiped at her wet upper lip, her breath misting the steel plate of her gauntlet. Numb, she felt first on the verge of vomiting, and then as if she were strangely detached from herself. She watched her wine-cup tip out of her fingers and bounce, spilling liquid across the trestle table, soaking all the papers neatly laid out.

The Faris swore, leaping to her feet, calling out, knocking over the table. Four or five boys—Visigoth pages or serfs—ran into the garden, rescuing the documents, wiping the table, mopping wine from the general's mail hauberk. Ash sat and stared with oblivious eyes.

Serfs *bred* as soldiers. Is that what she's saying? And I'm just some brat that somehow wasn't killed? Oh, sweet Jesus, and I always thought slaves and bondsmen beneath contempt—

And my voice isn't . . .

Isn't what?

Isn't the Lion? Isn't a saint?

Isn't a demon?

Christ, sweet savior, sweet sweet savior of me, this is worse than devils!

Ash gripped her left hand into a fist under the table, digging steel plates into flesh. Then she could look up, focused by the pain, and mumble, "Sorry. Drinking on an empty stomach. Wine's gone to my head."

You don't know. You don't *know* that what she hears is what you hear. You don't *know* it's the same thing.

Ash looked down at her left hand. The gauntlet-glove across her palm showed red blots, soaking into the leather.

The last thing I want to do now is carry on talking to this woman. Oh, fuck.

I wonder what would happen if I just told her? That I *do* hear a voice? A voice that tells me what tactics I can use in a battle?

If I tell her, what happens next?

If I don't know the answer to that question, then I certainly shouldn't ask her!

She was struck, as often in the past, with how time itself slows when life is knocked out of its rut. A cup of wine, in a garden, on a night in July; it is the kind of occasion that passes rapidly and automatically at the time, and falls out of memory instantly. Now she minutely registered everything, from the three-legged oaken stool's front leg sinking gradually into the daisy-thick grass under her weight, to the slide of plate over metal plate in her armor as she stretched her arm out to take the wine bottle, to the long, long intensity of the moment before the Visigoth general ceased being mopped down by her serfs and turned her bright head again toward Ash.

"It's true," the Faris said conversationally. "I do speak with the war-machine. My men call it the Stone Golem. It's not stone, and it doesn't move like these"— a little shrug, as she indicated the stone-and-brass figures bearing the torches —"but they like the name."

Caution reasserting itself, Ash put the bottle down and thought, If I don't know what the result of telling her I hear a voice will be, then I shouldn't tell her until I *do* know.

And certainly not until I've had time to think it through, talk it through with Godfrey and Florian and Roberto—

Shit, no! They just think I might be a bastard; how can I tell them I was born a slave?

Her lips stiff with the deceit, Ash said, "What would be the use of a war-engine like that? I could take my copy of Vegetius[65] onto the battlefield and read it there, but it wouldn't help me win."

"But if you had him there with you, alive, and you could ask the advice of Vegetius himself, *then* it might?" The Visigoth woman picked at the front of her fine mail with a fingertip, gazing down. "That's going to rust. This bloody wet country!"

The pitch torches hissed and sputtered, burning down. Golem stood, cold statues. Trails of pine-smelling black smoke went up into the night sky. The recurved-bow crescent of the waning moon sank behind the hedges of the garden. Ash's muscles ached. Every bruise from her arrest smarted. The wine fizzed in her head, making her sway a little on the stool; and she thought, If I'm not careful the drink will work, I shall be telling the truth to her, and then where will I be?

"Sisters," she said, blurrily. The wooden stool lurched forward. She came to her feet, rather than fall sprawling, and halted with one armored hand outstretched, catching the Visigoth woman's shoulder for support. "Christ, woman, we could be twins! How old are you?"

"Nineteen."

---

[65]*De Re Militari*, written by the Roman Vegetius, became the standard training manual for the later mediaeval and early Renaissance era.

Ash laughed shakily. "Well, there you are. If I knew the year I was born, I could tell you. I must be eighteen or nineteen or twenty-ish by now. Maybe we *are* twins. What do you think?"

"My father interbreeds his slave stock. I think we probably all look alike." The Faris's dark brows frowned. She reached up with her bare fingers and touched Ash on the cheek. "I did see some others, as a child, but they went mad."

"Went mad!" A flush spread up over Ash's face. She felt the heat of it. Entirely unplanned, entirely genuine: her face grew red. "What am I supposed to tell people? Faris, what do I say? That some crazy lord-*amir* down in Carthage is breeding slaves like *stock*, like *animals*? And that I was one of them?"

The Visigoth woman said softly, "It still could be a coincidence. One shouldn't let a likeness—"

"Oh, fucking hell, woman! We're *twins*!"

Ash looked into eyes exactly the same height above ground as her own, the same dark color, searching her features for kinship: for the curve of lip, shape of nose, shape of chin, a pale-haired foreign woman with the sunburn and odd scars of military campaigns, and a voice that, while not quite her own, might (she supposed now) be her own voice as others heard it.

"I'd rather not have known," Ash said thickly. "If it's true, I'm not a person, I'm an animal. Bloodstock. Failed bloodstock. I can be bought and sold—by *any*body—and I can't say a word about it. By *law*. You're a farm animal too. Don't you *care*?"

"It isn't news to me."

That brought her up short. Ash closed her hand over the woman's mailed shoulder, squeezed once, and let go. She stood swaying, but upright. The high hedges of the *hortus conclusus* shut out Basle, the company, the army, the world in darkness; and Ash shivered, despite armor and the padding under it.

"It doesn't matter to me who I fight for," she said. "I signed a contract with you, and I suppose this isn't enough to break it—assuming all my people here are unharmed, and not just Thomas. You know I am good, even if I don't have your 'Stone Golem.' "

The lie came with an ease that might have been role-playing, might have been numbness, but in any case, Ash felt, couldn't delude anybody. She pushed on doggedly:

"I know you've razed half a dozen essential commercial cities in Italy, I know the Swiss Cantons are wiped out as a fighting force, and that you've frightened Frederick and the Germanies into surrender. I also know the Sultan in Constantinople isn't currently expecting trouble, so your army is intended for Christendom—for the kingdoms north of here."

She let her gaze rest on the general's face, trying to detect any emotion. An impassive face looked back at her, chiaroscuro shadows shifting across it from the light of the golems' torches.

"Intended for Burgundy, Daniel de Quesada said, but I expect that means France as well. And then the *rosbifs*? You're going to be over-extended, even with the numbers you've got. I know what I'm doing, I've been doing it for a long time; let me get on with it. Okay? And then sometime in the future, when I'm not under contract to you, I'll let your Lord-*Amir* Leofric know exactly what I think of him breeding bastards."

—*And this would probably work with anyone else*, Ash concluded in the privacy of her own mind. How like me is she? Is she going to spot when I'm lying? For all I know, this would sound like bluff to anyone, let alone a sister I didn't know I'd got.

Fuck me. A sister.

The Visigoth general bent down and picked up the Brazen Head from where it dented the turf, shook it, shrugged, and placed it back on the trestle table beside Ash's sallet. "I should like to keep her as my sub-commander here."

Ash opened her mouth to reply, and registered the "her." "Her," not "you." That, and the precise diction, and the woman's unfocused eyes, brought a sudden stab of realization to her gut: *She is not talking to* me.

Fear flooded her body.

Ash took two steps back, skidded on the frosty grass and stumbled backwards down the grassy bank, barely keeping her footing, falling, ramming her back hard into the marble surround of the fountain. She heard the metal of her backplate creak. A copper taste flooded her mouth. She blushed, blushed red as fire, as hot with shame as if she had been publicly discovered having sex; feeling in the one second *it was never real until now!* and in the next, *I never expected to see someone* else *doing this!*

Golem stared down from the top of the bank. The nearest one to Ash now had a spider's web linking its arm to the hedge, a frost-rimed white strand running from trimmed privet leaves to the shining brass mechanism of its elbow. She stared at the featureless oval face, the hen's-egg shape of the head delineated by guttering torches.

The Faris's voice protested, "But I would prefer to use her and her company now, not later."

She is not talking to me. She is talking to her voices.

Ash blurted, "We're under contract! We're fighting for you here. That was the arrangement!"

The general folded her arms, now with her head raised, watching the southern constellations in the sky over Basle. "If you order me to, then I will."

"I don't believe you hear voices at all! You're a bloody

heathen. This is all play-acting!'' Ash made an attempt to climb back up the steep bank; the soles of her riding boots glided over the cold grass, and she slid down, pitching forward in a rattle of metal, catching herself on her hands, and gazing up from on all fours at the Visigoth woman. ''You're putting me on! This isn't *real*!''

Her protests were verbal floodwater. She stuttered, jabbering, and in the most private part of her mind, thought *I must not listen!* Whatever I do, I mustn't speak to my voice, I mustn't listen, in case it is the same—

—in case she'll know if I do.

Between keeping up a continuous protest and the clamped-shut determination in her mind, she neither heard nor felt anything as the Visigoth woman continued to speak aloud into empty air.

''Yes. I'll send her south on the next galley.''

''You will not!'' Ash got quickly and carefully to her feet.

The Visigoth general lowered her gaze from the night sky.

''My father Leofric wants to see you,'' she said. ''You'll reach Carthage within a week. If he doesn't keep you long, I'll have you back here before the sun moves into Leo.[66] We shall be some way further north, but I can still use your company. I'll send your men here back to your camp.''

''*Baise mon cul!*''[67] Ash snapped.

It was pure reflex. In the same way that she had played camp's-little-mascot at nine, so she knew how to play bluff-mercenary-captain at nineteen. Her head swam.

''This wasn't in the contract! If I have to take my people out of the field now, it'll cost you—I've still got to

---

[66]On 24 July.

[67]French, lit. ''kiss my arse.''

feed them. And if you want me to go all the way to fucking North Africa in the middle of your war . . ." Ash
made an attempt at a shrug. "That wasn't in the contract
either."

And the second you take your eye off me, I'm out of
here.

The Visigoth woman picked up Ash's sallet from the
table, stroking her bare palm over the curve of metal from
visor to crest to tail. Ash automatically winced, anticipating rust on the mirror-finished steel. The woman knocked
her knuckles against the metal thoughtfully, and pushed
the visor down until it clicked.

"I'm giving some of these to my men." A brief glitter
of laughter, her eyes meeting Ash's. "I didn't order Milano razed until I'd cleared it out first."

"You can't get better than Milanese plate. Except for
Augsberg—and I don't suppose you've left much of the
south German foundries, either." Ash reached up and
took her helmet from the woman's hands. "You send
word to me out at the camp when you want me to board
ship."

For a whole second, she was convinced that she had
done it. That she would be allowed now to walk out of
the garden, ride out of the city, put herself squarely in the
middle of eight hundred armed men wearing her own livery, and tell the Visigoths to go straight to whatever might
be the Arian version of eternal damnation.

The Visigoth general asked, aloud, "What do I do with
someone that my father wants to investigate, and I don't
trust to escape if I let her leave here?"

Ash said nothing aloud. In that part of her self where
voice was potential, she acted. It was no decision, was
gut-level reflex, taken in despite any risk of discovery.
Passive, Ash listened.

A whisper—the merest whisper of a whisper—sounded

in her head. The quietest, most familiar voice imaginable—

"Strip her of armor and weapons. Keep her under continuous close guard. Escort her immediately to the nearest ship."

V

A NAZIR[68] AND his guards kept a literal grip on her, walking from the castle garden down through the streets, to a long tall row of four-story houses that Ash recognized from her scouts' reports as the main Visigoth headquarters in Basle. Mail-covered hands held her arms.

Above the lime-washed plaster and oak beams of the gables, the stars were being swallowed up in darkness. Dawn coming.

Ash made no effort to break their hold on her. Most of this *nazir*'s unit were young, boys no older than her, with tan-creased faces, and tight bodies, and long legs with calves thin-muscled from being so much on horseback. She gazed around at their faces as they hustled her into the nearest building, through an oaken door. If not for the Visigoth robes and mail, they could have been any men-at-arms from her company.

"Okay, okay!" She stopped dead in the entrance, on the flagstones, and shaped her mouth into a smile for the *nazir*. "I have about four marks in my purse, which will

---

[68]"Nazir": a commander of eight men, the equivalent of the modern army's squad-leader (corporal). Presumably a subordinate of the *'arif* commander of forty (platoon leader) that the text mentions earlier.

buy you guys drinks, and then you can come and tell me
how my men are doing.''

The two soldiers released her arms. She felt for her
purse and realized that her hands were still shaking. The
nazir—about her age, half a head taller, and male, of
course—said, ''Motherfucking mercenary bitch,'' in a
fairly businesslike tone.

Ash mentally shrugged. Well, it was either that or *she's
our boss's double*! and I get treated like the local demon . . .

''Fucking Frankish cunt,'' he added.[69]

House guards and servants came out into the hall, carrying candles. Ash felt a hand jerk at her belt as she was
shoved forward, knew her purse would be missing when
she looked for it; and then in a clatter of boots and shouted
orders in Carthaginian, she found herself bustled toward
the back of the house, through rooms full of armed men,
down stone-floored passages, into a tiny room with an
iron-barred door made of two-inch thick oak, and a window about a foot square.

Two solemn-faced pages in Visigoth tunics indicated
they were to help her off with her armor. Ash made no
protest. She let herself be stripped down to her arming
doublet and hose, with its sewn-in mail at armpits and
crutch; her request for a demi-gown brought nothing.

The oak door closed. A sound of iron grating down
into sockets told her that bars had been secured in place.

One candle guttered, its holder placed on the floor.

By its light, she examined the room, padding around it
in bare feet. The oak floorboards felt chill. The room was
bare, containing neither chair nor table nor bed; and the
window-slot had thumb-thick iron bars set into its walls.

---

[69]''Frank'' is an Arab term of the period, meaning ''Northern Europeans,'' and is certainly not Gothic.

"Fuckers!" Kicking the door would hurt: she hit it with the heel of her hand. "Let me see my men!"

Her voice bounced back flat from the walls.

"Let me out of here, you motherfuckers!"

With the thickness of the wood, it was not even possible to tell if there was a guard posted outside, or if he could hear her if there was. She used the same voice she would have used to call orders across a battle line.

"*Cocksuckers!* Sweet Christ, I can *pay* a ransom! Just let me send a message out!"

Silence.

Ash stretched her arms above her head, and then rubbed at the sore spots where her harness had chafed. She missed both her sword and her steel protection so keenly that she could all but feel the shape of the metal between her hands. She backed across the room, slid down the wall, and sat beside the sole light: pale wax and primrose-yellow flame.

Her hands prickled, as if the blood in them was cold as the water in Alpine streams. She rubbed her palms together. A part of her mind insisted, no, it's not true, this is all some weird story, this isn't real life. You're a soldier's brat, that's all. It's coincidence. Your father was probably some Visigoth *nazir* who fought with the Griffin-in-Gold, and your mother was a whore. That's all: nothing out of the ordinary. You just look like the Faris.

And the other stunned part of her mind kept repeating: She hears my voice.

"Fucking hell." Ash spoke aloud. "She *can't* take me prisoner. I've got a fucking *contract* with the woman. Green Christ! I'm not going to Carthage. They might—"

Her mind refused to consider it. This was a new sensation: she tried to force her thoughts to consider being taken overseas to North Africa, and they slid away. Again and again. *Like trying to herd eels*, Ash thought, with a quick grin, and her teeth rattled together.

Maybe the Lion never came at all. *No*. No—our clerk made the miracle: the Lion did come.

But maybe nothing happened to *me*, there.

Maybe I just told the story of the chapel that way so often, I remember it like it did happen.

Ash's body shuddered, hands and feet cold, until she huddled up, tucking her hands into her armpits.

The Faris. She was bred to hear her tactical machine.

It *is* the same voice.

I'm—what? Sister. Cousin. Something. *Twin*.

Just something they discarded, on the way to breeding her.

And all I do is . . . overhear.

Is that all I've ever done? A bastard brat, outside the door, listening in to someone else's tactical war-machine, sneaking out answers for brutal little wars that the Visigoth Empire doesn't even notice . . .

The Faris is what they wanted. And even she's a slave.

After that she sat alone without food or drink and watched the candle-flame pouring a line of blackness up to where it suddenly broke and squiggled, playing sepia smoke over the low plaster ceiling, merging with the shadows. Her heart ticked off minutes, hours.

Ash rested her arms across her knees and buried her face in her arms. There was a hot wetness against her face. Shock comes after wounds in the field, sometimes a long while after; and here in this narrow room she feels it now: Fernando del Guiz is not coming.

She wiped her nose on her sleeve. What opportunities there might be, to talk herself out of the prison for a ransom, or pity, or by violence, would not present themselves now.

This was the Emperor's marriage, and he's got out of

it at the first opportunity that came along. No, that's not it—

Ash's chest aches. The hollow breathlessness wants to become tears, but she won't let it; raises her face and blinks in the candlelight.

—he's not here now because it was no coincidence he was in the town hall before I got captured. He was there to confirm where I was. For them. For her.

Well, you had him; you fucked him; you got what you wanted; now you know he's a weaseling little shit. What's the problem?

I wanted more than fucking him.

Forget him.

The wax candle melted down to a stump.

I'm prisoner here.

This is no Romance of Arthur or Peredur. I'm not about to scale the walls, fight off armored men with my bare hands, ride off into the sunshine. What happens to valueless prisoners taken in war is pain first, broken bodies second, and an unmarked, unchristian burial afterwards. I am in their city. They own it now.

A hot thread of disquiet rumbled her bowels. She rested her arms on her knees, and her forehead on her arms.

They might expect a rescue by my company. Soon. An attack, men-at-arms, not on war-horses in these streets, so probably on foot.

I'd better have got this right.

The sharpest and loudest noise she had ever heard shattered the house.

Her body froze in the instant of the sound. Her bowels moved. She found in the same second both that she lay on shattered oak floorboards, and that she knew what the noise was. *Cannon fire.*

That's *ours*!

Her heart leaped up as she heard. Tears ran down her

stunned face. She could have kissed their feet for gratitude. Another roar went up. The crack and thud of the
second explosion echoed off the bare rafters of the roof.

For long heartbeats she was back in the alpine crags,
where water falls down loud enough that a man cannot
hear himself speak, until out of the darkness and dust,
torches flamed and men walked—men walking in over
the remnants of lath and plaster and bloody rags of soldiers.

Black air swirled, dust clearing. Her room ended in broken beams and blackened limewash.

The back of the house gaped, blown away.

A great beam creaked and fell, like trees falling in the
wildwood. Plaster sprayed her face.

Outside the breech, in the torchlight in the open, stood
two carts and two light cannon dismounted, smoking from
their touch-holes still; and she squinted her eyes and made
out the bright blaze of Angelotti's curls, the man himself
striding up to where she lay, hatless, grinning, and speaking—shouting—until she heard:

"We've blown the wall! Come on!"

With the back of the house, the city wall was down
too; these houses all fortified at the backs, themselves
forming the wall around this part of the city.

Beyond them lay black fields, and the shrouds of forests
on moonlit hills, and men moving in armor, calling "*Ash!
Ash!*" both as a battle call, and to be known by their
fellows. She stumbled out of the rubble, cars ringing, her
balance gone.

Rickard tugged the sleeve of her arming doublet, Godluc's reins in his other hand. She made a grab for the big
gray gelding's bridle, face momentarily pushed against his
warm dappled flank. A crossbow bolt buried itself in old
Roman brick and sprayed the wreckage of the house with
fragments; men shouted, a rush of newcomers in mail and

white tunics scrambling over the fallen oaken beams.

Ash got one foot into Godluc's stirrup, swung herself up, loose points and mail flapping from her arming doublet, too light without her armor; and a little lithe man flew at her and caught her by the waist and bore her bodily onward right over her war-horse's back.

She fell, felt no impact—

Something happened.

I have bitten my tongue, I am falling, where is the Lion?

The picture behind her eyes was not of the Blue Lion banner, but of something flat and gold and meat-breathed, and a chill struck her fingers, her hands, her feet; dug deep into her sprawling body.

Feet stood to either side of her. Calves encased in shaped steel plate. European greaves, not Visigoth armor. Something flicked a glint of light past her face, into the air. Liquid spattered her cheek. An appalled shriek deafened her: the shriek of a man ruined in a second by the swipe of a sword, all life to come wrecked and spilled out on rubble; and a man close by her screamed, "My God, my God, no, no—" and then, "Christ, oh Christ, what have I done, *what have I done*, oh Christ, it *hurts*," and screams, on and on and on.

Floria's voice said "Christ!" very precisely and distantly. Ash felt the tall woman handling her head, warm fingers on her hair. Half her skull was numb. "No helmet, no armor—"

And another voice, male, saying above her, "—ridden over in the mêlée—"

Ash felt conscious through everything that was happening, although somehow she could not bring it to mind a moment later. Armored horses galloped; hand-gunners banged off their charges and then ran in the moonlight. She was tied with ropes to a truckle bed—how much later? while she screamed, and others screamed—and the bed tied to a wagon, the wagon one among many, moving down frozen, muddy, deep-rutted roads.

A flapping cloth across her eyes blacked out the moon. All around her, wagons moved, oxen lowed; and the screeches of pack-mules mixed with the shouting of orders, and a trickle of warm oil ran into her eyes, dripping down her forehead: Godfrey Maxmillian, in his green stole, pronouncing the Last Rites.

It was too much to hold. She let it slip from her: the armed company men riding outrider, the whole camp packed up and moving, the clashes of steel from behind, far too close.

Floria knelt above her, holding Ash's head wedged still between dirty-fingered hands. Ash had a moment's sight of the grease of unwashed skin blackening the woman's linen cuff.

"Stay still!" the husky voice breathed above her. "Don't move!"

Ash leaned her head to one side, vomiting, and then screamed, and froze: held herself as still as possible, pain flaying her skull. A strange new drowsiness possessed her. She watched Godfrey kneeling in the cart beside her, praying, but praying with his eyes open, watching her face.

Time is nothing but vomiting and pain, and the agony of the cart rocking and jolting in the ruts of the roads.

Time is moonlight: black day: cloud-obscured moon: darkness: night again.

What roused her—hours later? days later?—into a dreaminess in which she could at least see the world, was a mutter, an exclamation from one man to another, from woman to man and child, all down the lines of her company. She heard shouting. Godfrey Maximillian grabbed the sides of the cart and leaned out of the front, past Rickard driving the beasts.

What they were shouting, she finally made out, was a name, a place. Burgundy. *The most powerful of princedoms*, she voiced in her mind; and at a level of voicelessness knew that she herself had intended this, had ordered it, had made Robert Anselm privy to this her intention before ever going inside the walls of Basle after the Visigoth commander.

Trumpets sounded.

A brilliance dazzled her eyes. *This is the pass to purgatory, then.* Ash prayed.

Light broke on her, over the canvas roof of the ox-wain, sifting down through the white coarse cloth. Light brought out the grain of the wood, the wagon's thick oak plank flooring. Light manifested from the darkness the drawn cheek of Floria del Guiz, crouching over her wicker pack of herbs, retractors, scalpels and saws.

Not the color-leeching silver of the moon. A harsh yellow light.

Ash tried to move. She groaned with a mouth thick with saliva. A man's broad-fingered hand pressed flat on her breast, holding her still on the low bed. Light brought out the dirt in the whorls of his fingertips. Godfrey's face was not turned to her; he stared out of the back of the wagon.

A warmth gleamed on his pink flesh, under the road-dust, and on the acorn-color of his shaggy beard; and she could see, reflected in his dark eyes, a growing of this mad brightness.

Suddenly, a sharp line divided the rush-cushioned floor of the wagon and the strapped bed. Darkness over her body—shadow. Brightness over her blanket-covered legs, a line of light moving with the rocking motion of the wagon—sunlight.

She struggled, but could not raise her head. She moved her eyes only. Through the open back of the wagon glowed colors: blue and green and white and pink.

Her eyes teared. Through flooding water her eyes focused on distance—on green hills, and a flowing river, and the white walls of an enclosed town. The smell rose up and hit her, like a blow under her ribs from a quarterstaff: the smell of roses and honey, and the pungent warmth of horse- and ox-dung with the sun on it.

*Sun*light.

Nausea flooded up. Ash vomited weakly, the stinking liquid running down her chin. Pain fractured around the bones of her skull, brought more water to her eyes. Agonized, terrified of what the pain might mean, still she could only think, *it's day, it's day, it's the sun!*

Men with ten years' service cutting flesh on battlefields climb down to kiss the dirt ruts, bury their faces in dew-wet grass. Women who sew men's clothes and wounds alike, fall to their knees beside them. Riders pitch down from their horses' saddles. All, all falling on the cold earth, in the light, the light, singing "*Deo gratias, Deo adiuvante, Deo gratias!*"[70]

---

[70]Latin: "Thanks to God," "with God's help."

[E-mails found included in copy of text:—]

-- -- -- -- -- -- -- -- -- -- -- -- -- -- -- --

Message: #47 (Anna Longman/misc.)
Subject: Ash, archaeological discoveries
Date: 11/11/00 at 12.03 p.m.
From: Ngrant@   *format address deleted*
                           Other details encrypted by
                           non-discoverable personal key
Anna--

Anna, I apologise, for being out of contact for four days. It hardly seems like minutes, here! So much is going on—we've had television crews trying to get in. Dr Isobel has thrown what amounts to a security cordon around the area, with the local government's permission. So you may or may not have seen anything about this on non-terrestrial television. If I were Isobel, I wouldn't be so keen to have soldiers around an archaeological dig; when I think of what they could carelessly destroy, my blood does run cold, it is no mere figure of speech.

Before I do anything else, I *must* apologise for the things I wrote at the weekend about Dr Napier-Grant. Isobel and I have been old friends, in a rather spiky way, for so many years. I'm afraid I let my complete enthusiasm over the discoveries here reduce me to a babbling idiot. I hope you will regard everything I wrote as being in confidence.

I don't have Isobel's technical archaeological expertise, but she wants me to stay and give her more of the cultural background—all these finds are late 15th century. This is not her period, she's a Classicist. The 'messenger' golem we have here is being measured by the latest high-tech equipment, and *still* all that I can tell you, Anna, is that at some point in the past, this thing walked.

What I can't tell you is *how*.

There appears to be nothing to power it, and no means for anything to be fitted. Isobel and her team are baffled. She *cannot* believe that the 'golem' descriptions in the ASH documents are a coincidence or mediaeval fable. Anna, she WILL NOT believe it is coincidence.

I am baffled, too. You see, in many senses, we shouldn't be finding what we're finding here. Certainly, I believe I have the evidence for a late-Gothic settlement on the North African coast, but I have always known that the manuscripts' reference to 'Carthage' can be nothing but poetic licence. THERE IS NO CARTHAGE! After the Punic Wars, Rome destroyed Carthage completely. Carthage of the Carthaginians ceased to be an inhabited, powerful city in 146 BC. The great later Roman settlement, on this site, which they themselves called Carthage, was itself obliterated by Vandals, Byzantines, and the Arab conquest in the late 7th century AD—the ruins outside modern-day Tunis are a considerable tourist attraction.

"Delenda est Carthago," as Cato used to say in the Roman Senate, at every conceivable opportunity: "Carthage must be destroyed!" And so it was. After the Carthaginian army under Hannibal was wiped out by Scipio, Rome had the inhabitants of Carthage deported, the city demolished, and the area ploughed under and sown with salt, so that nothing could ever grow there again—a little excessive, possibly, but at this point in our history it was a toss-up whether we were going to have a Roman Empire or a Carthaginian Empire, and, having been victorious, the Romans methodically made sure they wouldn't have any trouble from that area again.

History eradicates thoroughly. Until a decade ago, we did not know for certain which of the ruins on the ten-miles stretch of coast around Tunis was any of the Carthages! I am now having to speculate that the Visigoth expedition from Iberia itself resettled a site that they, like the Romans before them, also CALLED Carthage; and that it was within a reasonable distance of the same location. If this didn't happen until quite late in the day—not until the High Middle Ages, perhaps—then that might account for the sparse documentary evidence of it. I intend to seek more in the way of Islamic sources to support this.

My theory, I THINK, remains intact. And now we have technological evidence to back it up!

--Pierce

Message: #48 (Anna Longman/misc.)
Subject: Ash mss., media projects
Date: 11/11/00 at 12.27 p.m.
From: Ngrant@ *format address deleted*
Other details encrypted by
non-discoverable personal key

Anna--

I forgot to check my previous mail! Shi Sorry. *Sorry*.

Isobel just downloaded your e-mail herself and is extremely interested in the TV project you propose—if not entirely flattered by your description of herself. She said, "This woman makes me sound like Margaret Rutherford!" A remark which, I may add, despite her being only 41 and merely having a predilection for old black-and-white film comedies, *does* make her sound like Margaret Rutherford. (Fortunately for British television, Isobel is rather more chic.)

We are discussing what might best be done, given a certain tension between the dumbing-down effect of television upon scientific enquiry, and the undoubted attractions of gaining popular publicity for archaeology and literature. And, if I can be honest, discussing the attractions that publicity holds for me. I should not mind my fifteen minutes of fame, no, not at all! Especially since it seems that someone else would be paying me for the privilege. I assume we will receive a fee of some kind?

Isobel wishes to consider her options and consult with her team, and the university. I should be able to get back to you later today. Now that I am certain I understand the uses of the Internet, I am forwarding the next section of 'Ash'. You will want to look it over while we hammer out some of the fine details here.

--Pierce

Message: #49 (Anna Longman/misc.)   *Previous message?*
Subject: Ash Project   *Hard copy presumed missing?*
Date: 11/11/00 at 12.44 p.m.
From: Ngrant@   *format address deleted*
                                  Other details encrypted by
                                  non-discoverable personal key

Ms Longman--

I am reluctant to teleconference with your editorial committee. The
phone lines here are not good, and moreover I doubt they are secure.
I will fly back to talk in person as soon as I can take a break from the
site. I would be obliged if you could put me in contact with an
association of literary agents, or 'media' agents, assuming that there
is such an association; my University will then be in a position to enter
into negotiations.

I see no reason why we should not reach agreement. Footage from
our videocam team is being sent digitally back to my department at
██████ University, and processed there. I suggest that you liaise with
my departmental head, Stephen Abawi, about any use of research
footage for publicising Dr Ratcliff's edition of 'Ash'.

At Dr Ratcliff's suggestion, I am encouraging the team to film more
of the actual 'felt experience' of this dig, in addition to our
archaeological findings. This may need to be limited in scope, as the
soldiers do not like to be filmed and small bribes are not always
sufficient to placate them. However, it will, as Dr Ratcliff points out,
be necessary to have this footage if a documentary is to be later
constructed from our time here.

It is possible that Dr Ratcliff and I may collaborate on a documentary
script. I am considering using quotations from the previous editors of
the 'Ash' material. Are you familiar with Charles Mallory
Maximillian's 1890 edition?—

. . . the great mediaeval spoked Wheel of Fortune is always turning; the Goddess Fortuna always sweeping up each man in turn from beggarhood to crowned king, to falling fool, and back to the darkness below the wheel, which is death and forgetfulness. In 1477, upon the field of Nancy, Burgundy vanishes from history and memory, lies as cold and dead as the frost-bitten corpse of Charles the Rash, who had been the shining Prince of Christendom, and whose own enemies thought, for two days, that they beheld the body of a mere peasant soldier, so wretched, filthy and torn it was. We recall a golden country. Yet, history has turned, and the past is lost . . .

Here on the coast of Tunisia, the Wheel is turning again.

--I. Napier-Grant

Message: #63 (Pierce Ratcliff/misc.)
Subject: Ash, documents
Date: 12/11/00 at 1.35 p.m.
From: Longman@   *(format address and other details non-recoverably deleted)*

Pierce--

Thank Dr Napier-Grant for her mail.
    Your news about the messenger-golem find is stunning. I don't know what to make of it. I'll tell you WHY I don't know what to make of it.
    You've found mobile golems.
    I've lost the Angelotti manuscript.

--Anna

Message: #50 (Longman/misc.)
Subject: Ash mss.
Date: 12/11/00 at 2.38 p.m.
From: Ngrant@

*format address and other details
non-recoverably deleted*

Anna--

I don't understand. How can you LOSE the Angelotti text? It's in four major world collections! Explain!

--Pierce

Message: #66 (Pierce Ratcliff/misc.)
Subject: Ash, mss.
Date: 21/11/00 at 2.51 p.m.
From: Longman@

*format address and
other details non-recoverably
deleted*

Pierce--

No. It isn't,

I wanted to check on this 'forgotten invasion' of yours for myself.

If you weren't out in Tunis with Dr Grant—if this turns out NOT to be golems—I'm pulling the book. I mean it. THERE IS NO ANGELOTTI MANUSCRIPT!

The problem isn't that a 'Visigoth invasion' seems to have been swept under the historical carpet.

The PROBLEM is that since I wanted to check the Angelotti text myself, I phoned the Metropolitan Museum of Art, and the Glasgow Museum.

The Glasgow Museum no longer hold a copy of the Latin text attributed to one 'Antonio Angelotti'.

Both the British Library and the Metropolitan Museum now classify it as Mediaeval Romance Literature. As FICTION, Pierce!

WHAT IS GOING ON HERE?

Message: #54 (Longman/misc.)

Subject: Ash/Angelotti mss.

Date: 12/11/00 at 9.11 p.m.

From: Ngrant@ *format address and other details non-recoverably deleted*

Anna--

I contacted Bernard at the Glasgow Museum. He tells me he doesn't know where their Angelotti text is, they may no longer shelve it, or it 'may' be out on loan to some other institution. He asked me why I wanted to study something so patently useless to the historian, since it's a presumed 17th century FAKE.

I don't understand what is happening!

Both Charles Mallory Maximillian and Vaughan Davies had no doubts whatsoever about the veracity of this manuscript! In 1890 and 1939 it was catalogued as an ordinary 15th century document. When I consulted it, it was in the CATALOGUE under that designation! This is not like anything else that has ever happened to me in my academic career! They CAN'T have re-classified it in the past six months!

I can't get anyone to talk to me on-line, and I CAN'T leave here. If I go off-site, I won't be allowed back on again. You're going to have to take this on for me. For our book.

--Pierce

Message: #69 (Pierce Ratcliff/misc.)
Subject: Ash, texts
Date: 12/11/00 at 9.22 p.m.
From: Longman@   *format address and other*
                            details non-recoverably
Pierce--   *deleted*

Jesus Christ Pierce what next? If one of your manuscripts is a fake, but
the golems are real?

   I'll do what I can on-line, and by phone tomorrow morning. I really
don't understand this.

   Give me a list of documents to check.

   Okay, I can understand that maybe Victorian historians weren't so
rigorous as modern ones. There are such things as faked manuscripts.
But there've been two editions besides yours: if Charles Mallory
Maximillian was lax, surely Vaughan Davies should have spotted
something?

--Anna

Message: #55 (Anna Longman/misc.)
Subject: Ash, texts
Date: 13/11/00 at 00.45 a.m.
From: Ngrant@   *format address deleted*
                            text encrypted by non-discoverable
Anna--   *personal key*

Yes, Vaughan Davies should have discovered if any of the documents
were invalid. You are kind enough not to say it, but, so should I.

This is a list of the principal authenticated documents that I have
been working from:

The WINCHESTER CODEX, c.1495, Tudor English translation
of mediaeval Latin original (1480s?). Ash's childhood.

The del Guiz LIFE, c.1516, withdrawn, expurgated and reissued 1518. German original. Plus a version by Ortense Man-
cini, 17c playwright, in which she mentions that it is translated
from a 16c Latin manuscript—we have no trace of this. Covers
Ash's life 1472–1477.

The CARTULARY of the monastery of St. Herlaine, c.1480, translated from the French. Brief mentions of Ash as a novice c.1467–8.

'PSEUDO-GODFREY,' 1478(?), a German text of dubious
value, found in Cologne in 1963; original paper and ink, but
possibly a contemporary forgery, cashing in on the popularity
of the 'Ash' cycle of legends. Ash's life c.1467–1477.

The ANGELOTTI manuscript, Milan, 1487; appended at the
end of a treatise on armour owned by the Missaglia family.
Ash during the period 1473–1477.

'FRAXINUS ME FECIT', possible autobiography of Ash,
therefore written down no later than 1477; if a biography,
between 1477 and 1481(?). Covers Summer 1475(6?)-autumn
1476.

The two previous editions of the 'Ash' material are:-

Charles Mallory Maximillian (ed.) ASH: THE LIFE OF A FE-
MALE MEDIAEVAL MERCENARY CAPTAIN, J Dent & Son, Lon-
don, 1890, reprinted 1892, 1893, 1896, 1905.
      This contains translations of all the above, excluding 'Pseudo-
Godfrey' (and, of course, 'Fraxinus'). CMM does include the

17th century poems by Lord Rochester supposedly based on episodes from the del Guiz LIFE; later research indicates this is unlikely. CMM was a widely read and reputable scholar of his period, holding the Mediaeval History Chair at Oxford.

Vaughan Davies (ed.) ASH: A BIOGRAPHY, Victor Gollancz Ltd, 1939. Not reprinted. Plates lost.

Contents as CMM. There was also rumoured to be a pirated paperback edition, a facsimile reprint done by Starshine Press in San Francisco (1968), but I have not seen it.

This original 1939 edition itself exists only in incomplete form in the British Library. The publisher's warehouse was bombed during the war, destroying stocks, and cutting short a popular vogue for Vaughan Davies' book—after all, it is not every history book that is written by a man with his scientific, as well as historian's, credentials.

That's all I have on file; I think there may be one or two confirmatory mentions in contemporary letters, but I don't have the data with me.

I've now completed the next translation of the del Guiz/Angelotti 'Ash' material, and will sent it to you after this.

Isobel, of course, is insisting that I IMMEDIATELY finish 'Fraxinus me Fecit' for her, and she wants the translation done meticulously—so, I think, do I; but she knows that.

Please contact me. I DO NOT UNDERSTAND what is happening here. I have been an academic for twenty years; I do not believe I could make an error—or a series of errors—of this magnitude.

--Pierce

Message: #73 (Pierce Ratcliff/misc.)

Subject: Ash, documentation

Date: 13/11/00 at 10.03 p.m.

From: Longman@ *format address deleted*
Text encrypted by non—discoverable
personal key

Pierce--

I took a day's leave and spent it in the British Library. I didn't particularly want to explain at the office that there may be problems with your book—not when we've put it in the Spring catalogue.

I have grave problems with what I've found.

Some of the documents you mention, I just can't find—the Pseudo Godfrey, and the Cartulary (log-book, I suppose) of this St Herlaine monastery. I can't find any record of the monastery either.

I've managed to trace the German del Guiz 'Life', but you won't like it, Pierce.

In 1890, it was classified under 'Late Mediaeval History'. Charles Mallory Maximillian was obviously being completely above-board when he did his translation of it. By 1939, it was re-classified, this time as 'Romance Literature', along with the Nibelungenlied! I found a reference to your 1968 American printing of Vaughan Davies, which has the del Guiz manuscript in it, and the whole thing is classified under 'General Fiction'! And as far as the British Library's concerned now, they don't have any record of having a copy.

They don't have a record of any mediaeval manuscript by an 'Angelotti', either.

As far as I can see, this material was thought to be genuine in the 1890s, was discovered to be fake in the late 1930s—and Vaughan Davies just ignored this. What I can't understand, Pierce, is why YOU'VE ignored this.

Unless you can give me a convincing explanation, I am going to have to discuss this with my Managing Director.

--Anna Longman

Message: #60 (Anna Longman/misc.)
Subject: Ash, archaeological discoveries
Date: 14/11/00 at 11.11 a.m.
From: Ngrant@

*format address deleted
Text encrypted by non-discoverable personal key*

Anna--

I didn't ignore anything.

When I last consulted these documents, in the British Library, less than two months ago, they were classified under 'Mediaeval History'. There was NO suggestion that they might be anything else.

Please do nothing rash.

If these documents are so unreliable—why is the ARCHAEOLOGICAL EVIDENCE backing them up?!

--Pierce

PART FOUR

August 13, 1476 AD–August 17, 1476 AD

THE GARDEN OF WAR

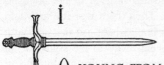

Ȧ YOUNG WOMAN'S body lay on a mattress stuffed with goose-down. Whether this was too soft, she too unaccustomed, it was not possible to tell. She stayed unconscious. She nonetheless rolled a little from side to side, and as her head turned it could be seen that she had a shaved patch over her left ear, hair sheared away from the swollen skull. A fine silver stubble grew back.

To stop her moving, they tied her with linen bands to the wooden frame of the bed. She seemed hot, with a fever, and restless. Someone washed and combed out and plaited the rest of her hair into two loose-woven braids, so it should not turn into impenetrable sweat-glued tangles.

Sometimes there were angry voices over her. A swearing-out of devils, or a fierce quarrel between soft-voiced women. Someone trailed oil over her forehead, and it rolled down the bridge of her nose and over her slashed cheek. When the linen sheet was taken back, half her body was spotted with black bruises, and a poultice of comfrey and Self-Heal was strapped to her right ankle, and another to her right wrist.

Someone washed her body with water from a silver basin.

Bees wove around the room, in the bright air between white walls, and back over the sill where climbing flowers nodded. A soft, rhythmic murmur of doves sounded beyond the window. Being washed and turned, she saw out

339

of the window to the birds, blazing white in the sun, one of them with golden beams shining from its head and back and golden eye: the Holy Spirit nesting in the dovecot, along with the other doves. Then there was fire and pain and shouting, and she was bound back on the bed with new linen, and the world went away to the sound of an angry voice that rose up the registers from contralto to alto to shout.

All the time, there was the light.

It came first always with a cold pink and yellow glow, through the night-shuttered windows. It grew, slanting, into bars of brightness: as bright as light down the edge of a sharpened blade. And light shook from the surface of the water in the jug that stood on an oaken chest beside the bed, dancing in blotched reflections on the white curving plaster of the ceiling.

Once a wing brushed her, white and stiff as a swan's feathers, but with all quills edged with gold like the leaves of a manuscript. Two voices spoke over the bed, debating about angels and those wandering spirits of the air that are devils, or perhaps old pagan gods worn weak with lack of worship.

She saw beyond the ceiling of the white cell a stacked rise of circles, circle within circle, each rimmed with faces and wings, and behind the saints' faces thin gold rings, a knife-scratch thin, haloes hot as the metal poured in a goldsmith's furnace. She sought, but could not find, a Lion.

The light, slanting the other way, drenched the room in gold. Chill shivered her, and hands brought up the linen sheets. A sharp clear-skinned face bent over her, short hair turned to rose-gold.

"D—"

Too soft a croak: and water from a wooden cup was spilling down her mouth and chin, soaking the sheets, leaking into her mouth, pricking a way between surfaces of dehydrated flesh. She felt in one instant the roar of pain through her flesh. Hurt leg, hurt arm, battered body, and her unbandaged hand jerking in its linen bands.

Fingers freed her. She felt for as much of her body as she could reach. Body, whole; no more damage to leg and arm than she has had before. A spurt of pain in her head. She touched her cheek, which flared with pain, and probed with her tongue to find the shattered roots of two back teeth in the upper left of her mouth.

''Did Thomas—''

''Thomas Rochester is alive! He's alive. And the others. Baby—''

More water at her lips, this with a stench of some herb in it. She drank, would she, would she not, but lay, fighting sleep, for as long as it took for the light to begin again, dew-wet and chill, at the shutters of the window.

Memories of darkness pushed at her, of a black sky, and an endless night, and lands growing winter-cold in the middle of harvest time.

''They'll be following—''

''Hush . . .''

Sleep took her down so fast that what she said was slurred, incomprehensible to anyone present:

''I will not be taken away to Carthage!''

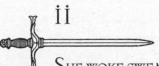

ii

SHE WOKE SWEATY and warm. A dream of terror slid away from her, like water vanishing through sand. Ash opened her eyes as delirium became sudden clarity:

Shit! How many days have I been sick? How long will it be before the Faris comes after me, or sends a snatch-squad—?

The voice of Floria del Guiz, above her, said, "You got stepped on by a horse."

"So much for the glory of battle . . ." Ash strained to focus her open eyes. "Sod this for a game of soldiers."[71]

"Bloody idiot."

The wooden-framed bed creaked as weight came down on it. Ash felt her body hoisted up by warm, strong arms. Time blipped: she thought she felt another body in the bed besides hers; then realized that the warm torso and breasts under the linen shirt pressed against her cheek were Florian's; that the woman surgeon was cradling her, and that her own body was weak as water.

Florian's quiet voice buzzed in Ash's ear, transmitted more by vibration through the flesh and bone of the surgeon's body than by sound. "I suppose you want an honest answer to how badly you're injured? Seeing as you're the boss?"

"No . . ."

"Damn right you don't."

You should have washed, Ash thought dimly, smelling a warm stench of old sweat on the surgeon's clothes. She let her head fall back limply against Florian's breasts, the bright white cell swimming before her eyes. "Oh *shit* . . ."

The weight of their two bodies was pressing them together on the goose-down mattress, into a valley in the center of the bed. Ash gazed up at a plastered white ceiling, her eyes tracking the black dot of a bee as it buzzed

---

[71]*Hoc futui quam lude militorum.* I quote Vaughan Davies' idiosyncratic translation of the mediaeval dog-Latin text.

into the room. The pressure of the woman's arms around her felt inexpressibly welcome.

"You're tough as shit," the rough voice above her said. "That's more significant than anything I can do for you."

In the room's hush, Ash heard a distant choir. A noise of women's voices singing mass. The tiny room filled with the scent of lavender: she guessed it must be growing close by.

Nothing in the room was hers.

"Where's my fucking sword? Where's my armor!"

"Yeah, that's my girl!"

Ash shifted her gaze to Floria's face. "I know I'm going to die before I'm thirty. We can't all be Colleoni[72] or Hawkwood.[73] How close have I come?"

"I don't *think* your skull's cracked . . . I've sewed you up. Said the right charms. If you'll take my advice, you'll stay in bed for the next three weeks. And if you will take my advice, it'll be the first time in five years!" The surgeon's cradling arm tightened. "I really can't do anymore for you. Rest."

"How many leagues are we from Basle?" Ash demanded. "What's happened to my company?"

Floria del Guiz heaved a sigh that Ash felt against every rib.

"Why can't you be like my other patients and start with

---

[72]Bartolomeo Colleoni (1404(?)–1475) had died the previous year. A famous condottiere, employed largely by the Venetians from 1455, he lived until the age of 72, still active Captain-General of the Venetian forces, and discouraged by the Most Serene Republic from traveling north of the Alps from his castle at Malpaga, in case the Milanese should immediately attack Venice in his absence! Those who truly wanted to see the great captain—for example, King Edward IV of England, in 1474—travelled to him.

[73]Sir John Hawkwood, famed English mercenary and leader of the White Company (1363–1375), saw long and profitable service in Italy and died old (in 1394).

'where am I'? You're in a convent, we're outside Dijon, in Burgundy, and the company's camped about a quarter of a mile *that* way.'' Her long dirty finger stabbed the air above Ash's nose, indicating a direction out of the cell window.

"Dijon." Ash's eyes widened. ''That's a *fuck* of a way from the Cantons. We're the other side of Franche-Comté. Good. Dijon . . . You're a fucking Burgundian, Florian, help me out. You know this place?''

"I should do." Floria del Guiz's voice sounded acerbic. She sat up, lurching Ash's body uncomfortably. "I have an aunt living six leagues from here. Tante Jeanne's probably at court—the Duke's here.''

"Duke Charles is *here*?''

"Oh, he's here. So is his army. And his mercenaries. You can't see the meadows outside the town for military tents!" Florian shrugged. "I suppose this is where he came to after Neuss. It is the southern capital.''

"Have the Visigoths attacked Burgundy? What's happening about the invasion?''

"How would I know? I've been in here trying to keep you alive, you silly bitch!''

Ash grinned helplessly at her surgeon's total disregard for military matters. "That's no way to talk to your boss.''

Florian shifted around under her in the bed, until she could look Ash directly in the face. "I do, of course, mean 'you silly bitch, *boss*.' "

"That's much better. Fuck." Ash tried to tense her muscles to sit up, and flopped back, her face screwed up in pain. "Some fucking surgeon you are. I feel half dead.''

"I can arrange the other half any time you like . . .''

A cool palm laid itself against Ash's forehead. She heard Floria grunt, vaguely dissatisfied.

The surgeon added, "There's a pilgrimage up here

every day, with a good three-quarters of the men trying to get in to speak to you. What's the *matter* with these guys? Don't they know a convent when they see one? Can't they even wipe their own arses without you being there to tell them to do it?''

"That's soldiers." Ash pushed her hands against the mattress, trying to sit up. "Shit! If you've been saying I can't see them because I got a crack on the head—"

"I haven't been saying anything. This is a *convent.* They're *men.*" Florian smiled wryly. "The sisters won't let them inside."

"Christ, they'll think I'm dying or dead! They'll be off to sign up with someone else before you can say *condotta*!"[74]

"I don't think so."

With a long-suffering sigh, Floria del Guiz got out of the bed and began to hold up Ash's torso and heap pillows under her shoulders and head. Ash bit her lip to keep from vomiting.

"You don't think so—why not?"

"Oh, you're a hero." Floria grinned crookedly, moving to stand beside the cell window. The white daylight showed up purple flesh under her eyes, and lines cut into the flesh at the sides of her mouth. "You're the Lioness! You saved them from the Visigoths, you got them out of Basle and into Burgundy; the men think you're wonderful!"

"They *what*?"

"Joscelyn van Mander is quite dewy-eyed. You military types are too damn sentimental; I've always said so."

"Fucking hell." Ash felt the goose-down pillows give under her as she leaned back, dizzy. "I had no right to go wandering into Basle looking for the Faris, and even

---

[74]The Italian "contract," from which the condottiere took their nick-name.

if I did, I put my men in danger. You name it and I fucked it. I really fucked up, Florian. They must know that!''

"If you walk down there today, they'll throw rose-petals under your feet. Mind you," Floria remarked thoughtfully, "if you walk down there today, I may be burying you tomorrow."

"A hero!"

"Haven't you noticed?" The surgeon delicately pointed upwards. "The sun. You've brought them back to the sun."

"*I* brought—" Ash broke off. "When did the sun come back? Before we got to Burgundy?"

"As we crossed the border." A frown compressed Floria's brows. "I don't think you understand me. The sun's only shining *here*. In Burgundy. It's still dark everywhere else."

Ash licked her lips, her mouth dry.

No, that can't be—it *can't* only be here!

Ash absently pushed Floria's hands away as the woman tried to put a wooden bowl to her lips. She took it in her own hands and sipped, frowning.

They put out the sun. But not here in Burgundy. Why Burgundy?

Unless the Eternal Twilight spreads where . . .

Where the armies from the land Under the Penitence successfully invade. No, how could that be?

Maybe it's not just here that there's the sun, but in all the lands north of what they've conquered—France and the Low Countries and England—where the eternal twilight hasn't yet spread? Shit, I need to be up and talking to people!

"If the guys think I got them *out* of trouble," Ash continued her progression of thought, "—Green Christ only knows why!—then I'm not going to tell them different. I need all the morale on my side that I can get.

Bloody hell, Florian. You're Burgundian, aren't you? What are our chances of getting another contract here, given that I made a sterling effort to off the Duke not so long ago?''

Ash gave a small smile, her lips wet with the clear spring water.

''Would your Tante Jeanne get us an in to court?''

Floria's expression closed like a door shutting.

''You'd better see Robert Anselm today,'' she remarked. ''It probably won't kill you. It might kill him if you don't.''

Ash blinked, her attention disrupted from the Visigoths. ''Robert? Why?''

''Who do you think rode over you at Basle?''

''Oh, *fuck*.''

Floria nodded. ''He'll be sitting outside the convent gate about now. I know this, because he's been sleeping out there.''

''How long have I been here?''

''Three days.''

''How long has he been out there? Don't tell me. Three days.'' Ash put her head in her hands and winced as her fingers came into contact with the shaved patch of her scalp and the painful irregularity of catgut stitches. She rubbed at her eyes. She was suddenly conscious of being dressed only in a stale night-shirt, and of needing the nightsoil pot. ''Then who's been running my company!''

''Geraint-the-Welsh-bastard.'' Floria widened innocent eyes. ''Or at least, that's what they seem to think his name is. With Father Godfrey. He seems to have it all under control.''

''Does he, by God! Then it's more than time I was back in charge. I don't want the Lion Azure turning into Geraint ab Morgan's company while I sit on my arse in some damn convent!'' Ash rubbed the heel of her hand over her face. "You're right, sod you; I'll get up tomorrow, not today. I still feel like there's a horse treading on me. I'll see Roberto. I'd better see the *maîtresse* of this place, too. *And* I'm getting dressed."

The surgeon eyed her sardonically, but made no comment except, "And with all your boys outside these walls, you expect me to act as your page, I suppose?"

"You might as well learn to be a page. You're a crap surgeon."

Floria del Guiz blurted out a laugh, an open guffaw completely different from her usual mordant chuckle, plainly taken by surprise. She whooped and thumped the flat of her hand against her thigh. "You ungrateful cow!"

"Nobody loves an honest woman." Ash's mouth moved into an unwilling smile, remembering. "Or maybe I'm just a wayward wench."

"A *what?*"

"Never mind. Christ, I'm well out of that!"

And I'm staying as far away from the Faris *as I can get.*

Okay, maybe we *are* far enough away to be safe. For the moment. What do I do now? I don't know anything like enough about this situation!

Ash swiveled her legs around with difficulty and sat on the edge of the bed. Blood thundered in her ears, drowning out the sound of doves cooing beyond the window. She swayed where she sat.

"Poor bloody Robert. It would have to be him. Find me a chair, or at least a stool with a back to it. I don't want him to see me looking as if the Grim Reaper will be getting the next audience with me!" Ash stopped, adding suspiciously, "This is a convent? I'm not putting on a dress!"[75]

---

[75]Original text, "kirtle."

Florian laughed, moving past her toward the oak chest against the far wall. She trailed her fingers across Ash's unshaved hair affectionately and lightly: Ash hardly felt the touch.

"I sent down to Rickard for your gear. The Soeur wouldn't let me bring a sword within the confines of the convent, but," Floria's head emerged, her hands clutching shirt, doublet, and hose, "you've got your green and silver, and a velvet demi-gown. Will boss be content with that?"

"Boss will do just fine."

Once past the squalidness of the nightsoil pot, and half laced into her clothes, Ash began to find it less disturbing to have a woman acting as her page. She grinned. "Why I've being paying you all these years as a *surgeon*, when—"

She broke off, as a nun entered the cell.

"Soeur?"

The big woman folded her hands at her waist. A tall, tight wimple robbed her face of all context, left it nothing but an expanse of puffy white flesh in the sunlight. Her voice sounded gravelly. "I'm Soeur Simeon. You're staying in bed, my girl."

Ash wriggled her arm down the sleeve of her doublet and leaned against the upright of the back-stool while Floria laced it tight at the shoulder. She spoke as if the room wasn't swimming around her.

"First, I'm seeing my second in command, Soeur."

"Not in here you're not." The nun's lips compressed into a hard line. "No men within the walls of the convent. And you're not yet fit to go out."

Ash felt Floria straighten up. Her voice came from above Ash:

"Allow him in for a few minutes, Soeur Simeon. After all, you let *me* in—and I know what's important for my patient's health. Good lord, woman, I'm a surgeon!''

"Good lord, woman, you're a *woman*," the nun rapped back. "Why do you think you're allowed in here?"

Ash chuckled at the almost audible wuff! of the wind being taken out of Floria del Guiz's sails.

"That fact, *ma Soeur*, is completely confidential. I know I can trust a woman of God." Ash put her hands flat on her thighs and managed to sit reasonably confidently. "Bring Robert Anselm in secretly if you must, but bring him in. I'll get through my business as fast as possible."

The woman—the nun's habit robbing her of her age, as well; she might have been anywhere between thirty and sixty—narrowed her eyes and surveyed the whitewashed sick room and its disheveled occupant. "You've been used to having your own way for quite some time, haven't you, *ma fille*?"

"Oh yes, Soeur Simeon. It's far too late to do anything about it."

"Five minutes," the woman said grimly. "One of the *petites soeurs* will be in here with you for decency's sake. I shall go and organize some prayer."

The door of the whitewashed cell closed behind the big woman.

Ash blew out her lips. "Whoa! *There* goes a born colonel of the regiment!"[76]

"Look who's talking." Floria del Guiz went to rummage in the oak chest again, and emerged with a pair of low boots. She knelt, thrusting them onto Ash's feet, and Ash looked down at the top of her golden head. She made as if to reach out and touch the disguised woman's hair, then drew her hand back.

---

[76]In the original text, "*triarii* [veteran] of a legion," but a modern version gives a more immediate referent.

"I'm all in tangles," she said. "Smarten me up, will you?"

The tall woman took a horn comb out of her purse and stepped behind her, undoing her loose braids. Ash felt a gentle, painful tugging as the comb worked its way up from the bottom of each hank of silver-fair hair, unthreading sweat-solidified knots. Her head began to throb. She shut her eyes, feeling the warmth on her face of the sun through the window, and the movement of warm summer air. *First I need to arrange for the company to survive in Burgundy. What are we living on?—Christ, but I feel sick!*

The comb stopped snagging her yards-long length of hair. Floria's fingers touched her cheek, which ran with salt tears. "Hurts? It will, with a head-wound. I could cut this lot off."

"You could not."

"Okay, *okay* . . . leave *my* head on my shoulders!"

Time blipped again.

Floria's voice spoke quietly to someone else in the sick-room. Ash opened her eyes to see another nun, in the same dull green habit and white wimple, who met her eyes as they focused, and stepped across the room to offer her water in a wooden cup.

"I know you." Ash suddenly frowned. "It's difficult to tell without the hair, but I *know* you. Don't I?"

Off over toward the window, Floria chuckled.

The little nun said, "Schmidt. Margaret Schmidt."

Ash's cheeks colored up. She said in a voice both weak and incredulous, "You're a *nun*?"

"I am now."

Floria crossed the room, sliding her hand over the woman's shoulders as she passed her. She bent down to feel Ash's forehead. "Dijon, boss. You're in the big convent outside Dijon." And then, when Ash only looked bemused, "the convent for *filles de joie* who become *filles de pénitence*."[77]

Ash looked at the little nun, whom she had last seen in the whorehouse in Basle. "Oh."

The other two women smiled.

Ash made an effort, and managed to speak. "If you change your mind before you take the last vows, Margaret, you'll be welcome in the company. Say, as surgeon's assistant."

Floria's face, as she glimpsed it, held an expression somewhere between awe, cynicism and unease; but mostly one of surprise. Ash shrugged at her and, at the resulting twinge, put her hand up to her head.

The woman from Basle made a courtesy. "I make no decisions until I see what life in a nunnery is like, seigneur—demoiselle, that is. So far it isn't so different from the house of joy."

A rap sounded at the door.

"Bugger off," Ash said. "I'm seeing Robert on my own."

She closed her eyes for a moment, finding it restful, letting the opening and closing of doors go on without her. From other wounds, she recognized this weakness. Knew more or less how long it would take to pass. Too long.

What am I? The Faris says, just a piece of rubbish. Just the same as a male calf you slaughter when it's born, because it's useless, because all you want is heifers to keep in milk.

But you hear a voice.

And that's all it is? Some brazen head, away in North Africa, some . . . some *engine* they've made, that spits out Vegetius and Tacitus and all the ancients on war? Just a—

---

[77]Contemporary records survive for this.

a *library*? Nothing more than tactics out of a manuscript, there for the asking?

Ash smothered a giggle under her breath, not willing to let out the tears that pricked behind her eyes.

Sweet Christ, and I've trusted my life to it! And the times I've read bits out of *De Re Militari* and thought, no, there's no way you should do *that* tactic under *those* circumstances—what have I been listening to?

Ash felt a strong temptation to speak, aloud, and ask her voice those questions. She shook off the impulse, opening her eyes.

Robert Anselm stood in front of her.

The big man was out of armor, in hose patched at the knee, and a demi-gown undone over a laced Italian doublet: all in blue wool and all looking very much slept in, and slept out of doors at that. He carried an empty dagger scabbard at his belt, thrust through the loop of his leather purse.

"Uhh . . ." Robert Anselm reached up suddenly and grabbed the velvet hat off his head. He turned it between his big hands, thumbs absently pressing the pewter Lion badge on each revolution. His gaze fell.

"Are we safe? Where are we encamped?" Ash demanded. "What's the situation here—who's the local lord, under the Duke?"

"Uh." Robert Anselm shrugged.

Ash's head twinged, as she put it back to look up at him. He immediately dropped into a crouch in front of her stool, his forearms resting on his knees, his head lowered. Ash found herself looking at the salt-and-pepper bumfluff growing out around the edges of his scalp.

I could tell you you're a fucking idiot, Ash thought. I could hit you. I could say *what the fuck do you think you're doing, leaving my company to run itself?*

Her stomach growled, appetite returning. *Bread, wine,*

and about half a dead deer, for preference ... Ash put one hand up to shield her eyes from what was becoming painfully bright sunlight at the window. The air grew hotter. This must be morning moving on toward noon.

"You never saw what I did at Tewkesbury, did you?" she said.

Anselm's head came up. His expression was mottled, under the dirt, a strained white-and-red, unpleasant and unhealthy-looking. He rubbed the back of his neck. "What?"

"Tewkesbury."

"No." Anselm's shoulders began to untighten. He put one knee down on the floor to keep himself steady. "Didn't see it. I was on the other side of the battle. I saw you at the end, wrapped in the standard. You were dripping."

Dripping *red*, she remembered, feeling again the wet cloth, the scratch of heavy embroidery, the sheer exhaustion of wielding a poleaxe. A razor-edged blade on a six-foot shaft. An axe that bites as hard into metal and body-parts as a domestic axe does into wood.

"That worked," she said measuredly. "I knew I had to do something at that age to get noticed. I was far too young for command, but if I'd waited and done something remarkable at sixteen or seventeen—it wouldn't have been remarkable. So I took and held the Lancastrian standard on Bloody Meadow." Now she lowered her gaze, catching Robert Anselm with an expression of pure distress on his features.

"I got two of my best friends killed doing that," Ash said. "Richard and Crow. I'd known them for years. They're both on that slope somewhere. Buried in the ditch the White Rose dug afterwards. And you rode over me by accident. That's what we *do*. We kill people we know, and we get killed. And don't tell me it's bloody stupid.

There aren't any ways to get killed that are sensible!''

Anselm yelled, "I'm getting *old*!"

Ash's mouth stayed open.

Robert shouted, "That's what those little shits have started calling me! 'Old man.' I'm twice your age; I'm getting too old for this! *That's* why it happened!''

"Oh, fucking hell.'' His hands were shaking and she grabbed at them, feeling his warm flesh clammy; and she tightened her grip as hard as she could, which was far less than she expected. "Don't be stupid.''

He wrenched his hands out of hers. Ash grabbed at the sides of the stool. Her head swam.

"I'm sorry, all right?'' he yelled. "I'm sorry! I'm *sorry*! It was my fault!''

The sheer volume of his shout brought her lip snarling back against her teeth. She winced at the pain; winced as the cell door banged open and back against the wall, Floria del Guiz grabbing Anselm's arm, yelling; him throwing her violently off—

"That's *enough*!'' Ash took her hands down from her ears. She breathed in and lifted her head.

Margaret Schmidt stood in the doorway, looking anxiously back along the passage. Floria had both her long-fingered hands tight around the big man's biceps again, straining to drag him out of the room. Robert Anselm's feet were planted firmly apart, his shoulders braced wide, and his head bullishly down; *nothing short of six men is going to throw him out of here*, Ash reflected.

"You, go and tell the Soeur Maîtresse nothing is the matter. You,'' her finger jabbed at Floria, "let go of him; *you*''—to Robert Anselm—"shut your fucking mouth and let me *speak*.'' She waited. "Thank you.''

"I'll go,'' Floria said, with distaste at her own embarrassment. "If you send her into a relapse, Robert, I'll geld you.''

The surgeon left the room, closing its door upon herself, Margaret Schmidt, and a number of other nuns attracted by the break in their monotony.

"Now you've had a chance to yell at me for getting hurt," Ash said gently. "Feel better?" The big man nodded, sheepishly. He stared intently at his own feet.

"Have you really been sleeping on the convent steps?"

His shaven head dipped. The big shoulders came up, slightly, in a minuscule shrug.

"I turn forty this year. Two choices," he said, apparently addressing the floor. "Get out of this while I'm alive, or stay in the business. Stay as a woman's commander, or get my own company. Christ, woman, I'm starting to feel old. Please don't tell me Colleoni rode into battle when he was seventy!"

Ash shut her mouth. "Well . . . that is exactly what I was going to say. You telling me you're out of here, is that it? Bottle gone?"

"Yeah." He did not sound goaded into a confession, but flatly honest.

"Yeah, well, tough shit. I need you, Robert. If you want to go and start your own company, that's different, you can go, but you're not leaving mine because you've scared yourself shitless. Got that?"

Robert Anselm reached out for her insistent hand. "Ash . . ."

"Get me into that bed, or I'm going to throw up again. Jesus Christ, I hate head wounds! Robert, you're not going. Sometimes I *do* think I couldn't run this fucking company without you." Her hand knotted around his. She pulled herself up off the stool onto her feet. She stood, swaying, not needing to accentuate it.

Robert Anselm muttered sarcastically, "Yeah. You're a poor weak woman." He dipped and scooped his other arm under her knees, lifting her bodily, and carried her the few feet to the bed. With one knee dinting the mattress, he lowered her down. ''You won't trust me after this. You'll say you will, but you won't.''

Ash relaxed down into goose-feather softness. The white ceiling swooped, circling. She swallowed a mouthful of sour saliva. To have her body supine and cradled brought such relief that she let out a long breath and shut her eyes.

''Okay, so I won't. Not for a while. Then I will trust you again. We know each other too well. Like she said, if you leave, I'll geld you. We're in deep shit now, and it needs sorting!''

He arranged her neatly in the bed, not unused to handling the wounded. Ash opened her eyes. Robert Anselm seated himself sideways on the edge of the bed, his head turned toward her, and suddenly frowned. ''She?''

''No. It wasn't her who said that, was it? Not the nun. *He*. Florian did.''

''Mmm,'' Robert Anselm said absently. The way that he sat, arms spread, hands down supporting his weight, occupying all the space around himself, was so purely Anselm that she had to smile.

''It's all very well to sound so certain, isn't it?'' Ash said. ''Get back and run the company. If that works, then they haven't lost confidence in you. As soon as I can get up without falling over, I'll come and sort out what we're going to do next. We won't have long to make up our minds here.''

He gave a curt nod and stood up. As his weight left the mattress, she felt suddenly bereft.

Her head pulsed with pain. ''We've just run like fuck. We don't have a contract here in the Duchy. Do this wrong, and my lads'll be deserting in droves by tomorrow . . . If you fuck up my company, I'll have your bollocks,'' she snapped weakly.

Robert Anselm looked down at her. "It'll be under control. Next time," he crossed to the cell door, "wear a bloody helmet, woman!"

Ash made an Italian gesture. "Next time, *bring* me one!"

Robert Anselm stopped on the threshold. "What did the Faris say to you?"

Fear punched in under her breastbone, flooding her body. Ash smiled, felt the falsity of it, let her face find its own expression of distress, and croaked, "Not now! Later. Get that asshole Godfrey up here, I want to talk to him!"

What had been background pain flared, throbbing, until water began to run out of her eyes. She took little notice of what was said or done then, except for someone putting a bowl to her lips, and since she smelled wine and some herb she swallowed it in great gulps and then lay praying until—not soon enough—she fell into a drugged sleep.

Her sleep became troubled less than an hour later.

Pain seared into her head. She froze, lying as still as possible, swearing at Floria whenever the surgeon came near her, her body broken out in a cold sweat. When the light dimmed, she felt it to be from the pain in her head. A male voice told her repeatedly that it was only evening, was sunset, was night, was the dark of the moon; but she shifted on the hot bolster, fangs of pain biting into her head, jamming her mouth shut with her fist, her own teeth breaking the skin of her knuckles. When she did give way and scream, when the pain became too bad, the movement blasted her into some region that she recognized: a place of blazing physical sensation, complete helplessness, complete inescapability. She had it one heartbeat, forgot it by the next; knew it for a memory, but not now what it was a memory of.

"*Lion*—" Her pleading voice choked in her throat,

barely above a whisper: "By Saint Gawaine—by the Chapel—"

Nothing.

"Hush, baby." A soft voice, man or woman's, she couldn't tell which. "Hush, hush."

Still in a frozen whisper, she snarled: "Are you a fuck ing *machine*? Answer me! Golem—"

"No suitable problem proposed. No available solution."

The voice in her secret soul is unemphatic, as it has always been. Nothing of the predator in it, nothing of the saint?

Pain swarmed over every cell of her body; she whispered, despairingly, "Oh *shit*—!"

Another voice, Robert Anselm's, said, "Give her more of that stuff. She won't die of it. For bloody Christ's sake, man!"

Sharp and rapid, Floria rapped out, "You can do this? Then you do this!"

"*No*; I didn't mean—"

"Then *shut up*. I'm not losing her now!"

iii

SHE MUST HAVE slept, but didn't realize it except in retrospect.

Predawn light made a gray square of the window before her eyes. Ash groaned. Her palms were cold with sweat. The bed-linen smelled stale. As she moved her shoulder, she felt wool against her cheek and realized that she was still fully dressed. Someone had undone her points, loosening her clothing. Stabs of pain entered her skull with every breath she took in, with every tiny movement of her body.

"I must be getting better, it hurts."

"What?" A shadow rose and bent over her. The chill dawn illuminated Floria del Guiz. "Did you say something?"

"I said, I must be getting better, it's starting to hurt." Ash found herself sounding breathless. Floria put the familiar bowl to her mouth. She drank, spilling half on the yellow bed-linen.

An odd sound became, as she recognized it, someone scratching at the sick room door. Before Floria could rise from beside her, the door opened and someone came in, carrying a pierced iron lantern. Ash turned her head away from the stabbing light. She bit down on a breath as the movement jolted her head. Carefully, she slitted her eyes and peered at the doorway.

"Oh, it's you," Ash muttered as she recognized the newcomer. "I don't know what the Soeur was complaining about—this fucking convent's *full* of men."

"I am a priest, child," Godfrey Maximillian protested mildly.

"Good God, am I that ill?"

"Not now." Floria's hand pressed down on her shoulder. Ash kept herself from crying out. The surgeon added, "You did too much yesterday. That won't happen today. This is the long boring bit. The bit you never like. The bit where boss tries to get up before she should. Remember?"

"Yeah. I remember." Ash momentarily grinned, catching the tall, golden-haired woman's smile. "But I'm bored."

The surgeon narrowed her eyes at Ash. There was a

look on her face that Ash suspected meant she would be
getting a smart cuff around the ear about now, if not for
her state of health. *Maybe I'm not well, at that.*

"I've brought you a visitor," Godfrey said. The surgeon glared at him, and he held up one broad-fingered
hand reprovingly: "I know what I'm doing. She's anxious
to meet Ash, but she has to travel on from the convent
later this morning. I told her she could come and speak
with the captain for a few minutes."

Floria held an expression of skepticism as they talked
across Ash's bed. The growing light brought their faces
out of the dimness: the big bearded man, and the laconic
man who was a woman. Ash lay and listened.

Godfrey Maximillian said, "It's still me, too, Fl—my
child. You used to believe that I had some skill in my
art."

"Priesting isn't an art," the surgeon grumbled, "it's a
fraud practiced on the gullible. All right. Bring your visitor in, Godfrey."

Ash made no attempt to sit up in the bed. Floria put
the pierced lantern on the floor, where its light would not
be so harsh. A blackbird spoke out of the emptiness beyond the window. Another called—a thrush, a chaffinch;
and in a space of three or four heartbeats, a loud noise of
birdsong echoed in the dawn. Ash's head throbbed.

"Fucking twittering *birds*!" she complained.

"Capitano," a woman's clear voice said. Ash recognized the sound of someone moving while wearing armor:
metal plates rattling and clacking, mail chinging.

Ash raised her eyes and saw a woman of about thirty-
five beside the bed. The woman wore Milanese-style
white armor, with a wheel-pommel sword belted at her
waist and an Italian barbute helmet tucked under her arm,
and had a considerable air of authority.

"Sit down." Ash swallowed, clearing her mouth.

"My name is Onorata Rodiani, Capitano.[78] Your priest said I must not tire you." The woman stripped off her gauntlets to move the back-stool to the other side of the bed. Her little finger and ring-finger of her right hand were crooked, both repeatedly broken and set.

She seated herself on the back-stool and sat carefully erect, dipping her head out of her bevor so that she could turn her chin and see whether her scabbard was scraping the cell wall behind her. Satisfied that it was not, she turned back, smiling. "I never lose a chance to meet another fighting woman."

"Rodiani?" Ash squinted past the throbbing in her scalp. "I heard of you. You're from Castelleone. You used to be a painter, didn't you?"

The woman rested her hand up beside her face. It took Ash a second to note she was cupping her ear, and to realize that she should speak more loudly. The side of the woman's face was speckled black with impacted powder. Deaf from gunfire.

"A painter?" Ash repeated.

"Before I became a mercenary." The woman's white teeth showed in the dimness as she smiled broadly. "I killed my first man as a painter. In Cremona—I was painting a mural of the Tyrant at the time. An inopportune rapist. After that, I decided I liked fighting better than painting."

Ash smiled, recognizing a public story when she heard it. *It's not that easy.* The woman's loose dark hair would show pure black in daylight. The lines of her tanned face promised plumpness in old age. *If she reaches it,* Ash

---

[78]Onorata Rodiani, a historical character, has obviously been incorporated in this text out of a conviction that these two women *ought* to have met. In fact, Rodiani is reported as dying, after a long career as a mercenary, in the defense of her home town, Castelleone, in AD 1472.

thought, and reached her hands out from under the sheet. "Can I see that?"

"Yes." Onorata Rodiani handed her barbute over.

Ash took the weight, the pull on her muscles shooting pain through her head, and rested the helmet on the bolster beside her. She poked at strap, rivets and helmet liner with an inquisitive finger and ran the pad of her finger around its T-shaped opening. "You like barbutes? I can never *see* out of the damn things! I see you've gone for rose-head rivets as well."

The woman's left thumb stroked the disc pommel of her sword. "I like brass rivets on a helmet. They polish up bright."

Ash rolled the barbute back toward her. "And Milanese vambraces? I've always used German arm defenses."

"You like Gothic armor?"

"I can get more movement out of their vambraces. As for the rest of it, all fluting and edge-work—no. It's frilly armor."

There was a snort from the doorway, where Floria and Godfrey stood talking in undertones. Ash glared at them.

"So. You want to see my sword?" Onorata Rodiani offered. "I wish I could show you my war-horse, too, but I have to leave this morning for the war that will come to France. Here."

The woman stood and drew. That sound of sharp steel sliding against the fine wood that lines a sword-scabbard brought Ash up on her elbows. She struggled to get her back up against the bolster, finally sat, and reached her hand out for the hilt. She ignored the pain that made her eyes water.

France? Ash thought. Yes. The Visigoths have more men and supplies than I've ever seen; they're not stopping where they are now. After the Swiss, and the Germanies . . . France isn't a bad guess.

The Faris is equipped for a full-scale crusade.

"So how many lances do you have?" Ash flicked the wheel-pommelled sword in her hand. The thirty-six-inch blade, wide at the hilt and tapering to a needle point, slid through the air like oil through water. A living blade: the feel of it worth every pang in her scalp. "Christ, that's sweet!"

"Twenty lances," the woman said, and added, "Isn't it?"

"I see you've gone for hollow-grinding on the blade."

"Yes, and didn't I have to stand over the blade-smith to make him do it properly!"

"Oh God, never trust an armorer." Ash lowered the blade and sighted along it, testing its trueness by eye, and found herself focusing on the grinning face of Godfrey Maximillian. "What's the matter with *you*?"

"Nothing. Nothing at all . . ."

"Well, get my guest some wine, then! You want her to think we don't have any courtesy around here?"

Floria del Guiz linked her arm through the priest's. She murmured, "We'll get some wine, boss. We'll be right back. Honest."

Ash flipped the blade upright in her hand. A sliver of dawn light flashed off the scratched, mirror-bright steel. There was, she noted, a distinct curve to one edge of the blade, near the hilt, where battle nicks had been polished out on a grinder. A man could have shaved with the weapon's edge.

"Nice work on the grip," she commented appreciatively. "What is it, brass wire over velvet?"

"Gold wire."

At the door, leaving, her priest said something to her surgeon that Ash did not quite catch. Floria shook her head, smiling. Ash lowered the sword, scooping up the

linen sheet on her left hand, and rested the blade across
her muffled finger.

"Balances about four inches down . . . I like 'em blade-
heavy, too. I bet it really cuts." She raised her head, glaring at Godfrey and Floria. "*What?*"

"We'll leave you to it, child. Madonna Rodiani," Godfrey bowed. Behind him, Floria was grinning for some
reason that Ash did not understand, but obscurely felt
might be best not inquired into. Godfrey smiled blandly
at her. He said, "I'll just tiptoe away now. Florian will
tiptoe away."

Ash heard Floria mutter something that sounded very
like: "*Everybody* will tiptoe away! My God, these two
could bore for Europe . . ."

"You," Ash said with dignity, "are interrupting a professional discussion. Now fuck off out of my cell! And
while you're getting us wine, you can find me breakfast
as well. Bloody hell, anybody would think I was an *invalid.*"

It was pure pleasure to forget the armies over the border, forget the nightmare of Basle, for however short a
time.

"You can't be fighting the war in your head every hour
of the day; not and win when it does come to a battle."
Ash grinned, all decisions temporarily in abeyance.

"Madonna Onorata, stay for breakfast? While we eat,
I want to ask you what you think about something in
Vegetius. He says stab with the sword point, because two
inches of steel in the gut is invariably fatal—but then,
your man may not fall over until he's had time to kill *you.*
I often use the edge, and cut, which is slower, but maybe
takes a man's head clear off, after which I find he generally doesn't bother me again. What's *your* preference?"

She was quite genuinely not afraid of injury.

When she had worked out, to her own satisfaction, that

she probably would not die on this particular day—this despite having known men who walked around for several days after a blow on the head, only to drop dead for no reason that anyone could see (despite the company surgeon's covert rummaging in the contents of their brainpan)—having decided this, and having suffered the extreme unpleasantness of having her two broken back teeth filed down flat, Ash to all intents and purposes forgot her wound. It became one of many.

That left her with nothing to do but think.

Ash leaned her elbows on the nunnery window's edge, gazing out into the confusion of a wash-day in the enclosed courtyard. The stench of Cuckoo Pint starch filled her nostrils. She smiled ruefully at the peaceableness of it.

Behind her, someone entered the cell. She didn't turn, recognizing the tread. Godfrey Maximillian came to stand at the window. She noticed he glanced reflexively up, as Florian and Roberto and little Margaret had, at the sun in the sky. He looked to be burned red across the cheekbones.

"Fl-Florian says you're well enough to talk business."

"Now you're doing it! She does, does she? That's damn good of her."

A sparrow darted down, dipping its beak for the crumbs she held on her palm. Ash chirruped as it fluffed brown feathers at her, watching her with one black, pupilless eye.

She said, "I suppose we're deemed, de facto, to have broken our contract with the Visigoths. The Faris certainly broken whatever agreement she had with me. I think we've chosen the side we're *not* going to be on in this war."

Godfrey said, "I wish it was that simple."

A sharp beak pecked her palm.

Ash raised her head, to gaze up at Godfrey Maximillian. "I know that just staying out of the way won't be good enough. The Visigoths are coming north anyway."

"They've come as far as Auxonne." Godfrey shrugged. "I have sources. We came through Auxonne, on the way from Basle. It's no more than thirty-five, forty miles from here."

"Forty miles!" Ash's hand jerked. The sparrow abruptly flicked into flight, dipping across the courtyard crowded with women. The sound of nuns' voices and the noise of water slopping in tubs drifted up to the window.

"That's . . . getting to the point where I'm going to have to *do* something. The question is, what? The company, first. I need the lads back on-line . . ."

A flash of sunlight on slate roofs, bright as a kingfisher's wing, took her eye. Past the convent wall, beyond strip-fields and copses, the white walls and blue slate roofs of a city shone clean and bright and clear under the midday light. Under the sun.

"Godfrey, I have to ask you something. As my clerk.[79] Call this my confession. Can I lead them into combat— if I can't trust my voice?"

One look at the frown creasing his face was enough.

"Oh yes." Ash nodded. "The Faris does have a war-machine, a *machina rei militaris*. I watched her speak to it. Wherever it is—Carthage, or closer at hand—it wasn't in the same place as she was when she spoke to it. But she heard it. And I . . . heard it. It's my voice, Godfrey. It's the Lion."

She kept her voice steady, but water stung the lids of her eyes.

"Oh, child." He cupped his hands around her shoulders. "Oh, dear child!"

"No. I can stand that. It was a genuine miracle, a gen-

---

[79]Priest. Most scholars (clerks) were also priests, in this era.

uine Beast, but—children imagine things. Maybe I wasn't
even present, I just heard the men talking. Maybe I made
up seeing the Lion myself when I started hearing voices.''
Ash moved her shoulders, freeing herself from his hands.
''The Visigoths, the Faris—she'll be suspicious now. Before, they had no reason to think anyone else could use
the machine. Now . . . they might be able to stop me doing
it. They might be able to make it *lie* to me. Tell me to
do the wrong thing, in the field, get us all killed . . .''

Godfrey's face showed shock. ''Christ and the Tree!''

''I've been thinking about it, this morning.'' Ash
smiled crookedly, there being nothing else to do but haul
herself together. ''You see the problem.''

''I see that you would be wise to tell no one about this!
This is Under the Tree.'' Godfrey Maximillian crossed
himself. ''The camp is rowdy. Disturbed. Morale could
go either way. Child, *can* you fight without your voice?''

The sun burned sparks from flints in the convent's wall,
glittering in the corner of her eye. A waft of warm air
brought her thyme, rosemary, chervil, and more Cuckoo
Pint from the herb garden. Ash looked at him flatly.

''I always knew I might have to find out. That's why,
when we fought Tewkesbury field—I never called on my
voice the whole of the day. If I was going to lead men
out to fight, where they could be killed, I didn't want it
depending on some damn saint, some Lion-born-of-a-
Virgin, I wanted it depending on *me*.''

Godfrey gave a choked sound. Ash, puzzled, looked up
at the bearded man. His expression wavered somewhere
between outright laughter and something very close to
tears.

''Christ and the Holy Mother!'' he exclaimed.

''What? Godfrey, *what*?''

''You didn't want it depending on 'some damn saint'—''
His deep, resonant laugh boomed out; loudly enough to

make some of the nearer nuns lift their heads and stare up at
the window, eyes squinting against the brilliance of the sun.

"I don't see what—"

"No," Godfrey interrupted, wiping his eyes, "I don't
suppose you do."

He beamed at her, warmly.

"Miracles aren't enough for you! You need to know
that you can do it by yourself."

"When there are people depending on me, yes, I do."
Ash hesitated. "That was five years ago. Six years. I don't
know that I can do without my voice *now*. All I do know
is, I can't trust it anymore."

"Ash."

She looked up to meet Godfrey's sobering gaze.

The priest pointed toward the distant town. "Duke
Charles is here. In Dijon. He's been holding court here
since he withdrew his army from Neuss."

"Yeah, Florian told me. I thought he'd've gone north
to Bruges or somewhere."

"The Duke is here. So is the court. And the army."
Godfrey Maximillian rested his hand over her arm. "And
other mercenaries."

What she had taken to be a distant continuation of Dijon's white walls, she now saw to be white canvas. Sun-
bleached tents. Hundreds of tents—more, as her eye ran
along their peaked canopies. Thousands. The glitter of
light on armor and guns. The swarming of men and
horses, too far away for livery to be distinguished, but she
could guess them to be Rossano, Hawkwood, Monforte,
as well as Charles's own troops under Olivier de la
Marche.

Sombrely, Godfrey said, "You have eight hundred
fighting men out there in the Lion Azure, not to mention
the baggage train, and they all talk. It's known you've

been with the Visigoths—and with their Faris-General.
Consequently, there are *many* people who are anxiously
waiting to speak to you, when you recover and leave this
place.''

"Oh. Shit. Oh, *shit*!"

"And I don't know how long they will wait.''

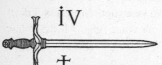

iV

THE NEXT MORNING'S heat laid a blue
glaze over the distant trees and turned the sky a hot, pow-
dery gray. Ash walked down between daisy-thick banks
and towering cow-parsley, leaving her demi-gown and
doublet sleeves behind, to where the Lion Azure had their
camp, the promised quarter of a mile beyond the convent
grounds. She came at it covertly through a copse of
birches, and the company's tethered cattle and goats, graz-
ing the rich water-meadow.

Ash scratched at one of the wicker pavises strapped to
the side of a baggage-wagon, some distance from the main
gate, making a mental note that Geraint's idea of how far
apart one should space pickets was sadly lacking.

"I shouldn't be able to do this . . .''

She stared at the camp beyond the wagons, the fire-
breaks between tents trodden down to dust, and the figures
of men in Lion livery mostly sprawled around dead fire-
pits, eating oat-porridge from wooden bowls.

Okay. What's been changed? What's different? Who—

"Ash!"

Ash tilted her head back, shading her eyes against the
sun, staring up at the top of the wagon. Heat crisped the

skin across her nose and cheeks. "Blanche? That you?"

A flash of white legs, and a woman swung herself out over the wagon-shafts and threw her arms around Ash. The yellow-haired ex-whore thumped her back. Tears sprang to Ash's eyes.

"Whoa! Steady on, girl! I'm back, but you don't want to kill me before I get inside!"

"Shit." Blanche beamed happily. White sunlight showed wet smears on her cheeks. "We thought you were dying. We thought we were stuck with that Welsh bastard. Henri! Jan-Jacob! Come here!"

Ash heaved herself over the wagon-shafts, jumping down onto the flattened straw that strewed this part of the camp further away from the knights' tents, and straightened to find her hand being wrung by her steward Henri Brant, and Jan-Jacob Clovet struggling to lace his cod-flap with his injured arm and thump her on the back at the same time. Blanche's daughter Baldina, a red-haired woman, dropped her skirts with aplomb and got up from the straw where she had been accommodating the man-at-arms.

"Boss!" she called croakily, "are you back for good?"

Ash ruffled the whore's flaming hair. "No, I'm marrying Duke Charles of Burgundy, and we're going to spend every day eating 'til we burst and fucking on swansdown mattresses."

Baldina said broadly, "Suits us. We'll make you a widow so you can. That's if that little limp-dick you married is still alive somewhere."

Ash made no answer, being engulfed in the wiry embrace of Euen Huw and a torrent of Welsh admiration and complaint, and finding herself at the center of a rapidly growing mob, made up of the company's boys, musicians, washerwomen, whores, grooms, cooks and archers, and being swept off—as she had intended—toward the center of the camp.

First of all the men-at-arms, Thomas Rochester threw his arms around her, his harsh face streamed with tears.

"Typical emotional *rosbifs*!" Ash thumped his back. Josse and Michael piled in on top of her, and half the English lances with them.

Fifteen minutes later, her head pounding and half-blind with renewed pain, Joscelyn van Mander was shaking her hand with a grip that left red imprints on her fingers, his blue eyes brimming with wetness.

"Thanks to Christ!" he blurted. He looked around, at the mob of men-at-arms and archers and billmen pressing close, and the knights elbowing in, all trying to reach Ash. "Lady, thanks to Christ! You're alive!"

"Not for much longer," Ash said under her breath. She managed to free her hands. One arm went comradely over Euen Huw's shoulder, and she rested her weight on the little Welshman; the other held Baldina's hand, the red-headed whore not willing to be parted from her for a second, mopping her face with the hem of her kirtle.

Lowering his voice for confidentiality, and breathing warm wine-breath in her face, Joscelyn van Mander interrupted. "I've been speaking to the Viscount-Mayor on behalf of the company; we have trouble with allowing knights into the town—"

Oh, *you've* been speaking on behalf of the company, have you? Uh-huh.

Ash beamed at the Flemish knight. "I'll sort it."

She grinned around at the thronging faces.

"It's boss!"

"She's back!"

"So—where's Geraint-the-Welsh-bastard?" Ash inquired, in a voice of piercing good humor.

Amid a roar of laughter, Geraint ab Morgan forced his

way through the crowd in front of the command tent. The big man was stuffing his shirt into the back of his hose, between a set of broken points. His bloodshot blue eyes flinched, seeing Ash in the middle of a throng of delirious admirers.

Geraint shoved out with both arms to clear a space, and thumped down on both knees on the earth in front of her. "It's all yours, boss!"

Ash grinned at the note of heartfelt relief in his voice. "Sure you don't want to keep my job?"

At this point, she knew exactly the answer he would make. Geraint didn't have any choice. She had chosen to come in by way of the menial members of the company, who had no chance, nor would ever have a chance, of competing for rank within it. Their genuine joy carried itself to the men, and that left the knights—given van Mander's *volte face*—with nothing to do but forget any quite viable ambitions that had started to grow in her absence, any unauthorized promotions and demotions, and cheer her to the echo.

In broad Welsh, Geraint said, "Stuff your fucking job, boss, have it and welcome!"

"Lightbringer!" someone shouted behind her, and someone else, Jan-Jacob Clovet, she thought, bellowed, "Lioness!"

"Listen up!" Ash loosened her grip and held up both hands for silence. The camp's failings could wait an hour, she decided. "Okay! I'm here, I'm back, and I'm going up to the chapel now. Anyone else who wants to give thanks for our deliverance from the darkness, *follow me*!"

She couldn't make herself heard for sixty seconds. Eventually she stopped trying, thumped Euen Huw on the back, and pointed. They moved toward the camp's main gate, at least four hundred strong; and Ash answered questions and asked for news and congratulated men recovering from wounds, all in one breath, under a staggering hot sky.

Being a chapel of Mithras,[80] it was naturally on separate land from the convent. Ash led the way uphill to the nearby copse, lost in the great crowd.

Trees in full leaf shuttered out the sun. Ash breathed a long sigh, not aware of how dazzled she had been by heat and light until now. She looked ahead, down the path, to where her officers waited outside the low, heavy masonry entrance: Floria, Godfrey, Robert and Angelotti, standing in sepia dappled shadow. She gave one very tiny nod of her head and saw them relax.

Floria fell in step with her as she came up to them, Godfrey on the other side. Angelotti bowed, he and Robert Anselm dropping back to let her pass.

Ash gave the two men a thoughtful glance over her shoulder.

Priests stood in the chapel entrance. She linked arms with Florian and Godfrey. Behind her, knowing there would be no room below, men-at-arms and archers were sinking to their knees on the leaf-mold, filthy men dappled with the sun's light through the green leaves, pulling off helmets and hats, talking at the tops of their voices,

---

[80]I find myself in agreement with Vaughan Davies's supposition in the 2nd edition of the ''Ash'' texts (published 1939), and can do no better than quote it:

''The oddities of religion apparently practiced among the fifteenth century cohorts of Ash bear no resemblance to contemporary Christian practice. A more robust age—indeed, an age less in imminent need of divine protection than our own—can afford religious satires which we should, perhaps, deem blasphemous. These scurrilous representations (which occur only in the Angelotti manuscript) are Rabelaisian satire. They are no more intended to be read as fact than are descriptions of the Jewish race poisoning wells and abducting children. The whole matter is a satire against a papacy which was, by the 1470s, not at all beyond reproach; and shows the feelings which would, in the next century, explode into the Reformation.''

and laughing. Junior priests of Mithras moved away from the entrance toward the groups of armed men, so that the service could be held here as well as below.

She fell in beside Godfrey, linking arms, going under the lintel and down the steps, exchanging the scent of dry woodland for the moist cold of the earth-walled passage. "So—what did you hear at court? Will the Duke fight?"

"There are rumors. No information I would trust. Surely he can't ignore an army forty miles away, but— But I've never seen such magnificence!" Godfrey Maximillian spluttered. "He must have *three hundred* books here in his library!"

"Oh, *books*." Ash kept a steadying hand on her clerk's arm as she reached the bottom of the steps and walked into the Chapel of Mithras. Sunlight slanted down through the bars above, casting the stone cave into floods of light and shadow. Roman mosaics under her feet depicted the Proud Walkers and the April Rainers in tiny pastel squares. "What am I going to care about Duke Charles's books for, Godfrey?"

"No, I don't suppose you will. Not in the present situation." He inclined his head, a smile partly concealed by his beard. "But he has the most wonderful Psalters. One illustrated by Roger van der Weyden, no less. He also has all the *Chansons du Geste*, child—Tristram, Arthur. Jaques de Lailang ..."

"Oh, what! Really?"

Godfrey chuckled, mimicking her tone. "Really."

"Now that's what's wrong with war," Ash said, wistfully, as they knelt in front of the great Bull altar.

"Ehh? Jaques de Lailang is what's wrong with war?" Godfrey murmured, puzzled. "Good lord, child, the man's been dead for thirty years."

"*No.*" Ash cuffed the priest affectionately. From the

altar, the Bull priest gave her a quelling glare.[81] She subsided to a whisper, aware she was still borne up by the
intensity of her welcome back to the company. They kept
up a constant chatter behind her. ''I mean what *happened*
to him is what's wrong with war. There you have him,
perfect gentle knight, wins all the tourney circuit matches
for years, been on every field of battle of note, a real
warrior chevalier—actually set up a knightly pavilion and
defended a ford with his lance against all-comers[82]—and
what happens to him?''

Godfrey searched his memory. ''Killed at one of the
sieges of Ghent, wasn't he?''

''Yeah—by a cannon ball.''

The blood bowl was passed around. Ash drank, bowed
her head for the blessing, and said formally, ''I give
thanks for my recovery and dedicate my life to continuing
the battle of the Light against the Dark.'' As the steaming
bowl continued around to the vast numbers of the company crowded into the chapel and queued back up the
steps, she murmured, ''That's what I mean, Godfrey. All
the virtues of chivalric war, and what happens to him?
Some damn gun-crew blows his head off!''

Godfrey Maximillian reached down with a broad arm
to haul her up off the flagstones. She took the necessary
help without resenting it.

''Not that I ever thought war was anything but a dirty
business,'' she added dryly. ''Why are Robert and Angelotti avoiding me, Godfrey?''

''Are they? Dear me.''

Ash pressed her lips together. The blessing concluding,
she waited while the white- and green-robed boys sang,

---

[81]Neither women, nor soldiers who were not officers, were permitted to
be present at the Mithraic mysteries.

[82]In AD 1450.

and then ascended up into the light between her lance-leaders—a mass of men in bright steel and brilliant linen, walking out into the wood with her, swatting buzzing insects away, and each of them desperate to have just one reassuring word with Ash.

"The riding-horses need exercise!" The company farrier.

"Twenty carcasses of pork, and nine of them off," Wat Rodway complained.

"Huw's archers keep brawling with my men!" An indignant fair-haired Sergeant of Bill. Carracci, she recognized, unusually fraught.

Euen Huw swore. "Bloody Italian bum-boys messing about with my lads!"

One of the female hackbutters complained, "And half my powder is left behind at Basle—"

Ash stopped dead on the path.

"Wait."

Her page, Bertrand, handed her her velvet bonnet. She heard the snort of horses and looked ahead. Beyond the brown trunks of trees and the arching green loops of briars, out in the meadow, war-horses were being held by grooms.

"Later," she ordered.

A group of armed men stood just within the copse's shade. Their banner hung limp and unreadable, but looked to be—she squinted—quartered squares of red and yellow, with white bars, mullets,[83] and either crosses or daggers. The men's livery jackets were white and murrey-colored.[84]

A hand under her armpit lifted her out of the discussion group and several yards on down the path from the crowd

---

[83]Not the fish. In heraldry, a five-pointed star.

[84]Murrey: a mulberry or reddish-purple color.

of her soldiers. Robert Anselm, without looking down at her, said, "I got us a contract. He's here. Meet your new boss."

"New boss?" Ash stopped dead.

She was no weight to stop Anselm, but the big Englishman let go of her arm and abruptly dropped to one knee in front of her.

A second man knelt on the dry leaves: Henri Brant. Antonio Angelotti thumped down beside him. Ash looked down at her steward and second in command and gunner. She put her hands on her hips. "Excuse me, my new *what*? Since when?"

Anselm and Angelotti exchanged glances.

"Two days ago?" Robert Anselm ventured.

"New *employer*," Henri Brant spoke up. "I had difficulty getting credit in Dijon. Prices are going up, now there's an army at their border. And I can't supply eight-score horses and a whole company on what there is left from Frederick!"

So how much *were* we forced to abandon at Basle? Shit.

Ash surveyed Henri's broad face. He still favored his right side a little, she noted, where he knelt. "Stand up, you idiot. You mean no food-merchant would give you credit unless the company had a formal contract with someone?"

Henri, getting to his feet, nodded agreement.

That's just about time for the news to get out that our last contract was with the Visigoths . . . Whoever it is, Ash thought, he didn't waste any time making his move.

Ash tapped the toe of her boot on the leaf-mulch floor of the copse. "Roberto."

The two men, kneeling before her, could not have been more different: Anselm still in his blue woolen doublet, face unshaven; Angelotti with his mass of gold hair falling below his shoulders and his gather-necked shirt spotless and of the finest linen. What they had in common were identical expressions of shifty apprehension.

"You said go run the company. I've run it." Robert shrugged where he knelt. "We *need* money! This is a good contract . . ."

"With a man that we know." Angelotti uncharacteristically stumbled over his words. "That Roberto knows, knew, knew his *father*, that is—"

"Oh, Christ, don't tell me it's one of your goddams!"[85] Ash glared. "There's a country I'm never going back to! Nothing but barbarians and rain. Roberto, I'm going to nail your ears to the pillory for this one."

"He's here. You better meet him." Robert Anselm got up, untangling his scabbard from a thorn bush. Angelotti followed suit.

"He's one of your fucking Lancastrians, isn't he? Oh, sweet Christ! On top of everything else, you want me to go and fight English King Edward for his throne. I don't *think* so." Ash stopped, scowled, suddenly realizing, *That would put me a thousand leagues and a good chunk of sea north of the Faris and her army.*

Maybe there's something in this. If I go to England, at the worst I die on the field of battle. Who knows what might happen in Carthage, if they ever found out that I hear—no!

She muttered, "Now, who's white-and-murrey?" and began to ransack her memory of the heraldry of dispossessed Lancastrian lords in exile from Yorkist England.

Robert Anselm coughed. "John de Vere. The Earl of Oxford."

Ash absently took her sword as Bertrand brought it, and

---

[85] With *rosbif, goddam* is a contemporary nickname for the English, at that time popularly supposed to be very foul-mouthed.

let the boy belt it around her waist. Dapples of sunlight shone on its battered red leather scabbard. Her green and silver doublet was still quite obviously an expensive garment: equally obviously, it had not been washed or brushed for nearly a week. And no armor, not so much as a jack of plates.

"The fucking Earl of fucking Oxford, and I look like I'm worth ten shillings a year. Thank you, Robert. Thank you." She gave the wriggle of her hips that settled her sword-belt comfortably at her waist. She looked keenly at him. "You fought in his household, didn't you?"

"His father's. His older brother, too. Then him, in '71." Robert shrugged uncomfortably. "I got us what I could. He needs an escort here, he says."

Ash glanced around for Godfrey and saw the priest in conversation with a man-at-arms in a murrey livery jacket with a white mullet on it. She could not very well approach her clerk at this point to ask him why a Lancastrian lord might be at the court of Charles of Burgundy, what he might want with a hefty contingent of armed mercenaries, and what, she ended in her own mind, he thinks of the Visigoth forces about forty miles away from here!

"His father, your old boss—he died in battle?"

"No. His father and Sir Aubrey—that's his brother—they were executed."

"Oh yippee," Ash said sourly. "Now I'm being employed by attainted nobility—he is under attainder, I suppose?"

Antonio Angelotti quietly put in, "Madonna, here he is."

Ash straightened her shoulders quite unconsciously. The annoying insects still buzzed, gold motes in the light under the trees. A horse snorted. The men with the de Vere banner jingled as they approached, their surcoats tied over light mail. There were a few burned-red faces under the helmets. Ash guessed the escort largely consisted of those who had recently displeased a sergeant. The man at the center of the group she could not see clearly, but she nonetheless hauled off her hat and went down on one knee as the escort parted and made way for him. Her officers knelt with her.

"My lord Earl," she said.

She was aware of the bulk of her company halted outside the chapel of Mithras watching her. She was fortunately too far ahead to hear much of what they were saying. The earth felt hard under her knee. A blink of pain went through her head. When a cool voice said in English, "Madam Captain," she looked up.

He might have been any age between thirty and fifty-five: a fair-haired Englishman with faded blue eyes and an outdoor face, wearing tall riding boots pointed to the skirts of a faded linen doublet. He stepped forward, extending a hand. She took it. He had bony wrists. Any doubts about strength were dispelled by his effortlessly bringing her to her feet.

Ash dusted her hands and looked shrewdly at the man. His doublet was Italian fashion, not so barbaric as she had feared; and if it looked as though he had been hunting all day across hard country in it, it had started life as an expensive garment. He was wearing a dagger, but no sword. She managed not to say *Mad English*!

"We're at your command, my lord Earl," Ash said, and also failed to add *Or so I'm told* . . .

"I find you recovered, madam?"

"Yes, my lord."

"Your officers have told me the strength of your company. I want to know your manner of commanding them." The Earl of Oxford turned on his heel and began to walk toward his horses. Ash muttered a brief command to Anselm, left him to get the company back to their camp, and walked briskly off in de Vere's tracks. His assumption that he did not have to tell anyone to follow him both amused her and impressed her by how correct it seemed to be.

At the wood's edge, she found her servants and the de Vere grooms vying for shade, and mounted with a minimum of fuss. Godluc shifted his great quarters under her, pushing for a gallop. She brought him up beside the Earl of Oxford's bay gelding.

Over the jingle of tack, the Englishman said, "A woman, most unusual," and smiled. He was missing a side tooth, and now they were out in the light she could see old white scars seaming his wrists and vanishing under the neck of his shirt. The dimple-puncture of an arrow wound marked one cheek.

He added, "They appear devoted to you. Are you a virgin-whore?"

Ash spluttered at his English translation of *pucelle*. She said cheerfully, "I don't see what damn business it is of yours. Sir."

"No." The man nodded. He leaned over in the saddle, offering his hand again. "John de Vere. You call me 'your Grace' or 'my lord.' "

Manners of the camp, not the court, Ash thought. Good. It always helps if they know something about soldiering. I must have seen his father around at some point; he looks familiar.

She shook his hand. His grip was solid.

Let's delay the questions for a bit. Until I have time to think about my answers.

"What is it you want my men to do, your Grace?"

"In the first place, I'm here to make a request of Burgundian Charles. If he refuses, you will form part of my escort to the borders, and back to England. I shall pay you off in London."

''How strongly are we liable to be refused?'' Ash asked thoughtfully. ''Does your Grace want me to put the Lion Azure up against the entire Burgundian military machine? I probably can get you to the Channel ports, in that case, but I don't particularly want to die to the last man, which is realistically what it would mean.''

John de Vere turned his pale blue eyes to her. His bay had a mettlesome look, barrel-chested and something wicked about the eye. He rode easy in the saddle. To Ash, all the signs said, this man is a soldier.

Almost demurely, the exiled Earl said, ''I'm here to find a Lancastrian claimant for the English throne, Henry late of glorious memory being murdered, and his son dead on Tewkesbury field.[86] The Yorkists don't sit so securely. A legitimate heir could dethrone them.''

Ash, knowing next to nothing about *rosbif* dynastic struggles after her own brief involvement five years before, remembered one fact. She shot John de Vere a confused glance.

Serene, he said, ''Yes. I'm aware that Duke Charles is married to the sister of Edward of York.''

''Edward of York, who's currently Edward, fourth of that name, King by the Lord's Grace of England.''

De Vere corrected her with immense authority: ''Usurping King.''

''So you're here, in the court of a prince married to the Yorkist King's *sister*, to find a Lancastrian claimant who's willing to invade England and fight against the Yorkist King for his throne? Yeah. Right.''

Ash eased herself back in her saddle, controlling God-luc's obvious desire to lie down and roll in the lush green

---

[86] 4 May 1471: Prince Edward, the only son and heir of King Henry VI, is killed in battle with Edward of York (afterwards King Edward IV of England) at Tewkesbury. Henry VI dies soon after, under suspicious circumstances.

grass they rode over. She couldn't look at the Earl of
Oxford for a minute, and when she did, she was no longer
sure whether or not he had been smiling.

"Remind me to renegotiate our contract if it comes to
that, your Grace. I'm pretty sure Anselm wouldn't sign
me up for that."

Actually, I'm pretty sure he'd like nothing better. Damn
Robert! He never gave up on his bloody English wars—
but he's not dragging me into them!

Not that I wouldn't like to be half of Christendom away
from here right now . . .

"Don't think of it as an act of lunacy, Captain." The
Earl of Oxford's weather-beaten face creased, amused.
"Or don't think of it as more lunatic than employing a
female mercenary in addition to my household troops."

Ash began to consider that under his English soldierly
exterior, John de Vere, Earl of Oxford, might be as reckless as a fifteen-year-old knight on his first campaign. *And
as mad as a dog with its balls on fire*, she thought dourly.
Robert, Angelotti, you're in deep, deep trouble.

The Earl said, "You came up from the south, Captain,
and were employed by the Visigoth commander. What
can you tell me? Within the terms of your *condotta*?"

Here it comes. And he's only the first. There's going
to be some interesting questions, and not just from mad
English Earls who happen to be employing me . . .

"Well?" de Vere said.

Ash looked over her shoulder and saw her own escort,
led by Thomas Rochester with her personal banner. They
were riding intermingled with the troops in murrey and
white.

The rest of the company, archers and billmen and
knights together all promiscuous, moved ahead with her
officers, walking and riding back to the camp.

"Yes, your Grace." Ash narrowed her eyes against the

sun, watching the column—from this illusory perspective, behind them, they did not appear to be moving forward: just a forest of polearms bobbing gently up and down. A multitude of steel helmets and bill-heads glinted in the Burgundian sunlight.

Ash said, "If you wish to inspect my company, there's wine in my tent. I'm considering what I can tell you, without betraying a previous employer." She hesitated, then said, "Why do you want to know?"

He appeared to take no offense, and she had used enough lack of ceremony to provoke him if he was going to be provoked. She thought, *Now we shall find out what he wants*, and waited, the reins tucked up in her fingers, her body swaying with Godluc's loose-boned walk.

"Why? Because I've changed my mind about my business since I came here." John de Vere switched to Burgundian French. "With this southern crusade rolling up Christendom like a carpet, and my lord princes of Burgundy and France squabbling instead of uniting, the Lancastrian cause is necessarily put into abeyance. What use would a Lancastrian king be on the throne of England if the next thing he sees is a fleet of black galleys sailing up the Thames?"

Ash dropped Godluc back very slightly, so that she could see the Englishman's face. His eyes, narrowing against the sun, showed deep-bitten crow's feet. He did not look at her, nor the rich miles of Burgundian countryside.

Over the noise of jingling tack, and Godluc huffing a long breath, the Earl of Oxford said, "These Visigoth men are good. Either they'll conquer us, disunited as we are, or we'll unite—and we might still be beaten. It would be bad war. Then there's the Turk waiting in the east, to come down and take the victor's spoils away from him."

His thin, bony knuckles whitened on his reins; the bay's head tossed. "Steady!"

"Your Grace hired me because I've been there."

"Yes." The Englishman brought his horse under control. The pale blue eyes lost their abstracted look and fixed on Ash. "Madam, you are the only soldier I can find in Burgundy who has. I'll talk to your officers, too; your master gunner in particular. First I'll hear details of what arms they bear, and their manner of war. Then you can tell me what rumors they have following them. Like this nonsense of a sky without a sun over the Germanies."

"That's true."

The Earl of Oxford stared at her.

"It's true, my lord." Ash found herself the more inclined to give him his title, since he was in exile. "I was there, my lord. I saw them put the sun out. It's only since we came here . . ."

She waved an ungloved hand, indicating the green sweep of grass running down to the water meadows; the wagons and tents and flying pennons of the Lion Azure camp; the sparkling water of the Suzon river; and Dijon's peaked roofs, blue tiles shining like mirrors under the summer sun.

". . . only here that I've seen the sun again."

De Vere reined in. "Upon your honor?"

"Upon my honor, as I honor a contract." Ash surprised herself with plain honesty. She tucked her reins under her thigh and pushed her linen shirt-sleeves up. Her skin was already reddened from the morning blaze, but she welcomed it, could not get enough of it, sunburn or not.

"Does the sun still shine on France, and England?"

Something in the intensity of her question must have got through to the Earl. De Vere said simply, "Yes, madam. It does."

Godluc dropped his head. White foam began to cream

his flanks. Ash cast a practiced eye to the horse lines (set up in that part of the camp that included trees and river) and considered their coolness and shade. The war-horses, separated out by long-suffering grooms from the riding mounts, looked fractious.

A figure came running out of the camp's wagon-gate as she watched, sprinting across the river meadow toward them—toward Thomas Rochester's Lion Azure banner, she guessed, and thus to herself.

His gaze on the running figure, the Earl of Oxford said, "And this war-machine of theirs? Did you also see that?"

"I saw no machine," Ash said carefully. The distant figure was Rickard.

"I'll tell you what I know," she said decisively. Then, with humor, "You hired me for what I know, your Grace. As well as for these men. And as far as I can, I'll tell you the truth."

"On the understanding that you have no more loyalty to me than to the last man who hired you," the Earl remarked.

"No *less* loyalty," Ash corrected him, and nudged Godluc and rode forward to where Rickard, long legs laboring, pounded across the grass and kingcups toward her.

Rickard halted, leaned forward with his hands gripping his thighs, breathing hard, and then straightened. Redfaced, he thrust a parchment roll up at her.

Ash reached down. "What's this?"

The black-haired boy licked parched lips and panted, "A summons from the Duke of Burgundy."

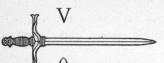

A**SH** BECAME CONSCIOUS of her pulse speeding up, her mouth rapidly drying, and an urge to visit the latrines. She closed her hand tightly around the Duke of Burgundy's scroll.

"When?" she demanded, not about to spell out some clerk's script word-by-word in front of a new employer. Seeing Rickard's bright red face, she loosed the water skin from her saddle and handed it down to the boy. "When does the Duke want us?"

Rickard drank, tipped a sparkling jet over his black curls, and shook his head, drops spraying. "The fifth hour past noon. Boss, it's almost noon now!"

Ash smiled reassuringly. "Get me Anselm, Angelotti, Geraint Morgan and Father Godfrey: *run!*"

Her voice cracked.

Straightening up in her saddle, she saw Robert Anselm just leaving the camp again, the Italian master gunner with him. As the boy pounded back past them, the two men strode through the thick, green grass toward her and the Earl of Oxford's retinue.

"Here they come—the lily-white boys," she remarked grimly, under her breath. *Robert, what have you got me into!* "My lord of Oxford, please you to accept my hospitality?"

The fair-haired Englishman eased his horse up alongside Godluc, gazing at the Lion Azure camp, which began, as they watched, to resemble a beehive kicked over by a donkey. With a slight smile, he murmured, "The

Earl of Oxenford[87] would be better advised to go away for an hour and leave you to put your men in order.''

"No." The grim edge didn't leave Ash's voice. Her gaze fixed on her approaching officers. "You're my boss, my lord. It's up to you now whether I obey this summons and go and see the bold Duke. And, if I do go, how I go, and what I say to him. It's your call, my lord.''

His faded brows lifted.

"Yes. Yes, madam. You may attend. I must decide what you say. Regrettably, it seems that I may have cheated you out of a contract richer than I can offer while Richard of Gloucester[88] holds my lands.''

And just how much are you paying us? Not a hundredth as much as Charles *Temaraire*[89] could, that's for sure. Shit.

"Stay and eat with me, my lord. You need to give me your orders. I can guest your retinue, too." Ash took a breath. "I intend to hold a muster now and take the roll, so that I can tell you our exact strength. Master Anselm may have told you that we left Basle in something of a hurry. You got a bargain. My lord.''

"Poverty is a worse master than I am, madam.''

Ash surveyed his frayed doublet and thought about being attainted and in exile. "I do hope so," she murmured under her breath. Then: "Excuse me, your Grace!''

As the men from his small retinue rode up to the Earl, Ash tapped Godluc's flanks with her spurs and trotted

---

[87]"Oxenford" is one of the contemporary versions of "Oxford."

[88]Seven years after the actions narrated in the "Ash" texts, Richard of Gloucester is crowned king of England, as Richard III (1483–1485).

[89]Duke Charles of Burgundy, like his forefathers—Philip the Bold, John the Fearless and Philip the Good—was known to his people by a cognomen. *Temaraire* has been subsequently translated, according to taste, as "Charles the Bold" or "Charles the Rash."

forward. She was aware of Florian walking up beside her stirrup and Godluc whickering at the surgeon. Her head began to ache. She halted before the panting figures of Robert Anselm, Angelotti, and now Geraint ab Morgan with them. She gazed over their heads from her saddle, at the camp, and sought with a critical eye to bring detail out of what was essentially a chaos.

"Jesus Christ on the Tree!"

Itemized, it was worse than it first looked. Men lay drinking around fire-pits gray with ash. Glaives and bills leaned in untidy heaps or rested unsteadily up against guy-ropes. Blackened cookpots were being prodded by half-dressed men-at-arms. Whores sitting up on the wagons ate apples and screamed with laughter. Euen Huw's lance's sorry attempt at guarding the gate made her cringe. Children ran and screeched far too close to the horse-lines. And the wall of wagons trailed down, at the river, to a mass of small shelters, blankets over sticks mostly, and no effort made to make fire-safety or a defense possible . . .

"Geraint!"

"Yes, boss?"

Ash scowled at a distant crossbowman with unlaced hose and a dirty white coif over stringy shoulder-length hair, who sat on a wagon playing a whistle in the key of C.

"What do you think this is, Michaelmas fucking Fair? Get that bloody lot kitted up, before Oxford fires us! And before the Visigoths get here and kick our asses! Move it!"

The Welsh Sergeant of Archers was used to being shouted at, but the genuine outrage in her tone made him swing around immediately and stomp off into camp, between the tents, lifting his big legs with remarkable alacrity over guy-ropes, and bellowing directions to each lance of men that he passed. Ash sat in her saddle, with her fists on her hips, and watched him go.

"As for *you*." She spoke to Anselm without lowering her head. "*Your* ass is grass. Forget dining with your old lord. By the time we come out of my tent, this camp is going to look like something out of Vegetius, and these dozy buggers are going to look like soldiers. Or you're not going to be here. Am I right?"

"Yes, boss—"

"That was a fucking rhetorical question, Robert. Get them mustered; take the roll; I want to know who we lost and what we kept. Once they're out in the field, get them practising weapons drill; half of them are lying around getting rat-arsed, and that stops *now*. I need an escort fit to walk into Duke Charles's palace with me!"

Anselm blenched.

She snarled, "You have one hour. Get to it!"

Florian, her hand resting on Godluc's stirrup, gave a deep, breathy chuckle. "Boss goes *bark!* and everybody jumps."

"They don't call me the old battle-axe for nothing!"

"Oh, you know about that, do you? I've never been sure."

Ash watched Anselm sprinting back to camp, conscious that, under her anguished concern that her men weren't secure, and under the level of fear about stepping into the premier court of Europe, some tiny inner voice was exclaiming *God, but I love this job!*

"Antonio, stay here. I want you to show the English lord your guns—I never met a lord who wasn't interested in cannon—and keep him out of my hair for one hour. Where's Henri?"

Her steward appeared at Godluc's bridle, limping, leaning on the arm of the woman Blanche.

"Henri, we're entertaining this English Earl and his

retinue in the command tent. Let's have fresh rushes, silver plates, and respectable food, okay? Let's see if we can set table for an earl's degree.''

"Boss! With Wat cooking?'' Henri's aghast, linen-coiffed face slowly changed to an expression of complacency. "Ah. *English.* That means he knows nothing about food and cares less. Give me an hour.''

"You got it! Angelotti, go!''

She turned Godluc with a pressure of her knee and rode slowly back to the murrey banner. The cloth drooped in the heat. The men-at-arms' faces under their helms shone wet and red. She thought, Every damn peasant is sheltering from the sun from now until late afternoon. Every merchant in Dijon is between cool stone walls, listening to musicians. I bet even the Duke's court are holding siesta. And what do we get?

Less than five hours to be ready.

"Madam Captain!'' de Vere shouted.

She rode up to the Englishmen.

The Earl of Oxford, speaking (as he had been speaking) in the Burgundian dialect of the Duchy, indicated his young knights and said briefly, "These are my brothers—Thomas, George and Richard—and my good friend Viscount Beaumont.''

His brothers all looked more or less in their twenties; the remaining nobleman a few years older. All of them had shoulder-length, curling fair hair, and a certain kinship of shabby leg-armor and brigandines and sword grips with the leather worn thin.

The youngest-looking of the de Vere brothers sat up in his saddle and said, in clear East Anglian English, "She dresses like a man, John! She's a strumpet. We don't need the like of her to get false Edward off the throne!''

Another brother, whose blue eyes squinted, said, "Look at that face! Who cares what she is!''

Ash sat her war-horse easily and surveyed the four brothers with a relaxed expression. She turned her head toward the remaining nobleman, Beaumont. With the English she remembered from campaigning there, she remarked, "No wonder they say what they do about English manners. You have anything to add to that, my lord Viscount?"

The Viscount Beaumont held up a gauntleted hand in surrender, eyes twinkling appreciatively. When he spoke, a missing front tooth made his voice appealingly soft-edged. "Not me, madam!"

She turned back to the Earl of Oxford. "My lord, your brother there isn't the first soldier to insult me for being female—not by about twenty years!"

"I am ashamed by Dickon's[90] lack of courtesy." John de Vere bowed from his saddle. To all appearances confident of her, he said, "Madam Captain, you know how best to handle it."

"But she's a weak woman!" The youngest brother, Richard de Vere, turning amazed pale eyes to her, blurted, "What can you do?"

"Oh, I get it . . . You think my lord didn't hire me for my fighting skills," Ash said bluntly. "You think he just hired me because he wants to question me about the Visigoth general and the invasion that's headed this way, and because you think Robert Anselm runs this company and commands it in the field. Am I right?"

One of the middle de Veres, Tom or George, said, "Duke Charles must be of the same opinion. You're a woman; what else can you do but talk?"

The Earl of Oxford politely said, "That is my brother George, madam."

Ash wheeled Godluc away to face the youngest brother.

---

[90]"Dickon" is the short, affectionate form of "Richard."

"I'll tell you what I can do, Master Dickon de Vere. I can reason, I can speak, and I can do my job. I can fight. But if a man doesn't believe I can command, or thinks I'm weak, or won't lie down after I beat him in a fair fight—which is the way I usually handle this with recruits—or thinks that any woman's argument is best answered by rape . . . then I can kill him."

The youngest de Vere's face colored up red from neck to hairline. Part embarrassment, part—Ash guessed—the realization that it was probably true.

"You'd be surprised how much trouble it saves." She grinned. "Honey, I don't have to convince you I'm not vermin. I just have to fight your lord brother's enemies reasonably well and survive to get paid."

Dickon de Vere, white-faced, stared, suddenly very upright in his saddle. Ash turned back toward the Earl of Oxford.

"They don't have to like me, my lord. They just have to stop thinking of me as a daughter of Eve."

There was a snort from the Viscount Beaumont, something in English so rapid between the four brothers that she couldn't follow it, and then the youngest brother flushed, burst out laughing, and only the two middle ones continued to glare at her. The Earl passed his hand across his mouth, possibly hiding a smile.

Ash narrowed her eyes against the sun, feeling sweat matt her hair under her velvet hat. A strong smell of horse and leather tack drifted up from Godluc; she felt it as something reassuring.

"Time for you to give me orders, my lord," she said cheerfully. And then, catching his eye, "This *is* my company, my lord Earl. All eighty lances. And I'd like to know something. We're too big for an escort and too small for an army—why *have* you hired us?"

"Later, madam. When we dine. There's time enough before you visit the Duke."

About to insist, Ash caught sight of Godfrey leaving a conversation at the camp gate with three or four shabbily dressed men, and a woman in a green habit. His wooden pectoral cross bounced on his chest as he strode across the grass, robe flapping at his bare heels.

"I believe my clerk wants me. Will it please you to have Master Angelotti here show you our guns? They are in the shade . . ." She pointed down toward the trees at the edge of the river.

Meeting de Vere's eyes, she became aware that the English nobleman was perfectly aware of the stratagem, perfectly used to such courtesies, and willing to consent.

Ash rose in her saddle and bowed as Angelotti took the Earl's bridle and led him toward the camp.

"Godfrey?"

"Yes, child?"

"Come with me!" She eased Godluc forward, Godfrey at her stirrup. "Tell me *everything* you've found out about the situation in Dijon, while I'm inspecting the camp. Everything! I have no idea what's going on in the Burgundian court, and I'm going to be standing in front of the Duke in four hours!"

Her command tent, when she reached it, was a scrum of servants rushing in and out, setting up a table, and strewing the sharp straw underfoot with sweet new rushes. Ash stomped behind the dividing curtain and dressed for the coming meal in extreme haste, knowing this would be the gear in which she would go before the Duke.

"It's *Burgundy*, Florian! It doesn't get any better than this!"

Floria del Guiz sat cross-legged on a chest, unimpressed. She rapidly lifted her feet up out of the way.

"You don't even know you'll be fighting with the Duke. Robert's mad Earl might take us God-knows-where."

"De Vere wants to fight Visigoths." Ash held her forearms up, speaking to Floria while taking no notice of Bertrand and Rickard tying the doublet's points down to her wrists. The sleeves puffed fashionably at the shoulders.

Bertrand whimpered. Ash fidgeted.

"I'm not going to look as good as I should—that bitch kept my armor!"

The surgeon drank from a silver goblet snatched from Henri Brant's servers. "Oh, wear what you like! He's only a Duke."

"Only a—fucking *hell*, Florian!"

"I grew up with this." The long-legged woman wiped sweat from her face. "So, you haven't got your armor. So?"

"*Fuck!*" Ash found no words to explain what putting on full armor does, no way to say to Floria, *But you feel like God when you've got in on!* And in front of all those people, all these bloody Burgundians, I want to do myself and the company credit—

"That was full harness! It cost me *two years* to earn the money to pay for it!"

A quarter-hour by the marked candle saw every chest turfed out, Bertrand in tears at the thought of repacking, and Ash with German cuisses strapped to her, thighs, Milanese lower leg-armour, a blue velvet brigandine with brass rivets showing dull against the cloth, and a polished steel plackart that, strapped around her waist over the brigandine, would come up in a point over her breastbone, to a fretworked metal finial. And be boiling hot.

"Oh shit," she said. "Oh shit, I'm having an audience with Charles of Burgundy, oh shit, *oh* shit . . ."

"You don't think you're taking this a *little* too seriously?"

"What they see—is what I am. And I'd rather worry about this than ...." Ash opened a small mirror-case in her hand, tilting the tiny reflective circle to try and see her face. Bertrand jerked her hair with his comb. She swore, threw a bottle at the boy, tugged her silver hair down loose over the injured part of her scalp, and stared into dark, dark eyes, the color of ponds in wild woods. The faintest tinge of sun colored her cheekbones, making her scars stand out the more pale. Apart from the scars, and the thinness that illness had given her, a flawless face stared back at her.

Don't worry about the armor, because that isn't what they'll be looking at.

Floria stepped out of two men's way, watching Ash give orders to lance-leaders and efficiently dismiss them. Her smile became sardonic. "You're going to court with your hair down? You're a married woman."

Ash gave the surgeon a reply she had been practising in her mind on her sick-bed. " 'My marriage was a sham. I swear to God that I am in exactly the same state now as I was before I was married.' "

Floria made a long, rude noise. "No, boss! Don't try that one here. You'll make even Charles of Burgundy crack a smile."

"Worth a try?"

"*No*. Trust me. No."

Ash stood still while Bertrand belted her sword around her waist. The brigandine's velvet-covered metal plates creaked as she breathed.

From the sepia shadows cast by canvas, the tall woman, said, "And what are you going to tell our noble Earl about meeting the Visigoth general? More than you've told me?

Christ, woman, is it likely I'm going to betray a confidence? We're all—"

"We?" Ash interrupted.

"—me, Godfrey, Robert . . . *How long do you expect us to wait?*" Floria wiped the top of one of Ash's four silver goblets with a grimy thumb and glanced up with bright eyes. "What happened to you? What did she say to you? You know, your silence is deafening."

"Yes," Ash said flatly, not responding to the woman's effortful flippancy. "I'm thinking it through. There's no point going off at half-cock. It could affect the company's future, and mine, and I'll call an officer-meeting when I've got it straight in my head—and not until then. Meanwhile, we have to deal with the Grand Duke of the West and a mad English Earl."

Two orders reduced the outer pavilion to order and got the side panels of canvas unhooked. The canopy continued to give shade; the open sides admitted stinging mites, white butterflies, and the swooping green metallic darts of dragonflies, and let a breeze blow over Ash's face from the rush-choked river.

She took a brief survey of the table, clothed in regrettably yellow linen. The silver plate shone bright enough to leave after-images on her retinas. Smart men-at-arms from one of van Mander's lances were forming a guard around the central area of the camp. Three of the camp women played recorders: an Italian air. Henri and Blanche stood with their heads together, talking heatedly.

As Ash looked, the steward wiped his red, streaming face on his shirt-sleeve, and nodded; this just as the sun caught bright golden curls beyond him, and she realized it was Angelotti leading the Earl's party back toward the command tent.

She saw John de Vere register the unusual fact of Blanche acting as a server, and Ludmilla's lance-mate

Katherine standing with her crossbow and a leash of mastiffs as part of the command tent guard.

Half as a question, John de Vere remarked, "You have many woman in your camp, madam."

"Of course I do. I execute for rape."

It jolted the viscount, she could tell from Beaumont's expression; but the Earl of Oxford merely nodded thoughtfully. She introduced Floria del Guiz with some care—but the Earl greeted the surgeon as a man—and Godfrey Maximillian.

"Please you be seated," she said formally, and let the servants place each man at table according to his degree, herself ceding the head of the table to John de Vere. The music ceased while Godfrey's rumble intoned a grace.

As she sat down, half her mind on how far the Visigoths might have advanced in six days, and the other half thinking how best to behave in Duke Charles's court with an invasion due, a memory clicked suddenly into place.

"Good God," Ash blurted, as Blanche and a dozen others put the first remove on the table, "I do know you. I've heard of you. You're *that* Lord Oxford!"

The English Earl quaked, with what, after a split second, she realized was laughter. " 'That' Oxford?"

"They put you in Hammes!"

Floria, on the far side of the table, glanced up from a dish of quail. "What's Hammes?"

"High-security nick," Ash said briefly, then colored, and began to serve John de Vere personally from the one large silver trencher they still possessed. "It's a castle outside Calais. With moats and dikes and . . . it's supposed to be the toughest castle in Europe to get free from!"

The Earl of Oxford reached over and slapped Viscount Beaumont heartily on the shoulder. "And so it would have been, but for this man. And Dickon, and George, and Tom. But you're wrong in one thing, madam, I made no escape. I left.''

"Left?"

"Taking my chief jailer, Thomas Blount, with me, as my ally. We left his wife garrisoning the castle until we should return with troops for the house of Lancaster."[91] John de Vere smiled. "Mistress Blount is a woman even you would find formidable. I doubt not but that we can go back to Hammes any time these ten years and find it still ours!''

"My lord of Oxenford's famous. He invaded England," Ash said to Floria. She sniffed back a laugh; no malice in it, only vicarious pride. "Twice. Once with the armies of Margaret of Anjou and King Henry." A mirthful snuffle. "And once on his own.''

"On his *own*!" Floria del Guiz turned an incredulous face to the Earl. "You'll have to excuse boss's manners, my lord of Oxford. She gets like this sometimes.''

"I was hardly alone," Oxford protested, deadpan. "I had eighty men with me.''

Floria del Guiz subsided in her chair, gazing at the English nobleman with wine-bright eyes and her infectious smile. "Eighty men.[92] To invade England. I see . . .''

"My lord the Earl took their Michael's Mount in Cornwall," Ash said. "And held it—how long, a year?''

"Not so long. From September of '73 to February of '74." The Earl looked at his brothers, whose loud voices were rising in easy talk. "They were staunch for me. But

---

[91] In point of fact, these events happened exactly as narrated here, but some eight years afterwards, in 1484. During the period covered by these texts, the Earl of Oxford remained a prisoner in Hammes castle. I suspect a chronicler of adding Oxford to the text, probably no later than 1486.

[92] Some sources give a figure of 400 men.

not the men-at-arms, once it was clear no relieving force would come from France."[93]

"And after that, Hammes." Ash shrugged. "*That* Lord Oxford. Of course."

"The third time, I shall put a better man on Edward's throne."[94] He leaned back against the carved oak chair. With steel under his tone, John de Vere said, "I am thirteenth Earl of a line that goes back to Duke William, that time out of mind were great lords and Chancellors of the realm of England. But since I am in exile, no nearer a king of Lancaster than you are near Pope Joan, madam, and since we have these Goths to contend against, then— 'that Lord Oxford' it is."

He raised his silver goblet gravely to Ash.

Ye Gods! So this is the great English soldier-Earl . . . Ash's mind ran on as she drank deeply of the indifferent red wine. "You reconciled Warwick the Kingmaker to Queen Margaret, too.[95] Good God! . . . Sorry to say, my lord, I was actually fighting on the opposite side to you on Barnet field in '71. Nothing personal. Just business."

"Yes. And now, madam, to our business," de Vere said bluntly.

"Yes, my lord." Ash gazed out from under the shading canopy, past the Earl, at the surrounding tents and pen-

---

[93]This is accurate. The English king, Edward, offered pardons to the men, but to Oxford and his brothers, only their lives. Oxford was incarcerated in Hammes shortly afterwards.

[94]In 1485, by winning the Battle of Bosworth for the then "Welsh milksop" Henry Tudor, Oxford put Henry VII of England on the throne (1485–1509).

[95]Richard Neville, Earl of Warwick, and Margaret of Anjou, wife to Henry VI of England; these inveterate noble enemies, having in 1471 spent the past fifteen years on opposite sides of the royal wars, were reconciled to an alliance by John de Vere.

nants sagging under the hot postmeridian sky. Her armor
kept her upright at the table. The brigandine's weight
didn't bother her, but the heat of it made her pale. Her
head began to throb again.

Between Geraint's tent and Joscelyn van Mander's pavilion, she saw the slope of green meadows and the gray
leaves of trees beyond at the water's edge. A distant flash
of blue took her eye: Robert Anselm, out in the field,
stripped to pourpoint and hose, shouting at men drilling
with swords and bills. Water-boys sprinted along the lines
of men. The harsh Welsh yowl of Geraint ab Morgan
sounded above the thunk of shafts hitting straw targets.

Let 'em practice in the heat! They won't be such bloody
layabouts tomorrow. Time this place started looking like
a military camp . . . Because if it doesn't, they're going to
stop thinking they're a military company. I wonder how
many I've lost to the whorehouses in Dijon?

The pavilion's marked candle showed it to be closing
on the third hour of the afternoon. She ignored the pulse
of anticipation in her stomach and lifted a cup of watered
wine, the liquid tepid in her mouth. "Shall I call my officers in, my lord?"

"Yes. Now."

Ash turned to give the order to Rickard, who stood
behind her chair, bearing her sword and second-best sallet.
Unexpectedly, Floria del Guiz spoke:

"Duke Charles loves a war. Now he'll want to attack
the whole Visigoth army!"

"He'll get wiped out, then," Ash said sourly, as Rickard spoke in an undertone to one of the many wagon-boys
serving as pages. Between servers, pages and two or three
dozen armed men with leashed dogs surrounding this end
of the pavilion canopy, the table formed an island of still-
ness. She leaned her arms forward, ignoring the stains on
the tablecloth, and caught John de Vere's blue eyes watch-

ing her. "You're right, my lord Earl. There's no chance of winning a battle against the Visigoths, without the princes of Europe united. And that's a fat chance! They must know what happened in Italy and the Germanies, but I guess they don't believe it can happen to them."

A stir among the guards outside the tent, and Robert Anselm strode in, sweating heavily, Angelotti on his heels, and Geraint close behind the two of them. Ash motioned them to the table. Viscount Beaumont and the younger de Vere brothers leaned over to listen.

"Officers' reports," Ash announced, pushing back her plate. "You'd better sit in on this, your Grace. It'll save going over things twice."

And give you a completely unvarnished view of us . . . well, let's not have any mistake about what you're getting!

Geraint, Anselm and Angelotti took places at table, the captain of archers regarding the remnants of food with wistful hunger.

"We've redone the perimeter." Robert Anselm made a long arm across the table and rescued a slab of cheese from Ash's plate. Chewing, he prompted thickly: "Geraint?"

"That's right, boss." Geraint ab Morgan gave the Oxford brothers a slightly wary look. "Got your men's tents set up in the river side of the camp, your Grace."

Ash wiped her wet brow. "Right—And where's Joscelyn? He's usually hanging about for command-group meetings."

"Oh, he's down there, boss. Welcoming them in on behalf of the Lion."

The Welsh captain of archers spoke entirely innocently and looked up with a welcoming grunt as Bertrand, at Ash's nod, served horn goblets filled with watered wine. Robert Anselm caught Ash's eye significantly.

"Is he, by God?" Ash murmured to herself. "Did your camp reorganization involve putting all the Flemish lances together?"

"No, boss, van Mander did that when we got here."

The tent pennants that she could see indicated, to Ash's practiced eye, that the entire back quarter of the camp was made up of Flemish tents, no other nation intermixed with them. Everywhere else was, as usual, a promiscuous mingling of homelands.

She nodded thoughtfully, her gaze absently on a passing group of women in linen kirtles and dirty shifts, laughing as they made their way toward the camp gate and—presumably—the town of Dijon.

"Let it go for now," she said. "While we're at it, though, I want double perimeter guards from now on. I don't want Monforte's men or the Burgundian lads coming in nicking stuff, and I don't want our lot going out getting rat-arsed all the time. Let 'em into town in groups, no more than twenty at a time. Let's keep the unpaid fighting down to a minimum."

Robert Anselm chuckled. "Yes, Captain."

"That goes for officers and lance-leaders, too! Okay." Ash glanced around the table. "What's the feeling in camp about this English contract?"

Godfrey Maximillian brushed sweat off his face with a quick gesture. With an apologetic glance to Anselm, he said, "The men would have preferred it if it had been something you negotiated in person, Captain. I think they're waiting to see which way you jump."

"Geraint?"

The Welshman said dismissively, "You know archers, boss. For once they're fighting on the same side as someone supposed to be more foulmouthed than they are! No offense, your Grace."

John de Vere looked rather grimly at the captain of archers, but said nothing.

Ash persisted, "No dissent?"

"Well . . . Huw's lance think we should have tried to get another contract with the Visigoths." Geraint didn't acknowledge Oxford. He said steadily, "So do I, boss. Outnumbered armies don't win the field, and the Duke's outnumbered and then some. The way to get paid is to be on the winning side."

Ash looked questioningly at Antonio Angelotti.

"You know gunners," Angelotti echoed. "Show us something we can fire at, and everyone's happy. Half my crews are off in the Burgundian army camp right now, looking at their ordnance—I haven't seen most of them for two days."

"Visigoths don't use much ordnance," Geraint observed. "Your boys wouldn't like that."

Angelotti gave his reserved smile. "There is something to be said for being on the same side as the big guns."

"And the men-at-arms?" Ash asked Robert Anselm.

"I'd say about half of them—Carracci and all the Italian lads, the English, and the easterners—are happy with the contract. The French lads don't like being on the same side as the Burgundians, but they'll wear it. They all think we owe the rag-heads something for Basle."

Ash snorted. "I've looked in the war-chest—*they* owe *us*!"

"They'll get stuck in, when the time comes," Anselm continued, amused. He frowned. "Can't answer for the Flemings. Captain, I don't get to talk to di Conti and the rest, now, I just get to talk to van Mander; he says it saves time if he passes orders on."

"Uh huh." In perfect understanding of the unease in Anselm's mind, Ash nodded. "Okay, let's move on—"

John de Vere spoke for the first time. "These dissenting

lances, madam Captain, how much of a problem will this be?''

''None at all. There are going to be some changes.''

Ash met de Vere's gaze. Something in her determined expression must have been convincing: he merely nodded, and said, ''Then you deal with it, Captain.''

Ash dismissed the subject. ''Okay, next . . .''

Beyond the men huddled around the linen table, beyond the peaked roofs of the tents, the forested limestone hills around Dijon glimmered green. Below the tree-line, in the valley, slopes glistened green and brown: rows of vines ripening in the sun. Ash slitted her eyes against that brilliance, attempting to judge whether this sun-in-Leo was still shining as strongly as on the previous day.

''Next,'' Ash said, ''the matter of what we're going to *do*.''

Ash glanced at Oxford. She found herself absently digging with the tip of her eating knife at the charcoal-black pastry that had coffined a cow-steak and cheese pie. Her blade scattered fragments on the cloth. ''It's like I said to you earlier, my lord. This company's far too big for you to want us just as an escort. But we're nowhere near big enough to take on an army—Visigoth *or* Burgundian.''

The English Earl smiled briefly at that. Her officers winced.

''So . . . I've been thinking, your Grace.'' Ash jerked her thumb over her shoulder. Where the tent-walls were removed, the long slope of pasture up to the city walls was visible, and the peaked roofs of the convent. ''While I was up there. I had time to think. And I came up with a half-baked idea that I want to approach the Duke with. The question is, your Grace, have you and I had the same half-baked idea?''

Robert Anselm rubbed his wet hand across his face,

hiding a grin; Geraint Morgan spluttered. Angelotti gazed at Ash from under ambiguously lowered oval lids.

" 'Half-baked'?" the Earl of Oxford questioned, mildly.

" 'Mad,' if you prefer." Excitement keyed her up, momentarily wiped out both oppressive heat and the effects of her injury. She leaned forward on the table. "We're not going to attack the entire Visigoth invasion force, are we? That would take everything Duke Charles has got here, and then some! But—why should we need to attack them head on?"

De Vere nodded, briefly. "A raid."

Ash dug her knife-point into the table. "Yes! If a *raiding* force could take out the head . . . a raiding force of, say, seventy or eighty lances: eight hundred men. Bigger than an escort, but still small enough to move fast, and to get out of trouble if we meet their army. And that's us, isn't it?"

Oxford leaned back slightly, his armor clicking. His three brothers began to stare at him.

"It isn't a mad idea," the Earl of Oxford said.

Viscount Beaumont lisped, "Only by comparison! Not as mad as some of the things we've done, John."

"And how does it help Lancaster?" the youngest de Vere brother broke in.

"Quiet! Ruffians." The Earl of Oxford thumped Beaumont on the shoulder and ruffled Dickon's hair. His worn, lined face was alive when he turned his attention back to Ash. Above him, the white canvas blazed gold, hiding the fierce southern European sun.

"Yes, madam," he confirmed. "We have been thinking alike. A raid to take out their commander, their general. Their Faris."

For a moment, what she sees is not the sun-drenched

camp in Burgundy, but a frost-starred pleasance[96] in Basle: a woman in Visigoth hauberk and surcoat wiping spilt wine from the dagged silken hem, her frowning face Ash's own. A woman who has said *sister, half-sister, twin.*

"No."

Ash, for the first time, saw the Earl appear startled.

In a very practical tone, Ash repeated, "No. Not their commander. Not here in Europe. Believe me, the Faris expects that. She knows damn well that every enemy prince wants her head on a spike right now, and she's well guarded. In the middle of about twelve thousand soldiers. Attacking her right now is impossible."

Ash looked around at their faces, back at de Vere. "No, my lord—when I said I'd had a half-baked idea, I meant it. I want to mount an attack on Carthage."

"Carthage!" Oxford boomed.

Ash shrugged. "I bet you anything you like, they won't be expecting that."

"For damn good reason!" one of the middle de Vere brothers exclaimed.

Godfrey Maximillian spluttered, "*Carthage!*" in a tone of outraged astonishment.

Angelotti murmured something in Robert Anselm's ear. Floria, as still as an animal scenting hounds, looked at Ash with a narrow, baffled, complaining expression on her smudged face.

John de Vere, in much the same skeptical tone as she had earlier spoken to him about his Lancastrain claims, said, "Madam, you were planning to ask Charles of Burgundy to pay you to attack the King-Caliph in Carthage?"

Ash took a breath. She leaned back against the upright of the back-stool, overheating under the canvas canopy

---

[96]Garden.

and held her goblet up for Bertrand to fill with watered wine.

"There are two things to be considered, your Grace. One—their King-Caliph Theodoric is sick, maybe dying. This I have from trustworthy sources." She momentarily met the gaze of Floria, of Godfrey. "A dead King-Caliph would be very useful. Well, a dead caliph is always useful! But—if there were to be a dynastic struggle going on back home, then I don't think the Visigoth army would be pushing their invasion north this campaigning season. They might even get recalled back to North Africa. At the least, it would halt them over the winter. They probably wouldn't cross the Burgundian border."

"Now I see why you hoped to speak to Charles, madam." John de Vere looked thoughtful.

Dickon de Vere spluttered something. Under cover of the English lords' increasingly loud talk, Floria del Guiz said, "*Are* you mad?"

"De Vere's a soldier, and he doesn't think it's mad. Not entirely mad," Ash corrected herself.

"It's desperate." Robert Anselm frowned, abstracted; reservations in his voice over and above what he was saying. He wiped his sweating, shiny head. "Desperate, not stupid."

"Carthage," Antonio Angelotti said softly, some expression on the master gunner's face that Ash couldn't identify. That worried her, needing to know how he would be on the field of battle.

Godfrey Maximillian looked at her. "And?" he prompted.

"And . . ." Ash pushed her stool back and stood up. The English lords' debate had reached shouting proportions, John de Vere thumping his fist repeatedly on the table, and her movement went unnoticed. Like birds disturbed in corn, her officers' faces lifted to her.

She thought, looking around the table, that no one who didn't know these men could have picked up the growing atmosphere of distrust—certainly de Vere and his Englishmen seemed unaware of it—but to her it was loud as a shout.

"Boss," Geraint ab Morgan said. "Are you telling us what's on your mind here?"

Ash said to Roberto, to Florian, to Godfrey, Angelotti, Geraint: "If their King-Caliph dies, it will give us breathing-space."

A look of settled disbelief closed up Godfrey Maximillian's expression. That was enough: she swung around, moved to stand with her hand against one of the tent-poles, staring out past the pavilion's spidering guy-ropes, past their shadows on the turf. Her eyes saw glimmering hot, brilliant, infinite sparks of sun on metal—silver platters, dagger pommels, sword blades in the meadow, the metal finial crowning the great standard-pole of the Lion Azure camp.

Ash turned. The sun dazzled her eyes: everything under the canopy now impenetrable with brown shadows, only a glimmer of white faces visible. She walked back inside, to the table.

"Okay. You're smart. *Not* the King-Caliph." She dropped her hand onto Robert Anselm's shoulder, closed it, feeling the rough blue-dyed linen of his pourpoint and the warmth of his body. "Although that would be a bonus."

She let her gaze move from Godfrey, who sat stroking his amber-brown beard, to Floria's face, to Angelotti's Byzantine-icon solemnity, Geraint's puzzled and impatient expression.

Beaumont said something in rapid English.

"Yes," Oxford added, raising his head from the discussion to Ash and, with a nod of acknowledgment, to the viscount. "You said, madam, that there are two things to be considered; what is the second?"

Ash nodded to Henri Brant. The steward bustled the servers and pages clear out of the tent. A sharp command got her the captain of the guard's attention: ordering the men-at-arms to circle the tent further off. She smiled to herself, shaking her head. *And still there'll be rumors before nightfall.*

"The second thing"—her expression took on a serious, pragmatic abstraction—"is the Stone Golem."

Ash leaned her fists on the tablecloth and looked around at her officers and the Earl of Oxford. "The *machina rei militaris*, the tactics-machine. *That's* what I want to raid."

Ash, watching Godfrey as she spoke, saw his dark, brilliant eyes blink. There was a furrow across his forehead: fear, condemnation, or concern—all unclear.

"Are you certain—" he began.

Ash gestured him to silence, not before she saw the look that Floria del Guiz gave the priest.

"We know the Faris hears a voice," Ash said quietly. "You've heard all the rumors about the Visigoth's Stone Golem. It talks to her from Carthage, it tells her how to win battles with her armies. That's what we need to take out. Not the Caliph. I want to raid to smash, burn and destroy this *machine* that she talks about. I want to wipe out this 'Stone Golem,' shut her damn voice up for good!"

A woodpecker began to hammer at one of the alders growing down by the river, the hard *toc-toc-toc* echoing through the humid air, sharper than the noise of men at sword-drill. Across the river, there was nothing to distinguish the bright southern afternoon horizon from the other three quarters of the compass.

Viscount Beaumont's blurred lisp asked, "How much does she depend upon this *machina*, and how much on her generals? Would the loss of it be such a loss to her?''

Before Ash could answer, John de Vere cut in. ''Have you heard anything else, since you set foot at Calais, but 'the Stone Golem'? Even if it only exists as a rumor, the *machina* is worth another army to her.''

''Then, if it is nothing but rumor,'' his brother George remarked, ''it can't *be* destroyed, no more than you can cleave smoke with a sword.''

Tom de Vere put in, ''And if it does exist, is it in Carthage, or with their woman-general? Or elsewhere? Who can say?''

Ash heard the woodpecker stop. Between tents, and over the palisades, she could see boys with slings down by the river bank.

Briskly, she said, ''If the war-machine was with her, we could have bought that information by now. It's *not* with her. If it's elsewhere—then it's so valuable to them that it can only be smack in the heart of the Visigoth empire, under a phenomenal number of guards, in the middle of their capital city.'' Ash paused and grinned. ''The city I'm suggesting we raid.''

Laconically, the Earl of Oxford said, ''If.''

''Anything this unique—that's where it's going to be, your Grace. Can you see the King-Caliph letting it out of the city? But we can buy that information, confirm it; Godfrey's got contacts with the exiled Medicis. You can find out anything from a bank.''

Wryly, John de Vere said, ''I have chiefly found them unwilling to be cooperative with exiled Lancastrians. I wish your clerk better fortune. Madam, what is the *machina rei militaris* doing for the Visigoths? Is it a vital target?''

''This invasion is being run by the Faris; she's vital but you won't get her; *she* believes her machine is vital. Any way you look at it,'' Ash said, pulling out a back-stool and sitting down again, "*she* believes it instructed her to beat the Italians and the Germans and the Swiss on the field."

She held out one of the dirty goblets automatically, forgetting there were no pages. She lowered the vessel. Making a long arm and grabbing the pottery jug herself, she splashed the goblet generously full of watered wine and drained it, aware that her face must be as heat-red as Anselm's and Oxford's.

Am I going to get away with this? she thought. This much and no more.?

"You are very anxious to go and die," the Earl of Oxford said gently.

"I'm anxious to fight, live, and get paid. I've got frighteningly little money in the war-chest, and"—Ash jabbed a finger at the Burgundian and mercenary tents visible down by Dijon's confluence of rivers—"there's too many other places my lads can go and sign on for better money. We need a fight. We got our asses kicked at Basle; we need to kick back."

The Earl of Oxford pursued, "A fight for something that may be a rumor, a phantasm, a nothing?"

No. I'm not going to get away with this much and no more.

"Okay." Ash swirled wine in her goblet, watching light ripple. She flicked a gaze up to de Vere, aware that he was quietly challenging her. "If I'm going to do what I plan, I have to have authority backing me up with money. And you're not going to give me authority or money unless you're convinced. It's this way, your Grace."

Godfrey Maximillian's brown hand touched his Briar Cross. Ash read Godfrey's face so plainly that it amazed her nobody else did. Only the Earl of Oxford's presence was stopping her company clerk from blurting out *Are*

*you going to tell him that you have heard her voice? That
you have always heard voices?*

Unexpectedly, the younger de Vere, Dickon, spoke up.
"Madam Captain, *you* hear voices. I heard your men say.
Like the French maid."

His voice rose at the end, a hint of a question; and he
flushed under his elder brothers' glare.

"Yes," Ash said, "I do."

In the outbreak of brass voices, English noble soldiers
shouting their conflicting views in growing excitement,
Ash momentarily put her face in her hands.

In the dark behind her eyes, she thought, And if the
Stone Golem *is* destroyed, does my voice and my life go
with it?

"Look at me, your Grace," she invited, and when the
English Earl did, she said, "And when you see the Faris,
you'll be looking at the same face. We are alike enough
to be twins."

"You are a bastard of her family?" Oxford's brows
went up. "Yes. That is possible, I suppose. How does it
concern this?"

"For ten years, I've thought I heard the Lion speak to
me." Ash, unawares, crossed her breast, her fingers brushing the bright pierced metal of the plackart. She met and
held each of their gazes in turn—Robert Anselm's considering frown, Angelotti's enigmatic lack of expression,
Floria's scowl, Geraint's sheer confusion, and the English
Earl's keen, weighing stare.

"For ten years, I heard the voice of the Lion speaking
in my soul, on the field of battle. That's why some of
them here call me 'Lioness.' When they think about it."
Ash's mouth took on a wry smile. "There's been campaigns when you couldn't move around here for God-
struck holy men hearing saints' voices; it isn't that
unique."

A ripple of male laughter went around the table.

Ash narrowed the focus of her attention to the attainted English Earl.

"This part I want kept quiet as long as I can," she said. "There's no way to keep it completely secret; you know what camps are like. My lord Oxford, I *know* the Faris hears a voice. *I* heard her speak to it. It isn't the Lion I've been hearing. It's their war-machine. She hears it because they bred her to. And I hear it—because I'm her bastard twin."

Oxford stared. "Madam . . ." And then, plainly dismissing doubt, and asking what he considered essential: "They know this?"

"Oh, they know it," Ash said grimly. She sat back on the stool, resting her hands flat on her armor. "That's why they bothered to take me prisoner in Basle."

Oxford snapped his fingers, his expression saying plainly *of course!*

Dickon de Vere said naively, "If your voices are on her side, *pucelle*, can you still fight?"

The reverberations of that question were visible on the faces of her officers. Ash smiled a close-lipped smile at the English knight.

"Whether I can or whether I can't, I can prove to you that it's the same voice—the same machine. If it *wasn't*"—she switched her gaze to John de Vere—"they wouldn't have been so damn anxious to find me in Basle. And they wouldn't want to drag me off to Carthage for interrogation."

A breath of humid air came up from the river, bringing the smell of weed and cool water over the sweat and stench of the camp. She reached out and gripped Floria's shoulder and Godfrey Maximillian's arm.

"Carthage wants me," Ash stated. "*I won't run.* I've

got eight hundred armed men here. This time I'm taking the fight directly to them.''

Her eyes glittered. She is keen, uncomplicated as a blade, with that frightening smile that she wears when she goes into a fight—frightening because it is serene, the smile of someone for whom all's right with the world.

"They want me in Carthage?—I'll *go* to Carthage!''

E-Mail hardcopies, found placed between pages of 3rd edition:

- -

Message: #135 (Anna Longman/misc.)
Subject: Ash, mss.
Date: 15/11/00 at 7.16 a.m.
From: Ngrant@ *format address deleted*
other details encrypted by
non-discoverable personal key

Anna--

Excuse this, I haven't slept, I have been on-line most of the night to universities around the world.

You're right. It IS all the manuscripts. The Cartulary of St Herlaine is lost completely. There is one copy of Pseudo-Godfrey in the fakes gallery at the V&A. The Angelotti text and the del Guiz LIFE are mediaeval romance and legend. I cannot find them documented as mediaeval history at any time after the 1930s!

From what I can download, the manuscripts they have on-line are the same TEXTS which I have been translating. All that's changed is the CLASSIFICATION from history to fiction.

I can only ask you to believe that I am not a fraud.

--Pierce

- -

Message: #80 (Pierce Ratcliff/misc.)
Subject: Ash, documentation
Date: 15/11/00 at 9.14 a.m.
From: Longman@ *format address deleted*
Text encrypted by
non-discoverable personal key

Pierce--

I do believe you. Or I trust you, which may be the same thing.

It isn't as if we didn't check out your academic record before we signed the contract. We did. You're good, Pierce. I know you can be good and still be mistaken, but you're good.

Doctor Napier-Grant's discoveries. Send me something. Download me images, something, I need something to show the MD, or this is all going to hell!

--Anna

Message:	#136 (Anna Longman/misc.)
Subject:	Ash, archaeological discoveries
Date:	15/11/00 at 10.17 a.m.
From:	Ngrant@

format address deleted
Other details encrypted by
non–discoverable
personal key

Anna--

Isobel doesn't have the slightest intention of letting photo images of the site, or of golems, on to the Internet. She says they would be global inside half an hour.

Her son, John Monkham, is flying back from Tunisia early this week. I have at last persuaded Isobel to let him act as a courier. He will bring you copies of the expedition's photos of the golem; but they will be in his possession at all times. Isobel is willing to authorise you to show them to your MD, before John brings them back to the site.

This is the best I can do.

--Pierce

Message: #81(Pierce Ratcliff/misc.)
Subject: Ash, archaeology
Date: 15/11/00 at 10.30 a.m.
From: Longman@   *format address deleted*
                                         Text encrypted by non-discoverable
                                         personal key
Pierce--

Give John Monkham my phone number, I'll meet him at the airport.
   I can't wait to see Ash's golem for myself. But I guess I'll have to.
While I'm waiting—have you thought of ANYTHING that can account
for what's happening?

--Anna

Message: #139 (Anna Longman/misc.)
Subject: Ash, texts
Date: 16/11/00 at 11.49 a.m.
From: Ngrant@   *format address deleted*
                                         text encrypted by non-discoverable
                                         personal key
Anna--

Frankly, no. I have NO idea why these manuscripts are now classified
under 'Fiction'. I'm at my wit's end.
   I HAD an idea. I thought, be philosophic. Occam's Razor—if the
simplest explanation for any event is the more likely to be true, could
it not be that it is the RECLASSIFICATION of the 'Ash' manuscripts that
is the mistake? You know how it can be, with databases on line; if
one university decides a document is a fake, that will cause a 'cascade

effect' through all the universities on the net. And documents DO become mislaid, and lost.

That thought consoled me through last night, when sleep was impossible. I saw myself verified. Sadly, this morning—to the mundane sound of lorries arriving on site—I realised it is a mere fantasy. A cascade error would not affect all databases. It would not affect those libraries that aren't computer-literate, either! No. I have no idea what's going on. When I gained access to the British Library manuscripts they were classified as 'Mediaeval History', plain and simple!

And I have no explanation for the apparent fact that these documents were reclassified in the 1930s.

I don't know what is going on, but I do know we are in danger of Ash vanishing into thin air, into a fantasy of history; of her proving to be no more (or no less) historical than a King Arthur, or a Lancelot. But I was—and I remain—utterly convinced that we are dealing with a genuine human being here, beneath the accretions of time.

What is truly perplexing to me, also, is that what we have found on this site authenticates not just my theory of a Visigoth culture in North Africa, but the STRANGEST aspects of that culture—the post-Roman technology, nine centuries on. While I assumed that my Visigoths were factual, the technology is something I had thought to be mythical! And yet, here it is.

Still inexplicable as regards how it functioned.

It's enough to make me think kindly of Vaughan Davies. You may not know quite how strange his Introduction to ASH: A BIOGRAPHY is—it's something one tends to ignore, because of the sheer quality of his scholarship and the excellence of his translations.

He suggested, on the subject of the 'accretions' to the various texts, that the difficulties arise not because Ash has accreted myths, but because she has disseminated them.

Let me copy in what I have with me:-

> (. . .)The hypothesis which I {Vaughan Davies} find myself
> compelled to accept is that, in the supposed history of 'Ash',
> this historian finds himself confronted with—among other

things—the prototype of the legend of La Pucelle, Jehanne of Domremy, more popularly known to history as Joan of Arc.

This theory may appear to defy reason. The 'Ash' narratives are set in what is clearly the third quarter of the fifteenth century. Certainly the manuscripts cannot be dated to any time before 1470. Joan of Arc was burned at the stake in 1431. To accept Ash as the prefiguration of Joan as the archetypal warrior-woman is surely lunacy, for Joan comes first.

It is my belief, however, that it is the legends of Ash, redeemer of her country, that we have transferred to the meteoric career of the young Frenchwoman who was, it must be remembered, a soldier at seventeen and dead at nineteen, having driven the English out of France; and not the history of Joan which becomes the 'Ash' cycle of tales. The reader will ask himself, how can this be?

A simplistic explanation could be offered. If the legends of Ash were in fact not late, but early mediaeval stories, then their reproduction again in the 1480s could be put down to popularity. With the invention of printing, the authors merely re-wrote her narratives in contemporary terms. It was common practice, for example in the illuminated manuscripts of the era, to reproduce scenes from Biblical and Classical history in fifteenth century costume, accoutrements and locale.

In this case, one would still have to account for the complete absence of any handwritten manuscript evidence of the 'Ash' cycle before 1470.

What explanation remains?

It is my belief that the 'Ash' stories are not fiction, that they are history—they are just not our history.

It is my belief that Burgundy did, indeed, 'vanish'; not in the apparent sense that it lost popular interest but can be discovered by a diligent historian, but in a far more final sense. What we have in our history books is only a shadow, remaining.

With Burgundy's disappearance, such a history of facts and events had to attach itself to something in the collective Euro-

pean subconscious: one of the things they sought out was an
obscure French peasant woman.

I am well aware that this requires the spontaneous creation
of the historical documentation of Jeanne D'Arc.

Accept this, and one begins to have a mental image of real
events flying out, in fragments, from the dissolution of Ash's
Burgundy. Fragments that impel themselves backwards and for-
wards, impaled along the timeline of history, taking on such
'local colour' as they require for survival. Thus Ash is Joan,
and is Ashputtel/Cinderella, and is a dozen other legends. The
history of this first Burgundy remains, all around us.

My hypothesis may be dismissed completely, of course, but
I consider it provable on rational grounds; (. . .)

I have always had a fondness for this extravagantly eccentric theory—the idea that Burgundy genuinely faded out of history after
1477, as it were, but that we can find the events of it in the mouths
of other historical characters; their actions in the actions of other
women and men throughout our history. Burgundy's portrait, as it
were, cut up and sprinkled like a jigsaw through history: still visible
for those who take the trouble to look.

Of course, it isn't a theory, as such. Plainly, although he says it is
his 'belief', this is merely a distinguished academic amusing himself
with speculations, and following Charles Mallory Maximillian's conceit
of 'lost Burgundy' to its logical conclusion.

The problem is that this is only *half* of his 'Introduction' to ASH:
A BIOGRAPHY. The theory is incomplete—what are his 'rational
grounds' for what he calls a 'first' Burgundy? We have no idea now
what Vaughan Davies' theory might have been in its entirety. I consulted a cheap wartime hardcover edition in the British Library and,
as you know, there appears to be no other copy in existence of this
second edition of ASH. (I presume that stocks were destroyed when
the publishers' warehouse was bombed during the Blitz in 1940.) As
far as I can discover through six years of diligent research, no complete copy now exists anywhere.

If you were to take the evidence of this partial theory, you might well say that Vaughan Davies was an eccentric. You may think he was a complete *crank*. However, don't dismiss him out of hand. It is not that many people in the 1930s who have doctorates in History *and* Physics, and a Professorship at Cambridge. He was obviously much taken with the high-physics theory of parallel worlds coming into existence. In a way, I can see why; history—like the physical universe, if the scientists are to be believed—is anything but concrete.

History is so *little* known. I myself, and other historians, make a story out of it. We teach in universities that people married at such-and-such an age, that so many died in childbirth, that so many served out their apprenticeships, that watermills and pole-lathes were the beginning of the 'mediaeval industrial revolution'—but if you ask a historian to say precisely what happened to one given person, on one given day, then we do not know. We *guess*.

There is room for so many things, in the gaps between known history.

I would throw up my hands and abandon this project (I don't need my academic reputation or my chances of getting published ruined) if I hadn't *touched* her golem.

I suppose that, also, I'm saying this by way of a warning. At Isobel's strict insistence, I am continuing the final translation of the centrepiece of this book—the document to which someone has (much later) added the punning heading 'Fraxinus me fecit': 'Ash made me'. Given Ash's lack of literacy, it seems likely that this is a document dictated to a monk, or to a scribe, with what omissions and additions and alterations we cannot know. That said, I am convinced that this document is genuine. It fills in the gap between her presence at the Neuss siege, and her later presence with the Burgundians in late 1476, and her death at Nancy on 5 January 1477. The 'missing summer' problem, as we have always known it.

I have reached the part which throws additional light on the del Guiz and Angelotti chronicles of Ash's time in Dijon. Translating now, with the golem only a few tents away from me—mere yards; the other side of a canvas wall—I start to ask myself a question. A serious question, although when I asked it before, it was a joke.

If the messenger-golems are true, what else is?

--Pierce

Message: #82(Pierce Ratcliff/misc.)
Subject: Ash, documentation
Date: 16/11/00 at 12.08 p.m.
From: Longman@   *format address deleted*
                                Text encrypted by
                                non-discoverable personal
Pierce--   *key*

If 'Angelotti' and the rest of the manuscripts aren't true, what else ISN'T?

--Anna